DANCE INTO DESTINY

DANCE INTO DESTINY

SHERRI L. LEWIS

www.urbanchristianonline.net

Urban Books, LLC
1199 Straight Path
West Babylon, NY 11704

ISBN–13: 978-1-60162-847-3
ISBN–10: 1-60162-847-1

First Trade Paperback Printing January 2008
First Mass Market Paperback Printing: February 2010
Printed in the United States of America

10 9 8 7 6 5 4 3 2 1

Distributed by Kensington Corp.
Submit Wholesale Orders to:
Kensington Publishing Corp.
C/O Penguin Group (USA) Inc.
Attention: Order Processing
405 Murray Hill Parkway
East Rutherford, NJ 07073-2316
Phone: 1-800-526-0275
Fax: 1-800-227-9604

Dedication

For Yvette.
I thank God for such a wonderful friend to
pursue purpose and destiny with.
Thanks for chasing the purple sky with me . . .

Acknowledgments

As always, first and foremost, thanks to my God. You're showing Yourself more faithful and perfect in my life every day. I have no human words to express my love . . .

Seems like I just wrote acknowledgments for *My Soul Cries Out*. In fact, as I'm writing this, it's due to release in about two weeks. I can't wait to hold a real book in my hands for the first time! If anyone sees me in Wal-Mart pushing a cart of groceries with my book in my hand, crying my eyes out, just know that I'm overwhelmed by this part of my dreams finally coming true.

To my bestest support and big sister, Joyce. I can't thank you enough for how much you believe in me and promote my work. Thanks for all your help and support with *Midnight Clear*, for all the emails you send out and for all the people you tell about my work. I can't wait until your first children's book comes out so I can return the love.

To Mommy, for agreeing to be my personal assistant for free. Thanks for all you do to keep me from going insane. To Daddy, for your continual support and encouragement. Hopefully I'll have a new manuscript for you to read soon. To Kelli, for creative inspiration. And to Jordan, for being the most beautiful niece in the world. I love you so much and can't wait to see who you're going to be in God.

To my best friend, Kathy—dude, thanks that I ALWAYS know that you're there . . .

To Allen, for always having a laugh or a song when I need one.

To Apostle Peterson and Pastor Viv—thanks for your support and endless intercession and for pushing me towards destiny.

To my beautiful, anointed sisters in Women of Destiny Bible Study (did we ever decide on a name for ourselves?). Words cannot express my gratitude for you guys. I am so honored that you come sit in my living room every week, listen to me teach (and actually take notes and look interested) and allow me to pray for you and speak into your lives. Thanks for your trust and for letting me be who God has called me to be. You are the beginning of the fulfillment of prophetic words spoken over my life for many years. Thanks for allowing me to do destiny! It's the most beautiful thing to watch each of you grow in God. I can't wait to see what you will become as we continue our passionate pursuit of His presence, purpose, and destiny. I love you all sooooo much!

To my mentor and Christian fiction shero, Victoria Christopher Murray. Your support is overwhelming. Thanks for the standard of excellence you set as a writer. You challenge me to continually perfect my craft. You know I'm trying to be like you when I grow up!

To Tia—my writing partner. Thanks for answering ALL my questions ALL the time and for your calm replies during ALL my freak-out moments. You notice how God keeps you right around the corner from me? He knows . . .

To my author friends—thanks for your friendship, encouragement, guidance and support; Kendra Norman Bellamy—for everything!!!! Marilynn Griffith—my bunkie (don't worry—your secret is safe with me); S. James Guitard—your brilliance at this thing amazes me; your willingness to share blesses me; Stacy Hawkins Adams—thanks for the endorsement and promotion—it means a lot coming from you; Jihad—thanks for ALL the advice—you got this thing down to a science; Claudia Mair-Burney—all I'm saying is can I get a bootleg copy of the second book?! Monique Miller—girl, let's just continue to figure this thing out together. Toni Lee—thanks for your support and best wishes on your debut novel also! And to the American Christian Fiction Writers—thanks for all you've taught me about this writing world.

To my aspiring author friends—it's only a matter of time. Rhonda Nain—thanks for brightening

my days with your emails; Monica McCullough—
this one's for you; Dee Stewart—any day now, I
feel it! Tyora Moody (also the BESTEST web
designer ever—thanks for the perfect website);
Michelle Sutton (thanks for all the reviews and
your overwhelming support—can't wait to return the favor); Shawneda Marks—girl, you
amaze me with the extent you're willing to go
to perfect your craft. God will reward that! And
the women of the Atlanta Black Christian Fiction Writers—okay, *now* who's next?

To my publicists at PowerFlow Media! Wow!
Thanks for all that you do. We've just started
and I'm already in places I never imagined and
would have never gotten on my own. I pray
God's blessings upon you!!

To Lisa and April at Papered Wonders—thanks
for making my promotional materials so beautiful. I pray God's continued blessings on your
business.

To my Urban Christian family—best wishes to
all my fellow writers as we embark on this journey together. Thanks to all the staff that sup-
ports us as we do what we do.

And by faith, I'm gonna speak those things!
Thanks to all the reviewers and readers who
made *My Soul Cries Out* such a great success.
Hope you like this one, too!

DANCE INTO DESTINY

Chapter One

"Quite honestly, Ms. Banks, if you're not able to bring your course grades up to a B average by the end of the semester, I'm afraid you're going to have to withdraw from the Master's program."

Keeva Banks stared at her counselor, watching her cheap, red lipstick bleed into the fine wrinkle lines around her lips. It was almost as if she were mesmerized by the words coming out of her mouth.

She wasn't.

She knew this was coming. Had been expecting it. Even still, hearing it out loud . . .

Keeva grabbed a lock of hair and twisted it around her finger.

Ms. Parker pulled a green file folder from her desk with Keeva's name printed on the front and began flipping through the papers in it. "I've received progress reports from each of your professors and I have to tell you, things don't look good." In a droning monotone voice, Ms. Parker delineated Keeva's impending failure.

Keeva felt her heart beat faster and her chest got tight. She tried to inconspicuously take a few deep breaths. Her therapist had taught her to practice relaxation techniques when she got emotionally overwhelmed. Keeva tuned out Ms. Parker's voice and fastened her eyes on her clothes. She had to focus on something—anything—to make it through this meeting without falling apart.

Ms. Parker's blouse was made of some cheapy, chintzy fabric with wide, horizontal brown and beige stripes. How could she have thought it matched the completely different shade of brown of her shapeless skirt? And didn't she know someone with her figure, or lack thereof, should never wear horizontal stripes? Not to mention that her skin was too sallow to wear brown anyway. Keeva tried to imagine her in a fitted pantsuit in maybe a nice peach color with makeup that actually matched her skin color. She shook her head. Even with a makeover, Ms. Parker was one of those women who just couldn't look much better.

Keeva glanced down at her own Donna Karan pantsuit. The rich, burgundy color accented her cocoa brown skin perfectly and the suit seemed cut to fit her petite, curvy figure. She had dressed carefully that morning, knowing she'd need to look good in light of the news she was about to receive.

She made her eyes go back to Ms. Parker's face, not wanting to appear rude.

"From what I understand, so far this semester you've made, at best, C's on your exams and you still haven't completed the project for your Research Methods class."

Ms. Parker paused as if waiting for Keeva to speak.

No way could she answer without her voice shaking. Or worse still, her bursting into tears. She nodded slowly, hoping that would be a sufficient response.

Ms. Parker's closet of an office seemed to be shrinking. And did they have the heat turned up in this part of the building? Keeva pressed her hand down on her knee to stop her leg from bouncing. She rubbed her sweaty palms on her pantsuit.

"I have to ask, Ms. Banks, do you really want this degree?"

What difference does it make what I want? Keeva sat up straight and pasted on a camera-pleasing smile. "Of course I want this degree. I wouldn't be here if I didn't." She hoped she sounded more convincing than she felt.

For the first time, and only for a minute, she thought about it. *Did* she want a master's in professional counseling?

How could she help anyone when *she* didn't have the answers? Keeva imagined herself counseling people, passing them tissue when they cried, patting their arms and giving them understanding looks in that annoying, empathetic way; bandaging them up to send them back into life to be bruised all over again. What was the point? Would she ever really change anyone's life?

Ms. Parker stood, came around to the front of her desk, and leaned against it.

Keeva watched her hips spread out wide across the wooden edge. She sat back a little. *Oh dear. Here comes the heart to heart.*

"Ms. Banks, is there something going on that you need to talk about? A problem affecting your academic performance?"

Keeva mustered her last bit of emotional stability to paste on another smile. "No, Ms. Parker. Everything's fine. Thank you for your concern, though."

And that was the worst part about it. There was nothing she could blame this on. She was healthy, all her needs were met; she had supportive parents, plenty of friends, and a wonderful boyfriend.

Her life was . . . perfect.

All she had to do was get this stupid degree, start her career, get married, have 2.5 children, buy a Volvo and a home in an exclusive neighborhood, and live out the rest of her years in Suburban Utopia.

What more could she ask for?

She reached down to pick up her Coach briefcase and stood. She had to get out of the office before she erupted. "I really appreciate you taking the time to speak with me."

That much was true. The last graduate program she flunked out of just sent a "warning" letter in the mail. It pretty much said get it together or else. Else had landed her here at Georgia State University.

Keeva flipped her shoulder-length hair and smoothed out her suit. "I assure you I'll do everything I can to pull it together. Things will be better by the end of the semester."

At least I hope.

Midtown Atlanta was a blur as Keeva drove to her apartment building. She couldn't wait to get to the haven she had created for herself. She loved her one-bedroom loft. The airy openness of it gave her room to breathe. The large floor-to-ceiling windows let in abundant sunlight that kept her numerous plants flourishing. The designer yellow paint gave the room a happy feeling and was further brightened by the red, leather couch and large modern art pieces on the exposed brick walls. Her place had an interior design magazine, art-deco feel to it.

Keeva winced as she imagined losing her apartment. She'd been there since her senior year at Spelman College. She and her boyfriend, Mark, then a senior at Morehouse, had picked it out together for her. If she flunked out again, her parents would withdraw their financial support and her penthouse loft, luxury car, and generous allowance would all be gone. There was no way her dad would call in another favor to get her into another graduate program.

Keeva dropped her briefcase off at the dining room table, ignoring the books begging to be read. She had to study, but needed to get rid of the heaviness that had been riding her since she stepped into Ms. Parker's office.

Keeva went to her bedroom and exchanged her pantsuit for some comfortable leggings and a T-shirt, and walked barefoot back into the living room. She pushed the furniture toward the kitchen, careful not to scratch her hardwood floors. They had been a must when she was looking for an apartment. Even though she had given up hope of a professional dancing career, she still loved to dance.

She flicked on the stereo and pushed the "skip disc" button until she got to her African drumming CD. The pulsing tribal rhythms connected with something deep within her.

Keeva inhaled slowly, breathing the music into her body. She began to sway back and forth until the music got into her feet, her body, and her soul. She moved around the room, slowly at first. Her movements grew bigger and stronger as she allowed herself to become enraptured in the music. As she leaped and twirled, the tension streamed out of every pore of her body. She danced herself into a frenzy until she reached a climatic point of release, and then lay in the middle of the floor.

She missed dancing.

Her mother enrolled her in her first dance class at the age of six so she could develop grace and good posture. Her father took her to see the Alvin Ailey dance troupe when she was ten. After that, all she dreamed of was being a professional dancer. She planned to audition for the troupe when she was seventeen, but her mother refused to let her. Neither of her parents thought a dance career was appropriate for Keeva. They thought she needed a professional career to support herself, and that she could dance in her spare time, as a hobby. After they canceled her audition, dancing became bittersweet for Keeva and she quit taking classes.

Keeva jumped when the phone rang. She stretched back out and stared at the ceiling. The hardwood floor felt cold against her hot, sweaty skin.

The answering machine beeped. "Keeva, this is Shara Anderson from your foundations class. I know you're probably bogged down with studying for your other classes, but we need to get this project started soon. Please give me a call when you get a chance so we can set up a time to meet."

Keeva rolled her eyes. In the midst of her mid-term exams, her stupid professor assigned a re-search project. He randomly grouped the class into teams of two and she ended up with Shara. Why was she calling her now? The project wasn't due until the end of the semester.

Keeva didn't know Shara too well. The most notable thing about her was how plain Jane she was. Her hair was always pulled back in a pony-tail and she wore no earrings, no makeup, no nothing. She had a pretty face and would prob-ably be nice looking if she fixed herself up a lit-tle. If she didn't wear jeans every day, Keeva would think she was one of those fanatical reli-gious people who thought it was a sin to wear pants or look good. Like God would send some-one to hell over a tube of lipstick and a pair of earrings. Shara definitely wasn't the kind of person Keeva associated with and she wasn't looking forward to the project.

She looked over at the clock. Mark would be dropping by in less than an hour to check on her. Keeva pulled the furniture back into place, then grabbed a quick shower. As she put on her makeup, she had to laugh at her new hair color. By some strange reasoning, probably a television commercial she had seen, she thought all she needed to fix her life was to spice up her hair color. She pulled her thick, brown hair, now with auburn highlights, up on top of her head and fastened it with a tortoise-shell clip. Mark liked her hair up.

As she poured a generous glass of wine, the buzzer rang, indicating that Mark was downstairs. A few minutes later, she heard him fumbling with his keys and went to open the door.

He pulled her into his arms. "Hey, how's my Princess?"

Somehow Mark had adopted her father's nickname for her. It was really a private joke between her and her dad. When she was growing up, he always thought Keeva's mother was too hard on her and wanted her to be perfect, like a little princess. He thought she should get to enjoy herself more and not worry about what fork to use or how to enunciate perfect English.

Keeva inhaled the strong, masculine scent of Mark's cologne and snuggled into his chest. "Fine, now. Do you want to come in or are we going to stand in the doorway all night?"

He kissed her on the nose. "You look beautiful as always. I love your hair like that."

She beamed at his compliment.

Mark took her glass so she could twist the lock on the door he could never seem to work. He took a sip and frowned. "Wine? I thought you were studying."

"I'm through for the evening. I was relaxing until you got here."

"You know I don't like it when you drink wine. How many times do I have to tell you that?"

Keeva clenched her teeth and turned to walk toward the couch.

He followed her. "All you had to do was wait until I got here. I know how to relax you."

She closed her eyes. *Oh, no—not tonight*. She searched her mind for excuses but couldn't think of anything. She took a deep breath and turned toward him, making herself smile. Demurely, she asked, "Really? How?"

"Come here, I'll show you."

Mark kissed her for what seemed like an hour. She knew him well enough to know what was next and wished she hadn't said she was finished studying. She slowly pulled herself away. She dodged his searching lips every time he tried to reengage her in another kiss until he finally gave a frustrated groan and said, "What?"

She lowered her eyes. She couldn't look in his face and lie. "I'm sorry, baby. It's that time of the month."

"Again? Wasn't that two weeks ago?" He was paying more attention to when her cycles were, probably because she was using that excuse more and more.

Truth was, she'd barely had a period since

she started getting Depo-Provera shots over a year ago. "You know that Depo has my cycles all crazy." She turned her back to him.

He rubbed her shoulders. "You know I hate that stuff. It's unnatural—all those extra hormones in your body. That's probably the reason for the extra pounds you've gained and your constant moodiness."

She whipped around. "What?"

"Don't get upset. I've noticed you've picked up a few pounds. And you're always irritable. I know school is difficult, baby, but you can't just let yourself go."

Keeva took a deep breath and pulled a strand of hair. "Mark, I'm really tired and I need to get some rest. I have to get up and study early in the morning. Thanks for coming by, but—"

He tried to smooth things over with a kiss. She stood there limp.

"Mark, I have a study group in the morning. I need to go to sleep." It wasn't *exactly* a lie. She did eventually have to set up a study date with Shara.

"You don't have to be so sensitive. I wasn't trying to hurt your feelings. I'm sorry, Princess." He slunk to the door like a sad puppy with his tail between his legs.

She walked over to kiss him. "I'm sorry. I'm just tired from all the studying. I'll feel better after a good night's rest. I'll call you in the morning, okay? I promise we'll spend some quality time together after midterms are over."

Mark accepted her apology with a kiss on the forehead. "All right, we'll make it a date."

Keeva closed and locked the door behind

him. She went to her dining table, sat down and flipped open a textbook. She had to make herself read at least two chapters before she went to bed. For the past few weeks, whenever she tried to study, she somehow ended up on the couch watching television. *Lifetime* always had a good movie on, one after another.

Later, as she undressed to get into bed, she stood in her full-length mirror and turned from side to side, trying to find the extra pounds Mark mentioned. She studied her twenty-five year-old, well-toned body, but didn't see any difference.

She pulled her favorite pair of jeans out of the closet. They were a size four and usually fit her perfectly. She pulled up the zipper. They fit the same way they always did. Mark probably noticed something she didn't. *Gotta start going to the gym.*

Keeva sat on the edge of the bed and opened her nightstand drawer to pull out a bottle of Ambien tablets. She didn't like having to depend on pills, but she had to get a good night's sleep. If she did her usual tossing and turning for hours, she'd never be able to study tomorrow.

She slipped between her satin sheets and started her deep breathing and meditation techniques, hoping for sleep to come. The pill would soon chase away images of her flunking out of school and losing everything she held dear.

Chapter Two

Why in the world did I agree to do this interview?

Shara Anderson stared at the television camera as if it were her archenemy. She had worked hard to get her hair slicked back into a ponytail that morning. All day, she'd made a special effort not to run her fingers through it like she usually did when she was nervous or upset. Otherwise, it'd be sticking up in some places with deep furrows in others. The only makeup she'd been able to find that morning was cracked and discolored. No telling how long it had been in her bathroom drawer. She'd ended up barefaced as usual.

"Do you really need to interview me? Isn't this supposed to be about the kids?" Shara almost pleaded with Cheryl Hanes, the Fox 5 News community focus reporter. She looked down at her jeans and sweatshirt, wondering if she should have dressed up.

"It is about the kids, but we need someone to tell the story." Cheryl looked down at her clipboard and back up at Shara. "Here's how it goes. I'll ask some questions and you answer as clearly and succinctly as possible. Make sure you talk in complete sentences as if the viewers haven't heard my question. If you don't like what you say or mess up, we can go back and fix it. Just act natural and talk normal, like we're friends."

A sympathetic smile peeked through Cheryl's professional demeanor. "Don't be nervous, you'll do fine. Pretend the camera's not even there."

Cheryl held the microphone toward her. "So tell us about your program."

Shara cleared her throat. " 'Run For Your Life' is a track program we started here at Kingdom Builder's Christian Church to reach out to the kids in the surrounding community. Teens from the neighborhood come here after school three days a week to run track or work out in the gym, and on alternating days we have a tutoring program. They have to make passing grades to stay in the program."

Shara knew she sounded robotic and staged, but how was she supposed to relax and act natural with that camera in her face? Cheryl coached her a bit and made her answer again. It came out better the second time and they moved on to the next question.

"When did you start the program?"

Shara paused to think about her answer so she wouldn't have to do it over. "I started the program as a class project almost a year ago. I'm in the Master's program for Education at Georgia State. Things went so well, we just continued it. It's turned out better than I expected. Across the board, the kids' grades are better. They get in fewer fights in school and in the neighborhood. Most importantly, their confidence and self-esteem have improved as well as their overall outlook on life." Shara started to feel more comfortable talking about her kids.

She pointed toward the track. "Davon there was having difficulty passing most of his classes and now he's maintaining a C average. He's convinced he can bring it up to a B average by next year."

The cameraman swung around to film the young teen as he rounded the track. Shara laughed to herself when she saw Davon glance at the camera, then pump his arms harder and pick up his stride, his jaw set with a determined look on his face.

Shara pointed to a tall, lanky youth with thick cornrows. "And that's Jamil. Before, he got into trouble in school all the time for fighting or acting out in class. In the last six months, he hasn't been in one fight. Now he's in competition with Davon to see who can make the best grades."

Jamil obviously didn't know the camera was fixed on him; otherwise he would have done something silly like make a face or perform his running man dance.

"And then there's Tangela Madison. She's the one I told you about."

Cheryl had asked if there was one teen they could do a special focus on with a follow-up segment later on in the year. She had explained that with all the negativity in the news, the station wanted to connect with the community and do "people stories." She wanted the teen most positively affected by the program.

Tangee was the obvious choice. She was Shara's fastest runner and most dedicated participant. She had gone from almost failing 8th grade last year to maintaining a B average in 9th grade this year. In her last two high school track meets, she was placed first in the 100-meter dash.

Cheryl turned toward the cameraman. "Get some footage of that girl over there."

Shara couldn't help but notice that Tangee's form was a little off as it had been the past few times she'd watched her run. She waved Tangee over. The young teen frowned. She wasn't any more excited about being in front of the camera than Shara was.

Cheryl gave Tangee similar instructions, and then started asking questions. Shara's pastor walked up as Tangee stammered out her answer. His interview was next.

Tangee pulled on the bottoms of her shorts and rocked back and forth on her heels. Shara made signs for her to stand still and put her hands at her sides.

". . . I never thought about going to college before, but now I'm definitely going. And if I keep doing so well in track, I should be able to get a full scholarship. This program has definitely changed my life," Tangee said.

That's my girl. Shara smiled and gave her a

thumbs-up from beside the cameraman. Tangee returned only a half-hearted smile and looked at the ground.

When Cheryl finished, Shara walked over and put an arm around Tangee. "You did great. I'm proud of you." She studied Tangee's eyes. "You seem a little tired. Wanna call it quits for today?"

"I'm cool, Miss Shara. I'ma finish."

"All right then, go ahead." Shara watched her drag back onto the track.

When she turned back, Cheryl had started interviewing her pastor. "Pastor Kendrick, it's so inspiring to see the work you're doing here in the community. How did you get started?"

Pastor Kendrick was only five feet eight, but seemed larger than life in front of the camera with his confident stance and strong smile. He gestured toward the church building behind the track. "We started off ten years ago with nine people in a classroom when this was still a Fulton County high school on the verge of closing. The Lord has blessed us with tremendous growth and we've been able to purchase the building from the city with a vision to completely revitalize this community. So far we've started a GED program and have received funding for a welfare-to-work program. Our next undertaking is an entrepreneurial development center for members of the church who want to start businesses. Hopefully, we can pump some finances into the community. One of our greatest focuses will be capturing the hearts of the young people. Shara's track program is just the start."

Cheryl asked a few more questions about Pastor Kendrick's motivation and the church and then motioned to the cameraman that they were finished. She turned to Shara. "We'd like to get some footage of the neighborhood. Care to ride with us? It'll only take a few minutes."

"Sure." Shara turned to Pastor Kendrick. "Keep an eye on the kids for me. You know how they can get."

"Yeah, I'll stay around. And Shara, thanks for doing this," Pastor Kendrick said. "I know it's not exactly your thing. I'm hoping the exposure will be good for us. Maybe the people in the community will watch and will want to come check us out. And you never know what rich philanthropist may watch and want to give a donation to our cause."

"No problem, Pastor. Anything to help."

Shara hopped into the front seat of the television station's SUV next to Cheryl while the cameraman sat in the back with the camera hoisted over his shoulder. She directed Cheryl to turn onto Martin Luther King, Jr. Drive.

They cruised the area slowly. The dilapidated buildings, debris in the streets, and grown men hanging on every corner drinking and talking trash looked worse to Shara as she watched it through Cheryl's eyes. It usually didn't bother her. Maybe in her seven years of attending the church, she had gotten used to it.

Shara pointed for Cheryl to turn at the stop sign. "You know it's funny. Even though this is in the middle of the inner city, it reminds me of home."

Cheryl turned onto Memorial Drive. "Where are you from?"

"A little town you've never heard of deep in the heart of South Georgia."

"That explains the hint of Southern twang you've got."

Shara laughed. "Yeah, when I first moved here for college, I worked real hard to get rid of it. The tiny bit left reminds me of where I'm from."

Cheryl looked out at a young woman dragging a toddler down the street. Even with the windows up, she could be heard screeching and cursing at the child. "How is this anything like rural Georgia?"

Shara looked out at several young men with their pants hanging off their bottoms, huddled in a corner "shaking hands" and looking over their shoulders to see who was watching. "The poverty, despair, and that overwhelming, choking feeling that no matter what you do, you'll never be able to get out."

"Get out?" Cheryl studied Shara's face as they stopped at a red light.

"Yeah. Get out. Make a better life for yourself. Live somewhere other than the little box of a neighborhood or town you seem to be stuck in. This neighborhood feels like that same depressing, stifling way home did."

Cheryl turned left and they headed toward downtown Atlanta. It was amazing how close the cosmopolitan downtown area was located to the impoverished area the church was in.

"Atlanta isn't the black mecca for the people in this neighborhood. The 'good life' is just as unreachable as it seemed to me when I was growing up." Shara looked up at the skyscrapers and office buildings. "Even though it's just a few city blocks away, it might as well be as far away as South Georgia."

Cheryl nodded and they turned onto Broad Street, back toward the church.

Shara wondered why the cameraman was pointing the camera toward her instead of out the window. "For me, getting an education and running track was my ticket to freedom. If I hadn't gotten a full scholarship to Georgia State University for undergrad, I probably would have never gotten out. I guess that's why my track and tutoring programs are so important. I want to help these kids escape. Tangee is me in high school all over again, just in urban Atlanta instead of rural south Georgia."

Cheryl turned toward the back seat. "Are you thinking what I'm thinking?"

The cameraman was still pointing the camera on Shara. "I'm way ahead of you."

"What?" Shara smoothed her hair back. *Would you get that durn camera out my face?*

Cheryl said, "I'm glad you rode with us. This is a great angle for the story. It'll make it deeper, richer. Do you have time to go back and do a few more questions and some shots with Tangee? I really want to focus on the two of you and use some of what you've told us."

Shara cringed. "More camera time?"

"You never know what might happen. Like your pastor said, some rich person may be watching and offer Tangee a full scholarship to the college of her choice. This segment may be her way out."

Shara let out a deep breath. "Okay. Let's do it."

Shara stood with an arm around Tangee in front of the church, her face aching from smiling, her brain tired from thinking of articulate answers to questions.

Cheryl said, "This is gonna be great. Okay, I think we're done with you, Tangee. We'll be back to interview you again in a few months. Keep winning those meets and keep your grades up and we'll have a great follow-up story."

"Yes ma'am." Tangee gave Shara a quick hug and jetted away as if she needed to get as far from the camera as possible.

"One more question, Shara, and I promise we'll be done."

Shara refreshed her smile. "Sure."

"It seems like you do so much here at the church with the kids and we know you're in grad school full time. What kinds of things do you do for fun? How do you unwind and spend your free time?"

"I . . ." Shara's smile faded into a frown. "I . . ." She bit her lip and wrinkled her nose, trying to think of something to say. She gave a nervous laugh. "I guess not much of anything."

Cheryl made a "cut" sign to the cameraman. "It's okay. We have more than enough to make a great story. Just trying to show you as well-rounded. I can't imagine you *would* have time for much else."

Cheryl shook Shara's hand with a strong grip. "Thank you so much. I have to say I really enjoyed doing this story. You're one of those inspiring people who makes us all want to be better. Keep doing all you're doing and best of luck with the program."

And best of luck with getting a social life too, huh? Shara could imagine the thought in Cheryl's mind. They said their good-byes and Shara turned to walk to her car.

As she rounded the corner to the parking lot, she spied Tangee sitting on the benches behind the church. At her feet sat a guy looking too old to be anywhere near her. Tangee was finishing off the end of a cornrow she was putting in his large Afro. This wasn't the first time Shara had seen him hanging around after track practice.

She made plans to talk to Tangee.

Poverty and lack of an education weren't the only things that could keep her from getting out of the neighborhood.

Chapter Three

Keeva closed her notebook as the professor finished her last class of the day. She decided to study in the library, knowing if she went home, she'd end up on the couch watching TV.

As she opened the door, the musty, dusty smell of old books and the quiet calm in the air beckoned her in. She sat down at a table in the corner facing the wall and opened her *Foundations* book. She sat forward in her chair so she wouldn't be too relaxed. The quiet hum of the heater and steady ticking of the clock were hypnotic enough to lull her to sleep.

Half an hour later, she'd barely finished the first paragraph and had no idea what she'd read. *Pay attention, Keeva! Stop daydreaming and get your head out of the clouds.* She could see her mother's face, stern and unyielding, one hand on her hip, the other held out with a finger pointing at her. That finger was the only rod of discipline Keeva had ever needed.

She rubbed her temples. The familiar band of a tension headache squeezed its vice grip around her head. She decided to take an inventory of exactly what she needed to do. As she turned through the pages of her syllabus, her stomach sank as she realized how far behind she was. What had she been doing?

Stupid *Lifetime* movies . . .

Was it possible to cover all the material in the small amount of time she had left? What if she couldn't? There was no way she could make a B in the course if she failed this test. Keeva imagined Ms. Parker's face, accentuated by her bleeding red lipstick, pointing a menacing finger in her face. What would she tell her parents if she flunked out? What would she tell Mark? What would she do with her life if she didn't get this degree?

Keeva pulled her hair. A few too many strands came out. She'd noticed more strands on her brush lately, too. She was so emotionally overwhelmed, she was losing her beautiful hair. Maybe she should increase her therapy sessions to twice a week.

The room was closing in on her. Her heart beat faster and faster as if it were going to leap out of her chest. She breathed deeply, trying to get enough air to her brain to get rid of the dizziness swelling in her spinning head. What was wrong with her?

"Hey, Keeva."

Keeva's eyes trailed upward, finally reaching Shara Anderson's smiling face.

"I'm not sure if you got my message or not. I called you on Friday," Shara said.

"Really?" Keeva frowned. "My answering machine must be acting up again."

"I wanted to set up a time to start working on the research project. I know it's early, but I want to get a head start on it. Waiting to the last minute to get stuff done makes me crazy." Shara smiled brightly.

What was she so happy about? Did she not have midterms right now? Keeva put on one of her most convincing fake smiles but her voice was tight. "I'd like to wait until exams are over. I wouldn't be able to give it much time now because I need to focus on studying."

Shara remained disgustingly cheerful. "Sure, well, my number is in the class roster. Give me a call when you're ready."

Instead of walking away like she should have, Shara stood there, looking at her a little too hard. "Are you okay?"

"Sure, I'm fine. Just, you know, studying for midterms." Keeva averted her eyes, hoping Shara wouldn't see the panicky look in them.

"Maybe you should take a little break. You don't look so hot."

Shara pulled up a chair, uninvited. Keeva flashed her a look, eyes narrowed and lips pursed. In spite of herself, she had inherited her mother's evil glares and sharp tongue. Her eyes swept across Shara's unkempt hair and bulky sweatshirt. She was about to tell her she didn't look so hot either, and not because she was studying too hard. She bit her tongue when she saw the genuine concern in Shara's eyes.

"I'm a little behind and need to catch up." Keeva hoped Shara would take the hint and leave.

She didn't. She looked at Keeva's book. It was from the class they shared. "Hey, I have my notes with me. Would you like to borrow them?"

"I took notes in class." Keeva tried not to sound defensive. Her notes were scant and full of doodles from daydreaming. She could use any help she could get right now, but didn't want to admit it to this girl. Who did she think she was anyway?

"Oh, I'm sure you have notes, but mine might be helpful. I'm real obsessive-compulsive when I study, so I re-do my notes from class combining them with notes from the book. I highlight things the professor concentrated on that I think may be on the exam."

Keeva stared at Shara. Was she for real? Talk about anal-retentive. She had to admit she needed help. She forced a smile. "Sounds great. I'd love to borrow your notes. Don't you need them, though?"

Shara shook her head. "I'm finished studying for that class." She took out a notebook and laid it on the table. "I'll be on the second floor studying for a few hours. I'll come back down for it before I go. If you find it helpful and don't get done in time, you can take it with you. Just let me know." She smiled one last cheerful smile and walked off with a little wave.

Keeva couldn't imagine having to work close-ly the rest of the semester with someone so aggravating. Was it too late to be reassigned to a new partner?

She looked at the perfectly neat handwriting on the front of the notebook, "Social and Cultural Foundations of Education—Shara Anderson." She turned the first few pages and was amazed at what she saw.

Shara had succinctly organized the material into outlines, and then expanded the outlines with brief text. As Keeva read over the notes, she began to feel as if she could get a handle on the information.

Two hours passed quickly. Instead of being disgusted that she hadn't accomplished anything, Keeva felt a glimmer of hope that she might actually pass.

Shara suddenly appeared. "Well?"

Keeva smiled a genuine smile. "Your notes are great. I feel like I understand what's going on now. It must take you hours to do that."

"I do a little bit everyday after class, while the information is still fresh in my head. I know I'm anal, but it works for me. Are you done or do you need to keep them?"

"If you don't mind, I'd like to keep them to go over them a few more times."

"No problem, just give them back to me in class when you're done." Shara headed toward the door.

Before she reached it, Keeva bit her lip, swallowed her pride and called out, "Shara?"

A few other students studying nearby gave her a dirty look for breaking their precious silence. Keeva gave them one of her nice-nasty smiles.

Shara turned and came back.

"Do you, uh, happen to have notes for any other classes? I was thinking, ummm, it would help me out a lot in my Family Systems and Research Methods classes," Keeva said.

Shara smiled. For some reason, her smile wasn't so annoying now.

"Well, actually I'm in the M.Ed program so I don't have any counseling classes. I did take the Research Methods course last semester and have my notebook at home." Even though they were in completely different programs, they still had some core courses in common.

They made plans to meet the next day so Keeva could get the notes and Shara left.

Relief flooded Keeva as she read through the notebook again. Must be some good karma she'd sent out coming back to her. She knew she'd be able to at least pass the tests, and if she focused hard enough, she might even eke out B's.

But was it enough to keep her in the program?

Chapter Four

On Friday afternoon, Shara stood at the edge of the track and cupped her hands around her mouth. "Time to hit the showers." One by one, the kids jogged toward her.

"Aw, Miss Shara, why we gotta take a shower?" Davon sniffed under his arms, as if to prove he didn't need to wash.

Shara shook her head and laughed. The boy acted like he was allergic to water. She swatted him. "Boy, you ain't going nowhere with me funky. We're going out for pizza tonight, remember?"

"Aw, yeah." The thirteen-year-old's eyes lit up and his pace quickened as he followed the other kids to the locker rooms.

She called after them, "And hurry up. We need to leave here in twenty minutes."

Shara frowned as Tangee jogged off the track last. "What's wrong with you? You're dragging today."

"I'm a'ight, Miss Shara. I caught a little leg cramp so I had to slow down some." Tangee rubbed her thigh.

"You sure that's all it is?" She studied Tangee's sunken eyes and pale cheeks. She wanted to believe her slower running times over the past weeks were due to leg cramps, headaches, or any of the other excuses Tangee had been giving.

Tangee nodded and looked away.

"Okay then, go ahead and get ready." As Shara watched Tangee limp to the locker room, she decided to talk to her after the pizza party.

Shara pulled the church van around to the back parking lot to wait for the kids to come out of the locker rooms. The heavy gym doors slammed open and she heard the loud arguments coming toward the van before she saw any of the teens.

"I get to sit in the front."

"You sat in the front last time—it's my turn."

"Unh uh, Tangee sat in the front last time and before that it was Deon."

"Tangee sit in the front all the time cuz' she Miss Shara's favorite."

"Well, I know it's my turn. I ain't sat in the front since we went to Six Flags last summer."

"Yeah, man and that was a long ride, so you don't get to sit in the front for a while."

"Whatever, man."

Eleven kids piled into the van. Jamil obviously won the argument, because he climbed into the front and flipped through Shara's CD case. The front seat argument was really about who got to control the music.

"Man, put on Tonex or Kirk Franklin."

Jamil turned around. "Yo, man, I'm the DJ and I play what I wanna play. When you sit in the front, you can run things, but for now—" he patted his chest, "I got this." He popped in a CD and started his signature head-bopping dance as the neo-soul gospel sounds of Lisa McClendon filled the van. The kid's choices in music had changed a lot since they'd been hanging out with Shara. They still listened to their favorite hip-hop artists, but also enjoyed Shara's contemporary gospel favorites.

"Aw, yeah." The head-bop dance was duplicated on every row of the van except the last. Tangee sat still in the corner, looking out the window. Shara thought she saw her wipe a tear from her eye.

When they arrived at Fellini's Pizza, the thick aroma of tomatoes, cheese, and spices drew them in. The kids fought over their seats at a large table in the back the manager prepared for their rowdy group every other Friday. He made it seem like he was taking extra care of his special customers, reserving a special section for them, but Shara knew he did it to keep her loud bunch away from the other customers.

Tangee usually sat next to Shara, but tonight she sat at the far end of the table. She only nibbled at a small piece of pizza when she usually competed with the boys for who could eat the most. Halfway through the meal, a terrified look came across her face and she jumped up and ran to the bathroom.

Shara followed her and found her there

retching over the toilet. When she finished, Shara placed a wet paper towel on her forehead and used another to clean her mouth. "You okay?"

Tangee nodded, but didn't look Shara in the eye as a single tear trickled down her face.

That said everything.

Shara's heart sank. *Oh, God no.*

Shara wiped the tear from Tangee's cheek and pulled her chin upward to meet her gaze. Tangee averted her eyes and burst into loud sobs. Shara pulled her close and held her, tears of her own slipping down her cheeks.

When Tangee stopped crying, Shara wiped the tears from her face and handed her some tissue to blow her nose. She wanted to give Tangee time to talk, but knew better than to leave the rest of the group unattended for too long.

"I'm going back out to the table. You go ahead and fix your face and come on back out. We'll talk later tonight, okay?"

Tangee nodded and stared at her shoes until Shara left.

No one at the table seemed to have noticed their absence. They were too busy arguing about who was the best, Ja Rule, Nelly, Naz, or Jay Z.

Davon was the loudest. "Man, Kanye West smoke all 'dem."

After a few more minutes, Tangee slipped back into her seat next to Jamil.

He turned and stared at her. "Yo, Tangee man, wassup wit' your face? You look a mess. Your eyes all red and puffy and your nose is bigger than it usually is." The rest of the kids laughed and Tangee looked like she was about to cry again. Shara was about to intervene when Lakita spoke up.

"Why don't you fools shut up? Always messing with somebody. You can see she upset. Come on, Tangee, let's go to the van."

Lakita had stepped out of character to defend Tangee. At eighteen, she was the oldest of the group and usually pretended she didn't want to be around. She never missed a day of practice or any pizza parties though.

Lakita walked up to Shara and held her hand out. "Miss Shara, I need the van keys. Me and Tangee tired of these fools and we ready to go. I don't know why I came wit' y'all anyway."

Shara was about to deal with her ever-present attitude, but the knowing look in the girl's eyes made her stop. She remembered Lakita's three-year-old son at home and handed her the keys. Lakita turned on her heels, rolled her eyes, and sucked her teeth, but put an arm around Tangee and led her to the van.

Shara rushed the rest of the kids through the remainder of their pizza and arguments and hurried them out to the van. She quickly squashed the squabble over the front seat and began dropping each of them off at their homes, leaving Tangee for last. When she pulled up in front of her apartment building, Shara turned the engine off and waited. Tangee sat there picking her fingernails.

Shara finally broke the silence. "Why didn't you tell me?"

Tangee put her head down.

Shara took a deep breath and smoothed her hair back. *Tell me what to do, God.*

Tangee sniffed. "I didn't mean to. It's just that . . . I know it was wrong . . . I know Jesus doesn't want me to . . ."

Shara put her hand on Tangee's arm. She had made a policy of never preaching to the kids, knowing it wouldn't help. Love said a lot more than "act right or go to hell" as she had heard so often growing up.

Tangee looked her in the eyes for the first time that evening. "I'm sorry, Miss Shara."

"I know, Tangee. The most important thing is where you go from here. You can beat yourself up all day, but it won't change anything. Forgive yourself and move forward. Your life is about to change a lot and you have to get ready. A lot of girls have babies and are still successful."

Tangee's mouth flew open. "Miss Shara, I can't keep this baby. I won't be able to finish high school or go to college. I meant what I told that TV lady. For the first time, I feel like I have a future—like I could end up somewhere different than this." She gestured toward her project building.

"What should I do, Miss Shara?" With tears clinging to the long lashes of her big, brown eyes, Tangee looked like she was four instead of fourteen. "I don't want to end up like my momma. I want to be somebody . . . like you."

The words cut Shara's heart like a knife. What could she say? Being a Christian, of course she didn't believe in abortion. But at the same time, could she tell this girl to have the baby and potentially ruin her future?

Shara felt guilty for even considering the unthinkable, but she wanted Tangee to have a chance. She remembered when she was a teenager and her best friend got pregnant at the age of sixteen. They had been friends since they were five and grew up in church together. When they got to high school, Antonia bucked against the rules and restrictions drilled into them in church. She started sneaking around with boys, and the next thing Shara knew, she was crying on her shoulder much like Tangee was.

Two years after Antonia had the first baby, she got pregnant again, and then had another baby sixteen months after that one. She never got to go to college like they'd always planned. She was now twenty-five and had four kids, all by different fathers. She worked at the local discount store back home and could barely make ends meet. Shara wondered what would have happened if. . . .

She shook the thought out of her head. She couldn't tell Tangee to kill her baby. "What about putting the baby up for adoption?"

Tangee scrunched her face as she looked down and smoothed her hands across her flat stomach. She shook her head.

They sat in silence for a few minutes. Tangee fiddled with the lock on the van door.

Shara asked gently, "What did your mother say?"

Tangee bit her lip and looked down at her hands.

Shara groaned. "You didn't tell her? What are you thinking?"

Tangee's eyes flashed. "That I want to stay alive. You have no idea, Miss Shara. If I told my momma, she'd beat me so bad." Her little body shook. "Then she'd put me out—she'd make me go live with my grandmother." Tangee burst into tears again.

Shara put her arm around her shoulder. "But you have to tell her. She's going to find out eventually."

Tangee clenched her fists. "That's why I didn't tell you. I knew you'd tell my momma. Promise me you won't tell her or I'll never come back to the program again." She cried harder, and then started coughing.

"Tangee, *please*. You're going to make yourself sick again. Stop crying. We'll figure this out, okay?"

Shara took some tissue from her purse and mopped Tangee's face with it. "Go in the house and get some rest. I won't tell her, but you're going to have to tell her. I know you think she'd put you out, but your mother loves you. After she got over being mad, she'd help you through this."

Tangee looked at Shara with fear and contempt in her eyes. "You don't know my momma." She got out of the van and trudged into her apartment building.

Shara sat there for a minute but was jolted out of her thoughts by a tap on the window.

"Hey, Church Lady. Don't you think it's a little late to be hanging out in the 'hood'?"

Shara started up the van as she nodded to

Belial. He was the neighborhood's drug runner. He wasn't a big time dealer or anything. He ran packages for the little money thrown his way to buy sneakers or games for his PlayStation. The people in the neighborhood didn't bother her too much, probably because they always saw her with the kids.

When she got back to the church parking lot, Shara was glad to see a blue Volvo next to her aging Honda Civic. God knew she would need to talk to Mother Hobbs, her spiritual mentor.

They met not too long after Shara came to Atlanta. After her freshman year in the dorm at GSU, Shara rented a room from Mother Hobbs until she graduated and took her first job as a schoolteacher. Mother Hobbs had taught in the Atlanta Public School System for thirty-two years. Her husband finally insisted she retire after one of her students was caught with a gun in school. She was now the church administrator.

Shara found Mother Hobbs in the church office. It used to be the principal's office when the building was a school and Shara was instantly transported back to her high school days whenever she entered.

"What are you doing here so late? You know I don't like it when you're here after dark," Shara said.

Mother Hobbs stood to give her a warm hug and then stepped back. "Chile, my mother is long gone, so don't even try it. What are *you* doing here so late?"

"I took the kids out for pizza and just finished dropping them off." She plunked her gym bag down and parked herself in a chair in front of Mother Hobbs' desk. "Whatcha doing?"

"Shara, it's Friday night. Why are you hanging out with a bunch of kids and then coming back here to hang out with an old woman?"

"Old woman? Please." She looked around the room. "Where?"

Shara could easily picture Mother Hobbs in one of those *Essence* magazine photo shoots of the older black women you'd swear were twenty years younger than their actual age. She'd stand tall and regal like a queen, eyes brimming with wisdom and mouth filled with laughter that she'd tackled life and conquered. Shara felt funny calling her "Mother" Hobbs at first. She definitely wasn't anything like the church mothers she had known growing up.

"Child, you need to get a life outside of this church. You're always here."

"Well, you're always here."

"I work here." Mother Hobbs fingered her silvery gray hair that cascaded down to her shoulders in small, neat dread locks. "Spending a Friday night with a bunch of kids. You act like you're their mother, or like you're trying to make up for the things their mothers don't or can't do. When do you ever have fun?"

"I enjoy my kids. That is fun."

"I'm talking about being with people your own age. And how are you gonna find a man hanging around a bunch of kids? That'll scare a man away."

"What makes you think I'm looking for a man?"

"Because you're a twenty-six-year-old woman who's not married. That's how I know."

Shara rolled her eyes. *Not this again.* "Look, I'm not here to talk about that. I need your help."

Shara told Mother Hobbs about Tangee's pregnancy. "I don't know what to tell her. It's like she's looking to me for an answer. It's scary to have that much influence in somebody's life."

Mother Hobbs shook her head. "Poor child. I really feel for her." Her tone changed. "But that's precisely what I'm talking about. As much as you love these kids, they are not your responsibility. That child has a mother who should be agonizing over this right now—not you. I understand your being upset, but it's not your job to come up with the solution."

Mother Hobbs rose and came around her desk to stand by Shara's chair. She ran a gentle hand over Shara's hair. She was constantly smoothing it down. Her habit annoyed Shara at first, especially since it was accompanied by scolding about how unkempt Shara looked. Mother Hobbs fussed about her fixing her hair or wearing makeup or dressing like a young woman instead of a tomboy who never grew up. Over time, Shara had grown to appreciate the motherly affection.

"So what am I supposed to do? Turn her away without any hope or direction?" Shara asked.

"It's not your place to tell her what to do. That's for Tangee and her mother to decide. You can offer prayer and God's mind for the situation if asked, but otherwise you need to pray and leave it at that.

Mother Hobbs walked back around to sit at her desk. "And don't spend all day and night worrying about it. Pray and give it to God. Carrying other people's burdens is the fastest way to spiritual fatigue, I know. You'll be all burnt out and won't be any good to anyone—not your kids, not yourself, not even God."

Shara nodded slowly.

"I'm not saying not to help people. I'm just saying make sure you get the mind of God for the situation. Some people you're meant to pray for and release. Others, He'll lead you to almost carry in the spirit, to 'labor until Christ be formed in them.' " Mother Hobbs quoted one of Shara's favorite scriptures from the book of Galatians.

"Is that what God told you to do with me?"

Mother Hobbs smiled. "You know what you need? Go out and have some fun tomorrow night. Why don't you ever hang out with some of the young women from the church?"

"I do sometimes, but . . ." Shara shrugged. She got up and moved over to her own small desk in the corner. She pulled out her stats notebook to jot down the number of kids at track practice. She then pulled out the financial record to log the expenses for the pizza party. Maybe if she looked busy, Mother Hobbs wouldn't push her about her nonexistent social life.

"But what?"

"I don't know." Shara rolled her eyes. "They're all right, but . . . the married women talk about their husbands and tell story after story about their kids. All the single women talk about is their man, getting a man, or the latest fine man who joined the church." She lowered her voice to a whisper. "Some of them even talk about sleeping with their boyfriends. Can you believe that?"

Mother Hobbs chuckled. "Have mercy on them, Shara. They still need to grow in God some."

"I'm not judging them or anything. I just don't want to talk about that. Or clothes or who's having a sale or who broke up with who or who's dating who or any of the other silly stuff they talk about."

"What do you want to talk about then?"

"The stuff we talk about. The Word and how to get closer to God and how to change these kids and this community. How to take over the world for the Kingdom of God."

"You can't be serious all the time. Those things are important, but you have to balance it out by relaxing and having fun." Mother Hobbs smirked. "Maybe if you found you a nice young man, you'd understand why women your age talk about them so much."

Shara put both notebooks back in her desk drawer. She didn't have much faith in her ability to find a "nice young man." Not that she was looking. She hardly ever thought about men or dating, let alone getting married. She knew she was supposed to be like her contemporaries, pining away for a man to fulfill her dreams, but she could care less.

Shara spent her childhood hearing from her father about the evils of the male species. To let him tell it, they were all devils, waiting to catch some young girl off guard so he could "have his way with her." When Antonia got pregnant, it confirmed her father's fears and seemed to validate his refusal to even let her near boys. She wasn't allowed to date until she was eighteen and in college, away from her father's control.

What happened when she finally could date and "fell in love" for the first time also contributed to her feelings about men. Her six-month relationship with Keith ended disastrously, leaving her heartbroken and bitter. It also left her wondering if her father's beliefs about men were true. That was years ago, and she hadn't been interested in being interested in any man since.

"Whatever, Mother Hobbs." Shara came back over to Mother Hobbs' desk and picked up her gym bag. "Tell you what. When you get a man, I'll get one."

"I told you 'bout that mouth of yours, getting smart with me. You know I had the best husband a woman could ever have, and even though he's gone, I still have enough of his love to last me the rest of my life." Mother Hobbs sighed. "I guess that's why I pester you so much. Love like that is the most beautiful thing in the world and everyone should get a chance to experience it."

"Maybe everybody's not meant to experience that kind of love." She gave the older woman a hug. "I gotta go, old lady. Don't stay here too late."

"Maybe I should be calling you Mother instead of the other way around."

Shara laughed as she walked to her car. For just a second, she allowed her heart to feel a pang. Would she ever experience love like that? She shook the thought out of her head. She didn't have time to long for some Mr. Wonderful who didn't exist. No, Shara was content with her relationship with God, her friendship with Mother Hobbs, her church and her kids.

Wasn't she?

Chapter Five

Keeva flipped through the pages of her exam and smiled. She walked to the professor's desk and laid it down, feeling like a weight had been lifted. It was her last exam and she'd done well on the others, too. It wasn't enough to keep her in the program yet, but at least it was a start. Now, if she could just finish her Methods project and do well on the Foundations project with Shara.

She felt like celebrating. She thought about calling Mark to go out for drinks, but didn't want to chance spoiling her post-exam high. She thought of calling a couple of her girlfriends, but didn't feel like hanging out with them either. Maybe she'd just celebrate by herself.

She walked out the door and found Shara waiting in the hallway.

"You're still here. You finished so long ago, I thought you'd be gone by now. Thank God it's over." Keeva gave her a genuine smile. "Shara, thanks for everything. I would have never made it without you."

"No problem. Glad I could help."

Shara had met Keeva every day in the library for the past week. In addition to letting her use her notes, her calm presence somehow helped Keeva concentrate. They took long chat breaks and had started to get to know each other. Keeva couldn't put her finger on it, but there was something about Shara she liked. She exuded this energy that made Keeva feel peaceful. And Shara kept her laughing by constantly pulling food out of her book bag and eating when the librarians weren't looking.

"You want to go out and celebrate? Drinks or dinner or something? My treat—I owe you big."

Shara looked at her watch. "I have to go to work for a couple of hours, but I'll be finished by six-thirty—seven at the latest."

"Perfect. I could take a little nap. I haven't slept in a week."

"Puleeze." Shara studied Keeva's face. "You don't look it. When I don't sleep for a week, it's obvious."

"Puleeze. When do you not sleep for a week? I've never met anyone so ridiculously organized and prepared."

They both laughed.

"What are you in the mood for? Drinks or dinner?" Keeva asked.

"I don't drink, but you know I love to eat, so dinner sounds good. It would also give us time to start talking about the project."

Keeva's eyes widened. "What are you, a machine? I'm not trying to talk about any project or anything that has to do with school tonight. I need to clear my head and relax."

"Okay, I promise, no school." Shara said. "I don't eat out a lot, so if you have any suggestions on where to go . . ."

"We could do Thai, or Japanese—I could do some sushi right now—or there's a cute little French Bistro . . ." Keeva stopped when she saw the expression on Shara's face. "What?"

Shara wrinkled her nose. "You eat raw fish? Blecchhh! I've never had Thai, don't eat sushi and the only thing French I want is fries. What about some good ol' American food?"

Now Keeva wrinkled her nose. "Eeeuuw! No way. There is this restaurant in Midtown I've been meaning to try."

They made arrangements to meet at 7:00.

Shara pulled into the church parking lot and headed around back to the track. As she turned the corner, she was dismayed to see the kids gathered in a circle jeering and screaming. She knew them well enough to know there were two people in the middle of that circle either cussing at each other and getting ready to fight, or already rolling around on the ground trying to kill each other. Who was it this time?

When the first few kids noticed her, they got quiet and stepped back. As they cleared away, she could see Lakita with her hands on her hips, neck winding in a circle, braids swinging and eyes rolling as she told off whoever her victim of the day was. As Shara got closer, she no-

ticed today's prey was an equally troublesome
teenager who had also been a thorn in her side.
Shanique had her hands on her hips and was
rolling her eyes and popping her gum with
every curse word flying out of Lakita's mouth.

Lakita stopped mouthing off when the circle
broke up and some of the kids whispered,
"Miss Shara, Miss Shara."

Shara put her hands on her hips and tried to
keep her voice calm. "What is going on here?"

Lakita and Shanique tried to explain themselves. "Well, she said . . . well didn't nobody tell
her to . . . she think she so special . . . all she do is
talk about people . . . ain't nobody thinkin' 'bout
her . . ."

Shara massaged her temples. "You know
what, I don't even care. I'm not in the mood for
this today. I just finished a week of exams and
don't have the time or energy for any foolishness." She looked around at all the kids. "You
should be almost done with a mile by now. Instead I find you fighting?"

They protested, but she held up her hand. "I
would think by now I could trust you all to do
what you know you're supposed to do. Why
does an adult have to be around for you to act
like you got some sense?"

They all got quiet, shuffled their feet and
looked at the ground.

"Sorry, Miss Shara." Davon was the first to
speak up. He turned and started a slow jog
around the track. After a series of mumbled,
"Sorry Miss Shara's," they all headed off to do
their laps.

Shara heard Lakita say under her breath,

"Run, run, run. All we do is run. Don't nobody feel like running around no boring track all the time. I'm quittin' this stupid program." She headed toward the track, but defiantly walked around instead of jogging like the others.

Tangee walked up to Shara. Her complexion had a yellow-green tinge to it. "Sorry I'm late, Miss Shara. Can I still run today?"

"Yeah, we're just getting started. You okay?"

"I'm fine, Miss Shara." Tangee walked toward the track.

"Tangee?" Shara called after her.

She came back. "Yes?"

"Did you tell your mother?"

Tangee looked at the ground. "Yes, Miss Shara. I did what you said."

"What did she say?"

Tangee kept her eyes on her shoes. "You were right. She was mad at first, but then she say we gon' work it out."

Shara patted Tangee on the shoulder. "You see? I told you it would be all right. Now don't you feel better that you told her?"

Tangee nodded and started off toward the track again. Shara watched her struggling to lift her feet. She'd have to make sure Tangee saw a doctor soon.

Chapter Six

Shara pulled into the parking lot at the restaurant Keeva gave her directions to. She looked at the sign—*Spice*. It looked really posh from the outside. Shara knew any Midtown restaurant was going to be pricey. She hoped this wasn't one of those fancy spots where they charged twenty dollars for a plate nicely decorated with pretty food that didn't fill you up.

Keeva drove up beside her in a black BMW convertible. She took off some expensive looking sunglasses, put them in a black, leather case, and tucked it into the glove compartment. She refreshed her lipstick, fluffed her hair, and smiled at her reflection in the mirror. Shara rolled her eyes.

Keeva got out of the car. She looked Shara up and down and gave one of her strained smiles that made Shara wonder what she was really thinking.

"Just coming from work?" Keeva asked.

"Yeah, I just got here." Shara looked down at her clothes and back at Keeva. She followed Keeva into the restaurant.

Shara looked around at the modern, upscale decorum. The place was filled with twenty and thirty-somethings dressed in business suits, sipping fancy looking drinks, talking on cell phones, schmoozing and looking polished and cosmopolitan. She pulled up her baggy jeans and pulled her jean jacket tighter around her to cover up her wrinkled sweat shirt.

The hostess gave Shara a similar strained smile when she greeted them, but led them to their booth and put their menus down in front of them. "Your server will be here in a few."

Shara scanned the menu. She didn't see anything she would want to eat. She giggled at the thought of embarrassing Keeva by asking if the chef could make her a hamburger and fries.

The waitress walked up. "Good evening, ladies. Welcome to Spice. Can I take your drink order?"

"I'll have a glass of white wine," Keeva said.

"I'll have some cranberry juice," Shara said.

The waitress scribbled down the orders. "Let me tell you about the specials tonight. We have a . . ." She described the food as if she was describing art.

They both ordered the special. Shara hoped it wouldn't take long. "Could we get some bread or something? I'm starving."

The waitress nodded. "Of course."

Keeva sipped her water. "So, where do you work?"

"I run an after-school program for inner city kids at my church," Shara said.

Keeva looked impressed. "I don't see how you do it. Work and go to school? I'd never make it. I can't believe I decided to get a graduate degree. Undergrad almost killed me."

"What made you decide to go to grad school?"

"There was never really a question of whether I would. It was just a matter of what I'd be going for."

Shara looked at her curiously.

"My parents," Keeva explained. "It was just one of those expectations all my life."

Shara laughed to herself. Her parents had never pushed her to go to college because they were convinced that at any moment, the rapture was going to come. "So why counseling?"

Keeva paused for a minute, as if she wanted to know the answer to that question herself. "I always wanted to help people, I guess. Especially young people."

Shara had to hide her surprise. She had taken Keeva to be one of those self-absorbed people who didn't think about helping others.

"At first, I wanted to be a pediatrician, but then I volunteered at South Fulton Hospital after my freshman year in college and was totally grossed out by all the sights, sounds, and smells." Keeva shuddered. "By the end of my first day, the nurse I was working with pulled me aside and told me she didn't think medicine was for me. I was glad because I felt like she gave me permission not to be a doctor."

Shara wondered why she needed permission not to do something she didn't want to, but decided not to ask.

"So I switched my major to English. I love writing, but my parents were concerned about me being able to get a good job with an English degree, so I switched to psychology."

"Why psych?"

The waitress stopped by to drop off a basket of steaming bread. Shara ignored her burning fingertips and smoothed butter over a large slice.

Keeva once again looked like she was trying to come up with an answer. She finally smiled, as if remembering something pleasant. "Well, when I was thirteen, my mom got real exasperated with me and took me to a shrink."

Shara's eyes widened. "Why?"

"Please." Keeva waved her hand flippantly. "I can't think of any of the kids I grew up with who didn't have therapy at some point in their lives.

"I felt like my mom wouldn't let me do anything I wanted to, and wouldn't listen to anything I had to say. She always wanted me to do things her way and think the way she thought. I felt stifled and controlled. I guess I got depressed. I slept all the time and stopped eating and lost a ton of weight. My dad got worried, so they took me to a psychologist."

Growing up as a preacher's daughter, Shara could identify with being stifled and controlled by her parents. She had never gone to a psychologist for it, though.

"My psychologist was the most incredible

person I'd ever met. She listened to me and cared what I thought about and felt. Nobody had done that for me before. She made me feel that all my dreams were okay—that *I* was okay." Keeva had a faraway look in her eyes.

"She gave me what my mother never could—acceptance for who I was. With my parents, there was always this pressure—like I had to live up to something—like I would never be enough. The psychologist had this magical presence about her that made it okay to be me. The impression she made on me, I guess, is what made me want to be a therapist. I guess I felt that if I could do that for somebody . . ."

Keeva stopped suddenly, her face red. The waitress appeared again and set their drinks down in front of them. Keeva drained half of her glass of wine in one swallow. She tossed her hair and pasted on a smile.

Shara sensed her discomfort and could almost see her putting her mask back on.

"Could you excuse me for a minute?" Keeva said. "I need to make a quick run to the bathroom."

"Sure." Shara picked up another piece of bread as Keeva hurried away.

Keeva lingered in the bathroom for a few minutes, hoping Shara wouldn't expect her to continue the same line of conversation. Why had she told all that stuff to a casual acquaintance? She straightened her Dana Buchman suit, gave her hair and lipstick one last glance in the mirror, and exited the bathroom. When she got back to the table and sat down across from Shara, she looked at Shara's hair and clothes. *Why should I care what she thinks anyway?*

Keeva finished off the rest of her wine. She looked around for the waitress. When she caught her eyes, she raised her glass to indicate to bring her another. She turned back to Shara. "So—what made you go into education?"

Shara sipped her cranberry juice. "I always wanted to be a teacher. When I finished undergrad, I taught seventh grade for a year and then eighth grade for two years."

"That must have been interesting. Where did you teach?"

"Bunche Middle School."

"Wow." Keeva's eyes widened. "Weren't the kids bad? Don't they carry guns and beat up the teachers there?"

"They aren't bad kids. A lot of them come from broken homes and live in not-so-great neighborhoods, so the way they act is a reflection of what they see every day. When you get down to the core of them, they're regular kids just like in suburbia. They have feelings and dreams like any other teenager. I don't think it's fair to judge them because they don't grow up privileged with all their needs met."

Keeva couldn't help but feel that last comment was directed at her. "I wasn't judging them. You hear on the news all the time about, you know—"

"I'm sorry," Shara said. "I didn't mean it that way. I guess I hear that all the time and it frustrates me. They just need a lot of love and guidance. If people have preconceived notions about them, they won't give them a chance."

"So why did you leave teaching?"

"At first, I really enjoyed teaching, but eventually it became frustrating and depressing."

"Why?" Keeva couldn't imagine "Miss Smiley-face" ever being depressed.

"Most of the kids have really bad home situations. After they got to know me and trust me, they would share things with me. Like their parents being strung out on crack, or working multiple jobs and never being home, or beating them, or neglecting them. Some of the kids were practically raising their younger siblings and they were just thirteen or fourteen. Too many young girls confessed that their father, uncle, or mom's boyfriend had molested them. Their situations were so depressing. I couldn't imagine how they could ever have a chance in life. No child should have to grow up the way some of them do."

Keeva looked around to see where the waitress was with her second glass of wine. She was almost sorry she had asked Shara about teaching.

Shara continued, "It seemed like I wasn't making any difference in their lives. I felt like I had so much to give—not just math and science, but love and a sense of self. The system isn't designed for all that, though. It got frustrating."

Shara reached across the table and took yet another piece of bread. Keeva was sure she wouldn't have an appetite when the food came. She smoothed a whole pat of butter on it, making Keeva wonder how she maintained her tight figure.

"So I decided to get my master's so I could start my own school. I want to be able to create a place where kids can come and get their needs met on many levels. I want to help them understand they have a purpose for being here and then equip them with the personal skills they need to reach their God-ordained destiny."

Keeva couldn't help but feel a pang of jealousy as she noticed the glow in Shara's eyes. "That sounds great. I wish I could have been in that kind of program when I was a kid. Probably would have saved my parents a pretty penny in shrink bills." Keeva fidgeted with her silverware. "Sounds like you really know what you want to do and are really passionate about it. That must be a good feeling."

"Well, you too, right?"

"Oh yeah, I definitely want to help people. I'd love to help little girls know who they are and get on the right track." She knew her half-hearted answer sounded nothing like Shara's impassioned decisiveness.

"But?"

Keeva shrugged. She didn't dare answer for fear that she'd start spilling her guts again.

The waitress brought their food. Shara stared at her plate and then at Keeva.

"What's wrong?" Keeva asked.

Shara whispered loudly, "How can they charge you $22 for this little bit of food? This ain't gonna do nothing but make my stomach mad."

Keeva looked at her own plate. It was a perfect

sized portion of salmon, garlic mashed potatoes and steamed vegetables. She appreciated the chef's elegant presentation with the bright yellow, lemon butter sauce drizzled delicately around the edge of the plate. "Try it. It's more than it looks."

Keeva was soon embarrassed as Shara tore into her food, almost violently. Keeva looked around the restaurant, hoping she didn't see anyone she knew. She was glad when Shara stopped eating and looked up at her.

"Sorry, I haven't eaten anything since lunch."

She went back to inhaling her food. Keeva forced a smile. Her cell phone rang. She recognized Mark's number and frowned. She was supposed to call him after her exam, but forgot.

"Hi, honey."

"Where are you? I thought you were going to call me when you finished your exams today. I had planned to come over tonight. Why aren't you answering your cell?" Mark's voice cut through the phone like a knife.

Keeva held the phone away from her ear to avoid the barrage of questions. "I didn't hear it ring, sweetie. I'm at a restaurant and it's kind of loud."

"At a restaurant?"

Keeva grimaced. *Oops.*

"Who are you out with? I thought we were going to be together tonight. Keeva, this is very inconsiderate of you. Did you even think of calling me?"

"My exams went well, sweetie, thanks for asking. Listen, I'm in the middle of a dinner meeting with a classmate. We're tossing around ideas so we can get started on a project we're doing together. This was the only time she could meet this week. I'll call you when I get home tonight, honey, I promise. We'll get together tomorrow. Love you baby, bye." She hung up before he could say anything.

She knew he was seething at her practically hanging up on him, but she didn't feel like dealing with him right now. She was actually enjoying her dinner with Shara, in spite of the hungry horse act she was putting on across the table. Shara stopped eating for a second to give her a questioning look.

"That was my boyfriend. I guess I forgot we were supposed to be getting together tonight."

"Gee, I thought we were having a celebratory dinner. I didn't realize we were working on our project."

"It's just a little white lie. You won't tell on me will you?"

Shara made a zipping motion across her lips. "Your secret's safe with me." She scraped the last bit of sauce off her plate with a piece of bread. "I have to admit, the food was good, but I'm still hungry. That'll be enough to last me until I get home, though." She rubbed her stomach.

Keeva looked down at her own full plate. "Want some dessert?"

"No, I'm not much of a sweets person. I'm more of a meat and potatoes girl."

"Not me, I'm a sweet-aholic. Give me some chocolate and all is right with the world." Keeva started to eat slowly. "Are you originally from Atlanta?"

"No, I'm from a small town south of Macon. My father was the overseer of a group of churches in that region."

Keeva had to ask. "Are you one of those holy people?"

"Holy people?"

Keeva didn't mean to, but she found herself looking at Shara's hair and plain face.

"Oh, you thought my look . . . you mistook my style—or *lack* of style for . . . that's funny." Shara laughed. "No I wish I could I could use that as an excuse. I'm just lazy. I figure if I have to choose between an extra hour of sleep and getting up earlier to look like you usually do, I'd rather sleep."

"Like I usually do?"

"You know, all fly, dressed to the nines, full face of makeup, perfect hair. Don't get me wrong. I admire you. I wish I could always look like I stepped out of *Essence*. That never was my thing, I guess."

Shara pushed her plate away from her and plunked her elbows on the table. "I never grew out of being a tomboy. I had a big brother I adored and the only way I could hang out with him was to do what he did. So I climbed trees, jumped off of bunk beds to see if I could fly, went fishing, you know, all the normal boy stuff. Then I was involved in sports from junior high through college, so I wasn't too worried about being pretty then, either."

Now it made sense. A girl jock. One of those girls Keeva's mother would turn up her nose at and talk about how mannish they looked. She couldn't imagine how any mother would allow her daughter to get so wrapped up in sports that she didn't get to enjoy being a girl.

"Track was about all I could do for fun growing up," Shara said.

"What do you mean?" Keeva had to restrain herself from telling Shara to take her elbows off the table.

"In the denomination I grew up in, anything having to do with 'the world', so to speak, was off limits. That included movies, secular music, most television shows, bowling, playing cards, anything remotely related to having fun. Anyone who participated in such activities was surely going to hell."

"Wow. How could you stand it?"

"I couldn't. Being the preacher's daughter, I practically *lived* in church. We had morning and evening service on Sunday, prayer meeting on Tuesday, Bible study on Wednesday, choir rehearsal on Friday night and of course Saturday night was spent getting ready for church on Sunday. I literally had no life."

"I can't imagine." Keeva shook her head.

"When I was a little girl, it didn't bother me much. I had a lot of little friends in church so it was like a big club. Of course, as I got older, it wasn't so much fun. My brother and I missed out on *everything*. At first, the kids in school made fun of us, but then they felt sorry for us. They brought their tape players to school and let us listen to the latest music and tried to show us how to dance. They told us about all the latest movies in vivid detail. We saw all our movies 'secondhand.' " Shara laughed bitterly. "My father tried to console us by telling us all our friends were going to hell. Of course, that didn't make us feel any better.

"That's how I got into track in the first place. It was the only way I could wear pants or shorts. Even then, my mom had to beg my dad to let me. He was concerned about me running in shorts because there were boys at my meets, but I was so shy I guess he figured he didn't have anything to worry about."

"You were shy?"

"Just around boys. I was convinced every male, except my father and brother, was the devil incarnate. I was terrified of them."

Keeva laughed. "That must have been difficult to get over."

Shara's smile faded. "Yeah. Pretty difficult."

The waitress came by and noticed Shara's empty plate. She raised an eyebrow. "All done already?" She reached for the plate. "Can I take this?"

"Sure." Shara held up the empty bread basket. "Can we get a fresh loaf?"

She seemed not to notice both Keeva's and the waitress' reactions. "So how about you? Did you grow up in church?"

"Yeah, but not nearly as much as you did. To be honest, I think church was more of a political thing for my parents," Keeva said.

"Political?"

"Have you heard of David Banks?"

"The state senator?"

"Yeah, well that's my dad."

"Your dad is a state senator?" Shara looked surprised.

Keeva nodded.

"What was that like?"

Normally, Keeva would have enjoyed bragging about being a senator's daughter. Somehow she knew it wouldn't impress Shara the way it impressed her other friends. She wasn't a part of that world where it mattered. She decided to be honest. "It was pretty horrible."

"Horrible?"

"We had to live the perfect life. Think about it—the best way to discredit a politician is to bring up some scandalous thing he did in his past or some dirt about his family.

"My dad knew early in his law career he wanted to run for public office, so he started planning then. He married the perfect wife who would be good for his public image—someone who could throw parties, say all the right things and know all the right people. His only child had to be a perfect angel and go to all the right schools and participate in all the right activities."

Keeva pushed around the remaining food on her plate, remembering the few extra pounds she had to lose. "Everything had to be proper and perfect. I couldn't do anything that might 'affect Daddy's career.' Church was like everything else—the right thing to do. My parents didn't really get into it though. We didn't pray or read the Bible or anything like that."

"Do you still go now?"

"Occasionally . . . to be perfectly honest, and no offense, I guess I don't see the point."

Keeva's cell phone rang again. She looked at the caller ID and rolled her eyes. "What!" she hissed at the phone before answering. When she did answer it, her voice was saccharin sweet. "Hi honey, what's going on? I'm still in my meeting. It's running a little later than I thought."

"Keeva, honey, I miss you so much. We haven't had any time together. Are you coming home soon?" Mark sounded anxious.

She sighed. "Yes, dear. I'll be there in a little bit okay?"

"I'll be waiting for you." He had a slight mischievous tone in his voice that let her know what he was waiting for. Keeva jabbed the "off" button on her cell phone and jammed it into her purse.

"I'm sorry. If I don't go, he'll call every five minutes and drive us both crazy." She signaled the waitress to bring the check. "We'll have to get together again some time soon. I really enjoyed this," Keeva said it as if it surprised her.

Shara nodded and smiled like she was surprised too. "I enjoyed it, too. And we do have to get together soon, although maybe not under such pleasant circumstances."

Keeva looked confused.

"The project? Remember? Graduate school, professors, grades, all that stuff?"

"Oh yeah." Keeva groaned.

The waitress brought the check. Shara picked it up and her eyes bugged out.

"My treat, remember?" Keeva took the bill from her.

Shara didn't object. "Thanks so much for dinner. This was really nice."

"No—thank you. I never would have made it through exams if it weren't for you." Keeva pulled out her credit card and motioned for the waitress to take it.

"So, when are you available to start the project?" Keeva was actually looking forward to hanging out with Shara again. She was so different from her other friends. With them, everyone was always trying to outdo someone else. With Shara, she could just relax and didn't feel like she had anything to prove.

They made plans to meet on Saturday morning and got up to leave the restaurant.

The evening's conversation played in Keeva's mind as she drove home. In spite of the way she dressed and wore her hair, Shara was a nice person. Keeva reflected on what Shara said about her kids and her school. She focused on what she said about giving them a sense of purpose. That phrase stuck with her.

Her cell phone rang, pulling her away from her thoughts. She knew it was Mark and decided not to answer it, knowing she'd be home in a few minutes. Undoubtedly, he had already let himself into her apartment and was tapping his foot, checking his watch and looking out the window for her car to drive up.

Sure enough, when she put her key in the door, Mark opened it before she could even turn the knob and pulled her into his arms, holding her too tightly. "Hey, baby."

She peeled herself away from him.

"I missed you, honey. Come here." Mark kissed her almost fiercely, as if he was a starving man and she was a T-bone steak. She tried to pull away, but the more she resisted, the more intense he became.

"Baby, it's been too long." He whined like a little kid.

Keeva decided to give in. She didn't feel creative enough to come up with an excuse and if she just went along with it, it would be over soon anyway. She allowed him to lead her into the bedroom and take off her clothes. Her mind drifted.

She wished he had greeted her at the door, asking her about her day and her exams. She wished he would talk to her about his day and how he was feeling. She wished he would caress her hair and look into her eyes. She wished he would ask her what was bothering her lately and listen like he really cared.

She pushed those thoughts away and pretended to be there like always. Soon he was snoring heavily beside her, his arm draped over her waist like a restraint.

If she had trouble sleeping when she was by herself, it was worse when Mark spent the night. He snored like a bear. And he always put an arm over her waist or threw a leg over her thighs. He slept so heavily his body felt like a dead man and she got trapped in whatever position she was in when he fell asleep. If she tried to pry herself loose, it would partially awaken him and make him hold on tighter.

She stared at the ceiling. Would he stop snoring if she kicked him?

If she had any hope of getting some sleep tonight, she had to escape. She rolled over and over until she reached the end of his arm. He tightened his grasp, but she rolled out of his reach and onto the floor. He reached for her and mumbled something, then turned over without waking up.

She slipped into the living room and turned the television on. If she was lucky, she would find a good movie to drown out her thoughts. One of her favorites was on HBO. She watched *Sleepless in Seattle* until she fell asleep on the couch.

Chapter Seven

Shara stretched lazily in the bed. Since mid-term exams were over, she had Friday off.

"Good morning, Daddy God." She could feel God's presence in her bedroom. She felt so close to Him first thing in the morning. It was so still and quiet, it was easy to feel Him and hear Him.

She started talking to God as if He were physically sitting in the room with her. She talked to Him about her kids, especially Tangee, and prayed for each one of them; that He would take care of them, save them, and make happen whatever needed to happen in their lives for them to reach their destiny. She prayed the church would continue to grow and meet the needs of the community. She prayed she would continue to grow and become all that He made her to be.

Her mind drifted to Keeva. She thought of the panicked look on her face in the library. She thought of the emptiness in her eyes when she talked about her career plans during dinner. She didn't quite know how to pray for her. On the one hand, Keeva seemed to have it all together. Beneath the surface though, she seemed like she was going to crack at any moment.

Shara found herself praying, *God, please help Keeva. She needs to know You. She needs a sense of direction she can only find in You. Bring her to a place of relationship and intimacy with You. Show her who You really are and how much You love her. Change her life. Cause her to live the life You planned for her when You created her. Give her that sense of purpose she needs to make life worth living. In Jesus' name.*

Shara's thoughts drifted back to Tangee. She didn't know why, but she sensed something was wrong. She prayed for a while, but still didn't get any peace. She'd make sure everything was okay when she saw Tangee later at track practice.

When Shara was growing up, she thought of prayer in terms of what her father did in the pulpit on Sunday. Until she met Mother Hobbs, she never realized prayer was simply talking to God. She remembered one of the first times they prayed together. They had just finished having some deep biblical discussion at the kitchen table and Mother Hobbs asked Shara to pray before they went to sleep that night.

Shara, of course, knew she knew how to pray. Her father taught her. Halfway through her recitation, Mother Hobbs stopped her. "What are you doing?"

"I'm praying."

"Well, why are you talking to God like that?"

"Like what?"

"Like He's the King of England or something with all those thee's and thou's—like He's far away sitting on a big, golden throne and staring down at you with a rod of iron in His hand."

Shara wrinkled her nose. That *was* sort of how she saw God. "How am I supposed to pray, then?"

"Honey, God is not impressed with big words or catchy phrases. He doesn't want to hear your religious clichés. You know what He really wants?"

Shara shook her head. She wanted to know more than anything. "What?"

"He wants to be your friend. Talk to him naturally like you would your best friend. Tell Him what you're feeling—what's bothering you. Ask Him questions. Have a normal conversation with Him. Most importantly, be real with Him. What's the point of a relationship if you can't be yourself?"

Shara took those words to heart. From that night on, her prayer life and relationship with God had radically changed. Her "friendship" with God had grown over the years to the point where Shara now did consider Him her best friend.

As she pulled on her sneakers, she looked around her bedroom. Her apartment building was old, but they had kept things up nice. She still had most of the same furniture she'd brought from home when she left for college. Her old wooden twin bed and matching dresser were scratched but still sturdy. She still had her childhood bookcases, now buckling under the weight of her college and grad school books. Everything was old and country, but it gave her apartment a cozy feel.

Shara headed outside for a quick run. She loved jogging in her midtown Atlanta neighborhood. Even though her rent cost more than it would have if she lived in an Atlanta suburb, she needed the cosmopolitan pulse of the city around her. It served as a constant reminder that she'd succeeded in escaping South Georgia and that with God's help, she could accomplish anything else she put her mind to.

Tangee flashed across her mind again. The sense of foreboding she'd felt in prayer that morning was growing stronger.

What is it, God? What's wrong with Tangee?

Shara turned onto Ponce De Leon street and sped her pace, as if she was trying to outrun the sick feeling in the pit of her stomach. A late evening discussion at Mother Hobbs' kitchen table came to mind. Mother Hobbs was teaching her about intercession and related that sometimes, God would put someone in her spirit with such a sense of urgency that she'd feel spiritually "sick" unless she prayed for them. During those times she'd literally have to groan and travail for them in the spirit until God did something, or at least brought peace about the situation.

Was that what she was supposed to do about Tangee right now?

Shara turned onto Moreland Avenue. On days

she didn't have class, she ended her run in Inman Park and then stopped at the Starbucks in Little Five Points for tea and a muffin. She hoped the tea would settle her stomach. She would talk to Mother Hobbs later and they could pray for Tangee together.

Shara stood at the edge of the track, watching the kids do their laps. Jamil was rounding the corner, making a silly face as he ran by. Tangee came around holding her stomach. She stopped long enough to tell Shara, "I'm sick. I gotta go to the bathroom."

Shara figured she had to throw up again. Maybe God had been telling her that morning that Tangee was experiencing a lot of sickness with the pregnancy. When she came back from the bathroom, Shara would tell her she needed to see a doctor soon.

A few minutes later, Danae came running up with a frantic look on her face. "Miss Shara, come quick!"

Normally, Shara would have ignored her. Most of her girls were drama queens and over-reacted about everything. Seeing the fear in Danae's eyes though, she knew to take her seriously.

"What is it?" Shara asked.

"It's Tangee. She in the bathroom screaming and crying—and there's blood everywhere!"

Shara's heart froze. "Go into the church and tell Mother Watkins to call an ambulance." Mother Hobbs had to pick today to be out of the office.

Danae stood there, wringing her hands with a panicked look on her face.

"Now, Danae!" Shara screamed, bringing her out of her trance.

As Shara ran into the bathroom, she heard Tangee wailing. She found her sitting on the floor, rocking and holding her belly. Lakita was with her, trying to comfort her. Tangee had bloody streaks down her legs and a small pool gathered at her ankles. Shara ran over to them.

"Tangee?" She turned toward Lakita. "Wet some paper towels with hot water."

Shara cradled Tangee in her arms and whispered into her ear. "You're okay, sweetie. The ambulance is going to be here in a few minutes. You're going to be just fine. Nothing is going to happen to you." Internally she prayed every healing scripture she could think of. Her hands shook as she wiped away the blood, which seemed to be flowing faster by the minute.

"Lakita, go find out what's going on with the ambulance."

"Please, Miss Shara—in this neighborhood? It'll be tomorrow before they get here."

"Lakita, just do what I said. Go to the church office, NOW!"

Lakita sucked her teeth, rolled her eyes, and stomped out the door.

Even though she didn't appreciate Lakita's attitude, Shara knew she was right. "Tangee, sweetie, can you walk? We need to get you to the van so we can get you to the hospital."

Tangee kept crying and rocking.

Danae came rushing in the door. "Miss Shara,

the ambalamps is going to be a while getting here. They said unless she unconscious, having a seizure or chest pain, she's low priority."

"I know, Danae, go get Jaquell so he can take Tangee to the van.

Tangee stopped rocking. "No, Miss Shara, I don't want him carrying me. I got blood all over me." Danae stood there.

"Danae, did you hear me?" Shara tried not to scream at her.

Jaquell's six-foot tall frame lumbered through the doorway a few minutes later. He stopped when he saw Tangee. "What's wrong with her?"

"Don't worry about it, Jacquell. Just pick her up and take her to the van."

He backed toward the door. "Unh, uh Miss Shara, she got blood all over her. I ain't touching no blood. I ain't trying to catch no AIDS."

Shara took a deep breath, but it didn't keep her from yelling at him. "Boy, get your behind over here and pick Tangee up and put her in the van. I don't want to hear another word. Just *do* it!" Her voice echoed off the bathroom walls.

By the time they got to the van, Lakita had spread newspaper and towels over the first bench. Shara smiled at her with appreciation but Lakita looked away, obviously still angry with Shara for yelling at her.

"You should go to Atlanta Medical Center." Lakita sucked her teeth. "She could bleed to death waiting at County Hospital."

"Thanks, Lakita, good thinking." Shara paused. "Can you come with me? I may need your help."

Lakita looked up at her and halfway smiled.

"Yeah, Miss Shara. I'll sit in the back with Tangee while you drive."

Shara prayed the whole way to the hospital, trusting God that Tangee and the baby would be okay.

Chapter Eight

Hours had passed when Shara and Lakita approached the nurses' station in the ER for the fifth time. The nurse sitting there knitted her eyebrows and pursed her lips. Shara guessed she was sick of seeing her face because she snatched up the phone. "Let me see if I can get the doctor to come out and give you an update."

A few minutes later, a middle-aged man wearing a long white coat over his hospital scrubs came out to the nurses' station. "Ms. Madison? I'm Doctor Reisen. Your daughter will be fine. We were initially concerned she was having an ectopic because of the severity of her pain, but after a pelvic and transvaginal ultrasound, we were able to determine that she did, in fact, have an intrauterine pregnancy and has had a complete spontaneous abortion.

"She lost quite a bit of blood but her hematocrit is stable and she shouldn't require a transfusion. We'll be observing her a little longer to make sure she doesn't have any retained products, but she should be fine to go home this evening. You'll need to consider putting her on some form of contraception so this doesn't happen again. We would be glad to give her a Depo-Provera shot before she leaves. Just let one of the nurses know." He rattled off the information and then walked away as abruptly as he came.

Shara turned to the nurse still sitting there. "Could you give that to us in English?"

The nurse smiled sympathetically. "Sorry about that. He gets in a hurry when the ER is busy. Basically, your daughter had a miscarriage, and based on the ultrasound, everything came out on its own so she won't need any surgery. She bled a lot, but won't need a blood transfusion. We need to watch her a little while longer to make sure everything is okay. The doctor suggested a birth control shot. Have you ever talked to your daughter about birth control?"

Shara shook her head. "She's not my daughter. I'm her track coach."

"Has anyone notified her mother or guardian?" the nurse asked.

Shara shook her head. She had been so worried, she hadn't even thought about calling Tangee's mother. "No, I'll call her now." She sent Lakita to see Tangee while she pulled out her youth roster. The nurse directed her to a pay phone at the end of the hall and she dialed Tangela's mother's work number.

An unfriendly voice barked, "Housekeeping, may I help you?"

"Yes, I'm trying to reach Angela Madison please," Shara said.

Shara pulled the phone away from her ear as she heard the person yell, "Where Angie at?"

In the background, Shara heard a voice yell back, "She on break—'sposed to be fifteen minutes, but it's been twenty-five already." The person repeated the information to Shara and was about to hang up.

"Wait, it's an emergency! I'm at the hospital with her daughter. Can you find her please?"

"Oh Lawd, what done happened to Tangela? What that child into now? These kids these days always up to no good. Is she all right? Angie always be talking 'bout how Tangee won't—"

"Please! Can you just find her mother?"

"Well, you ain't got to be rude about it. I'm just trying to show a little concern. Hol'on."

Shara pulled the phone away from her ear again as the woman yelled even louder, "Angie, you need to come on back in here and get dis phone. Tangee at the hospital. It's a 'mergency."

After a few moments, Shara recognized Ms. Madison's voice in the background. She heard a string of curse words and then, "What is it now, Tangee?"

It took Shara a few seconds to respond.

While trying to figure out what to say, she heard, "Hello? Ain't nobody on this phone, Thelma. Stop playing. That ain't funny."

Shara made herself say, "Ms. Madison, this is Shara Anderson, Tangee's track coach. We're at

Atlanta Medical Center in the emergency room. I think you should—"

"What is it? What's wrong with her?" Ms. Madison almost sounded concerned.

"She started bleeding at track practice today." Shara took a deep breath. "She had a miscarriage."

Silence.

"What you mean, she had a miscarriage?"

"She lost the baby, Ms. Madison."

Shara pulled the phone away from her ear as Ms. Madison screamed, "Baby? What baby? You telling me Tangee pregnant?"

As she continued yelling and cursing into the phone, Shara realized Tangee hadn't told her mother. Listening to her, she could understand why. "Tangee said she told you. She is . . . well she *was* pregnant. She lost the baby."

"No, Tangee didn't tell me nothing about being pregnant. You mean *you* knew she was pregnant and didn't tell me?"

Shara's heart beat faster. What ramifications would this have for her program? Was she liable for not having talked to Tangee's mother?

"I think at this point, the most important thing is Tangee's okay. She lost a lot of blood but the doctor says she's stable. I think it would be good if you came on down here to the hospital and—"

"Oh you *think*, huh? I'll be at the hospital all right. As soon as I finish my shift. You tell that little heifer when I see her—it's *on*. Me and her. Done told that child all her life. . . ."

Shara pulled the phone away from her ear

and smoothed her hair back. This was going to be a long evening.

She hung up and went back toward the busy emergency area. There must have been a lot going on in Atlanta that night because the ER was packed. Orderlies were rushing by with gurneys holding patients that looked like they were at death's door. The overhead intercom kept ordering different doctors to different rooms. There were even people lined up on beds in the hallway.

Shara pulled back the little privacy curtain to Tangee's room. She walked over and sat on the side of the gurney and looked at Tangee's tear-streaked face. Lakita sat quietly in a chair next to her.

"Well, Miss Shara, at least I don't have to have a abortion now." Tangee wouldn't look at her.

Shara smoothed Tangee's hair back. "You okay?"

A few tears slid down Tangee's face, as she shook her head.

"Are you in pain?"

She shook her head again. "She's gonna make me go live with my grandmother down in the country. Ain't nothing to do and the people all dumb. All my grandmother do is make me go to church and I don't get to have *no* fun." More tears flowed down her face. "The schools ain't no good. I'll never get to go to college now."

"Maybe not, Tangee. We'll talk to her and see—"

Tangee sat up. "Don't try to talk to her, Miss

Shara. She don't listen to nobody and it'll only make things worse. She ain't gonna change her mind. I might as well pack my bags now. Good-bye track program, good-bye college, good-bye future."

Shara tried to tell her that everything would be okay, but Tangee kept shaking her head. "You don't know my momma," was all she would say.

The three of them sat there in silence for a while. Tangee fell asleep and Shara nodded off in the chair next to her bed.

The nurse kept coming back to check on them. She finally said the ER was busy and they would need the room soon. Tangee was going to be discharged, so if her mother didn't come soon, they would have to sit in the waiting area. Tangee put her clothes back on from her gym bag Lakita had grabbed before they left the church.

As they were about to leave, the curtain flew back. Ms. Madison came in, still in her house-keeping uniform. "Tangee! If I didn't think the people in this hospital would call Child Protective Services on me, I'd beat your tail right here in this room. All the times we talked about this? All you had to do was come to me. We woulda got you some birth control and all this wouldn't have happened. But you had to go sneakin' around behind my back with one of those li'l knucklehead boys."

Tangee burst into tears. "I'm sorry, momma. I didn't mean to—"

"Didn't mean to what? Have sex? Or get

caught 'cause you got pregnant? I always told you, Tangee. It only takes one time. All these years, did you ever hear anything I said?"

"Yes, momma, I'm sorry, momma. I promise I'll listen from now on, momma, whatever you say."

"From now on? Oh no, Miss Fast-tail, ain't no 'from now on'. You know what this means. You going to live with your grandma, now. Let's see if she can do anything with you, 'cause I'm tired. You need to be down in the country to keep your li'l hot tail outta trouble. You can go to church with your grandma every day. Maybe her Jesus can do something to help you."

She huffed and paced around the little room, then came back to face Tangee. She was clearly oblivious to the fact that there was another patient on the other side of the curtain. "I work every day to provide for you and this is what you do? Why ain't you go to County? I ain't got no insurance and I ain't got no money for no foolishness like this. You think I go to work to pay for hospital bills for some foolishness?"

Shara tried to come to Tangee's defense. "Ms. Madison, I—"

Ms. Madison whipped around to face Shara with pure fire in her eyes. "I don't want to hear nothing you got to say. You call yourself running a program to help these kids? Well, look like ain't nothing you doing working."

She looked Shara up and down. "I don't know who you think you are, trying to tell me how to raise my child. Have you fed her? Clothed her? Dealt with her mess? I bet you ain't even got no kids, so what you know about raisin' one? You one of them educated Negroes. Done read a book so now you think you can tell me how to raise my child. She probably got pregnant while she was supposed to be at your track program. Shoulda had her fast tail come home every day like she used to, but nooo—she had to run track and Miss Shara this and Miss Shara that."

She turned back to Tangee. "We'll see about that. Let's see how much track your grandma gon' let you run. Now git your stuff together. Let's go."

Shara spoke softly, not wanting to induce another tirade. "Do you need a ride home?"

Ms. Madison glared at Shara. "We don't need your help no more. Don't come around my house and don't call. Just leave us alone."

Shara started to say something again, but decided against it. She walked out of the room with her shoulders sagging and head down. Lakita followed her.

Shara turned to her. "I'll take you home."

"I'm all right, Miss Shara." Lakita held up her MARTA bus pass. "Why don't you go on home and get some rest."

"No, it's late. Anything could happen to you."

"Please." Lakita put on her tough face. "You think anybody gon' bother me?" She smiled. "Really, I'll be all right. You go on home."

Shara didn't have the energy to protest any further. She watched Lakita walk away.

She sat on a bench in the hallway. After a few minutes, her shoulders shook silently as she cried from deep in her belly. That old feeling she had those years as a teacher resurfaced. No matter how hard she tried, it wasn't enough. No matter how much she prayed for and loved these kids, life had a way of snatching them back into darkness and despair. Now what was going to happen to Tangee?

Shara felt a hand on her shoulder. She looked up to see Lakita standing there with a tissue in her hand. She accepted it and wiped her face.

Lakita barely spoke above a whisper, "It's not your fault, Miss Shara. You do right by us." She patted her on the shoulder. "Don't give up on us, okay?"

Shara nodded. They shared a silent moment and Lakita walked away again.

Shara finally got up and walked down the long hospital corridor and out to the parking lot. The cool crispness of the March night air whipped against her cheeks. She pulled her jean jacket tighter and quickened her steps until she got to the van.

She didn't feel like going home. After she traded the church van for her car, she drove up to an old, large house in Grant Park, rang the doorbell and waited. She heard footsteps and saw Mother Hobbs peering through the window.

The door opened. "Child, what are you doing here? It's after midnight." Mother Hobbs took one look at Shara's face and led her into the house. She sat her down at the kitchen table.

"What is it, child? What happened?"

Fresh tears poured down Shara's face as she told Mother Hobbs about the miscarriage and all the blood and how scared she had been. She told about how Tangee's mother acted on the phone and at the hospital—how she had blamed her. "And now I've lost Tangee forever," Shara sobbed.

Mother Hobbs put her arms around her, rocking her and smoothing her hair. "My poor baby girl." She patted her on the back. "Saving the world is hard work, huh?"

Shara laughed a little between sniffles and accepted the napkin Mother Hobbs gave her to blow her nose.

Mother Hobbs walked over to the kitchen counter and started fiddling with her large canisters. Shara knew she was mixing some herbs together to make one of her infamous pots of tea. Mother Hobbs hummed silently, no doubt preparing the words of wisdom Shara would need to deal with the evening's events. Shara rested her back against the wooden chair, calmed slightly by the humming.

A few minutes later, a medicinal fragrance of plants and flowers drifted into the air. Mother Hobbs poured two steaming cups and brought them over to the table with some shortbread cookies.

"What happened to Tangee is not your fault. All you can do is pray that the good you put into her stays with her—that she'll continue to dream and even with everything that's happened, she'll still get to go to college."

Shara bit into a cookie and crunched slowly. "It's not just Tangee. I'm beginning to wonder if I'm really making any difference with any of the kids. Sure they're doing something positive after school instead of hanging out on the street. But Tangee still got pregnant, Jamil got suspended from school last week for fighting, and if Lakita *does* graduate this year, her highest hope is to get a job at the mall so she can get clothes at a discount. It seems like—"

"Shara, what are you saying? Your program has been going on for less than a year. You can't expect everything to be better in that short period of time. You're fighting years of negative mindsets, poverty, hopelessness—not just in the kids, but also in their parents and their parents' parents. You're talking years of generational curses. It's gonna take a lot more than running after school and a little tutoring to change that."

"So what do we do? What hope do we have in fighting against that?"

"We remember who we have fighting for us and in us." Mother Hobbs stirred a large dollop of honey into her tea. Soon its sweet fragrance floated up from her cup. "The power of God is the only thing that can break those types of strongholds. Just keep praying and loving. I promise, you'll see a change—in time."

Mother Hobbs mentioning praying brought that sick feeling back to Shara's stomach. "Oh no."

"What?"

She told Mother Hobbs about the feeling she got in prayer that morning and how it got progressively worse as the day went on. "And instead of stopping to pray, I sat in Starbucks eating a blueberry muffin. If I had prayed like God was trying to get me to, this might not have happened."

"Shara, you don't know that. It might have been the Holy Spirit warning you about what was going to happen so you'd have the strength to face it as you did. Or maybe your brief prayer this morning was the difference between Tangee bleeding to death at home by herself versus in the bathroom where the other kids found her. You don't know what that feeling was about."

Mother Hobbs rubbed her back. Shara felt more relaxed as she sipped her tea. The warm steaming mug took the chill from her fingers. "What's in this?" she asked.

"One of my secret recipes—Chamomile, Valerian, and St. John's Wort. You'll sleep good tonight. You staying?"

Shara nodded.

Even though she'd moved out almost four years ago, she still came over to visit Mother Hobbs on a regular basis. Often, they'd stay up talking so late Shara would go up to her old room to sleep rather than go home.

Mother Hobbs always kept her room ready for her. Shara knew she missed her living there. Her own children had gone off to school, and then got married and started their own lives. They were all doing well, but were busy and only visited on holidays. She would never admit it, but Shara knew Mother Hobbs was lonely in that big house by herself. She had rented the room to Shara not too long after her husband passed.

She sometimes talked about selling the house and moving into a condo, but then she wouldn't have anywhere for her children and grandchildren to stay when they did come to visit.

Plus the house had almost tripled in value since Grant Park was experiencing massive gentrification and becoming an "in" neighborhood.

Mother Hobbs got up from the table. "Time for bed, baby girl. Try to sleep late. You need the rest." She glanced at the clock. "I do, too. I got my senior yoga and water aerobics classes in the morning."

Ever since Mr. Hobbs died unexpectedly of a massive heart attack, Mother Hobbs had made a concerted effort to exercise regularly. She even traded in her soul food for healthier fare. She planted a motherly kiss on Shara's forehead and went upstairs.

Shara sat for a few minutes more. She took off her shoes and padded through the house admiring the decorative crown molding, rich, brown hardwood floors, high ceilings, and oversized rooms. The toasty beige paint added warmth to each room. Mother Hobbs' antique furniture fit the house perfectly.

Shara tipped up the stairs and into her room. It didn't take her long to rummage through the drawer of clothes she kept at Mother Hobbs' to find some pajamas. She climbed up onto the antique four-poster bed, pulled up the comforter and lay staring at the ceiling. She felt relaxed from the tea, but still had trouble falling asleep. After tossing and turning for a while, she decided to pray.

Please, God, tell me what to do. I know You love these kids. I know You gave me a heart for them for a reason. Please help me to help them. I'm getting discouraged. I feel like nothing is helping. Help, God.

She lay praying and thinking about the kids for a few minutes. If what she was doing wasn't enough, then they needed to do more. She thought about all the ideas she'd had over the past year while working with the kids. Every time a problem or situation arose, it seemed like God gave her an idea for a program that would be a solution. As she continued to pray, God brought the ideas back to her remembrance.

She wanted to start a mentoring program to pair young people with adults in the church to shadow them in their careers. Many of the kids had not given much thought to their future. Some didn't realize that they should. Those who did have dreams never imagined they'd ever be able to achieve them. If they got to shadow someone doing what they dreamed, perhaps it wouldn't seem so unattainable.

She also wanted to do some sort of music program. She knew kids involved in the performing arts tended to do better in school and were more likely to go to college. Maybe they could even start a dance and theatre program.

Shara also wanted to throw Christian youth parties. Many kids thought when they got saved, they had to give up parties, music and dancing. She definitely felt like she missed out on those things when she was young.

Then she wanted to do a computer training class. None of the kids had computers in their homes, although they had PlayStation or Nintendo. Many of them didn't even have access to computers in school. Shara didn't understand how in the same school district, some schools could have a computer for each child, and others only had outdated computers in the library.

She also knew it would be important to get their parents involved at some point. It wouldn't do much good to make all these changes with the kids and then have them still go home to the same living environment. She wanted to do parenting programs and job training and . . .

She got excited thinking about it all. She couldn't wait to finish school so she could write grants and get funding to build the programs.

Shara thought about a sermon Pastor Kendrick preached recently about writing the vision down and making it plain. She sat up and turned on the little lamp on the nightstand beside her bed. Moving over to sit at the desk, she pulled a notebook out of her book bag to jot some of the ideas down. After she had written down everything that had poured into her spirit, she climbed back into bed filled with a strange sense of peace and hope. She would have to trust God that these were His ideas and that He would bring them to pass in time.

Chapter Nine

Keeva looked at the large silver clock on her wall. It was 11:30 AM. She and Shara had agreed to meet at 11:00 to work on their project. She hoped Shara didn't forget.

Keeva was about to pick up the phone when the buzzer rang. She buzzed the downstairs lock, and after a few minutes, opened the door to find Shara out of breath with her hair flying all over her head worse than usual.

"Sorry I'm late. I had major drama last night and ended up not falling asleep until about three in the morning. So, of course, I overslept," Shara said.

"Don't worry about it. Come on in." Keeva said.

"Your apartment is great. I love the big windows and high ceilings." Shara looked around as Keeva led her to the dining table. "How long have you lived here?"

"Almost four years. I love this place. I can't

imagine living anywhere else." *So you've got to help me get an A on this project.*

"Want something to drink?" Keeva walked to the refrigerator. "I have cranberry juice."

"Sure, that sounds great."

"What happened last night?" Keeva brought over two large glasses and sat down across from Shara.

As Shara described the events of her evening, Keeva's eyes grew wide and her mouth dropped. "Are you serious? How did you handle all that blood? I can't believe you kept a clear enough head to get her to the hospital. I probably would have fainted the minute I walked into the bathroom!"

"It wasn't so much the blood, although the blood did bother me. More than anything, what upset me was the feeling of loss for Tangee's future. She has so much promise and potential. I'm afraid she'll never get to become all the things she had learned to dream about."

Shara took a long sip of cranberry juice then set her glass down on the table. "If you take away someone's dreams, you might as well kill them. Without some sense of purpose and destiny and some hope for achieving it, what do you have? You know?"

Boy, do I . . . Keeva thought. In those few words, Shara had summed up everything that was wrong with her. The phone rang, pulling Keeva from her thoughts. She hurried to the kitchen to get it. "Hello?"

She rolled her eyes, but said sweetly, "Honey, I told you I had a study group today. Remember the project I told you about?"

She pulled her hair while listening to Mark rant. "I know, honey, but I have to get this done. I have to work with other people's schedules too. It's not that I'm . . . I understand honey, but . . ."

She held the phone away from her ear. "Yes, dear . . . yes, honey . . . Okay, I'll call you as soon as I'm finished."

She hung up the phone and stood in the kitchen for a few minutes, taking a few deep breaths. She put her smile back on and walked back into the dining area where Shara was bent over her notebook.

"Sorry about that. I guess we should go ahead and get started. Looks like I have plans later this evening," Keeva said tightly.

Keeva saw the look on Shara's face and felt the need to explain. "My boyfriend . . . he's a great guy. I haven't been able to spend a lot of time with him lately and—"

"I'm sure it must be hard for him to deal with you being in grad school and having such a demanding schedule."

"Actually, he should understand. He's in his second year of law school."

Once again, Keeva felt as if something she would normally brag about was totally lost on Shara. She relaxed and decided to be honest. "He can be demanding and inconsiderate at times, but he's sweet. I've learned in relationships you have to take the good with the bad."

Shara raised her eyebrows. "Maybe that's why I'm not in a relationship."

Keeva laughed.

For the next hour or so, they discussed the project. Keeva liked the way Shara's mind worked. She could tell Shara had been thinking about the project for quite some time. It was almost as if she didn't need to be there helping. She didn't mind. Her brain felt fuzzy when she even thought about it, so she was glad Shara had at least mentally completed a large part of the work.

As they discussed it, Shara asked for her opinion or ideas a few times. Keeva didn't have anything to add. She started pulling her hair and bouncing her leg. The more Shara talked, the more unintelligent and unprepared she felt. After Shara asked her for her input for about the fifth time, Keeva couldn't tell whether Shara was trying to embarrass her or what.

"Shara, I told you before, I really haven't worked on this at all. I was primarily concerned about getting through midterms. Just because you're organized and get everything done in time doesn't mean I've done my part. Maybe you'd prefer to have another partner to work with since I haven't done anything. I'm sure it's not too late to switch." She knew her tone was nastier than it should have been.

Shara looked as if she had slapped her. Keeva was instantly sorry because it was clear she wasn't trying to embarrass her. Shara sat there without saying anything.

Keeva said, "I'm sorry. I feel bad because I haven't done anything and you've practically completed the project. I didn't mean to . . ."

Shara still didn't say anything.

Keeva continued. "I guess I've just been a bit overwhelmed lately. It's just school and all . . ." Her voice cracked. She froze.

Get it together, Keeva! You will not cry in front of this girl! She tried to rein in her emotions, but when the hurt look in Shara's eyes turned to concern, it did her in. She burst into tears. "I don't know what's wrong with me. I . . . it's just that I . . . I've been . . . could you excuse me for a minute?"

Shara nodded.

In the bathroom, Keeva splashed her face with cold water and stared at herself hard in the mirror. *What is your problem?* What was she going to say when she went back out to the living room? *Don't mind me, I'm an emotionally unstable basket case?* She took a deep breath and walked back into the living area.

Shara stood at a large window. "You have an awesome view up here."

Keeva walked over to the window and started to speak, but didn't know what to say.

Shara said, "I know you don't know me and I don't know you all that well, but . . . in the past few interactions, I've noticed you seem stressed out. You don't have to try to explain that. Life is like that sometimes. Like I said, I know we don't know each other well, so don't feel like you have to, but if you ever need a listening ear with a silent mouth, let me know. Sometimes it feels better to get things out."

Keeva nodded and stared out the window.

Shara walked over to the dining table and began putting her books back into her worn book bag. "We can work on the project later. We got a lot done today and we have plenty of time. I know I'm being anal in wanting to get it done so soon."

Shara had her hand on the door when Keeva finally spoke.

"Shara?"

"Yeah?"

Keeva took a deep breath. "When you said what you said about losing dreams and not having a sense of purpose and destiny and all that stuff . . . well . . . where do you get your sense of purpose from?"

Shara smiled. "I thought you were going to tell me to lock the door on my way out." She put her book bag down and slowly walked back over to the window.

"I'd have to say I get it from God. My sense of self, why I'm here, what I'm supposed to accomplish in life, the vision and strength to do it . . . all that comes from my relationship with God."

Keeva furrowed her eyebrows. She had gone to church on and off most of her life and had never gotten any of those things out of it. "I don't understand what you mean."

"Why do you ask?"

Keeva stared out the window, focusing on nothing. A large tear trickled down her cheek. "I'm getting a master's degree in a field I'm not even sure I want to work in. I'm dating a man I'm not sure I want to be with. I can only stand my friends in small doses. I can't have a real conversation with my parents. Sometimes I look at my life and wonder how I got here.

"When I was a little girl, I had so many dreams about who I wanted to be and what I was going to do." She fingered the tassel on her window blinds. "The life I dreamed of is not at all the one I'm living now. I feel like I lost myself somewhere. The worst part is, I don't know how to get *me* back. I'm not even sure I know who *me* is."

There. She said it. She was finally honest with herself and gave words to her misery. "You talk so passionately about what you want to do. You're exactly where you want to be, doing exactly what you want to be doing. I can't imagine how beautiful that must be." Keeva shook her head. "All I know is that I don't want to live like this anymore."

Shara was silent for a few minutes. Finally, she asked, "What did you dream about being when you were a little girl?"

A sad smile crossed Keeva's face. "I wanted to be a dancer. From my very first dance class when I was six, that's all I ever wanted. When I dance, I feel alive and happy, like everything's all right with the world."

She told her about her tradition of seeing Alvin Ailey every year with her father and shared her disappointment when her parents wouldn't let her audition. "I haven't gone to see them since or any other dance troupe for that matter. The only time I dance now is here in my living room and that's only when I get really depressed. Which has been quite often lately."

"Is it too late for you to dance now? Could you still try out for Alvin Ailey or some other group?"

Keeva shook her head. "I've been out of the game too long. I'm completely out of shape and—"

"Out of shape?" Shara looked her up and down.

"In terms of dancing, yes. I still took some classes in my first few years of college, but I haven't danced since then. I would have to really work hard to get back in shape to dance professionally. Plus, it's a full time job. I couldn't do that and go to school."

"What if you took some dance classes just to do something you enjoy?"

Keeva stared out her window at Peachtree Street below. "Hurts too much. It just reminds me that I'm not living the life I want to live."

Shara was quiet for a few minutes then asked, "You mentioned you majored in English for a while because you like to write. Was that something you wanted to do professionally?"

Keeva nodded. "Yeah, I love to write. I have this really vivid imagination. When I was a little girl, I used to sit around and make up stories in my head all the time, I guess to escape my life. I used to get in trouble with my mom and all my teachers for daydreaming. I thought I might try my hand at it."

"So what happened?"

"My parents threw a fit. They went into this spiel about me not being able to find a job. They said I should do it as a hobby, but that I'd never be able to make a career of it. They said if I insisted on majoring in English, they'd pull my financial support so I could see how it felt to live on no money."

"What did you do?"

"What do you think? I changed my major to psychology and told them I planned to get a

PhD. Of course they were thrilled. My dad even bought me a new car the next week. That was my first BMW. I got the one I'm driving now when I got accepted into the PhD program at Emory. They threatened to snatch it so many times when I wasn't doing well there. Then—"

She stopped when she saw the look of surprise on Shara's face. "I started out in Emory's PhD program but couldn't maintain the B average. I didn't even get to the second year. I guess that's why I was freaking out over midterms here. I can't afford to flunk out of another program. My parents would kill me."

Keeva turned and leaned her body against the long window. "I was always an A student with maybe a B here and there. For some reason though, I couldn't pull it together then. My parents threatened me so many times to withdraw their financial support if I didn't do better, but even that wasn't enough. They were furious when I had to leave Emory."

She halfway smiled. "Even though Georgia State isn't as prestigious, I was secretly glad for the change. I can still become a therapist after a much shorter program and don't have to do a stupid dissertation."

Shara shook her head. "You can't live for your parents. No wonder you're so miserable."

Keeva stared at Shara.

"No wonder you failed at Emory and no wonder you're having so much trouble at GSU. You're forcing yourself to do something you don't want to do to please someone else. How can you expect to be happy? Meanwhile, you've put all your dreams to the side. How could you not be depressed? Keeva, you can't live like this. What are you gonna do—pursue a career you don't even want? How long do you think it would be before you go insane?"

Keeva stood there, feeling like she should go off. Normally, she would have come up with something rude and nasty to put Shara back in her place. That didn't seem right. She knew Shara was concerned.

Besides—she was right.

Keeva walked over and plopped down on the couch. "So what do I do?"

"Keeva, only you know the answer to that question. All I can say is follow your heart. Be true to yourself."

"That *sounds* good, but how?"

"For one, start doing some of the things you love. Take some dance classes—write a poem."

Keeva rolled her eyes. "Now you sound like my parents. 'Just do your artsy stuff on the side.'"

"That's not what I'm saying. All I'm saying is you gotta start somewhere. You may not end up dancing with Alvin Ailey, but you can still dance. Start writing again. Just do *something*. If you sit around and dream about it and never do anything, nothing will happen. Each day, take some small action in the direction of where you want to be." Shara walked over and sat at the other end of the couch.

"That's just it. I don't know where I want to be," Keeva said. "I have no idea what I would do with my life if I don't get this counseling degree. I have no idea how to support myself and make a living. I'm not sure I'm willing to be a starving artist."

Keeva looked around her apartment. "I guess you can tell—I'm used to having nice things. I'm not materialistic or anything, but I like knowing I'm gonna have a certain amount of money coming in."

"So you're saying you'd rather be miserable with a steady income, than happy doing what you love without the BMW and the fancy apartment?" Shara asked.

"No. Well . . ." Keeva paused. It sounded so shallow when Shara said it that way. "You're saying 'doing what I love.' I don't know what I love. I mean, I know I love dancing, but unless I'm gonna dance in a professional company, what do I do? I know I love writing, but I don't know if I can make a living at it. I don't even know if I'm that good."

"That's because you've never given it a chance. Explore it. Or do something with dance. You may not dance professionally, but there's gotta be something you can do—like teach or something. If all you do is sit around and lament about it or think about what you used to love, you'll never do anything. You'll end up in a miserable career with a miserable life."

Keeva hugged her yellow throw pillow. "You're right. I know you're right." She let out a deep breath and stared into space. "So what do I do? Quit the program? At this point, I might as well finish. But then what? How am I supposed to know what's next?"

Shara shrugged. "I only know one way to get direction for my life and that's to ask God."

Keeva didn't say anything. Maybe that God stuff worked for Shara, but it didn't make much sense to her. She didn't want to offend Shara by saying that, so she just nodded.

The phone rang.

Keeva knew it was Mark.

She turned to Shara. "You hungry? Mick's down the street has the best burgers and fries. We could eat . . . and maybe, you know . . . finish this conversation."

Shara smiled and nodded. They grabbed their stuff and left with the phone still ringing.

Chapter Ten

After track practice the next Friday, Shara grabbed her notebook and headed for the church office. She stopped to greet Mother Hobbs at her desk. After they chatted for a few minutes Shara asked, "Is Pastor Kendrick busy?"

"He's always free for you. Everything okay?"

"Yeah, everything's fine. I want to go over a few ideas with him."

Mother Hobbs gestured for Shara to go into his office.

Pastor Kendrick was talking on the phone, but motioned for her to sit down in the chair in front of his large oak desk.

Shara admired the new family picture on his desk with Pastor Kendrick, his wife, and their three children. She perused his tall bookshelf for any new books she might borrow. She noticed many of her favorite authors—Myles Munroe, Dutch Sheets, Rick Joyner, and Francis

Frangipane. Her eyes settled on a Jim Goll book she hadn't read before.

Pastor Kendrick hung up the phone. "How are you, Shara?" He stood to give her a fatherly hug and then sat down in his chair. "Mother Hobbs told me about what happened to Tangela Madison. I know that must have been difficult for you. Are you okay?"

"It was difficult, but I'm okay. Thanks for asking."

"Have you heard from her? Is she all right?"

Shara shrugged. "I don't know. Her mother made it clear I wasn't to call the house or come by. All I can do is pray for her."

"You want me to try to stop by?"

Shara shook her head. "I don't think that's such a good idea. It may be best to let her mother cool off a little first."

Pastor Kendrick nodded. "Let me know if there's anything I can do to help. I know Tangee has a lot of potential and it would be a big loss for her to not be able to come back to the program. Don't lose heart though, Shara. Those types of things can make you feel like giving up, but you're really making a difference in these kids' lives."

"That's what I wanted to talk to you about. I left that night feeling so hopeless and started praying about us being able to do more in the community. Not only for the kids, but for the parents as well. I feel that if we do more, we can make more of a difference."

She pulled her notebook out of her bag and showed him the notes she scribbled the morning after Tangee's miscarriage, now typed and organized. She discussed each program, how they could implement it, and outlined a time frame in which it could be done. When she finished, Pastor Kendrick sat back in his chair shaking his head.

"What?" Shara asked.

He didn't say anything for a moment, then got up and walked over to his file cabinet and pulled out a large binder. He showed her the front—"Vision for Kingdom Builders Christian Center."

She looked at him curiously.

"I always asked for God to send me like-minded people to help, but I have to say this is beyond what I expected."

He turned to a section in the notebook headed "Community Outreach/Youth." As Shara flipped through the pages, she realized their notes were almost identical, except Pastor Kendrick had several sketches of a very large community center and other sketches of classrooms and recreation rooms. On the last page it was signed, "Michael Kendrick, 1982."

"God gave this to you all those years ago?"

"Yeah, but He had to do some work on me first—character building. God is funny like that. He gives you a vision, and then allows everything in your life to fall apart so He can produce His character in you. I promise you, though, there's nothing more fulfilling than seeing your dreams actually start to materialize. It's amazing to dream something, then pray and believe, and one day, see it happen. Life doesn't get any better than that."

Shara nodded and lay his notebook on his desk.

"I'm glad to see you're so excited about the vision. Since you're here, I might as well tell you that we've reached a critical number of members where we can start hiring more staff. One of the first positions we want to fill is youth pastor. I want you to be a part of our search committee for a candidate. We really need your input because you'll be working very closely with this person."

Shara nodded. It would be nice to have a full-time person there to help out with all that needed to be done.

After she finished talking to Pastor Kendrick, Shara chatted with Mother Hobbs for a few minutes then left. She decided to stop at Blockbuster's on the way home to pick up a video.

She browsed the shelves of movies, already knowing what she would get. As she approached the counter, the employee who waited on her said, "Let me guess, *Sister Act II*." She smiled. It was her favorite movie and she had seen it a million times.

Travis was always on duty at the store on Friday nights when she came in to rent movies. They had chatted a few times and he seemed like a nice person. He always had a big smile and pleasant conversation for her.

"I have something for you. I kept it behind the counter—you haven't been here in a while." He pulled a video box from behind the counter and she glanced at the label on it. "*Sister Act II*, previewed copy, $6.99."

"You've bought this ten times with the number of times you've rented it. You might as well own a copy." She took it from him and pulled out some money.

"Don't worry about it. It's on me." Travis gave her a dimpled grin.

Shara blushed.

"How are the kids?"

"Fine. I just left them a little while ago."

Shara had brought her group of rowdy teenagers one night to pick out some movies for an all night video night at the church. The kids wanted to get horror movies and movies with adult themes Shara didn't think appropriate for a church youth group. It almost turned into a riot as they argued with each other and with Shara about what they were going to watch. Finally, Travis came over and convinced them the movies Shara recommended weren't so bad.

Shara was so grateful for his help, she came back the next day to thank him. He asked her about the kids and she had explained her track program.

"Hey, Miss Shara." He started calling her that after hearing the kids screaming her name across the store that night. "I picked out another movie I think you'll like a lot. It's called *Finding Forrester*. It's about this young black guy that lives in the 'hood that really has a talent for writing. He's not doing much with himself or doing well in school until he meets this old white guy . . ."

Shara wondered if Travis was so nice to all his customers. His special attention made her nervous. She quickly paid for the movie. "Thanks, Travis. See ya' soon." He seemed like a nice guy, but then again, so had her ex-boyfriend, Keith. Her smile darkened and she quickly walked out the door.

Chapter Eleven

A few weeks later, Shara rushed into Pastor Kendrick's conference room after track practice with the kids. One of their most promising candidates had flown in from Chicago and Pastor Kendrick had scheduled an evening interview so all the youth leaders could come after work to meet him.

"Sorry I'm late. I . . ." Shara stood speechless at the sight of the most beautiful man she ever laid eyes on standing to shake her hand. She must have looked like a complete idiot standing there with her mouth wide open.

Pastor Kendrick stepped up to her. "Shara, this is Quinton Mercer. Minister Mercer, this is Shara Anderson, one of the other youth leaders." She shook his hand.

"Hi, nice to meet you." His smile was warm.

Shara stood there looking at him.

Pastor Kendrick motioned. "Come on in and have a seat, Shara, you're just in time. We haven't started yet. We've just introduced every-one."

She looked around at the other youth lead-ers—Anthony, Tina, Nia, Malcolm, Danielle, and Terrence. A couple were missing. Her eyes set-tled on Mother Hobbs who had a big grin on her face.

Shara sat in the empty chair next to her, re-fusing to make eye contact. She smoothed her hair down, wishing she'd taken the time to brush it back. It was doing that wild thing it did by the end of the day. Out of the corner of her eye, she saw Mother Hobbs grinning wider.

Shara glanced down at his resumé on the table in front of her. *Bachelors in Finance from University of Arizona. Master's in Urban Min-istry from Moody Bible Institute while serving as a youth leader at True Revival Christian Church. Promoted to youth pastor after he graduated, did that for a year*... He definitely looked more promising than the other candidates thus far.

They had interviewed a few church mem-bers, but Pastor Kendrick said he wanted to bring in some fresh blood from the outside. They interviewed a few people from other churches in the city, but Pastor Kendrick said he didn't feel too good about "stealing" someone else's members. Plus, most of them had traditional views about how to minister to young people and Pastor Kendrick wanted someone with in-novative, new ideas.

Pastor Kendrick took his seat at the head of the large, oval-shaped conference table. "Let's go ahead and get started. Quinton, we're not formal around here so we'll ask you some questions to get to know you and please feel free to do the same."

Quinton nodded.

Pastor Kendrick asked, "What made you interested in interviewing for this position?"

Quinton sat forward in his chair. "I know God has called me to work with young people. I can't think of anything I'd rather do with my life. I believe there's nothing more important than to help a young person discover and pursue their destiny. I'm looking for a position that will allow me to do that."

Pastor Kendrick said, "Obviously, it's what God called you to do, but what makes you passionate about it?"

Quinton paused for a second. "I grew up in inner-city Chicago. I saw a lot of things growing up that were enough to make me angry and hopeless for the rest of my life. What bothered me most was all the wasted lives and wasted potential. It was like people's lives were finished before they even started.

"I decided as a kid I was going to get an education and get out of there and be somebody and then come back and help others become somebody. About a year after I graduated from college, I got saved and acknowledged God's call for me to help other young people out of that life of despair. I went back to get my Master's in Divinity so I could be well equipped to do so."

Everyone around the table nodded, impressed with his candor.

"There seems to be a one year gap in your resume here. Can you tell us what happened during that time?" Shara asked.

Quinton smiled and Shara noticed a deep dimple in his cheek. "Guess you don't follow sports, huh?"

Anthony Thompson, one of the other youth leaders, snapped his fingers. "I knew that was you, man!"

Everyone looked at Anthony and then back at Quinton for an explanation.

Quinton smiled modestly. "I played basketball while at University of Arizona and then got drafted into the pros when I graduated."

Anthony said, "You're too modest, man. You were at the top of your game, All-American. Yo, man, what happened? You played with Orlando for a year, then just dropped out of sight."

Quinton's smile faded and he looked down at the floor. "My baby brother got killed about six months into my rookie year. I got real depressed and unfocused and ended up getting hurt. I guess more than anything, his death led to me getting saved and really making the commitment to reach out to youth."

Everyone was silent.

Mother Hobbs finally spoke. "We're sorry to hear about your brother. It seems like you're using that pain and turning it into something good for the Kingdom of God. Bad things happen to everybody in this life. It's those who are able to take those trials and use them that rise to the next level in God. That shows a lot of spiritual maturity on your part."

Quinton nodded gratefully at her comment.

Pastor Kendrick said, "Tell us about your vision for working with young people."

Quinton explained, "I started quite a few projects at my last church. One of the most popular ones was the midnight basketball program for the young men in the neighborhood. We were in the inner city like you. I also started a mentoring program where we matched young people with adults in careers that the kids were interested in. They got a chance to see someone doing what they dreamed of doing. We also had an intense tutoring program where most of the kids improved to and maintained a B-average. It's a prerequisite to participate in any other program."

Shara stared at Quinton. His programs sounded familiar.

Quinton continued. "We had also just gotten some grant money to purchase some used computers to do a computer training class."

Quinton frowned. "One thing I didn't get to implement was an arts program. I wanted to get people from the church gifted in music, theatre, dance, and visual arts to start classes for the kids. Kids involved in the arts really perform well in every area of their lives."

Pastor Kendrick nodded and looked at Shara. "Your vision lines up with a lot of what we plan to do here. That's encouraging to hear. We'd be just getting the programs started here so it's good that you have experience with getting them off the ground."

Nia asked about the arts program Quinton

was interested in starting. While he explained, Shara could barely focus on his answer. Why was her head spinning?

After he finished answering Nia, Shara cleared her throat. "Looks like you had a lot of great things going on at your church. Why are you leaving?"

Quinton shifted in his seat and drummed his fingers on the table. "My ideas on how to minister to young people seemed to be a problem for my previous pastor. While they seemed logical to me, they were too 'radical and worldly' for the leadership at the church. I guess because I didn't grow up in the church, I didn't have the ingrained traditions they had. We couldn't come to an agreement about a lot of things."

Quinton seemed to be choosing his words carefully. "When I first started there, I was so excited about implementing the ideas I felt God had given me. After so many meetings where I was called into the pastor's office to talk about 'my methods', I got burnt out. My ideas were being stifled to death. It was time to move on— hopefully to find a place of like vision and spirit."

I knew this was too good to be true. "Can you give us an example of your 'methods' that caused such a conflict?" Shara asked.

Mother Hobbs kneed her under the table, as if to tell her to back off.

Quinton didn't appear intimidated. "One of the things I wanted to do was to create a Christian night club for the youth. Instead of them going to the club where there's drinking, smoking, and fighting, I wanted them to be able to have fun in a church environment. You know, throw on some Mary Mary, Tonex, or Kirk Franklin and let them go for it."

Shara's eyes narrowed. Why did it seem as if he had been thumbing through her vision notebook?

Pastor Kendrick looked at her again and smiled.

Shara pushed further. "What would you do if you found that your ideas clashed with the vision here?"

Mother Hobbs didn't hide her glare this time.

Quinton answered easily. "I learned from my last position that being on staff in ministry is very different from a secular job. It's like a marriage. In marriage, the partners have to have like vision and spirit. I would hope that before they committed to one another, they would take the time to explore what they consider to be their purpose and philosophy to make sure they're a good match. Even after discovering that, they would need to pray to make sure their union is God-ordained. Even if they feel like they're right for each other, unless God has put them together, it won't work.

"That's how I feel about my next position. I want to make sure I know there's a common vision and commitment to the things of God. Then I would hope the ministry leaders would pray as I would be praying to make sure it's the will of God."

Pastor Kendrick and Mother Hobbs nodded at each other in approval.

Pastor said, "Does anyone else have any other questions?" He and the other youth leaders turned to look at Shara. She looked around innocently as if she hadn't been grilling Quinton.

Terrence asked for more details on the midnight basketball program. Everyone laughed when Tina asked how soon Quinton would be willing to move.

Pastor Kendrick looked at Quinton. "Do you have any questions for us?"

Quinton nodded. "I only know what I've read about your ministry on your website. I'm very impressed with the rapid growth of your youth department and I'm interested to know what you attribute your success to."

Pastor Kendrick seemed impressed that Quinton had done some research. "I have to say it's the combination of a lot of hard work and innovation on the part of our youth leaders. Because of their devotion to intercession and their overwhelming commitment of time and energy, the young people have gotten excited and have begun reaching out to their friends. I feel like we're only seeing the beginnings of a great harvest of youth from this community."

Quinton said, "I'm glad to hear you mention prayer as a key. It's definitely the foundation of any successful ministry. What programs do you already have in place?"

"As I mentioned, we're just getting started. One of our most popular programs thus far is our track/tutoring program Shara started almost a year ago. I'll let her tell you about it."

Everyone turned to Shara. Quinton's eyes were intense. Shara couldn't help noticing how perfectly chocolatey-brown his skin was.

Mother Hobbs elbowed her.

Shara made herself focus on her answer. "We have a track program where the kids run after school and also a tutoring program on alternate days." She stopped and looked down at her hands. Why were they sweating?

Everyone looked at her, expecting her to go on and on about her kids as she usually did. After a few moments of silence, Mother Hobbs spoke. "Shara is being far too modest. Her track program sounds a lot like your basketball program. We've already noticed beautiful changes in the children's attitudes about themselves and toward others. Most of them have also brought their grades up considerably. Shara organized both programs in the few extra hours when she wasn't at school."

Pastor Kendrick added, "She's worked very hard to make it a success. Sometimes I think too hard. I'm sure she'll appreciate some full-time help. It's amazing that Shara has a lot of ideas for programs similar to the ones you mentioned. Perhaps she could tell you about them . . ." He looked at Shara who was still dumbstruck, ". . . at another time."

Quinton nodded and smiled at Shara. "I'd like that. It's always good to share ideas with someone of like vision and passion."

Shara looked down at the floor and then back at Quinton again. His teeth were absolutely perfect. Her stomach felt funny. Must have been that leftover pizza she had for lunch.

Pastor Kendrick stood. "Well, Quinton, unless you have any more questions, we'll have Anthony take you on the tour of our facilities. We have a lot of space here and we're renovating it room by room. Later I'll go over the long-term vision with you. I agree with you about making sure our visions match up to make sure this is a good fit."

Anthony seemed excited about giving Quinton the tour. As they walked out of the conference room he said, "Man, I remember your championship game against Kentucky . . ."

Pastor Kendrick shut the door behind them. "Is he perfect or what? God never ceases to amaze me. I ask Him for something and He sends me more than I could have expected. I'm glad we decided to keep looking."

The other leaders also gave their enthusiastic assent. Shara was quiet. Mother Hobbs watched her closely, frowning.

"Well Pastor, I don't see why we need to waste any time," Mother Hobbs said. "Why don't we invite him to stay around for the rest of the week so we can spend a few days with him? He can come to service on Sunday and see what it's like. I'd be more than glad for him to stay with me. If nothing else convinces him to join us, my home cooking and hospitality are sure to do the trick."

Pastor Kendrick looked pleased. "Thank you, Mother Hobbs. I'll bring him over later if he decides to stay."

After everyone left, Mother Hobbs smoothed Shara's hair down. "Are you okay? You don't seem yourself."

"I think I ate something that didn't agree with me today. My stomach is a little upset."

Mother Hobbs raised her eyebrows. "Oh

yeah, you have a real sensitive stomach when it comes to food."

Shara frowned. "What's that supposed to mean?"

"I don't think it's food that has your stomach upset." Mother Hobbs' eyes twinkled with mischief as she walked out of the conference room.

Chapter Twelve

Keeva leafed through the sale section of the paper and noticed there was a spring sale at Nordstrom's. She could use a good all day Saturday shopping outing. She needed a couple of pairs of shoes and wanted a couple of new outfits. She thought of calling her friend, Jade, to go, but wasn't in the mood for her. She decided to call Shara.

They had been hanging out a lot over the last few weeks and were becoming friends. They both said it seemed strange because they were so different, but they had enjoyed a lot of good conversations over good food. Keeva had finally gotten Shara to try Thai, Indian, and Ethiopian food. She hadn't quite convinced her on the sushi. Shara had persuaded Keeva her face wouldn't break out and she wouldn't gain fifty pounds if she ate French fries and pizza every once in a while.

Keeva dialed Shara's number, hoping she wasn't out running.

Shara answered after a couple of rings. "Hey, Keeva. You're up awfully early for a Saturday morning."

"The shopping bug bit me and woke me up. Want to go to Perimeter Mall with me? Nordstrom's is having a big sale."

Shara was silent for a moment. "Now, Keeva, why would we want to do that?"

"What do you mean?"

"Okay, this is how our day would go. We'd go to Nordstrom's and I'd fuss about how expensive everything is and how stuff is not worth the prices they charge and then you'd get frustrated. Then I'd take you to one of the stores where I shop and you'd try to hide your disdain, but you wouldn't be able to because your lip would curl up. Then you'd want to shop for ten hours and I'd be ready to leave. Then you'd try to get me to buy a skirt or dress or something girly and I'd get irritated. By the end of the day, we'd both be totally pissed off at each other. Why put ourselves through that?"

Keeva laughed. "Yeah, I guess you're right. That would be a disaster." She thought for a minute. She could go shopping some other time. She really felt like hanging out with Shara. "Want to do something else then?"

"Like what?"

"There's this great pottery place in the Virginia-Highlands area. You pick out a piece of unfinished pottery, like a cup or bowl or something and you get to paint it. They fire it and you can pick it up the next week. It's real relaxing—puts you in touch with your creative side."

"My creative side?"

"Come on. We're trying new things, remember? Have I led you wrong so far?"

"I guess not. All right. Tell me where and when."

Shara trailed behind Keeva as they perused shelves of cups, bowls, platters and all sort of unfinished pottery in the small eclectic shop. "My creative side, huh? I don't know about this, Keeva."

"It'll be fun. Come on. Pick something."

"I don't see what's so fun about painting pottery. If I want a cup, I can just go buy one. And look at these prices. I can get something already painted for what they're charging. I gotta stop hanging with you. You're gonna have me broke before—" She gasped.

Keeva turned around to see what was wrong.

Shara was almost hugging a large teapot. "This is perfect. A close friend of mine loves to make the most wonderful tea out of fresh herbs. She would love this." She turned the pot over. "Okay, this might be fun." She headed for the table they had picked out. Paint colors were lined up for them to choose from.

Keeva chose a large mug and sat down across from Shara. They painted in silence for a few moments.

Keeva finally broke the silence. "Shar?"

"Yeah, Keev." Shara bit her lip as she painted a large squiggle on the side of the teapot.

"How come you've never invited me to your church?"

Shara looked up. "I don't know. I guess because you told me you don't see the point of going to church, so I guess I didn't see the point in inviting you."

They painted in silence again.

"Yeah, but you see the point, right?" Keeva said.

"What point?" Shara's tongue stuck out of the corner of her mouth as she concentrated on painting the pot again.

"The point of going to church."

"Of course I do. Why do you ask?"

"Maybe there's something I'm missing. Seems like something so important to you that you believe so strongly in, you would want to share with someone."

Shara nodded and kept painting.

Keeva waited for her to answer, but she didn't. Keeva painted a large, yellow flower on the side of her cup. They both painted for a few minutes until Keeva broke the silence again. "Shar?"

"Huh?"

"After everything you went through growing up in church, what made you ever want to go back again?"

Shara put her teapot down. "What's up with the deep questions? I thought we were gonna paint and relax, you know, get in touch with our creative sides."

"Just asking. You have to admit, it's strange to go through all you went through and still want to go to church."

Shara let out a deep breath. "To tell the truth,

after I left home, I didn't want to have anything to do with God. I didn't want to go anywhere near a church. I didn't want to touch a Bible. I felt like I'd had enough of God and church to last me the rest of my life."

"So what happened? What made you go back?"

"Desperation, I guess." Shara rinsed her paintbrush and dabbed it in the purple paint.

Keeva waited for her to explain.

"When I first moved to Atlanta, I felt like the country mouse that'd moved to the city. I was lonely and depressed. I didn't want to go home on the weekends though, because I needed to be away from my parents and their rules." Shara examined the teapot, turning it from side to side. "I didn't have many friends and I had to work to put myself through school, so I was tired all the time. Then I met this guy and he became my first boyfriend. Things were better for a while, but then we got into a big fight and he spread all these lies about me and things got even worse.

"I started to feel guilty, like maybe God was punishing me for turning my back on Him, so I decided to go to church. That made things even worse. It was as if I had slipped back into my childhood. The pastor preached about all the sins we were going to hell for. He ended with a rousing homily on if we just hold on, everything would be all right. I was so tired of that 'hold on' theology. I wanted to know 'what about right now?'

"I was so depressed when I left that service, I didn't know what to do. I felt like I had tried the one thing that was supposed to work and it didn't. When I went to bed that night, I prayed that God would help me. Nothing fancy, I literally just said, 'God, help me.' From then on, my life started to change.

"Not too long after that, I ended up renting a room from this older lady. Over the past few years, she's taught me so much about God and spirituality. That's who the teapot is for. I started going to her church and it also radically changed my life."

Keeva couldn't imagine any church radically changing anyone's life. She had seen people "get saved" and be excited for about six months, and then settle back into their old life again. She had also seen people who regularly went to church more depressed and stressed than she was. Then she had met enough people who said they were Christians who were so full of hell, they made you not want to have anything to do with the church. For Shara to say God and church had radically changed her life and for it to stick . . .

It made her curious. She had never met anyone like Shara. She wasn't annoying like a lot of Christians she knew. She didn't say, "Praise the Lord," every other sentence and she never complained when Keeva played V103 in the car. She didn't act all holy and try to make Keeva feel bad because she didn't go to church. Her Christianity seemed to be a part of her life rather than something she felt the need to smother other people with. It made Keeva interested enough to at least see what Shara's church was about.

"Well, I think if you're gonna be the good Christian you claim to be, you should invite me to your church."

Shara looked up from her teapot. "Okay, you're welcome to come any time."

"Shara!"

"What?" She smiled. "Okay, tomorrow morning, I'll pick you up on my way. Let me warn you, though. It's not church like you're used to. And don't wear any fancy black people church clothes—no big hats or fancy dresses or stockings and heels. Wear something comfortable."

Keeva nodded, becoming even more intrigued. They painted for a few more minutes. This time Shara broke the silence.

"Keeva?"

"Yeah."

"When you said you didn't see the point of going to church, what did you mean?"

"Now who's asking the deep questions?" Keeva painted her name on the bottom of her cup.

"I guess it never really did anything for me. You hear a few songs and then a man gets up and gives an emotional speech. You may feel excited for a few minutes, you may even cry, but then what? I've never really heard anything in church that changed my life.

"I mean, like you said, they preach 'hold on.' Till what? Next week? Then what—hold on some more? What good does that do? I think a lot of church people use their religion as an escape. You hear some good preaching and good singing and it makes you feel better. Other people go to church to do penance for all the dirt they did during the week. And church people are so fake. I *hate* hypocrites. They judge you because you don't go to church, but their lives aren't any different. I've seen people say 'Praise the Lord' and then cuss you out in the next minute. It doesn't seem real to me."

Shara nodded. "I know what you mean. I felt the same way until I started going to my church. A lot of churches and church people give God a bad name. There's a scripture in the Bible that says the traditions of men make the word of God of none effect. That's so true. All our religious rituals dilute the reality of who God is and make a lot of people not want to have anything to do with Him. I had to learn to reject 'churchianity' and not Christianity."

Keeva frowned. "What do you mean by that?"

"A lot of what we do in church or believe about God has nothing to do with God. It does nothing to help us develop a real relationship with Him. It's just what we've always done, so we continue to do it that way. We have so many doctrines, rituals, and rules that are worthless. And it kills us, because it keeps us from the truth and reality of who God is.

"I guess that was my biggest problem with my dad's church. I grew up thinking I had to be perfect for God to love me. I always thought God was this mean ogre, far away in heaven, with a big stick in His hand, waiting to punish me. Anything that went wrong in my life had to be punishment for some sin I had committed. I must have thought a wrong thought, or I didn't pray enough or read my Bible enough. Over the past few years, I've had to unlearn all that stuff and try to find out who God really is. It wasn't easy. I literally had to be un-brainwashed. But to have the relationship with God I have now was well worth it."

Keeva looked puzzled. "You always use that phrase, 'relationship with God'. What do you mean by that?"

"God wants to have a friendship with each and every one of us. Look at it this way. When we first met, we didn't know each other. I had preconceived notions about you and I'm sure you had preconceived notions about me. But over time, we've started to get to know each other. We've talked, shared our thoughts, ideas, personal feelings—we've developed a relationship. It's the same way with God. He wants to talk to us and us to talk to Him." Shara explained further.

Keeva could tell she was really passionate about this God stuff. It made her all the more interested in going to her church and seeing what it was about.

By the time Shara finished, Keeva felt like she understood a little better. She wasn't sure *she* could have a relationship with God like Shara had, but with the way she had been feeling, it was worth trying.

When Keeva got home, her answering machine light was blinking. Eleven messages. She checked the caller-ID machine. All from Mark. She'd left her cell phone off all day, not wanting to be bothered.

She could predict what the messages said. The first one would be him asking her to spend the day with him. The second would be him wondering where she was. Messages three through eight would be him becoming progressively angrier, until he was almost shouting obscenities on message nine. Number ten would be him sheepishly apologizing for all the horrible things he'd said in three through nine and eleven would be completely pitiful, ending with him begging her to call as soon as she got in.

The phone rang. The caller ID displayed Mark's name and number. If she didn't answer it, he'd probably be there in ten minutes, planning to wait for her until she got home.

"Hello?"

"Keeva, where have you been? I've been worried sick about you. Why haven't you called?"

"Mark, I'm fine. I was with my friend, Shara. We had to finish our project."

Another white lie. Thanks to Shara's "analness," they had finished the project last week. Had she told him that or not?

"I thought you finished that a week ago."

Oops. "I thought we'd finished it, but Shara wanted to make some changes. She's a perfectionist. Anyway, I think it's done now. Sorry, baby, I should have called."

"Seems like you've been spending a lot of time with this Shara person lately. I sometimes wonder if you even want to be with me anymore."

"Mark, honey, please don't be insecure. I'm just trying to do whatever I have to do to make sure I don't fail this program. I would think you would understand and support me so I can do the best I can in school." There—she'd answered his guilt trip with one of her own.

"I'm coming over there, Keeva. I think we need to talk in person."

"No, Mark. I'm tired from studying and I want to go to sleep. I don't feel like talking."

"This is no way to maintain a healthy relationship. I'm on my way."

"I'm going to bed. I'm asking you not to come over. Can't you respect that?"

"Princess, we need to be together. All this time apart is bad for our relationship. We won't talk. I'll just hold you and we can both go to sleep." He hung up before she could answer.

Keeva slammed the phone down. She wanted to crawl into her bed by herself and get some sleep. She knew he would want to stay in bed half the morning, have sex a few times, and then go to Sunday brunch. She would have to explain why she was going to church, and why she wasn't going to the church they went to together sometimes.

She decided to try to fall asleep before he got there, although there was very little chance of that happening. She crawled into bed and put her satin sleep mask on. About twenty-five minutes later, he crawled into bed beside her. She pretended to be asleep. Maybe he would leave her alone and she could sneak away in the morning.

That was too good to be true. She felt his hands roaming. She debated—give in and get it over with or pretend to be dead sleep and not respond? She tried fake sleeping for a few minutes, but his roaming became more annoying.

Keeva pretended to be waking up. "Hi, honey, you're here."

Mark didn't even bother to answer. He kissed her and then rolled on top of her. She didn't bother to resist. It was amazing how fast he fell asleep afterward. She literally had to roll him off of her.

She turned toward her bedroom window and stared out of it. Depression settled into her chest. She felt a little better as she thought about visiting Shara's church the next morning. Shara's words from their conversation that afternoon came to mind.

Yeah—she definitely needed God to radically change her life.

Chapter Thirteen

The next morning, Keeva dressed as quietly as possible. She couldn't figure out what to wear. When Shara said don't dress churchy, did she mean business casual or jeans? Knowing Shara, she would show up with jeans on. It didn't matter. Keeva couldn't bring herself to put jeans on knowing she was going to church.

She settled on a pair of khakis and a pink dress shirt. She grabbed her purse and snuck out the front door. Mark was a deep sleeper. If he didn't have anywhere to go, he could sleep until noon. If church didn't last too long, she could get back before he woke up.

She waited outside her apartment building for Shara to drive up.

"I would have buzzed the buzzer. You didn't have to stand on the street waiting for me." Shara moved a pile of books out of the passenger's seat.

"Mark's upstairs asleep and I didn't want to wake him up."

Shara didn't say anything.

Keeva gritted her teeth. It felt weird to admit to Shara that her boyfriend had spent the night. That was probably a major sin in Shara's mind.

About fifteen minutes later, they pulled up at an old school building on Hilliard Street. This was the church? Shara led her into the sanctuary. Keeva was glad she had worn the khakis. Everyone had on very casual clothes.

The sanctuary was actually what must have been the school auditorium with a stage and stadium seating. The stage looked more like it was set up for a concert than a church service. There were drums, a base guitar, an electric guitar, and two, huge keyboards.

Keeva stopped Shara, as she seemed to be heading toward the front. "Where are you going?"

"I always sit on the front row. What's wrong?"

Keeva pulled back. "I don't want to sit at the front. Can't we just sit here?" She motioned to a row about halfway back. Shara shrugged and scooted down the row with Keeva following her.

After a few minutes, a small group filed out onto the stage and took their places behind the instruments and a row of microphones. Everyone stood up. The band started playing some real jazzy music that was *way* too funky to be church music. The group started singing a song about praising God with dancing. A group of

young people crowded down front around the
stage. They were singing and dancing *hard*.
They really seemed to be enjoying themselves.

A young man with baggy jeans and cornrows
took the mic and started rapping. The young
people down front danced even harder. Keeva
had never heard anyone rap in church before.
The band switched over to a calypso song.
Everyone went wild as the group sang something about the Lion of the tribe of Judah. The
kids down front did some coordinated steps.

After a few more equally rousing songs, the
band switched gears and played something slow.
The group sang, ". . . He's the Worthy Lamb of
God, glorify the Lamb."

The kids down front lifted their hands. They
seemed to be as serious as they were when they
were dancing. Many people had their eyes closed
and their hands lifted. Some people were sway-
ing back and forth with the music. Others were
kneeling, some were crying.

Whatever the statement, everyone seemed to
be trying to focus on God rather than on the
music and the singers. Keeva looked around.
She didn't know what to do. She didn't understand what the people were feeling and didn't
want to fake it. At the same time, there was
such reverence in the air, she felt as if it would
be rude to sit down. She stood there with her
hands at her sides.

She'd never seen anything like this at any
church she'd gone to. She was more used to
hymns, anthems and spirituals sung by a well
directed, robed choir. It was rare that anyone
said "amen" or "hallelujah" out loud, let alone

raise their hands or even think about getting "happy". Such displays of emotion were frowned upon.

The key changed and the lead singer said, "Come on, let's worship Him. Sing to the Lord out of your hearts. Let Him know how much you love Him." She sang in a strong contralto voice, "I love you Lord, and I lift my voice. . . ." Everyone joined in.

Keeva knew the words to the song. She took a deep breath and began to sing. The more she sang, the more she relaxed. Since no one was watching her, she decided to lift her hands and close her eyes, releasing herself a bit more.

When the next chorus ended, everyone was quiet and the music played on. The woman leading sang softly, "Now just sing a love song to the Lord, sing your own song . . ."

Keeva heard everyone around her begin to sing. Even though they all sang something different, it all flowed together harmoniously. She began to feel something. It felt like energy—electricity, flowing through her body. It was strong and heavy, and kept coming over her in waves. It felt like love and strength and peace, and every good feeling she had ever felt before in her life. She felt this deepness, this pulling, this overwhelming *something*. Whatever it was, it made her nervous.

Keeva opened her eyes. Shara seemed caught up in whatever it was too. Her eyes were closed and tears were streaming down her face. Keeva sat down and smoothed out her blouse and khakis. She shook off the warm, tingly feeling and flipped through the pages of her Bible, trying to distract herself from being drawn in again.

The music played on for a few minutes longer, then a short, stocky man took the microphone and said quietly, "Lord, we thank you for your presence. We bask in your glory. Speak to us and tell us what's on your heart."

He was casually dressed in a pair of black slacks and a beige dress shirt. He had been dancing off to the side of the stage while the band was playing.

Shara leaned over and whispered, "That's Pastor Kendrick."

Keeva looked at him. That was the pastor? She had expected someone older, in a preacher's robe, or at least a suit. Of course, nothing else she had experienced had been like a conventional church so why should the pastor be?

"Thank you, worship team. You guys keep taking it to another level. I don't want to waste this atmosphere. I'd like to get right into the Word." Pastor Kendrick paused. "Let me make an introduction first. Quinton, can you come up here?"

A tall, dark man in a perfectly tailored, blue pinstripe suit walked onto the stage. Obviously, no one had told him about the relaxed dress code.

Pastor Kendrick grinned from ear to ear. "I'd like you all to meet Minister Quinton Mercer. As many of you know, we've been in the process of hiring a youth pastor. We've met many candidates and finally God sent us Minister Mercer. We've spent the week getting to know each other. We've discussed our visions and both had time to seek the Lord. I'm pleased to announce he has agreed to join us as our new youth pastor. Please welcome him."

Keeva heard Shara's breath catch. Everyone rose and applauded.

A voice behind them said, "Girl, he is *too* fine. Is he married?"

"Now women of God . . ." Pastor Kendrick grinned mischievously as the applause died down. "Let me make an announcement. No, Minister Mercer is not married and he's informed me that he's not looking."

Everyone laughed.

"So please, do *not* pass him your phone number, don't offer to cook him dinner, and he's the YOUTH pastor, so don't try to schedule any counseling sessions with him."

More laughter.

"And don't be getting no revelations about 'the Lord sent him here to be my husband.' "

Everyone laughed. The voice behind them said, "Girl, just watch me. Give me a year, no, six months. I will be Mrs. Youth Pastor."

Pastor Kendrick motioned for Quinton to say a few words.

He cleared his throat. "Good morning. It's really good to see you all this morning."

The voice behind them said, "Naw baby, it's good to see *you*."

"I'm very excited about joining you all here. I am very committed to working with young people to help them become the best they can be and I am pleased that it seems like our visions . . ." he motioned to Pastor Kendrick, ". . . are so similar. I'm looking forward to serving you."

That annoying voice again. "Naw, baby, I'm looking forward to serving *you*. Where do I sign up to work with the young people?"

Keeva leaned over toward Shara. "Do you get to work with him? He's absolutely gorg— . . . he seems very nice."

Shara nodded. Keeva looked at her more closely. She had a weird look on her face. Had she been passed over for that position?

Quinton returned to his seat and Pastor Kendrick flipped through the Bible. "Let's get started. Turn in your Bibles to . . ."

The music played softly after Pastor Kendrick prayed. Everyone was quiet, taking in the message. Pastor Kendrick finally spoke. "I don't want to ruin this atmosphere. You can leave your tithes and offering in the baskets at the back on the way out."

That was the last straw for Keeva. At the church she went to, they took up at least *three* offerings—tithes and offering, building fund, and missionary offering. That was one of the things she hated about church the most—the preacher spending an hour begging for money. She leaned over to Shara.

"They don't take up offering?"

Shara shrugged. "Sometimes. They always have the baskets up front and at the back for people to put their money in if he forgets. When he really gets into the music or the sermon, it sometimes slips his mind. He teaches on tithes and offering on a regular basis, then leaves it up to us."

Shara waved to someone. "I want you to meet somebody."

She led Keeva to the front. She gestured to an older woman. She looked like a queen in her lavender African dress with a matching head wrap. She floated over to where they were.

"Keeva, this is Mother Hobbs, my friend I told you about. Mother Hobbs, this is my friend, Keeva. We go to school together."

Keeva extended her hand, but the older woman pulled her into an embrace.

"It's good to meet you, Keeva. I'm glad you joined us today. Did you enjoy the service?"

Keeva nodded. "It was very different, but that's probably why I enjoyed it so much."

"Good, I hope you'll join us again."

Mother Hobbs turned to Shara. "Looks like we've got ourselves a youth pastor. Listen, I was up all night cooking up a big welcome dinner for Quinton. Pastor Kendrick and Jenell will be joining us. I'd love to have you two come."

Before Keeva could consider accepting, Shara said, "Oh, no thanks, I have to drop Keeva off. We rode together."

Keeva knew she should get home to avoid an argument with Mark. She wanted to go to dinner, though. If this was the woman to whom Shara attributed her spiritual growth, she wanted to see what she was about. She also wanted a chance to see what the pastor was like in person. He seemed so sincere while preaching. But she had heard of a lot of ministers who could really preach, but secretly drank heavily, or stole the church's money, or were sleeping with all the women in the church. She wanted to see if he was the man of integrity he seemed to be.

"Actually, I don't have any plans, Ms. Hobbs. I'd love to come." Keeva smiled.

Shara shot her a funny look.

Mother Hobbs beamed. "Wonderful! You ladies can come on over and help me get everything set up. Quinton is going to hang around here for a while to meet and greet people, and then he'll ride over with Pastor Kendrick."

Chapter Fourteen

As soon as they entered Mother Hobbs' house, all sorts of wonderful smells greeted them. It reminded Keeva of Thanksgiving day at her grandmother's in Alabama. Shara set the table while Mother Hobbs got the serving dishes ready. Keeva tried to help but Mother Hobbs told her she was still considered company.

"You can help next time you come over." She sat her down at the kitchen table with a cup of chilled herbal tea.

Keeva fidgeted in her seat not knowing what to say. If Mother Hobbs was this great spiritual person, she might be able to tell Keeva she wasn't really a Christian or that she had slept with her boyfriend last night.

Mother Hobbs pulled her shoes off. "Girl, my feet *hurt*, you hear me? That's what I get for trying to be all cute wearing these heels. I'm too old for all that. But you have to admit, lavender pumps with my lavender dashiki? Mother Hobbs was fine today." With a bit of dramatic flair she added, "The price we women pay for beauty."

Keeva giggled and relaxed back into her chair.

Shara appeared from the dining room. "Yeah, you were cute and all, but I don't want to hear nothing 'bout your corns or bunions later."

"Oh please, Miss Bluejean. You wouldn't understand. Don't you be sassin' me either. You ain't as grown as you think you are. Respect your elders."

Shara laughed and disappeared back into the dining room with some glasses.

"That child is all mouth. Always got something to say."

Shara called out from the dining room, "I can hear you, old lady. Watch yourself."

Mother Hobbs pulled dishes out of the refrigerator and put them in the oven to heat up. "So you're in school with Shara? Are you in the Education program also?"

"Actually, I'm in the Professional Counseling program. I hope to work with young people too, but as a counselor rather than as an educator."

"I think that's even more challenging. I tell you, the state of our young people today is scary. It's good to see good people committed to helping them."

They chatted for a while with Mother Hobbs, sharing some of her horror stories from her last years teaching school. The doorbell rang. Mother Hobbs went to let Quinton, Pastor Kendrick, and his wife in. Shara came in from the dining room.

Mother Hobbs made introductions. "Keeva, this is Pastor and Mrs. Kendrick and this is Quinton Mercer."

Pastor Kendrick hugged her warmly, as did his wife. Jenell Kendrick was a petite woman with a round, pretty face and a dazzling smile. Keeva recognized her as the lead singer on the praise and worship team.

"I loved the music this morning. You have an awesome voice."

"Thank you. I'm glad you joined us today," Jenell said.

Keeva shook hands with Quinton, noticing he was even more handsome up close.

He bowed his head a little. "Nice to meet you, Keeva." She watched as he also shook Shara's hand.

"Good to see you again, Shara, isn't it? Both Pastor Kendrick and Mother Hobbs have been going on and on about you all week. I'm really looking forward to sitting down with you and tossing around some ideas," Quinton said.

Shara stood there, shaking his hand. Keeva elbowed her in the side, ever so slightly.

Almost as if startled, Shara said, "Yeah, I'm looking forward to that, too."

Mother Hobbs and Keeva both eyed Shara and then looked at each other, raising their eyebrows.

Mother Hobbs grabbed Shara's arm and directed her toward the kitchen. She motioned everyone else into the next room. "We almost have everything ready. Why don't you all go on in to the dining room? Go ahead and get comfortable. The food will be out in a minute."

They all sat around the large antique dining table while Shara and Mother Hobbs brought out the serving dishes brimming with food. Mother Hobbs had made oven-fried chicken, salad, string beans, greens, black-eyed peas, macaroni and cheese, candied yams and cornbread. Everything came straight out of the *Soul Food for a Healthy Heart* cookbook she got from her cooking class at the YMCA. It had taken a while for her to learn to make healthy food still taste like soul food, but she had now made it an art. Her secret was a variety of fresh herbs she grew in her little garden in the back yard.

Pastor Kendrick blessed the table and everyone fixed their plates. They were all quiet for a few minutes as they dug into their food.

Quinton said, "Church was absolutely awesome today. Is it always like that? I've never experienced anything like that before. The music, the Word, the freedom—man, I didn't know church could be like that." He frowned. "Somebody could have told me not to wear a suit, though."

"Oops, my bad, man," Pastor Kendrick said. "I forgot to mention that. I don't believe in having to dress up for church. I think God is happy with us being comfortable." He bobbed his head to an imaginary beat. "Besides, I can't get my dance on in no suit."

Quinton laughed. "That was an interesting order of service. Now that I think about it, all you do is praise and worship, and then the sermon. I've never seen a preacher not take up an offering."

"I know," Keeva said. "No announcements, no choir, no welcoming of the visitors. It was fine with me, though. Most of the time when they do all that stuff, I daydream anyway."

"That was precisely the problem," Pastor Kendrick said. "We found that our members from the neighborhood weren't usual church-goers. They kept coming to service late every Sunday. We changed service to a later time, thinking they didn't want to get up that early, but they still kept coming late. I finally got some feedback from a few of them and they said they didn't want to be bothered with all that other stuff. They just wanted to hear some good music and a sermon and go home. So we changed everything. I decided the most impor-tant elements were the worship to create the proper atmosphere, and the Word."

"That band is awesome," Quinton said. "Now that's a powerful evangelistic tool. Some people will come just for the music and then you slip them the Word. Who writes your music? I've never heard most of those songs before."

Pastor Kendrick nodded proudly toward his wife. "Jenell writes most of the stuff we sing. She's my little songbird."

Jenell blushed. "Oh sweetie, stop." He leaned over and kissed her on the cheek.

Mother Hobbs snorted as she spooned a large portion of macaroni and cheese onto Quin-ton's plate. "Don't y'all start all that mushy stuff. People are trying to eat."

Everyone laughed and Jenell blushed even more.

Keeva looked at Pastor Kendrick and then at Jenell. "Wow, you write the music? It was awesome. How do you come up with those songs?" she said.

"Most of them come out of my time with God. As I'm praying, reading the Bible, or spending personal time with Him, they come to me. Sometimes they come out of something my husband preaches or from life experiences. I love music, so my deepest feelings get expressed through song." Jenell had the same dreamy expression when she talked about God and music she had when Pastor Kendrick had kissed her.

"Have you ever thought of using your band for street ministry?" Quinton asked.

Pastor Kendrick looked up from his plate. "What do you mean?"

"Well, you pick a major street in the middle of your target neighborhood and set the band up with the amps, drums, guitars, singers and everything. You start a concert right in the middle of the street on a Friday night. The people gather around because they're interested and then you just *jam*. You don't even have anybody preach. At the end, let them know where you're from and invite them to church if they want to come. That was one of my ideas that got shot down at my old church."

Pastor Kendrick nodded. "Sounds like a good idea, man. We may have to look into that." He smiled. "This is gonna be good. I'm excited about you joining us."

"So when *will* you be joining us, Quinton?" Jenell asked.

"I resigned from my position at my last church a month ago, so I'm free. After spending the week with you guys, and especially after service this morning, I'm more excited about ministry than I've been in a long time. I'm ready to start *yesterday*."

Quinton's eyes had a fire in them Keeva recognized. It was that same passion she saw in Shara when she talked about God and her kids, the same look in Pastor Kendrick's eyes when he preached, and in Jenell's eyes when she talked about her music.

She looked around at everyone in the room. They were all so committed to this church thing and they each had this energy about them when they talked about it, almost a glow.

Mother Hobbs looked over at Quinton's nearly empty plate. "My goodness, you were hungry. Do you want some more?"

"If this woman feeds me any more food . . ." Quinton rubbed his stomach. "Pastor Kendrick, you ain't slick. I got you all figured out. I'm sure part of your plan to get me here was to have Mother Hobbs spoil me to death. She's waited on me hand and foot all week."

"Guilty as charged. But it worked right?" Mother Hobbs said.

"Oh yeah, too well. I think I've gained ten pounds since I've been here. She says this is all healthy food, but I'm not buying it. It tastes too good to be good for me." Quinton leaned back in his chair. "Yeah, I was gonna make a trip back here to go apartment hunting, but I think I'll move into my room upstairs permanently."

Everyone laughed except Shara, who feigned a scowl. "No way, Quinton. This is my house. You gotta find your own place to stay."

Mother Hobbs smiled at Shara's jealous daughter act. "Actually, Quinton, I was going to mention that you're welcome to stay here as long as you need to. Atlanta has a lot of different areas, each with their own character. You may want to live here a while before deciding where you want to move, especially with the traffic. You can spend a few months here until you make a decision."

"Actually, I plan to live in the neighborhood around the church," Quinton said. "I really want to get a feel for the community and the youth. I feel like I can serve them better if I'm living right there among them, seeing what they see, feeling what they feel, living like they live."

Everyone was quiet for a moment.

Pastor Kendrick finally said, "That's admirable, Quinton, and I really appreciate your commitment to the ministry, but that neighborhood isn't the best. Let's be real, man, it's downright bad. The drugs and so-called gangs have gotten a little better in the last few years, but still—there aren't any nice apartment buildings or anything there."

Quinton waved away his concern. "I grew up in Chicago's Cabrini Green Projects, man. There can't be anything here in Atlanta that can touch that. I don't have a wife and kids to think about, so it's not a problem. I see it as a strategy—infiltrate and conquer for the Kingdom."

Pastor Kendrick nodded his respect. "Okay, I'll help you in any way I can to find a decent place. I know you're anxious to get down here, so let me know when you want to come back to start looking."

Quinton rubbed his chin. "Actually, I think I'll take Mother Hobbs up on her offer. I'll stay over for a few more days and stake out the neighborhood. I had checked out an apartment building around the corner from the church the other day and need to get some more information on it."

"Do you have a lot of furniture to move?" Jenell asked.

"Not a bit. I bought my mom a house out in the suburbs of Chicago a while back. I'm gonna leave the furniture with her and get all new stuff. I need some help with that, though. If I try to furnish it myself, no telling how the place will end up looking."

Jenell's face lit up. "I'd love to help out. I love to decorate and I know where all the bargains are. I'm a professional shopper."

Pastor Kendrick held up a finger. "Quinton, beware. This woman will have you broke. Your place will be hooked up, but you won't have a dime left."

"Hush, Michael." Jenell swatted at Pastor Kendrick playfully. "Quinton, don't pay him no mind. You just tell me when you want to go."

"Thanks. I'll let you know." Quinton turned to Shara. "Since it looks like I'll be here a little longer, maybe we can meet some time this week. Maybe I can come to track practice."

Shara smoothed back her hair. "Sure, that . . . that would be . . . uh good. We meet Monday and Wednesday this week at 4:00, so umm that would . . . you could drop in any time."

"Great, I'll drop by on Wednesday."

Mother Hobbs got up from the table. "Who left room for dessert?" She returned with a German chocolate cake.

Quinton groaned. "Oh my goodness, that's my favorite. There's no way you can convince me that's healthy."

"The cake is made with egg whites and applesauce instead of eggs and oil. The icing—that's another story. Every once in a while, you have to just go for it."

She cut the cake into thick slices, put a large piece on a plate, and handed it to Quinton.

He eyed it and held his stomach. "On second thought, maybe I better not move in to your house, Mother Hobbs. I'd end up being one of those big-bellied preachers."

Mother Hobbs pushed the plate closer to him. "I was up all night baking this cake. Y'all better eat it. A little piece of cake ain't gonna hurt nobody."

"That ain't no little piece of cake. But if you insist . . ." Quinton took a bite and rolled his eyes back in his head. "Hallelujah, Glory to Jesus." He did a little quiver and shook dramatically. "Hondalashayah. Cake so good, it'll make you speak in tongues."

Mother Hobbs pinched Quinton's cheek. "Boy, you crazy."

They all chatted for a while longer over cake and coffee until Jenell looked at her watch. "Michael, it's getting late. We better go pick up the kids."

"Yeah, where are they?" Shara looked around as if she just realized someone was missing.

"They went out to dinner with the Patterson kids. They didn't know you were gonna be here, otherwise I'm sure they would have come. They love them some 'Miss Shara'," Jenell said.

"How old are your kids?" Quinton asked.

"Michael Jr. is eleven, Briana is ten, and Monique is eight. Can you say stair steps?"

Keeva stared at Jenell. She didn't look like she'd had three children. "How long have you two been married?"

Pastor Kendrick rubbed Jenell's arm. "Thirteen wonderful years. Feels like just yesterday . . ."

Jenell kissed his cheek. "Baby, you so sweet."

"Didn't I tell y'all about that mushy stuff?" Mother Hobbs fussed. "Keep on, hear? Next time we get together, you'll be saying '. . . Monique is eight and the baby here is two weeks old.'"

Everyone laughed except Jenell, who shook her head and patted her stomach. "No way. No 'ooops' or 'uh-ohs' for me. Three is all I need."

Everybody laughed.

Jenell continued, "Anyway, Miss Shara, you promised to take them to the movies next weekend and you know they never forget anything."

"I know. We're going. I promised to take them to Dave and Buster's too. I should let them spend the night. We haven't had a slumber party in a while."

Pastor Kendrick said, "Keep them for the whole weekend and we just *might* be talking about 'the baby is two weeks old.' Why stop at three?"

Jenell playfully punched his shoulder. "Unless you're gonna carry it, three is all you get, Michael Kendrick. I told you that when we first got married. Now come on, we gotta go."

She got up, picking up her plate and silverware. "Mother Hobbs, I hate to leave you with all these dishes. Do you need some help?"

"Now Jenell, you know better than that. Y'all go ahead and get the kids." Mother Hobbs took the dishes out of her hands.

Quinton stood to walk them to the door. He hugged Jenell and then Pastor Kendrick. "Peace, man, see you tomorrow."

Shara took the serving dishes to the kitchen. Keeva got up to help her. Quinton rolled up his sleeves. "I got it, ladies. Relax yourselves. Have a seat."

They looked at each other in mock amazement at his offer.

"What? A man can't do the dishes? Shoot, I can probably clean and cook better than all of you."

Mother Hobbs put her hands on her hips. "Is that so?"

"My mother worked two jobs for as long as I could remember. I had to do all the cooking and cleaning around the house while she was gone. I practically raised my three younger brothers."

"A man that can cook *and* clean?" Mother Hobbs reached up and patted his face. "You don't need no apartment, baby. You can stay right here with me."

Shara pretended to be hurt. "I see how you are, Mother Hobbs. Quinton comes along and you kick me to the curb." She pointed a threatening finger at Quinton. "You better not be sleeping in my room either."

"Your room?" he asked.

"That's right, the one at the top of the stairs."

Mother Hobbs laughed and stepped in between them. "Children, stop fighting. There's enough room and enough love here to go around." She walked over and pinched Keeva's cheeks. "If y'all don't behave, I'm kicking both of you out and Keeva is moving in." She planted a motherly kiss on Keeva's forehead.

Quinton pouted while he washed the dishes. Mother Hobbs sat Keeva down at the kitchen table and stood behind her, rubbing her back. There was something so soothing about her touch. Keeva closed her eyes for a minute. This was a good day. For the first time in her life, she actually enjoyed church. The sermon touched her in a way she couldn't explain. Dinner was fun. She enjoyed all the love and laughter. They were all real, down to earth people.

"Tired?"

Keeva opened her eyes to see Shara looking at her. "No. Relaxed. I guess we better get going. I totally deserted Mark today and I know I'm gonna hear about it when I get home."

"You must not have had your cell phone with you."

Keeva smiled a guilty smile. "I accidentally left it on purpose."

Shara made a zipping motion across her lips. "Your secret's safe with me."

They stood to leave. Quinton dried his hands and came over to say good-bye. He bowed dramatically. "My dear ladies, I do appreciate the pleasure of your company. Thank you so much for gracing me with your presence."

Keeva giggled and curtsied, extending her hand for him to kiss. Shara looked at them both with mock disdain and said, "Whatever," and kept walking toward the door.

Mother Hobbs gave Shara a hug. "Bye, sweetie. I'll see you tomorrow."

She gave Keeva a long hug. Keeva tried to soak in all the love she could while Mother Hobbs held her.

"Keeva, I hope this won't be the last time I see you." Mother Hobbs cupped her cheeks in her hands and looked into her eyes. "There's something you need that you can only get from God. If you seek Him, you'll find Him and your life will never be the same. I promise, life will be all you ever dreamed it could be. God can make every dead dream come to life." She gave her another hug and then stood on the porch while they walked to the car.

As they were driving away, Keeva asked Shara, "What did she mean by that? What did you tell her about me?"

"Nothing. I barely mentioned you. She has a spiritual gift, that's all."

"What do you mean? She's psychic or something?"

"No, not psychic, silly." Shara grinned. "Should

I come upstairs with you? Are you gonna get a beat-down from Mark?"

Keeva rolled her eyes. "Girl, please. He ain't crazy." She paused. "Well, he ain't *that* crazy."

They both laughed.

Keeva looked over at Shara. "Sooooo, what do you think about Quinton?"

"He seems very nice. I'm sure he'll be a great addition to the staff."

"You can't be *that* spiritual. Give me a break."

"What?"

"Girl, he is *too* fine. Don't act like you don't notice how fine he is. He looks just like Morris Chestnut."

Shara looked at her with feigned horror. "Keeva, he's a minister of the gospel."

"Minister or not, girl, that man is fine. I don't see how you're gonna work with him. You could barely talk to him without stuttering."

"What are you talking about? I didn't stutter."

Keeva mocked her, "Uuh, uum, we have track practice Monday and uh Wednesday." She bugged out her eyes and held her mouth open, pretending to be speechless for a second. "Uuh, umm, I'm looking forward to talking over ideas with you too."

"Whatever, Keeva!" Shara smiled. "Okay, maybe he threw me off a little bit. And I do admit, he is pleasant on the eye. But I ain't falling all over him or nothing. You won't hear me saying 'Just give me six months and I'll be Mrs. Youth Pastor.'"

"I know, wasn't that disgusting? I thought

you were going to turn around and tell her to shut up."

"I thought about it, girl. I had to catch myself."

They pulled up in front of Keeva's building. Shara parked the car and got out.

"What are you doing?"

Shara put up her fists as if she was about to fight. "I told you, I got your back."

Keeva laughed.

Shara gave her a big hug. "I'm glad you came with me today. It's a good thing you invited yourself."

"I'm glad too. Thanks." Keeva headed toward the front of her building but couldn't resist saying over her shoulder as she went in, "Have fun at track practice on Wednesday."

When she got upstairs, Keeva was shocked to see Mark sitting on the couch watching TV. She thought he would have been long gone. When she walked in, he raised the remote and clicked the television off.

"Keeva, what is this all about? You sneak out while I'm 'sleep and stay gone all day? I try to call and the cell phone rings in the next room? What's going on? Are you seeing someone else?"

"Mark, please." Keeva rolled her eyes. "Of course I'm not seeing someone else. I went to church with Shara and then we went to her friend's house for dinner afterward. I didn't sneak out. You were sleeping so peacefully, I didn't want to wake you."

"Didn't want to wake me? Went to church

with Shara? If you wanted to go to church, all you had to do was tell me. We could've gone to our church together." He folded his arms across his chest. "Is there something we need to talk about? I feel like we're on two different pages lately."

Keeva sighed and pulled her hair. "Maybe we do need to talk." She walked over to the couch, sat down, and took her shoes off.

"Mark, I don't know if you've noticed or not, but I've been very unhappy lately. I feel like—"

"You've been studying too hard, Keeva. I understand. I've been studying hard too, but that's no reason to—"

"No, that's not it. It's deeper than that. I've been feeling depressed lately and I've been doing some soul searching about my life and my future. I think—"

"You've been under a lot of stress. We've *both* been under a lot of stress lately. We need to spend more time together—be there for each other."

"You're not listening to me."

"I am listening. You've been stressed out. I understand."

Keeva pounded the arm of the couch. "Why can't you let me talk for a minute? Stop saying you understand and listen to me."

"Princess, you know I can't stand to see you upset. I hate to hear you talk about being depressed. I want to make you happy. Can't you let me make you happy?"

"Mark, you can't make me happy." She saw the hurt in his eyes. "I don't mean it like that. I have to have happiness from inside of me. I have to be happy with my life and I'm not happy right now. I feel like—"

"Honey, maybe Dr. Cohen is right. Maybe it is time to start some medication to get you through this."

Keeva got up from the couch and walked over and flipped on the television. Her wonderful-day feeling was fading. She wanted to salvage what was left of it. "Mark, I don't need any medication. I just need . . . never mind."

"What do you need? Whatever it is, I'll get it for you, Princess."

Keeva sighed and smiled at him. "Nothing, sweetie." She curled up next to him. "Let's watch a movie and fall asleep."

She felt him take a deep breath. He seemed relieved. He put his arms around her and held her tight. "I love you, Princess. You're going to be fine. I'll take care of you. I promise."

Chapter Fifteen

On Wednesday afternoon, Shara stood at the edge of the track, watching the kids run. She felt a presence beside her and turned to find Quinton standing there. She jumped. "Oh!"

"Sorry. Wasn't trying to sneak up on you."

She nodded. There was an awkward silence.

He cleared his throat. "So—these are the kids in your program?"

"Yeah."

"How many do you have participating?"

"Twenty-eight all together. We have about twenty regulars. We started out with more than that, but a lot of the older guys dropped out. I just lost one of my best girls, too."

"What happened?"

She told the Tangee saga one more time. Shara couldn't help wondering where Tangee was and what she was doing. Tangee's mother wouldn't give Shara the address or phone number at her grandmother's.

Quinton stared at her as she told the story. Shara smoothed her hair back. Was it flying all over her head?

"That must've been difficult. Seems like you cared a lot about her," he said.

"Yeah, I love all my kids, but I have to admit, Tangee was special to me."

"I know how that feels. I had a few special ones I lost to gangs and drugs and stuff. Then I felt bad when I had to tell the ones left I was moving here—like I was abandoning them. I wonder what's gonna happen to some of them now. Not to say I am solely responsible for what happens to them. I just know one caring adult can make all the difference in a kid's life."

"I know what you mean. I think we all have one adult we can look back on that really pushed us to be the best we could be. Mine was my track coach," Shara said.

Quinton nodded. "Mine was my high school social studies teacher. I remember in the tenth grade, he pulled me aside and made a big deal about how smart I was. He told me, 'don't let them pimp you to be their basketball star. Let it open doors and pave the road to the life you want to live.' He told me to focus on my education as much as I did basketball. He said I could really be somebody important and really make a difference in the world. I think about how much of a difference his words made with me and I try to take every interaction with a young person seriously. You never know when something you say or do may change someone's life."

Shara stared at Quinton, thinking about his

words when Danae, Shanique, and Lakita ran up.

"We're tired. Can we stop now?" Danae looked at Quinton. "Who this, Miss Shara? Your boyfriend?"

"No, he is not my boyfriend and that was rude of you to ask. You know better than that, Danae." She gave her a "you're gonna get it later when he leaves" look.

"This is Minister Mercer. He's going to be the youth pastor of the church. He'll be coordinating all the youth activities."

"What? You not gonna be working with us no more?" Danae looped her arm through Shara's and laid her head on her shoulder.

"Of course I'll be working with you guys. I'm not going anywhere." Shara patted Danae's head. "He's coming to help out. We'll be starting some other projects in addition to the track and tutoring program."

Lakita said, "Good, 'cause I'm tired of running all the time." She moved over and stood in front of Quinton. "I'm Lakita and this Danae." She rolled her eyes. "That's Shanique."

Shanique scowled at Lakita, then moved over in front of Lakita to get a better look at Quinton. Lakita stepped out from behind her with her hands on her hips. She was about to go off when Shanique said, "I know you! Your poster was on my brother's wall. You're a basketball player!"

Quinton smiled that modest smile of his. Shara wondered how often this happened.

"Tyreek! Come here! Hurry up!" Shanique motioned for him to come off the track.

"What? I ain't finished yet." He started to pass by and then stopped. "Aw, man, are you for real? Yo, Jamil, Davon, come here!"

One by one, all the kids came off the track and crowded around Quinton. He laughed and talked, seeming to make each one feel important all at the same time. Shara watched him interacting with them.

"You coming here for real, man? You gonna start a basketball program? Yo, man, dat's da bomb. Wait 'til I tell T-bone," Jamil said.

Quinton looked over at Shara, standing at the edge of the small crowd. "Look, y'all gonna get me in trouble with Miss Shara. You better finish your laps. She told me how you've been slacking lately."

"Naw, we ain't slacking. We doing right." Jamil said. They all raced back toward the track. Shara noticed they seemed to be jogging faster and with better form than she had seen in a while.

"They seem to like you already. I didn't realize you were famous like that. I'm not much of a basketball fan."

"It can get a little nerve racking. Strangers want to talk to you all the time and get your autograph and stuff. You can't go anywhere without someone recognizing you. People want to befriend you because you're famous and rich. You never know who your real friends are. It's been better lately though, since I've been out of the game for the past few years. Don't tell anyone, but I'm glad I got out of it when I did."

"Why is that a secret?" Shara asked.

"I don't know. People told me I was crazy for quitting. They couldn't understand why I would give up fame and fortune just like that. I caught a lot of flack from everybody."

"I thought you got hurt."

"I did, but after my surgery, I rehabbed my knee for a few months and was fine. I could've played again. After everything that happened though, I didn't want to go back." The dark look that moved into Quinton's eyes told Shara not to ask what he meant.

He shuffled his feet. "So, Pastor Kendrick has been telling me all about your plans for the youth projects. Sounds like we have a lot of ideas in common."

"Yeah, I was thinking that during your interview. It seemed like you were reading from my vision journal."

"Vision journal?"

Shara bit her lip. "I have this book where I write down all my ideas for things I want to do or that I feel God wants me to do."

"That sounds like a great idea. I might have to try that. My ideas sort of all run around in my head. That might help me to get them organized."

"Would you—" Shara hesitated. "Ummm, you want to see mine? It might, uh, give you some ideas on how to organize yours." She had never shown anyone her journal except for Mother Hobbs and Pastor Kendrick. Her dreams and ideas from God were very personal. Why had she offered to show them to a complete stranger?

"That would be great. I'd like that." He smiled and it seemed like the sun started shining a little bit brighter.

Shara smoothed back her hair.

After track practice, she sent the kids home and went into the church building. She hoped Quinton forgot or got preoccupied with something else, but he was sitting in the office talking to Mother Hobbs when she walked in.

Mother Hobbs looked up and smiled. "There you are. Quinton was waiting for you. Let me get out of y'all's way. Quinton, let me know when you're ready to go." She paused. "Or actually, Shara can drop you off. It's not too far out of her way. Is that okay with you, Shara?"

Quinton's back was to Shara so he couldn't see the evil glare she gave Mother Hobbs while saying, "Sure, no problem." She thought for a minute. "Actually, Mother Hobbs, I'm starving and would love some leftovers from Sunday. Why don't I grab my notebook and Quinton and I can talk at your house. Is that okay with you?"

"Of course, Shara. I'll meet you guys at the house."

"Ummmm, I need a few minutes to finish up some paperwork here. How 'bout I meet *you* guys at the house?" Shara bit her lip.

"All right, sweetie." Mother Hobbs gave Shara a concerned look. She had been in the office when Shara had proudly announced she was finished with all her stats for the youth program on Monday. "I'll have your plate ready by the time you get there."

After they left, Shara shuffled some papers around on her desk. She looked through her roster and came across Tangee's name. She thought about calling Ms. Madison to see how she was doing, but remembered her evil glares and words from that night at the hospital and decided against it. She took her notebook out of her drawer and headed for Mother Hobbs' house.

When she arrived, Quinton and Mother Hobbs were sitting at the kitchen table eating. As promised, Mother Hobbs had a huge plate of food coming out of the microwave for her.

"Oh my goodness, I can't eat *that* much!"

Shara hoped Mother Hobbs wouldn't mention that she'd seen her put away that much food and then ask for seconds on many occasions.

"I'm sorry, Shara. I guess I got carried away." She stared at Shara. "You know how I am."

The three of them chatted over dinner. After they finished eating, Mother Hobbs cleared the table. Shara saw her frown when she picked up her half-eaten plate of food. With her eyes, she begged Mother Hobbs not to say anything.

"Shara, why don't you and Quinton move on into the dining room and use that table? I'll clean up."

They moved into the dining room and sat down. Shara slowly opened the pages of her notebook, still anxious that she was sharing it with Quinton. She explained each of the programs.

Quinton carefully studied each page, nodding his head and reading. When she finished, he looked directly into her eyes. "This is absolutely amazing. It's as if you jumped into my head, looked at all my ideas and then organized them perfectly so they made sense. I know it's the same spirit talking to both of us, but this is unreal. It's almost as if we are meant to work together."

Shara shifted in her seat and pulled her eyes away from his.

"I can't believe you have timelines and detailed projections. Are you always this organized?"

"It's a sickness of mine I guess."

"No, this is great. A lot of people have dreams and goals, but never take the time to put them on paper and make any concrete plans. That's why most of the time they remain just that— dreams that never materialize. This is a dream with a plan to make it happen. That's an awesome thing."

Shara nodded, not knowing what to say next. The intensity of his gaze made her nervous.

Quinton reached over and turned the next page. "What's this?"

Shara pulled the notebook away from him. "Just another one of my ideas."

"Let me see. What is it?" Quinton gently pulled the notebook back from her. His hand brushed by hers. She pulled her hand back.

"It's just . . . it's my school."

"Your school? Gee, you dream big. I like that. May I?" Quinton waited until Shara nodded before reading the next section. When he finished, he looked at her. "This is really something. Where do you get this stuff from?"

Shara traced circles on the deep brown dining table. "Sometimes when I'm thinking about the kids, or praying for them, or spending time with them, ideas just come to me about how to . . . I don't know, make their lives better, I guess." Shara smiled thinking about them. "Wait 'till you get to know them, Quinton. They're such great kids. They just need—"

"A chance?"

"Yeah. They can be anything they want to be. *They* just need to know that. I want to—"

"Help them realize that?"

"Yeah." She nodded. "I wish I had a whole bunch of money to buy them books and send them all to college and send them on trips to broaden their horizons so they can—"

"Realize there's more to life than the ten block radius they live and go to school in?"

"Yeah." She nodded again. "Sounds like you know exactly what I'm talking about."

"Yeah." Quinton nodded and smiled.

"You know what bothers me? Here we are in our little corner of the world, but right around the corner there's another neighborhood with a whole 'nother group of kids that probably aren't being reached by someone else, and in other neighborhoods in other cities all over the country. Like you said, what's gonna happen to those kids you left behind?"

"You're only one person and you can only do what you can do. Feel good about that and trust God to take care of the rest. Otherwise, you get overwhelmed and burnt out. Then you're no good to anyone."

"Mother Hobbs is always telling me that. I guess it's like she says though—I want to save the world."

Quinton was looking at her with that intense gaze again.

"What?"

"Nothing." Quinton looked away. "I've never met anyone like you before."

"Yeah, I guess I'm a little strange."

"No, not strange, just . . . different."

Shara smoothed her hair back. What was Mother Hobbs doing? There weren't *that* many dishes in the kitchen.

As if Shara's thoughts pulled her into the room, Mother Hobbs appeared. "Quinton, sweetie, do you want some cake?"

"No, ma'am. I can't eat another bite." He leaned back in his dining chair and rubbed his belly. "I'm gonna have to run an extra five miles every day when I get back home to recover from this trip."

Mother Hobbs made a face. "You run, too? I don't understand that obsession. Shara runs almost every day. If you want to, you can run with her tomorrow morning. I'm sure she wouldn't mind coming to pick you up. It's at a God-awful hour, though. What is it, Shara, six in the morning?"

If looks could kill, Mother Hobbs would be dead—or at least in the intensive care unit.

Quinton said, "I didn't bring any exercise clothes or shoes. I didn't know I'd be here this long. I'll definitely take you up on that when I come back though, Shara."

"That sounds good." She forced a smile. Her mornings at the track were her special time with God and she didn't want to share them with anyone. She stood up. "I better get out of here. I want to do some reading before class tomorrow."

Quinton walked her to the door. "I guess I'll see you when I get back. I've found a place to live so I'm gonna tie up some loose ends in Chicago and then make my way down here for good."

"I'm surprised you found something that quick." Shara was glad he had picked out a place. She was looking forward to having Mother Hobbs and the house back all to herself.

"Well, they have to do some renovations. Pastor Kendrick was right. There was nothing in real good shape in the neighborhood. Mother Hobbs is letting me stay here until it's ready. It may take a month or two."

"That's some serious renovation." Shara frowned.

"Yeah. Hopefully it won't be any longer than that."

Mother Hobbs joined them at the door. "Don't even try to leave without giving me my hug."

Shara gave Mother Hobbs a hug and kiss. "Thanks for dinner. It was great as usual."

She awkwardly shook Quinton's hand and said a quick, "See you when you get back," and went out to her car. She pretended not to notice that Quinton stood on the porch watching as she drove away.

Chapter Sixteen

When she got home, Shara sat down at her dining table to study. She hadn't gone over her class notes for the day or done any reading. After about an hour, she realized she'd read a paragraph three times and had no idea what she'd read.

I must be tired. She never had problems concentrating. She got up to get ready to go to bed.

When she looked in the bathroom mirror, she noticed how rumpled her hair was. Had it looked like that all day? She never could get it to lie down smoothly. She put some water on it and tried to brush it down, but it got wavy and still didn't lay right. She looked in the cabinet under the sink for something to slick it down with. She didn't buy too many hair products and the only thing she could find was a jar of blue Bergamot grease—something she'd used since childhood. Shara scooped out a big wad and tried to slick her hair back with it. It gathered in a clump at the top of her head.

Great. It was definitely too late to wash her hair tonight. She tried to distribute the grease through her hair with the brush. By the time she finished, her hair was a wavy, greasy mess. She decided to tie it down with a scarf and see how it looked in the morning. Maybe she'd have some well-behaved waves like the guys did when they wore their "do-rags".

Shara took the scarf off the next morning, expecting magic. Instead, she found her hair was a matted down, wavy, greasy mess. She dug in the back of her cabinet and found her curling iron. She hadn't used it for years, but decided to give it a try. She turned it on high, hoping she could straighten the waves out with the heat.

She picked up a large lock of hair at the front of her head, wrapped it around the curling iron and waited for a few seconds. The smell reminded her of her press-and-curl days in her aunt's kitchen growing up. Shara knew if she'd just get a perm, her hair would lie down with no problem. She didn't like the idea of putting chemicals in her hair or being stuck going to a salon on a regular basis, though.

Exactly how long did it take to curl her hair? She heard the grease pop like frying bacon. Must have been long enough. When she unrolled the hair, part of the curl stayed attached to the iron. Shara gasped and her eyes grew wide. She had burnt her hair! She studied the charred piece of hair left sticking up out of her head. It was short and frayed.

Now she'd never get it to lie down.

What was she going to do? She didn't have any of those fancy scarves people were wearing these days. Even if she did, she wouldn't know how to tie it right, so it would probably look like an Aunt Jemima rag. She opted for a baseball cap. That would get her through the day, but she couldn't wear a cap for the months it would take for her hair to grow back to a decent length to reach her ponytail. She'd have to ask someone who knew what to do.

She picked up the phone and dialed Keeva's number.

"Hello?" A groggy voice answered.

"Keeva, it's me Shara. Are you asleep?"

"Am I what? What the . . . Shara? Do you have any idea what time it is? Is everything all right?"

Shara heard a male voice in the background say, "Who is it, honey?"

She realized Mark was there with Keeva. "Oops! Sorry, but this is an emergency. Can you meet me after class today in the lobby of the Ed building?"

"Shara, what's going on?"

"Nothing, I need a little help. Just meet me then, okay?"

"Okay. 4:00. Lobby. Ed building. Bye."

Shara put on her running clothes, pulled on the baseball cap, and headed outside.

* * *

Keeva's mouth flew open when Shara pulled off her baseball cap. "What happened?" As she listened to Shara's explanation, she covered her mouth to stifle her giggles.

"Are you laughing? Keeva, it's not funny!"

"Bergamot? Are you serious? If you were gonna fry your hair, why didn't you use some Crisco?" Keeva laughed harder.

Shara's eyes widened.

"Oh Shar, I'm sorry. I didn't mean to laugh. We'll fix it. I promise, okay?" She studied the piece of hair and began talking to herself. "It's too short to be a bang and the edges are too frayed to slick back onto a ponytail. I guess you could . . . well no, because . . ."

Keeva shook her head and took out her cell phone. She turned her back to Shara and walked away, as if she was making a secret call. She returned smiling. "Consider it fixed." She gave Shara a pensive glance. "There's one thing, though. You have to miss a couple of classes tomorrow morning."

Shara gave her a "that's completely out of the question" look.

"Please." Keeva rolled her eyes. "Consider it a mental health day."

Shara shook her head slowly.

"Come on. Dag, girl, do you always have to be Miss Perfect? Live on the wild side for just one day. We'll play hooky together. You can go to your first class and then we'll meet here at 10:30. You have an 11:00 appointment with my stylist. Don't worry, girl. Everything will be fine." She smiled knowingly. "Better than fine."

Chapter Seventeen

As Keeva and Shara entered the upscale Buckhead salon, a slim light-skinned man smiled at Keeva and waved wildly, walking toward them. He had on black leather pants and a lime green shirt, no—blouse with ruffles on it. As he got closer, Shara could see how "pretty" he was. Was that eyeliner and foundation he was wearing? He and Keeva embraced and kissed each other on both cheeks.

"Antone, this is my friend I was telling you about, Shara. Shara, Antone."

He shook Shara's hand lightly, eying her up and down. "Oh my goodness, Keeva, what do you think Antone is? Umh, umh, umh." He directed Shara toward his chair.

As Shara walked toward the chair, she eyed the expensive looking products lined up on the shelves and surveyed the shop's glamorous décor. She felt like she was in a celebrity salon and wondered just how much this was going to cost her.

"Sit down, dear. Let me look at what we're dealing with here." Antone pulled off her rubber band. "Oh my—look at this! It looks like a rat has been chewing on the ends of your hair. When was the last time you had your hair trimmed?" He got to the front of her hair and gasped. "What in the world happened here?"

He looked at Keeva, then at Shara's hair, then back at Keeva again. He called out to the receptionist, "Jackie, clear my schedule for the rest of the afternoon. This is gon' be a job. Thank God I'm good."

Shara seethed quietly in the chair, hoping Keeva was feeling the full effect of the evil looks she was giving her. Keeva laughed and made a silly face behind Antone's back.

Antone said, "Keeva, I am flattered at the compliment girl, but you know you gon' owe me for this one. You are truly putting my skills to the test. Why, I haven't seen hair like this since—"

"Antone!" Keeva seemed to know Shara wasn't going to take too much more. "Darling, you are the best. What do you think we should do? I thought about a bob or a short cut. The only problem is that Shara doesn't want to give up her ponytail."

"Shara, girlfriend, rubber bands are *not* your friend. Let Antone show you what's happening. They're like little razors, especially when you put them on real tight. They scrape away at the hair cuticle . . ." He continued his discussion on the perils of chronic rubber band use.

In spite of his rudeness, he seemed to know a lot about hair, so Shara decided to listen.

"All this hair back here is badly damaged and is going to have to come off. The front is *burnt* so it has to be cut, too. Don't worry, you're in the hands of a cutting master."

"But if you cut off a lot, I won't be able to pull it back anymore," Shara objected.

Antone rolled his eyes. "Hello, is anybody home? Did you hear anything Antone just said? No more ponytails, good-bye, no more." He gestured dramatically, as if he was throwing the ponytail away.

Shara wrinkled her nose. "What am I supposed to do with my hair then? If I can't pull it back, I'll have to curl it. You see what happens when I try to curl my hair."

Antone looked at Keeva. "You must think Antone is a miracle worker. What I'm 'sposed to do wit' her?"

He frowned and stared at Shara's hair. He turned her around in the chair a few times slowly, looked at her face, fluffed her hair, and then frowned again. He talked to himself under his breath. "Well if I . . . no because that'll make the . . . maybe if I . . . no that won't work either . . ." He squinted. "Your hair is just so . . . so dusty." He scrunched his nose like he smelled something bad.

"Dusty?" Shara's nostrils flared. "You know what? This was a mistake." She started to get up from the chair.

Antone put a hand on her shoulder. "Girl, stop

getting your little feelings hurt and sit down in that chair. Antone don't mean you no harm. I can *not* let you walk out of here looking like this. Now sit your little self down and let me do my job."

Shara acquiesced and settled back into the chair. "What do you plan to do?"

"I can cut it in a short style that you can curl once a week and it should keep pretty well. Or, you can always come here once a week to get it curled."

"I don't think that would work. I run everyday and by the time I finish sweating, my hair is all wavy and curly. It wouldn't last one day," Shara whined.

"Wavy and curly?" Antone looked at her through squinted eyes again. He clapped his hands together and then said with flourish, "I have the perfect style for you. Now watch me work."

Keeva walked to the door. "I'm going to get a manicure and pedicure. I'll be back in a few hours."

Antone waved her away with his hand. "Girl, take your time." He pursed his lips. "It may be a while."

When Keeva returned two hours later, Antone's makeup artist was applying a natural brown color to Shara's full lips.

Keeva gasped. "Antone, what did you do?"

Shara gasped. "Oh no, what *did* he do? He won't let me look. After I protested him chopping me bald, he turned me around and hasn't let me see the mirror since. Do I look bad?"

Now Antone gasped. "Look bad? One of

Antone's clients look bad? Antone is hurt—Antone is offended."

He waved away the makeup artist and turned Shara toward the mirror. His indignance turned to arrogance as he saw the look on Shara's face. "That's right, baby. Antone is *the one*. I accept your apology my dear, but don't *ever* let it happen again."

Shara stared at herself, speechless. If it weren't for the goofy look she knew she was wearing, she wouldn't have believed it was her staring back in the mirror. She lifted a finger to touch her hair and the person in the mirror lifted her hand also. Yep, it was her.

"Wow," was all she could say.

Antone went on and on in the background about being "the one."

"Wow," she said again, softly.

Keeva came up behind her and stared at her reflection with her. She beamed as if she had transformed Shara herself. "Wow," she said in agreement.

"Yes, Antone has skills. He is the original, the only." He stopped praising himself to answer Keeva's question. "I cut off Shara's hair to about half an inch. This child had a fit when she saw all her hair hit the floor." He paused and gave Shara a disgusted look. "I don't know why—it was all *dead*."

He turned back to Keeva. "Then I tapered the sides and back, and put on a clear glaze to get rid of the 'dustiness.' Then all I had to do was put styling gel on it and it naturally curled up in these beautiful little wavy curls, all over her head.

"Then she let Serge here wax her eyebrows . . ."

Keeva's eyes widened.

Antone narrowed his eyes. "I know, chile. She practically cussed him out after the first rip. He had to be begged to finish. Child almost lost her religion in here. You shoulda heard her." He sucked his teeth.

"You know she didn't want no makeup, but I persuaded her to let us do the bare minimum. A little eyeliner and lipstick and *voila*." He gestured grandly at Shara. "The beauty before your eyes. Antone has done it again."

Serge had to claim some of the glory. "It's a good thing she's a natural beauty and doesn't need much makeup. I picked the perfect colors to blend with her olive undertones. That perfect skin, those big eyes and full lips. What I would give . . . ."

Antone said, "The best thing is that she doesn't have to do anything to it. Just put some gel on it and go."

He looked at Shara in the mirror and fingered her little curls proudly. "You hardly even need a comb anymore." He paused dramatically, putting his hand to his chest. "My brilliance amazes me."

He put a hand on her shoulder. "Now, Shara, you'll need to get your edges tapered about every three weeks and a full cut about every six weeks, so call and make an appointment or come in with Keeva."

Shara didn't bother to complain that she was obligated to come to a salon on a regular basis. She looked and felt too good.

Antone put some products in a bag—shampoo,

hair gel, and the eyeliner and lipstick they had used on Shara. "Now you need to get you some nice earrings. You have to wear jazzy earrings when you have a short haircut. Keeva, girl, you know what to do. I'm putting her back in your hands."

He looked Shara up and down. "Why don't you take her to get some jeans that actually fit, or better still, some real jazzy clothes to go with her new hair cut? Do a total makeover. Ooohh," he squealed. "This is just like Oprah."

Keeva planted a kiss on Antone's cheek. "You are the best, forever and always. Put it on my tab, okay, love? I'll see you Saturday."

Chapter Eighteen

Keeva started up the car. She looked at her watch and said, "See? That didn't take long. We can probably get you to school in time for your afternoon classes."

Shara frowned. "Didn't you hear Antone? You're supposed to take me shopping for earrings and clothes."

Keeva turned the car off and looked at Shara. "What?"

"You know, the mall, shopping, that thing you do all the time?"

"Yeah, but . . . I thought we decided World War III would erupt if we ever went shopping together. Remember?"

"I know, but I promise whatever you tell me to do, I'll do. I'll be good."

"You're serious?"

Shara nodded.

Keeva started up the car again. "Well, all right then. Let's do it."

"Only one thing."

Keeva turned the car off again. "See. We haven't even pulled off yet and you're already giving me trouble."

"Just one thing and then I promise, I'll be good. I don't want to spend a lot of money. I'm a practical girl and don't believe in paying extravagant prices for clothes. Keep that in the back of your mind, that's all."

Keeva turned the car on again. "I have the perfect idea. Let's make a day trip of it. We can hit the outlets up I-85 North. We can still get the good stuff but at good prices."

As they zoomed up I-85 with the top down in Keeva's BMW with a Jill Scott CD playing, Shara relaxed back into her seat. She kept sneaking peeks at herself in Keeva's rearview mirror. Keeva finally grabbed the mirror and turned it toward her.

"Here, stop breaking your neck."

Shara laughed.

"So, what's your style? What kind of clothes do you want to get?" Keeva asked.

"I don't know. You know my style—you see it every day. Jeans and a T-shirt or a sweat-shirt."

Keeva looked at Shara. *Oh boy, this is going to be harder than I thought.* She said, "What kind of clothes do you think you want to get, or what do you think will look good on you?"

"I don't know. Honestly, I never really give it much thought. I wake up, I get dressed, I go. It's not a big deal to me. The most important thing is to be comfortable."

"So you're telling me we're driving an hour to

go buy more T-shirts and jeans? Is that all you've ever worn?"

Shara's light mood suddenly darkened. "No. Like I told you, when I was growing up, I couldn't wear pants or short skirts or anything tight or form fitting. After I left home, well . . ."

Keeva waited. Shara rubbed her hands together and fidgeted with the knob on the glove compartment.

"Well, what?"

"Nothing. I'm sorry. Maybe this was a bad idea. We haven't gotten too far. We can go back if you want."

"What's up with that? We're cruising with my girl Jill Scott, you're flirting with yourself in the mirror, and all of a sudden you want to turn around? What's that all about?"

"Nothing. Just let it go."

Keeva felt a wall suddenly erected between them. She nodded her head slowly as if she was realizing something for the first time. "I see how you are, Shara. I can share all my deep, dark secrets and cry on your shoulder, but you can't be real with me?"

Shara sat there, not saying anything.

"Help me out here. Is this a 'super-spiritual, I'm perfect and can't have any faults' thing? Or is it a 'you can trust me, but I can't trust you thing?' What—I'm not 'spiritual' enough for you to talk to?"

"No, it's not like that at all. I promise. It's just that . . ."

Keeva softened her tone, noticing how fragile Shara suddenly seemed. "What?"

Shara swallowed. Keeva noticed a tear trickle down her cheek.

"Oh, dear. Shara, I'm sorry. What is it?"

Shara started fidgeting with the buttons on the car door. Up, down, up, down. She appeared to be mesmerized by the motion of the window moving.

Keeva waited.

"When I first moved away from my parents, the first thing I did was go clothes shopping. You know how when something is forbidden, it makes you want it all the more?"

Keeva nodded.

"Well, I couldn't wait to get me some pants, tight ones, that showed . . . everything. I got a bunch of really short skirts and tight shirts."

Keeva couldn't imagine Shara in tight anything.

Shara kept fidgeting with the window. Up, down, up, down. "Remember, I told you about my first boyfriend?"

Keeva nodded.

"When we first got together, I told him I didn't plan on having sex until I got married. He was all shy and sweet, so I didn't think he would, you know, pressure me. He was impressed that I was a virgin. After a while, he decided he wanted to, you know. I guess I was afraid of losing him, so I started to let him get away with more and more kissing and touching and all that stuff. Then he became obsessed with being my 'first.' One night, we were studying and I had on one of my sexiest, short skirts with this little top with cleavage and all. We got to, you know, kissing and stuff, and . . . he asked me how long

I thought he was going to wait and I told him I didn't know what he was waiting for because I wasn't going to have sex with him and then he called me a tease and told me he hadn't wasted six months for nothing . . ."

Shara stopped. Up, down, up, down.

Keeva realized what Shara was trying to tell her. "He didn't."

Shara nodded, now with tears running down both cheeks. "I kept telling him no and tried to push him off me, but he was bigger than I was, and stronger."

"He raped you?" Keeva asked softly.

"He pulled up my little skirt and pulled my underwear down and got on top of me and put his . . . you know . . . on me, but I fought him. The harder he tried, the harder I fought. It was like he became a whole 'nother person. My sweet boyfriend turned into a monster right before my eyes. He ripped up my shirt and bloodied my nose and busted my lip, but he didn't . . . you know. So he cursed me out and called me a tease, and left. Then he spread all these rumors all over the school about me being a slut."

Shara fidgeted with the window again. Up, down, up, down. She wiped her face with the back of her hand. "I never told anyone before. Not even Mother Hobbs. So no, it's not that I don't trust you or think you're not spiritual enough."

"You never reported it?"

Up, down, up, down. "I was ashamed."

"Ashamed? Of what?"

Up, down, up, down.

Keeva pushed the button that controlled the

windows for the whole car to the off position. "Shara! Ashamed of what?"

"I knew if I had never started wearing all those tight, short clothes, it would have never happened."

Keeva turned off the CD player. "Shara, what he did was not your fault. It had nothing to do with you. He was a sick jerk that wouldn't take no for an answer. Your clothes had nothing to do with it. Even if you were still wearing your long skirts, he might have done it anyway."

Shara looked down at her hands with tears streaming down her face.

"Shara?" Keeva reached over and rubbed her arm. "It wasn't your fault. You didn't do anything wrong and you don't have anything to be ashamed of."

Shara wiped her nose. "I'm sorry. I didn't mean to fall all apart like that. I never talked about it before. I didn't realize it had affected me like that all these years I guess. I'm okay."

"You don't have to apologize, Shara. That's what friends are for, right?"

"Yeah—friends." Shara smiled.

They drove in silence for a while.

Shara looked in the mirror and wiped her eyeliner and patted her curls. "Look what you did. I was all pretty and you messed my face up. Now look at me."

Keeva gawked at her. "I think I've created a monster." With concern in her voice she asked, "You wanna go home now?"

"No. We're going shopping. I need some new clothes and new earrings to go with my new haircut." She pulled out her little bag from Antone. "Now how do you put on this eyeliner stuff?"

Four hours later, the two women emerged from the outlet mall with six shopping bags. Finding Shara some nice clothes was easier than Keeva thought it was going to be. As Keeva watched what clothes Shara picked, she decided her style was retro/Bohemian. They bought boot cut jeans with cute tops, long flowing skirts and casual dresses all in the proper colors to compliment Shara's skin tone.

Keeva was careful to pick clothes that fit Shara's shape that weren't too tight. She could tell Shara was self-conscious about showing her body, so she was careful not to push her to buy anything she didn't feel comfortable in.

Keeva noticed Shara's smile became brighter with each outfit she tried on. She primped and modeled in the mirror as she got more confident.

They rode home, satisfied what they had conquered at the outlet mall.

Shara was still primping in the rearview mirror. "So, you wanna go to church with me Sunday?"

Keeva paused for a second and fidgeted with the CD player. "I have plans. I have to uh, go to a meeting at eleven."

Shara was silent for a moment. "You know what, Keeva? I'm not Mark. If you don't want to go somewhere with me, just tell me no. You don't have to make up one of your little white lies."

Keeva bit her lip. "Sorry." She was glad she was driving and didn't have to meet Shara's eyes. "I don't know why I do that."

"If we're gonna be friends, I need you to be honest with me. I don't want you to ever feel like you have to go to church with me or believe what I believe or feel like I feel about God. Just be real, okay?"

"It's not that I don't want to go to church. I really enjoyed it, much more than I expected to. It . . . it made me feel funny. It challenged me and I don't know what to do with that."

"I understand. I felt the same way when I first started going. After my first time, it was two months before I went back again. Like I said, do what you feel."

Keeva let out a deep breath. "Thanks, Shara."

"For what?"

"For letting me be okay just being me. I don't get that often with my friends."

"Maybe you need new friends."

Keeva jumped as if she had been stung. "Ouch!"

"I didn't mean that to be rude." Shara sighed. "It frustrates me to see you trapped in this box. You have all this potential and beauty on the inside, but it's stuck because you let other people dictate who you are. I wish I could let you out of the box, that's all."

"Dag, Shara. Do you always have to be so honest?"

"That's the only way I know how to be."

Keeva put in her India.Arie CD.

Shara reached over and turned it up. "I like

your music. I hate most of the stuff out there these days. It's all about sex and booty and stuff, but your music is deep and soulful. I gotta get some of these CD's."

"I don't know. That might be too much too fast. New haircut, new clothes, new music. The folks at your church are gonna think I'm corrupting you."

"Are you kidding? When Mother Hobbs sees me, she's going to kiss your feet and declare you a miracle worker." She groaned thinking about it. "I don't even want to hear her go on and on about it."

"Oh, look at my baby girl! You're absolutely gorgeous!" Mother Hobbs had been going on like this for the last half hour. Shara made the mistake of stopping in the office before changing her clothes to go out to the track. Mother Hobbs kept patting her hair, pinching her cheeks, and making her turn around and around to model her new clothes.

"What happened to you?"

"Nothing. Just thought I needed a change." Shara shrugged.

"Child, please, I've been after you for years and then all of a sudden . . ." She narrowed her eyes. "Come on now, tell me the truth.

Shara laughed and decided to come clean. She told her about burning her hair and about her outing with Keeva.

After she finished laughing, Mother Hobbs said, "Wait a minute. You tried to use a curling iron? I've known you for all these years and didn't even know you owned a curling iron." She eyed Shara suspiciously.

"What?" Shara asked.

"Nothing. Nothing at all. Whatever the reason, I think you look absolutely beautiful." Mother Hobbs smiled with a mischievous twinkle in her eye. "I guess I don't have to worry about you finding a man anymore. I'll have to beat them off with a stick. They better know they got to come by me first."

"Whatever." Shara rolled her eyes. "What are you working on?" Mother Hobbs had a big stack of papers by her computer.

"Pastor has a big meeting with the city next week and we're trying to get all our numbers together. He's trying to get some more funding to renovate more of the building and to fix up the basketball court and resurface the track. He's adding all of Quinton's information to the proposal. He thinks that will really give us a boost."

"Superstar basketball player turns community activist. Yeah, I can see that." Shara flipped through some of the papers. "Did Quinton say when he was coming back?"

Mother Hobbs looked up from her typing. "Not exactly, why?"

"No reason." Shara shrugged. "I was wondering where we're gonna fit his desk. We're already on top of each other in here."

"Pastor Kendrick already thought of that. The guys have started fixing up the office next door. They should be finished with everything and ready to paint next week. That'll be Quinton's office. I think your desk will be moved in there, too."

Shara dropped the papers. "What? Why? I like working in here with you. I don't want to move."

"He's the youth pastor. You're the head youth leader. Makes perfect sense to me. You'll have much more room in there. I think Pastor has a bigger desk for you, too. This one will actually hold your computer and all your notebooks."

Shara tried to be excited about her new office and desk, but she wasn't sure she wanted to share with Quinton. She put the papers back in order and put them on Mother Hobbs' desk. She looked up at the clock.

"I'm gonna go change. I better get out to the track before I end up having to break up a fight."

"Shara—I really do think you look beautiful."

"Thanks, Mother Hobbs." Shara gave her a kiss on the cheek before she headed for the locker room. She called over her shoulder, "I guess you can't call me Miss Bluejean anymore."

Chapter Nineteen

It was Friday evening and Shara was bored. Keeva was going out with Mark so she didn't have anything to do. She thought of calling Danielle, one of the other youth leaders she was becoming friendly with, but she had left her number at the church.

Shara had decided to make a concerted effort to make more friends. Getting to know Keeva made her see how important that was. They had a lot of fun hanging out. She didn't have to be so serious about life and could relax, laugh, and have a good time—which she now realized was much needed.

Every once in a while, though, she hungered for a deep, spiritual conversation. She wanted to talk about destiny and vision, and get excited about all the dreams she had. She tried to avoid that conversation with Keeva because it seemed to send her into a blue funk. Talking to Keeva over the past months made her wonder what was worse: not knowing one should have a sense of purpose *or*, knowing that, but having no earthly idea what that purpose was.

Shara had noticed in spite of the fact that Keeva had joined her in her rigorous study schedule, school was getting harder for her. Keeva had mentioned that she was getting more and more frustrated as she was asking herself questions about whether this was really the career she wanted to pursue or whether she was doing it to make everyone else happy.

Shara couldn't imagine having to do something day after day, with hours of class and then additional hours of study, without being 100% committed to it. School got on *her* nerves, and she knew why *she* was doing it. All she could do was pray for Keeva and hope she would find God to rescue her from her misery.

Keeva hadn't been back to church with her since that first time and Shara hadn't brought up church or God to her at all. Was she being a true friend, allowing Keeva to wallow in misery when she had the answer she needed?

Shara had learned a lot over the past few years about bringing people to Christ. Before, her whole concept of witnessing was from what she learned growing up. Passing out tracts, badgering people and trying to convince them they needed to "get right with God or go to hell" was all she knew. Mother Hobbs taught her that was the best way to repel people away from God. Shara learned that being an example of a Christian through one's lifestyle was the best witness there was. Mother Hobbs taught her that intercession, then using whatever strategy the

Holy Spirit revealed was the best way to get someone saved.

So Shara continued to pray for Keeva and to be her friend—without preaching, without condemning, without judging. In her experience, that had never gotten anyone saved anyway.

Shara decided to get a movie. It had been a while since she'd been to Blockbuster's. She wandered through the stacks of movies until she finally picked *Mr. Holland's Opus*.

When she plopped her movie down on the counter, Travis looked up at her and said, "Did you find everything okay, ma'am?"

Shara stood there and smiled.

He looked at her with faint recognition in his eyes and then shock. "Miss Shara? What happened to you?"

Shara narrowed her eyes at him.

"I don't mean it like that. You look so different. You look, uh, nice."

Shara narrowed her eyes further, but then allowed a smile to creep through. "I'll take your surprise as a compliment, otherwise I might have to get offended."

"Did you leave your church or something?"

"Okay, now I *am* offended. What's that supposed to mean? Why does everyone think because I didn't wear makeup and earrings that I'm a religious nut of some sort? I run five miles a day, am a graduate student, and work."

Travis looked at her like he was seeing her for the first time. "I'm sorry, Miss Shara. I just assumed . . ." He scratched his ear. "So you run five miles a day?" He looked down at her legs.

"Hello? My face is up here. What is your

problem, Travis?" She watched his eyes as they roamed her body. This was precisely why she didn't like wearing shorts outside the house other than when she was running. No matter how much they tried, men couldn't hide the dog inside.

He shook himself out of his lusty stupor. "Nothing . . . I . . . you can't expect to make a total change and not have somebody notice, that's all." He smiled. "This is a good movie. You've never seen it before? It's one of my favorites. You'll enjoy it." Now he looked like the Travis she knew.

"Thanks." She picked up her movie and walked toward the door. She could feel him watching her.

"Hey, maybe we should get together and watch a movie sometime." He spoke in time to catch her before she walked out the door. "We seem to have the same taste in movies. It would be fun."

Shara returned to the counter with her hands on her hips.

He continued. "Actually, I've been thinking lately that it's time for me to get my life together. How 'bout I come to your church this Sunday? We could go out for dinner afterward." He flashed a charming smile.

Shara got up close so no one else behind the counter could hear. "Travis, we've been chit-chatting about movies as long as I've been coming to this store. You never wanted to watch movies together before. I've invited you to church several times and all of a sudden you want to go? If I didn't know any better, I'd think that had more to do with my *butt* than you wanting to get your life together. Do you have any idea how shallow that is?"

She gave him one of Keeva's nice nasty smiles, turned on her heels and walked out the door. She'd definitely have to go to the video rental store down the street from now on.

Shara walked into her apartment in time to catch the phone. "Hello?"

"Hey, Shara."

"Hey, Keeva. I thought you were out with Mark."

"He had to cancel—study group or something. I'm getting together with a group of friends to go out for drinks. Wanna go?"

Shara didn't really like the idea of going out for drinks or the idea of meeting some of Keeva's friends, but Travis' roaming eyes had ruined her Blockbuster mood. She didn't want to stay home with that yucky feeling.

"Sure, I guess. Where are you going?"

Keeva gave her directions to a place called Café 290. Shara had wanted to change into a pair of baggy jeans and a T-shirt, but she didn't feel like seeing Keeva's lip curl up or her fake smile. She pulled on a nice fitting pair of black jeans and a lavender knit top and was on her way.

When she pulled up at Café 290, Keeva was already there in the parking lot, standing next to a tall woman with a long, flowing weave in front of a red Lexus. She was waving at a light-skinned woman driving up in a green Jaguar.

Shara wanted to keep on driving, but realized Keeva had seen her when she waved in her direction.

She pulled into a spot next to them and got out.

"Shara, this is Jade and this is Heather. Lisa's on her way."

Keeva's friends shook her hand and looked her up and down. Compared to them, Shara might as well have worn her jeans and T-shirt. Jade had on a stylishly cut, olive green pantsuit that blended with her light green eyes. Heather had on a tight fitting black Lycra dress that showed off all her curves. She might have been pretty if she didn't have so much makeup on. Keeva was her usual stylish self, wearing a long, black skirt and a mustard, short-sleeve sweater. Shara looked down at her own outfit.

Keeva waved again. "There she is."

Shara figured this was Lisa driving up in a red sports car. The petite woman got out, pulled her short skirt down over her ample hips, adjusted her left shoe, pulled up her bra, and then walked over to where they were. "Watch out ladies, I'm a woman on a mission. I gotta get me some tonight!"

Keeva made the introductions and they walked into what Shara realized was a bar. It was filled with smoke and well-dressed, black professionals, looking like they were on the same mission as Lisa. Shara sat down at their table between Jade and Lisa, across from Keeva.

The waitress came over to their table and took their drink order. "Two Long Island Ice teas, two white wines, and a cranberry juice."

Heather started chair dancing to the live jazz music playing in the background. "Girl, I am so glad it's Friday, I don't know what to do. If I had to face another day at work this week, I might pull out my weave."

Lisa giggled. "I know what you mean. I'm beginning to think I should have gone to grad school like Keeva, 'cause this nine to five is kicking my butt."

"Please—grad school ain't no better." Keeva sucked her teeth. "You gotta go to class all day and then you gotta come home and study. At least with work, when you're done, you're done."

Lisa looked at Keeva. "I don't know what kind of job you think you're gonna have."

Jade looked over at Heather. "Hello, are you here with us or here with him?"

Heather was making eyes at a tall man at the next table. "Girl, he is *too* fine. I might have to get his number." She leaned in and lowered her voice. "You know I need a spare, especially since Darnell ain't been acting right."

"A spare? What are you talking about?" Lisa looked over at the man Heather was admiring.

"Girl, you don't get one man, you always get two." Heather flipped her hair. "That way if Number One don't act right, you always have Number Two waiting in the wings."

"You go, girl. That's what's up," Lisa said.

Heather leaned in again. "Girl, what you think? Does he look like a five-minute man or an all-night-long man? Lord knows I don't need another five-minute man. I need somebody who can satisfy *all* my needs."

Shara squirmed in her seat. She saw Keeva watching her.

Heather continued, "How much money you think he makes? I don't need no broke man either."

Jade looked over. "Well, the shoes are Ferragamo, the suit looks like Armani. I'd say he's paid. His friend don't look like he's doing too bad either. I might have to talk to him."

Lisa and Heather looked at each other then back at Jade. "I can't believe you're looking at another man. What about Andrew?" Heather asked.

Jade sipped her wine and rolled her eyes. "He started to get boring, and then he got laid off. Girl, you know he can't afford me if he ain't got no j-o-b."

Lisa gave her a high-five. "Girl, I know that's right!"

Keeva shook her head at them.

"What, Keeva?" Jade snapped. "Just because you got Mr. Perfect doesn't mean you should look down on the rest of us. If I had a man like Mark . . ." She smiled.

"What?" Keeva raised her eyebrows.

"Let's just say I wouldn't be hanging out with y'all tonight." Jade finished off her wine. Lisa and Heather laughed nervously.

Heather finished off her Long Island Iced Tea. "Shara, you're awfully quiet. Maybe you need a little drinky-drink so you can relax and have some fun."

Keeva shifted in her chair as the women turned their attention to Shara.

"No thanks. I don't drink," Shara said.

Heather smiled. "I feel you, girl, I'm not supposed to drink either, but I figure since my problem was with prescription pills and not alcohol, a little drink here and there shouldn't hurt." She motioned for the waitress to bring her another. "So how do you and Keeva know each other? She's never mentioned you before."

Keeva spoke up, "We're in school together. Shara was a teacher and now she's getting her degree to be a principal. She's gonna run her own school."

Lisa swirled her drink. "I feel you, girl. I know teachers don't make no money. You had to go back so you could get yours, huh? My cousin is a teacher and all she makes is $28,000 a year. I don't see how she can live on that. She talks some junk about the kids being our future and how it's not about the money; it's about making a difference in someone's life. Yeah, right. She ain't fooling nobody but herself. Don't nobody want to be that broke."

"So how much do principals make?" Jade asked.

Shara pulled her purse over her shoulder and stood up. "You know what, Keeva? I've got to go." Her eyes darted around the table. "It was nice meeting all of you. Have a good evening." Shara walked away without looking back.

When she was almost to her car, she heard Keeva's voice behind her.

"Shara, wait!" Keeva ran across the parking lot to meet her at her car. "What's wrong?"

Shara spun around to face her. "Are you serious?"

"Okay, I'm sorry. My friends . . . I don't know what to say. I didn't think they would—"

"What possessed you to invite me to hang out with them?" Shara turned her key in her car door. "I don't understand you, Keeva. You're not like those girls in there. You're a real person with real depth and real feelings. I guess maybe I shouldn't judge them like I initially judged you. Maybe there is some real depth to them, but who has the time to dig beneath all that crap to find it? Thanks for trying to show me a good time, but next time, leave me at home."

Shara got into her car and put her key in the ignition.

"Shara, wait. Please!" Keeva put her hands on Shara's window. "I don't know why I thought you would like them. Most of the time, *I* don't even like them. Please don't be mad."

"I'm not mad, Keeva. I just didn't enjoy that."

"To tell you the truth, I didn't enjoy it much either."

"Then why do you hang out with them?"

"I don't know. We've been friends since freshman year of college and we get together every now and then."

Shara let out a deep breath. "Keeva, I'm gonna take off. I'll talk to you tomorrow."

"Wait. You wanna go get something to eat?"

"No, Keeva, I just want to go home." She noticed the disappointment on Keeva's face. She sighed. "You can come over if you want. I rented a movie and we can stop at Fellini's."

Keeva smiled. "Pizza sounds great." Keeva headed toward her car.

"Don't you need to tell them you're leaving?"

"Nah. I think after a while, they'll figure it out. Or who knows, if they keep drinking, they'll never realize I'm gone."

Shara laughed. "All right. I'll meet you at my house."

Chapter Twenty

Shara was doing her Saturday morning cleaning a week later when the phone rang.

"Hey, Shara." It was Keeva. "The pottery place called me. Our pieces have *been* ready. You want me to come by and get you so we can pick them up? We can take Mother Hobbs her teapot afterward. I want to see her face when she gets it."

Shara looked at the pile of dishes in the sink and thought of her overflowing laundry basket. "I can't, Keeva. I really need to clean my apartment."

"Come on, Shar. You can clean later. Please?"

Shara hadn't spent any time with Mother Hobbs lately. "All right. I'll be ready when you get here."

When they pulled up at Mother Hobbs' house an hour later, Shara was glad to see her car, as they hadn't bothered to call before dropping by.

She knew Mother Hobbs' water aerobics and yoga classes ended a couple of hours ago, and she usually spent Saturday afternoons cleaning or working in her herb garden.

Shara rang the doorbell. When the door opened, she staggered backward a little, bumping into Keeva. "What are you doing here?"

It was Quinton.

"Well, hello, Miss Shara, glad to see you, too," he said.

Shara hadn't remembered him looking so good. "I'm sorry. I didn't mean it like that. I just . . . I wasn't expecting you . . ."

Keeva pushed past Shara and gave Quinton a hug. "Quinton, it's great to see you. Excuse my friend here. She has no manners. Are you back for good?"

"Good to see you too, Keeva. Yep, I'm getting settled in here for a little while and then hopefully it won't be forever before my place is fixed up in the 'hood."

He stepped over to hug Shara, but she lifted the large gift bag she was holding up to her chest. He stepped back, letting his arms fall back to his sides. "You brought me a present? I'm touched."

"No, it's for Mother Hobbs. Where is she anyway?"

"She's at the grocery store. I drove in last night and you know her. She insisted on having plenty of food to fatten me up with. She should be back any minute now."

Shara looked over at Mother Hobbs' car in the driveway.

Quinton said, "I let her borrow my truck. She

said she wanted to go to the grocery store in style."

Keeva raised her eyebrows. "Really? What kind of truck do you have?"

"Just a regular ol' SUV."

He turned toward Shara. "You look great. Doing that natural thang, huh? I like your hair like that."

"Thanks." Shara smoothed her hair back and got a handful of styling gel. She kept meaning to try a dry mousse she'd seen in a magazine.

Mother Hobbs pulled up in a black Cadillac Escalade. She had shades on and had her locs pulled up high on her head. She slowly pulled the sunglasses off and looked over at them, posing elegantly.

Shara shook her head. "Look at her. She is too much."

"Oooh, nice truck." Keeva walked down the sidewalk as Mother Hobbs was getting out. Mother Hobbs got out and gave her a big hug and kiss.

Quinton looked over at Shara. "What do you think?"

"It's okay. Well actually, it's a little—"

"Ostentatious? I know. It was one of the few luxuries I allowed myself when I first got paid. I didn't go crazy and buy up everything like most of the other rookies, but I figured after riding the el and buses and walking all my life, I deserved a little 'sump'n sump'n.' I'm over it now. I'll probably sell it soon. Wouldn't be wise to park it in my new neighborhood."

Quinton walked down the porch steps. "Don't you dare touch a bag."

Mother Hobbs had opened the back of the truck and was getting the groceries.

"Go on in the house, I'll bring everything in," Quinton said.

Mother Hobbs gave Shara a hug. "Girl, did you see me? Didn't Mother Hobbs look good?" Her eyes lit up when she saw the gift bag. "Is that for me?"

"Yes, Mother dear," Shara answered. "Come on in the house so you can open it."

Shara, Keeva, and Mother Hobbs sat at the kitchen table while Quinton brought in the groceries. Mother Hobbs squealed when she saw her teapot. "Oh, Shara, this is beautiful. It's absolutely perfect."

"You can't put it on the burner. You have to boil the water on the stove and then pour it over the herbs in the pot."

"Child, who you tellin' how to make tea?"

Keeva put her little gift bag on the table. Mother Hobbs squealed again when she opened it. "What did I do to deserve all this love? A new teapot and cup, a jazzy new SUV to ride around town in, a big, strong man to carry my groceries. I'm special today."

They all laughed. Mother Hobbs got up and put the groceries away and started pulling out pots. "What y'all want to eat? I'm gonna cook up a big dinner for everybody. Get out the kitchen now, let me do my thing."

They moved back out onto the porch.

"Hey, Quinton, are you going to take us for a ride in the truck?" Keeva asked.

"Sure, you guys could give me a little tour—

show me all the hotspots in the city. I don't know where anything is besides Mother Hobbs' house and the church."

"Cool, let's roll. I'll show you Atlanta according to Keeva Banks."

Quinton came around the side of the truck to open the door for them. Keeva sat in the front to navigate.

"Okay, the key to Atlanta is this. You have a big circle with a cross through the middle. The circle is 285. The cross is I-20 intersecting with I-85 and I-75. They run together for a while, but then split at the top and bottom. In the city itself, you have a million streets named Peachtree something. There's Atlanta itself and then the surrounding suburbs that make up the metro area like Stone Mountain, Lithonia, East Point, College Park . . ."

Keeva gave Quinton a layout of the city and told him about the different areas. They drove for a couple of hours and made their way to Midtown's Peachtree Street.

They crossed Ponce de Leon. "This is the Fabulous Fox Theatre." Keeva pointed. "All the good stuff comes here. I live right down the street a couple of blocks."

Quinton read the marquis. "The Alvin Ailey dancers. Have you guys seen them before? They're great."

"Yeah, they are, aren't they?" Keeva sighed.

Shara spoke up from the back seat. "I'll have to check them out. Keeva's always saying how good they are."

Quinton looked back at Shara. "Are you

kidding? You've never seen the Alvin Ailey dancers before? How long have you lived in Atlanta?" Quinton looked over at Keeva. "Is she for real?"

Keeva giggled. "I've been working on her lately, trying to get her 'culturified.' She's trying to sneak me Jesus. We both have our own little private agendas going on here."

They all laughed.

Quinton asked, "So do you guys want to go check out Alvin Ailey?"

"I don't think so. I used to go all the time, but . . . no, I think I'll pass," Keeva answered.

Quinton looked over his shoulder. "What about you, Shara? You want to check them out with me?"

"I think I'll pass too, Quinton," Shara answered.

"Brotha can't get no love around here. That's all right. I guess I'll settle for dinner after church tomorrow."

"I won't be at church tomorrow," Keeva said.

Quinton looked over his shoulder. "Shara, I guess you won't be able to join me either."

"I have to clean my apartment tomorrow. That's where I'm supposed to be now, but Keeva kidnapped me. We are having dinner tonight though, when we get back to Mother Hobbs house. Remember?"

"Oh yeah, well, I guess that will have to do."

Mother Hobbs had a feast ready by the time they got back to the house. Quinton rubbed his stomach. "Oh boy, here we go again."

They ate, talked, and laughed until it got late.

When it was time for Keeva and Shara to leave, Quinton walked them to the door as if he were now head of the house. He hugged Keeva. "Good to see you again and thanks for the tour." He turned to Shara. She stiffened a little as he hugged her. "So I guess I'll see you tomorrow?"

She nodded and smoothed back her hair. "Yeah, tomorrow."

Chapter Twenty-one

When Shara opened her eyes when worship ended in service the next morning, she was surprised to see Keeva standing beside her, lifting her hands. She had felt someone slip into the seat beside her, but was too caught up in the presence of God to look and see who it was.

"What are you doing here?" she said in a loud whisper while giving Keeva a hug.

"What—I can't come to church?" Keeva turned to hug Mother Hobbs who was sitting on her other side.

Shara gave her a wide grin.

Pastor Kendrick came to the podium and pulled out his Bible and some notes.

"Good morning, saints. Wow, with worship like that, I can push right on into the Word. I feel like the atmosphere is ripe and ready and I pray that your hearts are good ground that will take in this Word and produce 100-fold. Turn in your Bibles to . . ."

Shara noticed that for the first few minutes of his sermon, Pastor Kendrick was struggling. She looked over at Jenell who appeared to be equally puzzled.

"I'm sorry, folks. I have to obey the Holy Spirit. I had one message all planned out to share—notes and everything, but the Lord is leading me in another direction. I don't know why, but I know Him well enough to know He knows what He's doing." He laid his notes aside. "Walk with me now, I'm hearing this as you are, so I'm gonna trust the anointing is going to take over because I have no idea where I'm going."

"Preach, Pastor!" several members encouraged.

He smiled and flipped through his Bible. "Okay, we're going to look at several scriptures. Turn to John 18:28-37. I promise if you follow me, this will all make sense."

He read the scripture and then paraphrased. "Basically, Jesus is about to be crucified and He's being questioned before Pilate and is not saying *anything*. Finally, Pilate, the Roman governor, looks at him and says 'I don't know if You realize what's up here, man—but these people are trying to kill You. You ain't got *nothing* to say? Are you a King or what?'

"Jesus is real cool and says, 'Yeah, I'm a King. In fact, to this end, I was born, and for this reason I came into the world.' Key phrase saints, *'to this end I was born, and for this reason*

I came into the world.' Jesus knew *exactly* why He was born and *exactly* what He came into the world to do."

Pastor Kendrick started doing that little pacing thing he did when the Word got good to him. "All right, now turn to John 4:34. I promise if you follow me, this will all make sense."

He read the scripture, then summarized, "Okay, here Jesus has been talking to the woman at the well and the disciples just came back from grocery shopping. They're telling Jesus, 'Yo, man, you looking a little tired. You need to eat a little 'sump'n sump'n.' Jesus tells them He has food they don't know nothing about. So the disciples wonder if someone else went and bought him some chicken wings or a fish sammich or something. Then He busts this revelation on 'em, 'My food is to do the will of Him who sent me and to finish His work.' "

Pastor Kendrick paused. "I need you all to catch that. Jesus was saying, my food, my sustenance, my nourishment, that which keeps me alive—is to do what God sent me to do and to finish His work. How many of you have ever gone without food for any period of time? Think about how your body feels when you do that. How long do you think you could actually *live* without food?"

He flipped through his Bible again. "Another scripture. I promise if you follow me . . ."

". . . this will all make sense," the congregation said in unison.

Pastor Kendrick looked up. "Have I said that before?"

Everybody laughed.

"Okay, turn to Esther 4:14. Esther is after Ezra, which is after Nehemiah."

Pages could be heard turning.

"It's before Job which is before Psalms and Proverbs."

Pages turning.

"It's on page 624 in my Bible."

Everybody laughed.

"While you're finding it, let me set things up here. The Jews were God's covenant people, but they were really hardheaded—like most of us. They had a problem with putting other 'gods' before God—like most of us. God kept warning them and warning them, but they didn't listen—"

". . . like most of us," the congregation said in unison.

"I didn't say that." Pastor Kendrick laughed. "So finally, He allows them to be taken into captivity by other nations. Before, they had their own land and their own kings and government, but now, because of their disobedience, they're living subject to another government. Whew, that's a whole 'nother sermon in itself." He stopped and jotted down a note.

"Anyway, this particular set of Jews were living under a Persian king by the name of Xerxes. He has this party so he could show off all his riches and majesty to the people for seven days. Now *that's* a party. He gets drunk and decides to show off his wife and sends for her. Well, his wife, Queen Vashti refuses to come. The king's wise men are like, 'Yo, King. If you let her get away with dissing you like that, then all the wives all over your kingdom are gonna start dissing their husbands too. We can't have that.' So Queen Vashti gets put out the castle and the king starts this search for another queen. All these virgins are called together for him to pick from. They go through all these beauty treatments for a whole *year*."

He smirked. "I guess I shouldn't complain when Jenell spends half the day in the beauty shop."

The congregation laughed. Jenell crossed her eyes and stuck out her tongue at him.

"Long story short, God gave favor to this little Jewish girl, Esther, and she became queen. Well, everything was all good until the King's right hand man, Haman, starts ego-tripping. He gets mad because Esther's cousin, Mordecai, won't bow down to him and honor him. So he finds out that Mordecai is a Jew and instead of just punishing Mordecai, he decides to kill all the Jews. Haman goes to the king and gets him to sign a death sentence for all the Jews in his kingdom. So Mordecai sends word to Esther, 'Yo, you need to do something, shawty, or me and all us Jews are gonna get kilt.' "

Everyone laughed. Mother Hobbs shook her head. "That boy is crazy. I don't see that in my Bible."

"Esther sends word back and says, 'Look, Cousin Mordy, you don't understand how things work in the castle. If I go to the king and he didn't call for me, I could get killed. He ain't even thought about me in a whole month. The only way I get to talk to him is for him to extend his golden scepter to me.'

"Well, Mordecai sends word back, 'Girl, you

ain't special! Don't think just because you queen, you ain't gonna die, too. You're a Jew like the rest of us. If you don't do nothing, God will send deliverance for the Jews from another place, but you and your family will die.' "

Pastor Kendrick stopped pacing and came back to the podium. "Okay, saints, here's the key verse. Mordecai says to her in verse 14, 'who knows whether you are come into the kingdom for such a time as this?' Basically, he says to her, how do you know it's not your destiny? The whole reason you were born was for this moment. God gave you favor to become queen for this reason."

He put down his Bible. "Long story short, Esther risks her life and goes in to the king and intercedes for her people. She saves all the Jews in the kingdom from being put to death. In that, she's a type of Christ. She was born for the salvation of her people. Her entire destiny—her reason for living—was to save her people from destruction. Jesus was saying the same thing in those scriptures. His entire purpose, his destiny, his reason for living, was to do the will of God and save people—*us*—from destruction."

Pastor Kendrick wiped his forehead.

"One last thing, and then I'm gonna close. We won't turn there, but you know the story of Joseph. He was sold into slavery by his brothers, and ended up in Potiphar's house. Then Potiphar's wife framed him because he wouldn't get busy with her, so he ended up in jail. His life was hard—slavery, then prison for years and years. Finally, he ends up interpreting a dream for Pharaoh and becomes second in command in the whole kingdom of Egypt. There was a famine throughout the land and long story short, God gave Joseph a plan to save everybody, including his whole household who eventually multiplied and became the people of Israel. God preserved the patriarchs of the Jewish nation—which eventually gave birth to Jesus Christ himself—through Joseph. That was his whole destiny, his whole purpose. He had to go through a whole bunch of hell in his life, but that hell led him to where God ordained him to be, and he ended up saving an entire nation."

Pastor Kendrick stopped pacing. "I want to ask the question of each of you. For what reason were *you* born? Why are *you* here? What is *your* purpose? What did God send *you* to the earth to do? 'Cause let me tell you something. If you're not living for the purpose that God ordained you to live for, you're not living. Jesus said it was His food to do God's will. If you're not doing God's will, what are you feeding on?

"That's why some of you are so miserable. You're not doing what God created you to do. Five days a week, you're depressed because you spend all day doing something you weren't meant to. Meanwhile, the purpose of God lies dormant within you. And you wonder why your hair is falling out and you're having panic attacks and you can't sleep. Stop giving all that money to the psychiatrist and the psychic. Stop living the life others think you should live or that the American dream dictates."

Keeva shifted in her seat and looked at Shara.

Shara leaned over and whispered, "No, I didn't

talk to him about you. It's the Spirit of God speaking through him."

Pastor Kendrick walked to the other side of the stage. "That's our problem—chasing the American dream, some fabricated idea of success. Fancy cars, big houses, and material wealth. If that's success, then why are so many rich people miserable? Why are so many so-called successful people miserable? You want real success? You want real life? You want real joy and real happiness? Find out what God put you here for and pursue it with all your heart. The prosperity will follow you, instead of you chasing it. I promise you, you'll know joy that you never imagined. I can just see God now, designing each one of us, putting inside of us exactly what we need to fulfill our destiny. Think of all the untapped potential inside of you."

He slowed down and came back to the podium. "I'm gonna say this and then I'll close. You'll never know who you really are until you know who *God* says you are. You'll never know why you're here unless *God* shows you. It's like Myles Monroe says, 'if you want to know the purpose of a thing, you have to consult the manufacturer.' God is the master designer and manufactured you with a specific purpose in mind. If a blender can't blend, it's worthless. If a vacuum cleaner doesn't vacuum, it's worthless. If your washing machine doesn't get your clothes clean and your dryer doesn't dry, they're worthless. If you're not doing what God made you to do, what is your worth?"

Shara looked over and noticed Keeva trembling.

Pastor Kendrick said, "One last thought, and then I promise I'm gonna close. Esther's purpose and destiny was to save her people from destruction. Joseph's purpose and destiny was to save an entire nation, and the future Jewish nation from destruction. I didn't talk about Moses, but you know the story. His purpose and destiny was to deliver the people of Israel from bondage. Look at Joshua—his purpose was to lead God's people into their promised land. And finally Jesus . . . His whole purpose and destiny—the reason why he was born and the reason He died was to save the *human* nation from death and destruction. Think about this. Who were you put here to save from destruction? Whose deliverer are you? If you don't find the purpose of God for your life, what people may end up being destroyed? Or will it be like Mordecai told Esther. If you don't do what you're supposed to do, God will send deliverance through somebody else, but you'll die. How many of you are 'dying' because you're not living the life God made you to live?"

Tears streamed down Keeva's face. Shara reached over and took her hand and held it tightly.

Pastor Kendrick closed. "Jesus said, 'I came to give you life and that more abundantly.' If you don't have Him, you're missing out on life. You may have life, but not the best life you can have. There are some here God has been speaking to today. You've felt like the living dead. You've felt empty, like your life has no meaning or purpose, like you're just going through the motions. If you accept Him, and truly follow

Him . . . If you seek Him for your purpose and destiny, I promise life will be more than you ever dreamed it could be. If that's you, then you can come to the altar and we'll pray for you. Don't leave here today without him."

People streamed to the altar. Pastor Kendrick, Jenell, Quinton, Shara, and some of the other ministers prayed for each one individually. Mother Hobbs got up to move toward the altar, but Keeva caught her hand as she was leaving.

Shara could hardly concentrate on the person she was praying for as she saw Keeva sobbing in Mother Hobbs' arms. She finished ministering to the person and walked over just in time to hear her friend accept Christ into her life.

Chapter Twenty-two

On Wednesday afternoon, Quinton stepped over to the track from the basketball court to speak to Shara. "Where are the boys for basketball practice? Didn't they know we were supposed to start today?"

Shara looked over at the court. What was he talking about? There were at least ten boys there. That was a good turnout for the first day. "Quinton, they're waiting for you over there."

"Yeah, but they're all little boys. The oldest one is twelve. Where are the teenagers?"

"They don't participate much. They spend most of their time hanging out on the street. They don't think it's 'cool' for them to be involved in church programs."

Quinton walked back over to the basketball court to play with the kids that were there. Shara stepped over from the track to watch for a few minutes.

One of the young boys threw Quinton the

ball and he dribbled a few times and then took off across court and did a slam-dunk. On the next play, one of the boys threw the ball up for a basket, but Quinton slammed it away, blocking the shot. On the next play, he easily stole the ball away from a boy having some difficulty dribbling. He did another slam-dunk and held on to the basket for a while.

Shara fumed on the side of the court. What was wrong with him? Did he know anything about working with kids? Was he trying to show off for her or what? She let this go on for a few more plays, and then noticed the boys getting frustrated.

She marched onto the court with her hands on her hips. "Quinton, what are you doing? You can't play with these kids like that."

"Shara, I know what I'm doing." He smiled. "Could you get off the court, please?"

She stood there with her hands on her hips. Who did he think he was? She had a good mind to tell him off. She couldn't believe they had hired someone who knew absolutely nothing about working with kids.

He started dribbling again and headed toward the basket.

"Minister Mercer, may I speak with you for a second?" Shara said through tight lips.

He ignored her. He did another slam-dunk and came back. "Woman, get off my court." He grinned. "I know what I'm doing."

Her eyes blazed at him.

His twinkled at her. He winked and then said loudly, "What? You want summa this?"

Shara stepped back. Was he challenging her

openly in front of the kids? She opened her mouth to tell him off, the best way she knew how, but then noticed he was looking past her. She turned to see who he was talking to.

A large group of teenage boys had come over and had been watching Quinton play. He gestured to the court in a challenge. "What's up? You want summa this?"

They had been standing across the street on their favorite corner. Quinton must have noticed them when he first got to the court. Obviously, his showing off had been for their sake, not Shara's.

Shara recognized some of these boys. They had come to the track when she first started her program, but didn't want to be involved. They preferred to hang out in the bleachers and jeer at the ones that did participate. She remembered one day that was particularly bad.

"Why y'all runnin'? Ain't nobody chasing you. I don't see why anybody would want to run around in circles all day . . ." One of the older teens had said.

A few of her boys had quit the program because of their teasing. Obviously, it was important to them to maintain their respect in the neighborhood.

Shara approached the rowdy bunch and told them if they didn't want to participate, they needed to leave the track. One of them got right up in her face and sneered at her. "What you gon' do about it, Miss Church Lady? You don't run things around here, we do. You ain't runnin' nobody off this track. If I leave, it's cuz I want to. You feel me?"

Shara had the good sense to be afraid. She stood there, not knowing what to say, hoping they didn't notice her shaking.

Jamil had come to her rescue. "Yo', T man, Miss Shara cool. Don't step to her like that— she good people." He shifted from side to side like he did when he was nervous, right before a race.

"Well man, you need to tell her not to step to me." T-bone looked Jamil up and down. "Man, you need to come wit' me. We got some bidness to take care of." He looked at Shara when he said 'bidness', as if to let her know it was none of *her* business.

Jamil went into one of his little clown acts, shuffling and running, looking behind him like someone was chasing him. "Naw, man, I got to get my run on. Nigga never know when he need to run real fast. Know what I'm sayin'?" He picked up his knees and pumped his arms, running in place dramatically, as if his life depended on it. The older group cracked up.

T-bone shook his head and laughed. "Nigga, you crazy. All right stay here and get yo' run on, man. You right, you probably will need it some day." His smile faded. "Soon, if you don't come correct."

Shara read these last words as a threat. Jamil obviously did too, because he stopped his clown act. "I got you, man, I got you."

They slapped hands and the older group left, each one seeming to feel the need to give Shara a threatening look as they passed. She wanted to stare each one of them down to let them know she wasn't intimidated, but Jamil elbowed her and ever-so-slightly shook his head to let her know that wasn't cool.

Shara didn't have time to warn Quinton about all this, because the boys had already come around the fence and were talking the talk that black men talk when they get on a basketball court—pure trash.

Quinton took off his T-shirt to reveal a basketball jersey underneath. Shara noticed his broad muscular chest and strong chiseled arms.

The boys noticed the jersey.

Their trash talking turned to praise and admiration. "Quinton Mercer? Number 37? Orlando Magic? Man, you my nigga!" one said.

Another one put his hands to his mouth. "Orlando is down two points; eight seconds left in the game; ball is in play, Anderson throws to Mercer; five seconds left on the play, Mercer comes down the inside lane; two seconds left, Mercer puts up a three pointer—whoosh! Game goes to Orlando!" Two of them slapped hands and they all cheered, barking loudly.

Quinton smiled. "Yeah, that's me, but what y'all got?"

They shuffled their feet. "Aw, man, ain't nobody ballin' wit' you. You were Pro. Yo man, what happened? You played one season and then dropped out of sight."

Quinton put the ball down and pulled up the right leg of his long shorts. He showed them a long scar on his knee. "Tore my ACL, man. Didn't even get to finish the season."

They all joined in expressing their version of sympathy. "Aw, man, that's whack, that's jacked up. All that hard work and trainin' . . ."

"All that money, man? You woulda been fat paid, mad cheddar, set for life. Fly crib, rollin' in a Benz, all the honeys just throwin' it at ya. Bling bling, baby!"

"Man, I'm still gonna be paid. I didn't just play ball at Arizona. I got my education."

"Yeah right, man, whatever. What's your education got against the NBA? Education don't get you paid like that."

"Man, life ain't all about the honeys and the bling, bling. Keep living and you'll learn that. But you li'l niggas stallin'. Ain't nobody trying to ball with an old, crippled man?" He shot the ball from where he stood at mid-court. Whoosh! All net.

The older boys looked at Shara and the younger kids gathered behind her. "If she get these babies off the court, we'll take you, man."

Quinton nodded at Shara to take the younger kids off the court. Shara started to lead them back to the church, but they protested.

"Aw, Miss Shara, can't we watch?" one pleaded.

Another said, "We wanna see them get dropped!"

One of the older boys started toward him, like he was going to hurt him and then laughed when he darted back behind Shara. Shara stared at him, feeling confident with Quinton standing on the court with her.

"What, Church Lady? You got something to say?"

Quinton stepped in front of him. "What's up with that? Man, if I ever catch any one of y'all disrespecting Miss Shara, it's *on*; me and you."

The teen sucked his teeth. "Why man, that yo' lady?"

"Naw, man, she ain't *my* lady, but she is *a* lady, so you treat her with respect." Quinton bounced the ball. "Now y'all gon' ball—or fight with ladies and babies?"

After many games of basketball, the boys all slapped hands with Quinton.

"If y'all want some more, you can meet me back here day after tomorrow. You up for that?"

"Yeah, man, we'll be here. Friday afternoon."

After the boys left, Quinton walked back over to where Shara stood at the edge of the court. "Looks like we have some new participants."

Shara's eyes lit up. "We'll need to get them signed up so we can have a roster. They'll have to bring in their report cards to monitor their grades. We also have to get parental consent for them to participate, and—"

"Wait a minute, slow down. Let me get 'em hooked first. Right now, they're just ballin'. In order for them to make a commitment to making good grades and all, I need to earn their trust. Give me a little while on that, okay?"

Shara nodded. She couldn't seem to keep her eyes off Quinton's chest and arms so she decided to focus on her shoes. "I like the way you handled them. I've had a few run-ins with them that didn't go too well. They seem to respect you a lot." She kicked at a pebble on the ground. "One thing though, do you have to call them nigger?"

"Here we go again." Quinton pulled his shirt over his head.

"What do you mean by that?"

"First day on the job and somebody's already questioning my methods."

"Quinton, I'm not questioning your methods. Like I said, I like the way you handled them. All I said was I don't understand why you have to use that degrading word."

"It doesn't have to be degrading. For these guys, it's a term of endearment, brotherhood, solidarity. I have to get into their world. I can't just be a minister and quote scripture to them. Like Paul said, I have to become all things to all people."

"Okay, if you say so."

He tilted his head to the side. "Trust me, okay?"

The younger boys who had been on the court earlier came running over to Quinton. They had gone to the playground after they got bored watching him play the older boys.

"Mr. Quinton, we wanna play too." They gathered around him, pulling on his shirt. "Please, can you play with us? Only don't beat us this time."

Quinton laughed and took his shirt off again. "All right, I promise I won't beat you guys this time." The smallest and youngest of the bunch pulled the leg of Quinton's shorts. "Mr. Quinton, can I play? They say I'm too small to play."

Quinton squatted down to his height. "What's your name, li'l man?"

"My name Tiquan Davis, but everybody call me Li'l Booboo."

"Tiquan Davis, do you think you're too small to play?"

The young boy stuck his chest out. "Naw. I can take all dem."

Quinton stood up. "All right, Tiquan Davis, you can be on my team. We'll take 'em together." He lifted Tiquan and carried him over to the court. He whispered in his ear, pointing to the court and to the basket. Tiquan nodded and grinned.

Shara watched as Quinton played with the boys. The aggression with which he'd played only moments before was now gone and he was gentle and playful. He threw Tiquan the ball and then ran over to lift him up so he could slam-dunk. He purposely missed when he shot baskets, feigning frustration at his lack of skill. He let the boys steal the ball from him while dribbling and then took a long time to catch them so they could get to the basket and shoot without any defense. When the score was tied at 7/7, he told them his knee was bothering him so they would have to leave the game tied. He lifted Tiquan up on his shoulders and declared them all winners. They all came cheering and running back over to where Shara was.

"Miss Shara, did you see us? Did you see the

basket I hit? Did you see me steal the ball from Mr. Quinton? Did you see my three pointer?"

"Yeah, I saw you guys. You got game. Maybe you need to teach Mr. Quinton here some of your tricks because he looked a little sloppy out there." Shara smiled up at Quinton who was spinning Tiquan around in circles.

"Yeah, Miss Shara. They were too much for me." Quinton stopped and staggered, pretending to be dizzy.

"Mr. Quinton, can we start our own team too?" one of the boys asked.

"Of course. You didn't think we were going to leave you guys out did you?"

They ran shouting back to the church building.

Shara called out after them, "You guys get your stuff together and get loaded up in the van so we can get you home."

"Yes, Miss Shara," they screamed back.

"Looks like you got yourself two basketball teams. Can you handle that with everything else?" Shara looked down at her feet again, hoping Quinton would put his shirt back on.

"That's what I'm here for. It's my full time job. I get concerned about you, though. I don't see how you do everything here *and* school. I remember how difficult it was for me. It doesn't get to be too much?"

"Are you kidding? This is what keeps me going. Every time I get overwhelmed with school, I spend time with my kids and remember why I'm in school. It actually makes it easier, focusing on the purpose for it."

Quinton pulled his shirt over his head. "Man, I'm starving. Want to get some dinner?"

"I have to take the kids home. The guy that usually drives is out today."

"Want me to do it?"

"You don't know where they live, and trust me, they'd have you lost trying to go around the corner."

"Want me to ride with you then?"

Shara pinched her nose. "No offense, Quinton, but you just played two hours of basketball." She smiled mischievously. "I think the only place you need to be is in the shower."

"Oh you got jokes, huh? I was gonna hit the shower real quick. Give me ten minutes."

"Really, I got it. I need to go ahead and get them home. It's later than usual and I don't want their parents to worry." Shara smoothed her hair back.

"Okay. I guess I'll see you Friday then?"

"Yeah. See you Friday."

Chapter Twenty-three

Shara stood in front of her new full-length mirror, trying to decide if she needed to change clothes. She was taking Keeva out for a surprise evening for her birthday. Keeva had taken her to so many new places and showed her so many new things, she wanted to do something to pay her back.

She had on a deep brown, knit dress Keeva had persuaded her to buy that hugged all her curves in all the right places. She couldn't decide if she was comfortable with the low neckline. It was a bit more cleavage than she was used to. After she admired herself in the mirror for a while, she decided it was okay.

When she pulled into Keeva's parking lot, she was already outside waiting for her. Shara parked the car and got out. "We're walking tonight."

"Where are we going?"

"You'll see in a minute. Just come on."

They walked a few blocks up Peachtree until they came to Third Street. Shara stopped.

When Keeva saw the marquis for the Fox Theatre and realized what was going on, her eyes grew wide. "You didn't!"

"I did."

"Shara, I can't believe you did this. Why?"

"I don't know. I guess because of the look you get in your eyes when you talk about the infamous Alvin Ailey dancers."

"Wow. I can't believe it. Shara, thank you so much."

As they waited in the lobby of the theatre, Shara looked around. She had never seen so many beautiful black people in her life. She stared at all the gorgeous women and oh-so-fine men. They looked like they could be celebrities with their stylish haircuts and jazzy clothes. She felt self-conscious for a few moments until she remembered her reflection in her mirror. She realized somehow Keeva had transformed her into one of these beautiful black people.

They settled into their seats and chatted until the lights dimmed and the curtains opened. Keeva sat forward in her seat and clasped her hands together.

Shara didn't know what she enjoyed more, watching the dancers or watching how much Keeva enjoyed them. Her face took on a dreamy glow Shara had never seen before. She was oblivious to everything going on around her and seemed completed absorbed in every movement, every turn, and every leap in every scene.

* * *

They went to a Café Intermezzo afterward. Keeva sat down at the table they picked and inhaled deeply. "Umm, Sumatra, chocolate, hazelnut, amaretto—don't you love coffee shops?"

Shara shrugged and sat down across from her. "So did you enjoy the show?"

Keeva's countenance brightened. "Aren't they amazing? I could watch them all night."

"It was beautiful. You could feel their passion and emotion. I got lost in it. I had never been to anything like that before." Shara picked up the coffee menu. Her eyes widened. "Are you serious? How can they charge you that much for a cup of coffee? That's ridiculous."

Keeva rolled her eyes and took the menu from Shara. She waived a waiter over and ordered a cappuccino for the both of them. "I gotta teach you to appreciate the finer things in life. Like Alvin Ailey tonight. I can't believe you've never seen them. I can't believe I've gone so long without seeing them."

Shara wrinkled her nose. "Maybe because I'm not used to seeing stuff like that, but I didn't always understand what they were trying to say. It was beautiful, but what was the message?"

"That *is* the message—the beauty of it. It doesn't have to tell a story." Keeva frowned. Shara had obviously missed the whole point. "That's what's wrong with black folks—we always want a story, some drama, a soap opera. We can't appreciate art for the sake of art. We don't go to a museum and look at a picture and appreciate it for its beauty. We got to know the story behind it and what it means."

Shara wagged her neck in classic ghetto fashion. "Well excuse me, Miss Hoighty-Toighty-High-Society, that I'm common black folk and didn't get it. I'm just saying—"

"You don't have to get offended."

"I'm not offended, although that was offensive." Shara lowered her voice. "I appreciate that it was beautiful. It must really be something to be able to evoke that type of emotion. It must feel awesome to be able to talk with your body, to be able to express that much passion through movement. I'm just saying, imagine if it was for Christ."

Keeva rolled her eyes. "Are you that spooky and deep? Does everything have to be spiritual? Can you ever step outside the box and do something other than church? You can't even appreciate art. I don't—"

"Now who's getting offended? Why are you so sensitive about it?"

"Because I love dance. I love to watch it and I love to do it. Now you're telling me I can't enjoy it because it's not spiritual?" Keeva gripped the table. "I don't believe I have to give up something that beautiful because I want to have a relationship with God. I don't believe salvation has to be devoid of beauty and art and life and—"

"I'm not saying that! I know you think I'm Miss Holier-Than-Thou, and I also know you think that salvation means giving up everything that brings you joy, but you're wrong on both counts. If you would hear me out—"

Shara lowered her voice as the waiter brought over their coffee and a small container of sugar, honey, and Splenda. "Something to sweeten your coffee? Although, you probably don't need anything sweet . . ." He smiled directly into Shara's face. She blushed.

Keeva let out a loud breath and stared down the overly attentive waiter. "No thank you, we're fine." Keeva gave him her nice-nastiest smile. "Now be gone," she muttered under her breath as he walked away.

He looked back at the table and flashed a suave smile at Shara. She looked away quickly.

Keeva's eyes widened. "I can't believe you're flirting with the waiter! Girl, he *is* fine, though. Did you see that behind? Oops! You probably don't look at those things. You were probably looking at his spirit."

"What's up with all the spiritual throw-offs? And I was not flirting with the waiter!" Shara lowered her voice. "He *does* have a perfectly round butt though, just like an apple. I'd love to take a bite—"

Keeva coughed and spit the large sip of cappuccino she had just taken across the table. "Why Minister Shara, I'm shocked, I'm appalled. I'm—"

"Disgusting!" Shara wiped up the mess with a napkin. She laughed. "Can't take you nowhere, Miss High-Society. Didn't they teach you in charm school or etiquette school or wherever you rich kids go, not to spit your food across the table?"

They both looked at each other and cracked up.

The waiter sauntered over with a towel. "Do you ladies need some help?"

Keeva said dramatically, "Look at me, I'm so clumsy. I spilled coffee all over the table.

Shara's mouth dropped. "Spilled?"

"Oh, Shara, I've gotten coffee all over your dress." Keeva looked at the waiter's nametag. "Malik, could you help her out? She'll never forgive me if that stain doesn't come out."

Malik ever so softly brushed the front of Shara's dress with his towel.

She stiffened and blushed profusely, grabbing the towel. "I'll get it." She kept one hand over her cleavage and used the other to rub the coffee stain.

Malik laughed. "I'm sorry, I didn't mean to . . ."

Keeva was sorry about the scene she had created, especially since it was making Shara so uncomfortable. "Malik, perhaps you could get us some seltzer water. That's usually good for getting stains out."

He stood looking at Shara.

"Malik?" He shook his head and looked at Keeva as if she was speaking Greek. "Seltzer water?"

"Oh—yeah, I'll be right back with that."

Shara kicked Keeva under the table. "I can't believe you told him to fondle me!"

"He didn't fondle you. He barely touched you!" Keeva laughed. "Anyway, I thought you wanted to bite his apple, Miss Thang. What happened?"

"I was joking. I didn't mean—"

She shushed as Malik brought the seltzer water. Mercifully, he sat it down and walked away without lingering. Shara grabbed the bottle and poured some on the towel and wiped the stain on her dress.

Keeva mopped the rest of the coffee off the table with some napkins. "I'm sorry. Sorry about Malik and sorry about what I said about your spirituality." She took a deep breath. "I guess I'm intimidated by you sometimes. I've never met anyone so into God. I guess sometimes it makes me feel bad about me. I know I should be more spiritual and should pray more and read my Bible more. I do admire that about you. But I honestly think you could use more balance in your life. Not that I think you should go around biting the buns of flirtatious waiters."

Shara narrowed her eyes at Keeva, but then smiled. "I'm sorry too, for calling you Miss Hoighty-Toighty-High-Society. I guess I'm not used to all these fancy people and their expensive lifestyles, fancy food, and schnazzy clothes." She paused. "I still can't believe you told him to fondle me though."

"I didn't tell him to fondle you!" Keeva glanced over at him. "He is *extremely* cute though. You should get his number."

"For what?"

"He seems interested. You guys might want to hook up, go out."

"For what?"

"What do you mean for what? Are you telling me you don't date?"

Shara shrugged. "I don't see the point of dating. Why waste time with someone you're not gonna marry?"

"How do you know if he's the one you're supposed to marry if you don't date him?"

"I dunno. You just know. You can tell whether someone's *the one* or not. You know your soul mate."

"Soul mate?"

Shara put the cap back on the seltzer water. "I think the whole problem with relationships in this country is that people don't really know what love is. They have this Hollywood image of it. Think about the movies. Two people meet, they have this physical attraction and 'chemistry'—whatever *that* is. Before they even know each other good, they sleep together, get used to each other and then make a commitment based on what? Good looks and good sex? How much time do they really take to get to know each other though? And people wonder why the divorce rate is over 50%."

Keeva emptied another packet of Splenda into her cappuccino.

"What I want is a soul mate. Someone I can be totally real with—transparent and vulnerable. I should be able to share all my fears, dreams, feelings, who I really am and trust that it's safe because he loves me for me and vice versa. We should be behind each other 100 percent, supporting each other so we can each realize our life dreams together. Maybe I'm being too idealistic, but if it's anything less than that—I don't want to be bothered."

Keeva nodded, refusing to let herself think about her relationship with Mark.

Malik looked over at the table and winked at Shara. She blushed and looked away quickly.

Keeva studied her reaction. "Shara, remember when you told me about being shy around guys and I asked you if it was difficult to get over?"

"Yeah." Shara looked at her hands.

Keeva tried to ask as gently as possible. "Have you really gotten over it?"

Shara sighed. "I don't think so. To be honest, I guess I don't really have any experience with being comfortable with men. If it's under normal circumstances I'm fine, but if I feel like they're interested in me, or if I'm interested in them, I get all goofy inside. I can't relax and be myself."

"If a prerequisite for finding your soul mate is being yourself, then you're in trouble."

"I guess when the time comes, I'll find a way to get over it. I guess I would need to feel totally safe and comfortable, like that person would never hurt me."

Keeva stared at Shara. "Now *that* is being too idealistic. In relationships, people get hurt. It comes with the territory. Most of the time, it's not on purpose, but it still happens."

"I don't know, Keeva. I guess I'm afraid. Maybe I need God to send me someone real loving and sweet who can be patient with me and my issues."

"I'm sure God will do that for you." Keeva took a sip of her cappuccino. "Maybe He already has."

"What are you talking about, Keeva?"

Keeva smiled innocently. "Nothing, Shara."

Shara's eyes got big. "What?"

Keeva took one last slurp on her cappuccino. "Nothing. Nothing at all."

Chapter Twenty-four

One Friday evening after track practice, Shara gathered her things to leave the church office as a group of youth leaders came in. Terrence, one of the boys' basketball coaches, came up to her desk.

"Hey, Shara. A group of us are going bowling tonight. Want to go?"

Shara didn't like the way Terrence was looking at her up and down, all shifty-eyed. She stepped back a little. "No thanks. I think I'm gonna get some rest this evening."

Quinton walked over as she was declining the offer. "Oh come on, live a little. Have some fun."

"No thanks, Quinton. I've had a long week. I need to recuperate and get some stuff done around the house."

"Shara, it's Friday night. You can rest tomorrow."

"I don't know how to bowl. I've only been once and I wasn't very good at it."

Terrence gave her that look again, making her skin crawl. "Don't worry. I'm a pro and can teach you all you need to know."

Shara was about to decline once again, sure she didn't want Terrence to teach her anything when Quinton said, "Come on, a whole group of us are going. All the youth leaders are going to be doing activities together some weekends so we can get to know each other better. As your boss, I'm ordering you to go."

"All right, Quinton. Whatever."

When they got out to the parking lot, Quinton looked over at her car. "Why don't you ride with me? No sense in us taking two cars. I'll bring you back here afterward."

Before she could protest, Quinton was holding the door for her, helping her up into his truck. He got in and passed her a stack of CD's. She thumbed through his collection. He had a lot of the same CD's that Keeva had—Musiq Soulchild, Jill Scott, India.arie, Erykah Badu, Angie Stone, and Lauryn Hill. He also had some jazz CD's—Joe Sample, Chick Corea, George Duke, Miles Davis, and Rachelle Ferrell. Then he had many of the same gospel CD's she had—Israel Houghton, Mary Mary, Yolanda Adams, Donnie McClurkin, Kim Burrell, and several of Fred Hammond's, who was Shara's favorite. She noticed a CD by Joann Rosario. She remembered this was a new artist released on Fred Hammond's new label a while back. She had been meaning to check it out. She handed it to Quinton.

"Oh yeah, this is one of my favorites. It has this Latin, urban flavor to it. I played it to death when I first got it. You'll like it."

Shara had a habit when she first got a new CD; she'd listen to a little bit of each song to see if she liked it. It took a few minutes to figure out the buttons on Quinton's CD player.

He finally pointed out the "skip to the next track" button. "You do that, too? I used to drive my roommates in college crazy doing that. That and playing a song over and over."

Shara smiled. "You do that, too? Mother Hobbs used to swear I was trying to drive her out of her mind doing that."

It was rare she liked most of the songs on a CD, but Shara was enjoying this one so far. She started at the beginning and let the CD play. She leaned back and relaxed a little. She liked being up high, sort of towering over the other cars. "This is nice."

"What the truck or the music?"

"Both." She turned the music up a little.

Quinton bobbed his head. "This is a great hook." He sang a little bit of the song. "Are those some of the best lyrics you've ever heard or what? Needing His Spirit like we need to breathe? I'm feeling that." Quinton sang a little more.

He had a nice voice. Shara liked the lyrics too. They expressed exactly how she felt about God. "This is a great CD. I've got to get it."

"You want to take mine? With CD's I really

like, I have this extravagant habit of buying one copy for the truck and one for the house."

Shara looked at him like he was crazy.

He held up his hand to ward off her disdain. "I know. I'm changing a lot of my lifestyle habits left over from being a rich superstar athlete. Honestly though, I'm a very practical person. There are only a few things I splurge on. For the most part, I'm quite a scrooge."

"I've been called a scrooge many a time."

They said simultaneously, "I think it's from growing up poor."

They looked at each other and laughed.

Quinton gave her a sideways glance. "What you know about growing up poor? You had a mom *and* a dad and your father was a pastor wasn't he?"

"A district elder actually. You know that old school religion, though. The poorer you are, the more spiritual you are. My dad swears all these prosperity preachers out here are going straight to hell and taking all their members with them. You know, money is the root of all evil."

"Actually, the Word says the *love* of money is the root of all evil, not money itself."

"Yeah, *I* know that. My dad reads a different Bible, I guess. It took me a while to get over that poverty mentality. I *do* think some of these name-it-and-claim-it preachers take it too far. They make money and getting stuff the focus of everything. It seems like *that* becomes their gospel. The focus needs to be right. God gives us wealth to—"

"Build his Kingdom?"

"Yeah. Not for our own personal gain. Some people have made God their cosmic Santa Claus who exists solely for the purpose of blessing them. They seek His hand—"

"Instead of His face. I know. It gets sickening sometimes."

"Do you always do that?"

"What?"

"Finish people's sentences."

Quinton thought for a moment. "Well, actually no. In fact, never. Maybe we think alike or something. Seems like when you talk, or stuff you write is stuff that's been in my head too."

"Whatever, Quinton." She turned the music up a little more. "This is really a slammin' CD. I think I am gonna *borrow* it. I need to jam to this while I'm cleaning my apartment. Speaking of, how's your place coming? Are they almost done?"

"Not even close. It'll probably be another few weeks."

"Was it *that* bad off to begin with?"

Quinton looked sheepish. "I have to admit, that's another area where I'm extravagant. I really like having a nice place to live. I promise that's it though. I only splurge with my automobile, my music and my home, and okay, maybe my clothes. But that's it. Well, maybe with books too, but that's really all. Maybe with furniture too, but that goes under my home, so that doesn't count. And, maybe I have expensive taste too when it comes to restaurants. But really, that's it."

Shara laughed. "You may need to go back to

being a superstar athlete with your extravagant taste, even if it is just a 'few' things."

"Naw, I'm 'scraight'. I wasn't a finance major for nothing. I made some wise investments when I first got paid and I got a few things up my sleeve now. I ain't like regular black folk who spend money they don't have cause they 'have to have something' or to keep up with the Joneses. You can believe if I'm spending, I've got a full Excel spread sheet on my entire financial situation for the next twenty years already figured out."

They pulled up at the bowling alley. "Don't you dare touch that door."

She obediently waited for Quinton to come around and open it. He extended his hand to help her down. "There you are, madam. Watch your step."

"Such a gentleman. I'm touched."

When they got into the bowling alley, the rest of the group had already paid and were getting their shoes. There were about ten of them altogether. They crowded into their booth. Terrence squeezed into a small space between Shara and Tina. Tina was petite and rather pretty. Shara hoped it was Tina that Terrence was trying to get close to. She realized she was wrong when he slipped an arm around her and said, "Watch me close. I'll teach you all you need to know to become a pro bowler."

She removed his arm from her shoulder and edged away from him, but bumped into Anthony who was on her other side.

Quinton sat at the score table. He watched Shara squirming and Terrence breathing down her neck. He patted the chair next to him. "There's a seat over here. You guys look crowded."

Before Shara could move, Tina jumped up to get the seat next to Quinton.

"Thanks, Quinton." She patted his arm, her hand lingering for a minute.

A few people took some turns, not really doing too well. Anthony was shame-faced over his score. He tried to play it off. "I'm just getting warmed up."

Terrence got up and walked toward the lane. He winked at Shara. "Watch me now."

She smiled one of Keeva's nice-nasty smiles and rolled her eyes when he turned his back. He knocked all the pins down, and then hit eight pins on his second turn. He came back grinning. "That's all there is to it. You want to go next?"

Quinton got up. "I'll go next." He got his ball and stood for a few minutes like he was contemplating the perfect shot.

Tina watched as he bent over. "Um, um, um. God is good, all the time."

Quinton knocked all the pins down. He got almost all the pins on his second turn. He came back over to their booth, but stood this time.

Tina took her turn next. She seemed to need a lot of time to concentrate and was bent over with her butt in the air for a while before sending the ball down the lane. She only hit two pins. "Ooops, guess I need to try a little harder." On her second turn, she posed even longer, but the ball went into the gutter. "Oh dear, maybe Shara's not the only one that needs help. Quinton, you seem to have the hang of this. Show me?"

"Oh no, not me, Terrence is the pro bowler here. Yo, T, help the lady out."

Tina scowled a little, but recovered as Terrence demonstrated for her a couple of times how to position her legs and line up the ball.

Quinton looked over at Shara. "Ready?"

"I guess." She stood.

On her first try, the ball went into the gutter almost as soon as she let it go. On her second try, it went halfway down the lane before hitting the gutter. "See? Told you I couldn't bowl."

Quinton laughed. "Don't worry about it. Practice makes perfect. You'll get it."

Everyone took his or her turn again. Tina took her second turn and somehow managed to knock almost all the pins down.

"Gee, Terrence gives really great lessons." Quinton had the slightest hint of sarcasm in his voice.

Tina bit her lip and giggled. "Yeah, I'm starting to like this game."

Shara picked up her ball again. Terrence walked up behind her. "Let me show you how." He put one hand on her waist and the other on her arm. "It's all about having good form."

Shara moved aside and handed him the ball. "Why don't you just show me?"

He shrugged his shoulders and took the ball from her. He demonstrated the swing a couple of times and then handed the ball back to her. He stood behind her watching as she sent the ball into the gutter again.

7 .7

Terrence laughed. "Really, you gotta feel it to get it right. Let me show you. I promise I won't bite." He put his hand on Shara's waist again and held her arm. He guided her through a swinging motion a few times. "Loosen up, Shara." He moved closer.

Shara stiffened and moved away again. "I think I got it, Terrence."

He moved toward her again. "Let me show you one more trick."

"I think she's got it, man," Quinton called out.

"I know man, but she's so stiff. If I can get her to loosen up, it will really improve her game."

Quinton's voice was a little firmer. "Really Terrence, she's got it. You've taught her everything she needs to know."

Shara looked gratefully at Quinton and moved to throw the ball down the lane. She wanted to get it out of her hand so she could go back to her seat. She hit three pins this time.

"See, man, I told you she had it." Quinton eyed Terrence as he returned to his seat.

Shara purposely sat on the end seat next to Nia so Terrence couldn't sit by her again. She sat there quietly as the next few bowlers took their turns.

After a few minutes, Quinton looked over at her. "Shara, I hate to be such a party pooper, but I'm exhausted. Do you mind if I go ahead and take you back to your car?"

Shara was on her feet with her purse on her shoulder before he could finish.

Terrence rose also. "Don't worry 'bout it, man. I'll take her back to her car."

"No really, I'm tired too. I'll catch a ride back with Quinton. You go ahead and finish your game." Shara walked away before he could say anything else. Quinton followed as they headed to his truck.

Quinton opened the door and reached to help her in. She ignored his hand and grabbed onto the door to balance herself.

Quinton rolled out of the parking lot. "I'm really sorry about that, Shara."

"Why are you sorry? You didn't do anything."

"I know, but I talked you into going. You were obviously following your instincts when you told him no the first time. I didn't know he was like that. You wouldn't think that a guy from church—"

"He didn't do anything but help me with my form. Don't worry about it."

"I know, but you were obviously uncomfortable and it was inappropriate."

"Like I said, Quinton, *you* didn't do anything. Just drop it." Shara inched a bit closer to the door.

Quinton turned the music up.

Shara turned it back down. "Tina seems nice. She's pretty too. I think she likes you."

"What was your first clue? The way she practically sat in my lap, or her loud, ignorant comments about how great my 'form' was. No thanks. I know her type. Can't be bothered."

Shara relaxed a little. She turned the music back up.

Quinton started skipping songs.

"Hey, I was listening to that." Shara pushed his hand away.

He pushed her hand back. "Woman, don't you know what happens when you touch a black man's radio?" She giggled. He kept flipping. "There's a song I want you to hear."

It was a slow, worshippy song. Shara relaxed as she listened to the lyrics. It was a song about being in the presence of God. Shara closed her eyes.

Quinton sang a few lines.

"That's nice." Shara said with her eyes still closed.

"What, the lyrics or my voice?"

"Both," Shara said shyly. She turned the music up a bit more. Quinton sang the rest of the song.

"How many times have you listened to this? Do you know all the words?"

"Just about." The next song was up-tempo and funky. Quinton turned it up. "This is my jam."

"You've said that about almost every song."

Quinton bobbed his head to the music. "I know. What can I say? It's a nice CD. Hey, have you heard Tonex?"

"Are you kidding? He's the kids' favorite. He's been the start of many a parking lot dance party."

"Yeah? They dance in the parking lot?"

"You should see them go at it. They're something else."

Quinton rubbed his chin. "We really should plan a dance party for them. Get a DJ with all gospel hip-hop and rap and stuff. It would be a lot of fun."

Shara was amused at his excitement. "For you or for them?"

"Both." He grinned.

They talked about ideas for the party until they arrived at Shara's car. The ride back from the bowling alley seemed quicker than the ride there. Shara knew to wait this time for Quinton to help her out of the car. "Here you are, madam. Safely back at your destination." He kissed her hand.

She pulled it away quickly. "Thanks, Quinton." She lowered her eyes.

He held her car door for her as she got in.

"Wait." He went back to his truck. By the time he returned with the Joann Rosario CD, she had already pulled off.

Chapter Twenty-five

Quinton plunked his keys on the kitchen table.

"Quint? That better be you," Mother Hobbs called out from the living room.

"What are you doing up? Isn't it past your bed time?"

"Boy, I ain't that old. Where you been?"

"Me and Shara and the other youth leaders went bowling." Quinton sniffed. "Umm, that smells good. I gotta get me a cup of that tea."

"You don't want any of that. That's my special women's tea. I'll fix you something else."

"Maybe I need some of that. Will it help me understand women better?" He plopped down in the living room chair and rubbed his hand across his face.

Mother Hobbs slowly closed her Bible and sat it on the couch next to her. She took a deep breath. "Quinton, normally I mind my own business, but since I like you so much, I'm gonna help you out on this one. If you ever mention this conversation to anyone, I'll deny it to my death."

Quinton leaned forward to hear whatever wisdom she was about to share.

"Imagine the church you just left, but in rural South Georgia. Now make it ten times more conservative and a hundred times more religious. The women can't wear pants, makeup, or jewelry, and wear long skirts every day. They can't even wear their toes out. Now imagine a pastor who preaches Sunday after Sunday against the evils of sex, convincing young girls that men are evil demons lurking in dark corners waiting to take advantage of them. Now imagine that pastor is your father and you grew up in his house and in his church. Does that make things make more sense?"

"Who and what are you talking about, Mother Hobbs?"

"I'm talking about the object of your unrequited affection. Although I'm not so sure it's really unrequited."

"You got some serious herbs in that tea, old woman. I have no idea—"

Mother Hobbs held up her hand to let Quinton know his innocent protest was wasted on her. "Please, boy. Ain't nothing wrong with my tea. And ain't nothing wrong with my eyes, either."

Quinton crossed his legs, then uncrossed them. He rubbed his hands together. "Okay, so what do I do?"

Mother Hobbs snorted. "If I have to tell you that, maybe you do need some of my tea."

Quinton gave an exasperated sigh.

"You got it bad, huh?"

Quinton grabbed a pillow off the couch and smothered his face with it. He lowered it to his chest and hugged it. "I didn't know it could be this bad. All day, all night . . . my brain won't focus . . . I feel totally out of control."

"Um hmm. I knew it. The minute she got this new look, I knew she'd have men chasing after her."

"No, it's not that. I mean, that's nice and all but . . . I've never met a woman like her. I'm used to gold-diggers and empty-headed women with no idea what they want out of life other than a husband. Even when I got saved, most of the women I met in church weren't really serious about God. Some of them come to church just to find a man. They're no different from women out in the world. But Shara . . ."

His voice softened when he said her name. "No, it wasn't her looks. When we were sitting at the dining room table that night and her hair was all over her head and she had on her big jeans and big sweatshirt—she was showing me her journal and showing me her soul. She stole my heart. I couldn't stop thinking about her the whole time I was in Chicago. And then when I came back and she came ringing the doorbell . . . the look was the icing on the cake."

He put the pillow over his head and moaned. "I have to admit, I'm not used to a woman not falling at my feet. I swear, if she doesn't feel anything for me . . . I'm gonna have to find a new job in another city."

Mother Hobbs chuckled softly. "My, oh my.

Ain't this something? Now Quinton, I told you I don't meddle in other folks business. All I'll say is don't pack your bags."

Quinton sat up on the edge of his chair. "Has she said anything about me?"

"No."

He flopped back in his seat, putting the pillow over his face again.

"But she doesn't have to. I know her very well."

Quinton pulled the pillow away from one eye and peeked out at Mother Hobbs. She laughed, shaking her head. She patted the seat on the couch next to her. He moved his lanky body next to her, hugging the pillow tightly.

"You're going to have to be patient, loving, and gentle."

He listened intently for her to finish. She didn't say anything else.

"That's it? That's all the advice you're gonna give me? Patient, loving, and gentle? You're supposed to be helping me here."

"Quinton, I promise, that's all the help you need." She winked at him and patted his cheek.

"Yeah?"

She nodded. "Yeah."

Chapter Twenty-six

Shara ran into Keeva leaving the education building after class. They were finishing up finals and were about to start their summer classes.

"Hey, wanna get something to eat?" Shara asked.

Keeva smiled the biggest smile Shara had ever seen on her face. "Nope, can't make it. I have a dance class."

"What?"

Keeva looked like her face was going to burst open. "Yep. I'm starting modern classes twice a week for the whole summer. I wanted to do a little African and jazz too, but I figured I better start slow."

"That's great. I'm proud of you." Shara gave Keeva a hug. "Listen, speaking of dance. We're having this big summer kick-off dance party for the kids at church. Quinton and I wanted to know if you would help chaperone."

"Quinton and I?"

Shara punched her arm playfully. "Don't start. He's the youth pastor, I'm a youth leader. That's all there is to it."

"I don't know. I kinda like the way it sounds."

"Stop playing, Keeva. Do you want to help us out or what?"

"When is it?"

"Friday night."

Keeva frowned. "Why the short notice? Mark and I already have plans."

"Come on. You have to come." Shara bit her lip. "Can't you go out with Mark on Saturday?"

"What's up with you?" Keeva's eyes widened. "Oh, I get it. You don't want to be there alone with Quinton. I'm the buffer person."

Shara punched her again playfully. "It's nothing like that. We have to have a certain number of chaperones per kid and we're expecting a lot of kids to show up. Pleeeeease!"

"Mark would kill me. Do you know how many times I've blown him off to hang out with you? I already told him you and I would be working on a summer project on Tuesdays and Thursdays so I could go to my dance classes."

"Why?"

"I don't know. I didn't feel like having that conversation with him I guess. I'm excited about dancing again and I don't want anything to mess that up."

Shara had long made a policy never to press Keeva about the things in her relationship with Mark that seemed *so* wrong. She pressed her lips together to keep the question from slipping out.

"I know, Shara. Please, just don't say anything."

Shara made a zipping motion over her lips. "Your secret's safe with me."

On Friday night, Shara changed clothes four times before getting exasperated. She pulled off her jeans and laid them across the bed. *What does one wear when chaperoning a youth party?* Why did she care anyway?

She finally settled on jeans and a blue knit top with spaghetti straps. She admired herself in the mirror for a second. "You go, girl, with yo' fine self."

As she was heading out the door, the phone rang. "Hello?"

"Shara?"

"Keeva? I thought you were going out with Mark."

"I sorta told him one of my little white lies. I wanted to be there for you tonight. Can you pick me up on your way?"

"Yeah, that's great." Shara let out a deep breath. "I mean not about lying to Mark, but great that you can go. I'll be there in about twenty minutes."

"Great. I'll be downstairs when you get here."

Keeva was pacing back and forth muttering to herself when Shara drove up. She slammed the car door when she got in.

Shara raised her eyebrows. "Are you okay?"

"Mark got mad at me for canceling. We had a *huge* argument. That means I'll have to make it up to him later."

"How?"

Keeva stared at her. "What planet are you from?" She shook her head. "Let's just go have a good time. I hope the music is good because I really need to dance."

"How were your dance classes this week?"

Keeva's face changed from dark to bright. "Absolutely awesome! It was like I never stopped. It felt soooo good. I felt like I was me again. It felt like I—"

"Came home from a long journey after being away for a long time?"

"Yeah." Keeva thought and smiled. "Yeah."

Shara slapped her palm to her forehead. "I can't believe I did that."

"What?"

"Finished your sentence. That's one of Quinton's annoying habits I guess I picked up."

"Quinton's habits, huh?"

Shara narrowed her eyes. "Do you get a special joy out of teasing me about him or what? I told you, he's the youth pastor, I'm a youth leader. We work together. That's all."

"Am I sensing an 'I wish it was more than that' in your voice?"

"No! What is it with you and Mother Hobbs? We've become friends and we work well together. That's all, and no, I don't wish it was any more than that. That would really complicate matters."

"That means you've thought about it then?"

"Keeva! Don't say another word until we get to the church."

"What—am I on punishment or something? Am I one of your kids now?"

"Yes, you're on punishment. Sit there and don't say anything. And wipe that smirk off your face, too."

"Okay, but thou protesteth too loudly."

"Keeva!"

"Okay, I'm shutting up. I won't say another word about you and Quinton. Except that I think—"

"Keeva!"

"OKAY!"

They were silent for a few minutes until Shara couldn't help herself. "Except that you think what?"

"Unh uh. I'm not saying a word. Lips are sealed. Keeva Banks is quiet as commanded."

"I'm taking you right back to your apartment to be with Mark if you don't tell me what you were about to say."

"Nothing. Except that I think you guys would make a great couple."

"Whatever, Keeva. It's not like that."

"Come on, you have to admit it. Being around you guys is weird. You think alike, you're passionate about the same things, you're both so into God, you love the same music. I won't mention the fact that he is FINE! You can't tell me you haven't thought about all that."

"No, I haven't." Shara was silent for a few seconds. "Okay, maybe a little. Okay, maybe a lot. Okay, maybe it's starting to completely and totally take over my every thought." Shara squeezed her forehead as if she was trying to squeeze the thoughts out of her mind.

"I knew it!" Keeva smirked.

"Whatever, Keeva."

"I knew it, I knew it, I knew it! I *told* Mother Hobbs—"

"You talked to Mother Hobbs about me and Quinton?"

"We really didn't talk about it. She pointed to you staring at Quinton in the pulpit with these dreamy eyes and I nodded at her and gave her one of those 'yeah, I noticed it too' looks and that was it. I promise."

"When was I staring at Quinton in the pulpit? I wasn't staring at Quinton in the pulpit. Oh my goodness! Do you think anyone else noticed? I'm never going to church again."

Keeva laughed. "Would you chill out? Look at you. You're a nervous wreck. I shouldn't have even said anything. I should have let you two go on, playing this 'I don't really feel anything' game until you both implode. Now you're gonna be all goofy tonight."

Shara knitted her eyebrows. "You're right. I *am* going to be all goofy and then he's gonna notice and . . . oh I just can't go."

Keeva giggled. "You are hilarious."

"Keeva, this isn't funny! Help me! I don't want to be all goofy."

Keeva stopped laughing and patted Shara on the arm. "Shara, just be yourself. Don't be afraid of the way you feel. I'm sure he feels the same way about you, too."

"I can't believe you said that! You're supposed to be helping me, not making it worse. Now I'm going to be watching him to try to figure out how he feels about me and then I'll be all goofy because of how I feel about him. Thanks a lot. You've set this evening off to a great start."

Keeva giggled, but patted Shara again, sympathetically. "No you're not. You're gonna relax and be yourself, and you're gonna have a good time tonight." She gritted her teeth. "And I'm gonna have a good time tonight and dance and not think about Mark James not even one time."

Shara kept shaking her head and mumbling to herself until they pulled up in the church parking lot. She turned off the car and sat there. "I'm not going in."

"Stop being silly. Yes you are. By the way, you look great. Those jeans really fit you nice—they show off all your curves and stuff."

Shara's mouth flew open. "Keeva, I hate you with every fiber of my being."

"Yeah, I love you too. Now come on."

Chapter Twenty-seven

When Shara and Keeva walked into the gym, Quinton was talking to a young man who must have been the DJ. He was setting up a table with electronic equipment and some huge speakers. Quinton waved and walked over to where they were. He gave Keeva a hug.

"Hey, glad to see you. Shara said you couldn't make it."

"Last minute change of plans." Keeva smiled. "You gonna be my dance partner tonight?"

"Please. I would dance circles around you."

Quinton stepped over to hug Shara. When he stepped back, he said, "You look great this evening, Shara. You gonna save a dance for me?"

Shara smoothed back her hair. "Oh . . . no, uh, I'll leave the dancing up to you and Keeva. Somebody has to, uh, keep an eye on the kids."

Quinton pointed toward a large table off to the side. "Let's get this stuff set up. Can you guys get the punch and the snacks ready?" Quinton walked around to some of the other youth leaders and assigned tasks to them also.

After an hour of preparations, they were ready for the kids to arrive. Quinton took one last walk around to make sure everything was set up and then came over to where Shara and Keeva were standing. "I think everything is ready."

"Everything looks great, Quinton. It'll be fine," Keeva said.

He rubbed his chin. "Do you think they'll show up?"

Keeva patted his arm. "They'll come, Quinton. Relax."

Tina came up behind Quinton and linked her arm into his. "All the decorations are done. Do you need me to do anything else?"

"No, Tina, I think we're fine. Thanks, though."

She didn't let go of his arm. "If you need anything else done, let me know. Save me a dance later?"

Quinton unhooked her hand from his arm. "I'm not much of a dancer, Tina. I'll probably be keeping an eye on things with the kids. I'll let you know if anything else needs taking care of."

As she walked away, Keeva nudged Shara. "Who is that?"

Quinton overheard and answered. "An annoying, persistent individual."

Shara grimaced and turned her back. "Speaking of annoying, persistent individuals . . ."

Terrence walked in the back door to the gym.

Quinton looked at his watch. "Gee, he's just in time not to help."

Shara kept her back turned. "He's not coming over here is he? I am *so* not in the mood for him."

Quinton grinned. "Don't worry, Shara. He won't be bothering you tonight or any other night for that matter."

"Why?"

"He just won't."

"How do you know?"

"I just do."

Shara narrowed her eyes at Quinton. "What did you do?"

"Don't worry about it. Just know he won't be bothering you."

The front door of the gym opened and about twenty kids poured in.

"Gary must have just gotten here with the van. He's got one more group to bring." Quinton signaled to the DJ.

The DJ started playing a gospel rap song. "It's time to get your *PRAAAAAISE ONNNNN*!"

Quinton started moving to the music. "Gospel Gangstaz. That's my jam!"

"Everything's your jam, Quinton," Shara said.

He stopped dancing. "You got a problem with that?"

She laughed. "No, Quinton. Jam on."

He started dancing again.

The kids that came in headed straight for the food and punch. They stood around the table eating for a while then broke off into small clusters, talking. A second group of about eighteen

more came in the front door. A few more strag-
gled in here and there. All of them stayed away
from the dance floor.

Quinton nodded. "Good turnout."

Keeva looked around. "I guess kids aren't any
different than when we were kids. I wonder
how long they're gonna stand and hold up the
walls. We need to set this off." She held out a
hand to Quinton. "Come on, Quint."

His eyes widened as he gave Keeva an 'I'm
not going out there' look.

"You're as bad as these kids. Shara, come on.
Quinton can stay here if he wants to. I'm sure
he's afraid of getting embarrassed by us."

"Embarrassed? Please. It's *on*. Let's see what
you got." Keeva and Quinton headed for the
middle of the gym.

Shara stayed behind. "You guys go ahead. I'll
watch."

Quinton was suave and smooth, and didn't
do much in the way of steps, but looked good
doing the little bit he was doing. Keeva started
out slow and low key with him. She then ap-
parently got bored and did some more complicated steps.

The DJ put on Tonex's song, " 'Bout A Thang",
and it was all over. Keeva came unglued and
pulled out some fancy hip-hop steps. Quinton
was obviously in over his head, but continued
his suave dance, not even bothering to try to
match Keeva's skill. The kids gathered closer to
watch her.

Shanique inched closer and closer and finally started dancing with Keeva, matching her

step for step. Keeva did a turn and then a faster step. Shanique stayed right with her. Then it was Shanique's turn to do a complicated step-turn rhythm that Keeva matched with ease. Pretty soon, all the kids were gathered around them in a circle, cheering them on.

Shara was impressed. Keeva could really dance. Quinton rejoined her on the sidelines.

She smiled up at him. "What was that you were saying about 'it's on, let me see what you got?'"

Quinton held up his hands. "Man, she got skills a brotha didn't even know about. I can't mess with her. That girl there, though." He pointed at Shanique. "She's giving her some trouble."

Shara eyed Shanique who was giving it all she had. The other kids were loosening up and dancing in their circle around Keeva and Shanique. Jamil obviously decided to take them on and pushed his way into the middle of the circle. Shara soon wondered if he had a bone in his body because he seemed to be able to twist and shake his body in ways that shouldn't have been possible. When he jumped up in the air and landed in a split, all the kids cheered.

Quinton shook his head. "Okay see, I'm totally out of my league."

More of the kids decided to show their skills. Keeva was able to keep up with whatever they did.

Quinton turned to Shara. "What—you don't dance? You're the only one left holding up the walls here."

"I don't see you out there anymore either since you got showed up, so don't even try it."

Quinton looked Shara up and down. "I figure you a church girl, so you oughta be just about my speed." He bowed and extended his hand as an invitation for her to dance.

Shara blushed. "Stop playing, Quinton."

He left his hand out. "Aw come on now. You ain't gonna leave a brotha hangin' like that are you?"

Shara giggled at his pitiful, rejected look. She slowly reached out to take his hand and then followed him over to where everybody else was dancing.

Her timid, self-conscious style matched his smooth, easy one, and they danced for a few songs. She relaxed and began to enjoy herself. Every once in a while, she'd let herself go and do a more complicated step.

Quinton looked impressed. "I see you got skills, too. Just holdin' out on me, huh? I appreciate you trying not to embarrass a brotha. That's more than I can say for your friend there." They both looked over at Keeva who was still dancing with the kids.

"She is out of control," Shara said.

Keeva had a group around her she was taking through some steps slowly, showing them the movements. After they mastered the steps, the whole group did them up to tempo. They all got excited and slapped hands when they conquered a step. Soon, they did a whole sequence of steps as a group. It looked like something out of a music video.

Danae was waving wildly and screaming over the music. "Miss Shara! Look at us—watch this!"

Shara looked at Quinton and nodded toward the kids. "Come on."

The DJ started the song over and they started their dance from the top. Shara was impressed at the steps Keeva put together and how well she had taught the kids to do them. When they finished, Keeva walked away, but the kids grabbed her and begged her to dance some more. She pleaded with them to let her go get something to drink.

Keeva gulped down a whole cup of punch and then held her cup out for Quinton to pour some more. "I can't believe how thirsty I am." She gulped the second cup down and held the glass out for one more.

"I wonder why? You danced like a wild woman for at least an hour straight." Quinton waited to see if she would want some more punch.

"Was it that long? It didn't feel like it." Keeva pulled her sweaty shirt away from her skin.

"Where did you learn to dance like that?" Shara said. "I thought you were a modern dancer—all 'culturified' like you say."

Keeva fanned herself. "Girl, you'd be surprised at what you pick up watching BET and VH1 all night when you can't sleep."

Danae and Shanique ran up to get some punch. Danae latched her arm into Keeva's. "Miss Keeva, you da bomb! Will you be our dance teacher?"

Shanique linked her arm into Keeva's other arm. "Yeah, Miss Keeva. Miss Shara said she was finding us a dance teacher and we want you. You dance better than Janet Jackson."

"I'm not that good. Tell you what. Let me talk to Minister Quinton and Miss Shara. I don't want to make any promises until I talk to them."

"Puleeeeze!" Danae begged.

"Danae! She said we'd talk about it." Shara pulled the girls off Keeva and directed them back to the dance floor. "Now y'all go ahead and dance. Go on." They went back to the group of kids that were going through Keeva's dance sequence again.

Quinton looked at Shara. "You're such a little mother."

"What's that supposed to mean?"

"Nothing. I like the way you handle the kids, that's all. They respect you a lot and listen to whatever you tell them to do. That's rare."

Shara smiled shyly. She ignored Keeva's grinning.

Tina came over to the punch bowl. "Quinton, I thought you weren't dancing. You weren't just being shy with me, were you? I saw you out there. Is it my turn?"

Quinton put his hand on his chest. "Whew—I'm exhausted. I don't think I can dance another step. Thanks though, Tina."

Tina shot Shara an evil look and walked off.

Shara turned to Keeva and gave her a 'did you see how she looked at me?' look. Keeva gave her a "I know girl, what's her problem?' look.

Anthony came over and asked Keeva if she

wanted to dance. She looked at him like she was sizing him up. "You think you can hang?"

"I can hang. Come on. Let me show you what I got."

Shara and Quinton were soon stifling laughter as they watched from the edge of the dance floor. Anthony had *three* left feet and no rhythm, but was dancing with attitude as if he was the world's greatest dancer. Keeva obviously decided to take it easy on him and kept it slow. They danced for a few songs, and then Keeva came back over to where Quinton and Shara were.

"Girl, was he pitiful or what?" Shara asked.

"Oh, don't say that, girl. He was cute. Don't anybody tell him he can't dance either."

Shara leaned in close. "Uh oh, Miss Keeva, you're not playing the 'don't get one man, always have two' game, are you?"

"Girl, please. I barely want the one I got. I was just dancing."

The kids left in big groups as they had come when Gary announced it was time for them to load up the van. Danae and Shanique came over and begged Keeva once more to be their dance teacher.

"Time to go, ladies," Shara said.

"Wait, Miss Shara, we'll stay and help you clean up. You can drop us off. Miss Keeva, can you take us home if we stay and help?"

"You guys know better. Come on, let's go," Shara said.

They both gave Keeva a big hug before they left. "Thank you, Miss Keeva. We love you, Miss Keeva. See you soon, Miss Keeva."

Keeva waved as Shara dragged them to the door.

Most of the other youth leaders left to grab a late dinner at IHOP. Keeva nudged Shara in time for her to see Tina's arm looped through Terrence's as they walked out the door together.

"She finally caught her one. Now she can leave your man alone," Keeva said.

"Would you stop saying that?" Shara was only slightly annoyed.

She looked around the gym and sucked her teeth. "I can't believe everybody is leaving. I guess they think some magic fairy is gonna come in here and clean all this stuff all up. Keev, do you mind staying around to help? I can't leave Quinton with all this mess."

"Can't leave Quinton, huh?" She grinned and dodged Shara swatting at her.

Quinton came over with a huge trash bag. "You gotta be kidding me. They all left? Man, black folk is trifling. You'd think church people would be different, but they just as trifling." Quinton continued muttering under his breath as he went around the gym picking up trash.

When they had everything cleaned up, Quinton came over to where Shara and Keeva were packing up the decorations. "Thank you so much for staying to help. I would have been here 'til tomorrow if you'd left. You have to let me take you guys out to get some dinner."

Shara looked at her watch. "It's too late to eat and I have to get Keeva home."

"Shara, please." Keeva rolled her eyes. "I need some food after all that dancing. And it is not late. I swear, you are such an old lady."

Quinton laughed. "I'll take that as a yes?"

"I'm in. Miss Fuddy-Duddy can do whatever she wants to."

Shara rubbed her hands together nervously and followed Keeva and Quinton out the door.

Chapter Twenty-eight

They pulled up at the IHOP and noticed some of the other youth leaders were finishing and getting ready to leave.

Malcolm asked, "Y'all just now getting here? We're all through eating."

"Somebody had to stay and clean up." Quinton had a bit of an edge to his voice.

"My bad, man. Why didn't y'all say nothing? We would have stayed and helped."

"Why should I have to say anything? You guys saw the mess before you left. How did you think it was gonna get cleaned up?" Shara put her hand on Quinton's arm, hoping to calm him down a little.

He took a deep breath. "Don't worry about it, man. You guys will have clean up duty next time."

Quinton and Malcolm slapped hands and Malcolm and the others left.

Quinton started muttering under his breath again about black folk being trifling.

Shara steered him toward their table. "Let it go, Quinton. It's not worth being upset over."

"You're right. I just can't believe he had the nerve to say—"

"Quinton, let it go." Shara patted his arm again as they sat down.

"All right, Miss Shara. But only 'cause you said so." He flashed her a Kool-Aid smile as he flipped open his menu. "Now what us gon' eat?"

Keeva ordered a chicken Caesar salad. After studying the menu, Shara ordered a salad also. Keeva gave Shara a 'I can't believe you ordered a salad' look, but Shara refused to make eye contact with her. Quinton ordered steak and eggs and a double order of pancakes.

Keeva gawked. "You can't possibly eat that much."

"Yes, he can. You should have seen him at the bowling alley. He put away a whole pizza by himself."

"You guys went bowling?" Keeva asked.

"A bunch of us went after a youth meeting. It was spur of the moment. Anyway, we didn't stay very long," Shara said.

"Yeah, I had to rescue Shara from the evil Terrence's advances."

"Whatever, Quinton. We left because we got tired."

"Yeah, right, Shara. If we hadn't left, I think I would have had to rescue Terrence from you. You looked like you wanted to crack his head open with that bowling ball."

Shara laughed. "Yeah, the thought did cross my mind. What did you say to him anyway? He didn't come within twenty feet of me tonight."

"I told him he needed to step off."

"That's all?"

"I sorta told him we were seeing each other and if he ever stepped to you again, he'd have to deal with me."

Shara's mouth flew open. This obviously struck Keeva as funny. Shara had to kick her under the table to stop her from laughing.

"I can't believe you told him that."

"Why? It worked didn't it?" Quinton pouted.

"I'm sorry, Quinton, I didn't mean it like that." Shara patted his hand. "Stop pouting. I appreciate you handling Terrence for me. He gives me the creeps."

"What did he do?" Keeva asked.

"He called himself teaching Shara how to bowl, when he was really just trying to feel all over her. I thought I was gonna have to punch him in his face."

"My hero." Shara smiled at Quinton and he blushed and fidgeted with his silverware. Keeva looked at Quinton, then at Shara, then back at Quinton again and smiled.

Quinton snapped his fingers as if he was remembering something. "I gotta take my boy Jamil to get him some sneaks tomorrow. He ended up the school year with all B's and C's. I told him next year we're going for all A's and B's."

"I see you got a little pet, huh?" Shara asked.

"Yeah, that's my boy. I guess he reminds me of my little brother."

Shara looked at Quinton. He never mentioned his brother. "Really? How?" she asked, gently.

"I don't know. They don't look anything alike. I guess following me everywhere, wanting to go everywhere I go, treating me like I'm the world's greatest guy. He's always running behind me, asking me questions, talking about his future and all the stuff he wants to do when he gets out of the projects. That's how Quintell was."

Shara had never even heard Quinton say his brother's name before. She said, "Jamil's a great kid. He's so smart. If I could get him to stop clowning all the time, he could really get somewhere."

"Yeah, he is a jokester. I think he does that to cover up for all the stuff going on inside of him and around him." Quinton fiddled with the butter dish on the table. "Quintell was like that, too. That boy was so funny. I don't care how bad I felt or what was going on, he could always make me laugh."

Quinton looked around for the waitress. "Man, I'm hungry. Can they bring me out some toast or something? I'm ready to start eating this butter."

When the waitress brought their food, Quinton dug in before she could get the plate on the table good.

"Dag, Quinton, were you hungry or what?" Shara said.

Keeva stared at her. "He eats like somebody else I know."

"Ouch!" Keeva rubbed her shin where Shara kicked her again.

Quinton looked up from his food. "You okay? What happened?"

Keeva winced. "I banged my ankle on the metal thingee under the table."

Quinton dug into his food again. Shara picked at her salad. The smell of the steamy syrup and butter rising up off of Quinton's pancakes made her mouth water.

Quinton finally came up for air after half his pancakes and steak were gone. He looked over at Shara's plate. "You want some of my food?"

"No, I'm fine. I really wasn't that hungry." At that moment, Shara's stomach rumbled. Keeva didn't catch her giggle before it escaped so she pretended to be having a coughing fit.

Quinton patted her on the back. "You okay?"

"Yeah, I think a crouton went down the wrong way." Keeva took a sip of water. She jerked her leg out of the way before Shara could kick her in the shin again.

Quinton looked under the table. "What's wrong, Keeva?"

"Nothing, just a little leg spasm, you know, from all the dancing," she lied.

Shara coughed and cleared her throat. "Speaking of dancing, Miss Keeva. Are you gonna be our dance teacher?" Shara linked her arm through Keeva's and mocked Danae. "Puleeze?"

"She is so cute. What's her name again?" Keeva asked.

Shara rolled her eyes. "Danae? Cute? She is spoiled rotten."

Quinton raised his eyebrows. "And who made her that way?"

"I may have had a little something to do with it." Shara gave a guilty grin. "Okay, I admit, since Tangee left, she's become my little shadow."

"Her little brother is equally cute," Quinton said. "Tiquan—that's my little basketball buddy. He's always begging me to take him home with me. I wish I could. He tries to be such a little tough guy because the bigger boys always make fun of him." He got a faraway look in his eyes. "He kinda reminds me of Quintell, too." Quinton attacked his pancakes again.

Shara watched him closely while talking to Keeva. "I can't believe Shanique, though. She never gives me anything but attitude and lip. She was all hugged up on you and didn't want to leave you. I've never seen her like that before." She thought for a minute. "I wonder where her cut-buddy, Lakita, was tonight. She usually never misses anything we have. I'll have to check on her tomorrow."

Keeva studied Shara and Quinton. "You guys really love these kids, huh?"

"Yeah," they said simultaneously and smiled.

Shara pushed her lettuce around on the plate. She had picked out all the chicken and eaten it. "They're something else. There's nothing more rewarding than seeing them grow. Like when their grades come up, or when they start talking about going to college and dreaming about what they can become. It's amazing what a little love will do. It makes all the work worth it."

Keeva thought for a moment. "I think I'll do it then. What would it be? Two classes a week?"

"Really?" Shara said.

Keeva nodded slowly. "Yeah. I want to do it. I *need* to do it. I don't know what it feels like to make a difference in someone's life."

"You've made a difference in my life. A huge difference," Shara said.

"What do you mean?"

"You're my friend. Friends always make a difference."

"I know. But I'm talking about life-changing stuff like with you guys and the kids."

"You've changed my life a lot. I used to be a little church mouse that never did anything. Now I've seen Alvin Ailey, eaten Thai food, and even sushi—although I'm not sure it counts if it doesn't stay down."

They all laughed.

"That's not to mention all the other changes," Shara said.

Quinton looked up from his pancakes. "What changes?"

"Nothing, Quinton." Shara blushed.

Quinton shook his head. "See, that's why I hate hanging out with women. Always got little secrets. Didn't your momma ever tell you it was rude to keep secrets? Y'all ain't slick. You kicking Keeva under the table and her laughing and pretending she's coughing. Quinton Mercer ain't no fool. Keep your little secrets. Don't nobody care." Quinton pouted.

Shara patted his arm. "You are such a big baby, Quinton."

She turned to Keeva. "Seriously, though.

That would be great. Two times a week would be perfect. We have to see what room we could use."

Keeva's eyes lit up. "The gym would be best because of the wood floor. The only problem is there's no mirrors. I'd like the girls to be able to see themselves when they dance. It does a lot for their self-esteem."

"I don't know about that, Keeva. Money is kinda tight in terms of renovations. We're trying to get this big grant now, but it will be months before we find anything out and then even longer before the money comes," Shara said.

Quinton finished off his pancakes and dropped his napkin on his plate. "It shouldn't be a problem. I'll mention the mirrors to Pastor Kendrick tomorrow. We may even be able to get another room done with hardwood floors and mirrors. I'm not so sure we want mirrors on the walls of a basketball court. That's an accident waiting to happen."

Shara eyes bugged out at Quinton. "Do you know something I don't know? Last I heard we were having a major budget crunch."

Quinton rubbed his chin. "Pastor and I have been discussing alternative sources of funding. It shouldn't be a problem."

"If you say so, Quinton," Shara said.

They sat and worked out the details of Keeva's dance classes and then stood to leave.

Shara looked at her watch. "Can you believe it's one in the morning?"

Quinton put an arm on her shoulder and led her toward the door. "I know. We have you out way past your bedtime. Tomorrow is Saturday. You can sleep late."

Quinton walked them to Shara's car. He gave them both a hug and a kiss on the cheek and watched until they drove away.

Keeva sighed. "He is absolutely wonderful. What are you waiting for?"

"What do you mean what am I waiting for?"

"I don't know, make your move, jump his bones, do something!"

"You are so silly. Quinton and I are friends."

"Whatever, Shara."

"Quinton's a really nice guy. He treats me the same as everyone else. He's a gentleman, that's all."

"Are you trying to convince me or yourself?"

Shara's voice got quiet. "I don't want to like him and think he likes me and then find out he really doesn't like me. I'd rather him surprise me by liking me than for me to think he likes me, but he really doesn't like me like that. Know what I mean?

Keeva laughed. "I think I understand, Shar. Don't worry about it, okay? I know these things." She rubbed Shara's arm. "He likes you."

Chapter Twenty-nine

"Dance class? What do you mean?" Mark came over on Saturday morning for brunch. He sat at the table reading the newspaper while Keeva made crepes in the kitchen.

"Mark, I've told you about this before. By the time you and I met, I had pretty much stopped dancing. But before then, dancing was my life. I want to start dancing again. Actually, I've started dancing again.

He frowned. "What?"

"I'm taking classes twice a week now, brushing up on my skills, getting back in shape."

"Well, if it's important to you, then I'm all for it."

Keeva smiled. She hadn't expected that response from Mark. "Oh and . . . I'm also going to teach some dance classes."

Mark looked up from his newspaper. "Where?"

"At a community center."

"Where?"

Here we go. "It over on Hilliard Street, off Edgewood."

Mark frowned. "Where is that?"

Keeva walked toward the kitchen and poured herself some juice. "Down the street from the school. Near Grady Homes.

Mark put his newspaper down. "Keeva, that's a terrible neighborhood. Why would you want to teach there? How did you get involved with this anyway?"

Keeva sat down at the table and told Mark about the program at the church. She talked about all the wonderful things they were already doing and the changes in the kids, but he frowned the whole time. She made the mistake of getting too excited and telling him about how much fun she had with the kids at the dance party.

"You were in that neighborhood at night? Keeva, that's insane!"

"Mark, it's perfectly safe. The neighborhood has gotten a lot better in the past few years since the church has been there. Nobody bothers us and the parking lot is fenced in." Keeva walked back into the kitchen to finish the crepes.

"Who is us?"

"Well, Shara runs the program with Quinton, who's—"

"Shara." His lips tightened. "I should have known. Ever since you met this Shara person, you've ceased to make any rational sense. You start going to this weird church and staying out all times of the night and now you want to hang out in that neighborhood and teach dance classes to a bunch of hoodlum kids?"

"They're not hoodlum kids. You don't even know them. Why would you say something like that?"

"I don't understand. If you want to help children, why don't you teach dance classes in Buckhead or Dunwoody or somewhere safe? Why do you have to teach bad kids?"

"They're not bad kids. People assume they're bad, but they're regular kids like you and I were. They just need someone to take an interest in them and help them do something with their lives." Keeva was surprised at how much she sounded like Shara.

Mark sighed and picked up his newspaper. "I don't think it's a good idea. If you want to teach dance, that's great. Find somewhere else to do it." He turned the page and started reading.

"I've already made a commitment. I'll be starting the classes in a couple of weeks."

Mark put the newspaper down. "So I don't get any say-so in this at all? Why bother to tell me then?" Mark's voice echoed off her 12-foot ceilings.

Keeva slammed down the skillet. "I bothered to tell you because I thought you might be interested in what I was doing. Not for you to control me and decide whether I should do it or not."

Mark jumped. "Okay, Princess, I'm sorry. Don't get upset. You don't have to slam things and yell."

"Oh, you can yell, but I can't? And stop calling me Princess."

"What in the world has gotten into you?" Mark came into the kitchen and put his arms around her. "I'm worried about you. All these changes and now you're yelling at me. This is not like you to behave this way."

"Mark, you don't even know what's like me." Keeva pulled away from him and picked up the pieces of mushrooms and green peppers that had flown out of the skillet.

"Princess, I mean, Keeva, please. There's nothing so bad that we can't talk about it or work it out." He pulled her toward him and kissed her.

She pulled away, wiping her mouth. "Is that your answer for everything, Mark?" She put the juice and eggs back into the refrigerator. She'd never been this honest with Mark. She smiled when she turned her back to him. "I'm teaching this class. If you'd prefer, in the future I won't tell you what I'm doing."

"That's no way to have a relationship." He walked up to her slowly. "If that's what you want to do, then go ahead. But if something happens to you, I don't want to hear about it."

"Fine, you won't."

"Are you going to behave like this for the rest of the morning?"

"Like what?" Keeva didn't mean to snap at him, but once she decided to let her real feelings show, it was hard to put them back in the box.

"Like this whole different person I've never met before. Like you hate me and don't want me anywhere near you. Like my mere existence irritates the heck out of you. Like—"

"I get the point." Keeva took a deep breath.

"Mark, we need to make some changes in our relationship."

"Our relationship is fine, or at least it was fine until—"

"Until what?"

"I don't understand the person you're becoming. I talked to Jade the other day and she said you left in the middle of having drinks because of this Shara person. We haven't had our monthly Sunday dinner at your parents' in months. You're moody all the time and short with me. You won't make love to me anymore. Can you talk to me about what's going on?"

Keeva held Mark's hand. "Sweetie, when I try to talk to you, you don't listen. When you do listen, you get agitated and upset. I don't feel like we're getting anywhere."

"What are you suggesting we do then?"

Keeva looked away and let out a long sigh. "I don't know what the answer is."

"You're not thinking about ending the relationship are you?"

The panicked look on his face was too much for Keeva. She put her arms around him. "No, I'm not thinking about ending the relationship." She bit her tongue at that lie. Truth was, she had been thinking about it quite a bit lately. Not for long because it was a scary thought. They had been together for such a long time, that whether good or bad, he was a part of her life. She kissed his cheek and sent him back out to the table. She finished the crepes and he went back to reading his newspaper as if nothing had happened.

She joined him at the table and they ate in silence for a while.

"Mark, it's not that I don't want to make love to you anymore. It's just that . . ." Keeva let out a deep breath.

"What, sweetheart?" He reached out to touch her hand.

"I . . . I want to be celibate now, until I get married." She looked down at her plate.

He kept eating as if he hadn't heard a word she said. Then he spoke slowly. "I'm really trying to be patient with all these changes. I guess this is because of this new church of yours. Did you take some religious oath or something?"

"It's not a 'religious oath.' It's just that . . . you know, premarital sex is a sin."

"So now it's a sin. We've been together for almost four years and now it's some god-awful sin? That's what they teach in that crazy church of yours?"

"It's not a crazy church. And it has nothing to do with that church in particular. Any church would say the same thing. Remember when we went to church all the time when we first got together? Remember when we both decided we were going to wait until we got married because we wanted to be right with God?"

Mark smiled. "I remember." His smile faded. "That was a long time ago. We're practically married now. I don't understand why stopping now would make any difference."

"Honey, I realize I'm asking a lot. Can you understand this, though? I'm happier now than I've been in a long time, maybe ever. I feel like I'm coming alive after being dead. I'm finding out who I am and discovering what I like and what I want and don't want. I need you to allow me to do that, Mark. I need to figure out who I am and be free to be that person. If I can't do that in this relationship, then . . ." She left her next thought unsaid.

"Then what?"

"Then nothing. I need you to try to understand."

"I'll try, Keeva." He bit his lip. "The sex thing though, do we have to stop all at once, or can we gradually wean off of it because, well, you know."

Keeva laughed. Mark looked so cute and vulnerable asking her that. "I . . . promise me you'll try to understand that this celibacy thing is important to me and we'll go from there."

He seemed satisfied with that. He reached across the table and took her hand. "How'd I do?"

"What do you mean?"

"We talked. You told me how you felt. I listened. We didn't yell at each other and although we may not have arrived at a consensus, at least we somewhat understand each other."

"You did well, honey." Keeva rubbed Mark's hand. "You did well."

She avoided looking into his eyes so he wouldn't see her wonder whether it would be enough.

Chapter Thirty

Shara rounded the track, pushing herself a little harder. When she completed four miles, she looked at her watch. Her time was better than yesterday, but still not where she wanted it to be. As she did her cool down laps, she slipped into her usual routine of talking to God.

So many things had been on her mind lately she wanted to talk to Him about. She was excited about Keeva starting her dance classes. The basketball programs were in full swing. The grant would be reviewed soon, and if awarded, could make a big difference in how much the church could expand their programs. She sat on a patch of grass to do her cool down stretches. When she lifted her head up from a hamstring stretch, Quinton was there, looking down at her.

"Oh!" She jumped.

"Sorry, didn't mean to scare you."

"What are you doing here?"

"Why do I always seem to evoke that response in you? I came to run. Is that okay?"

"I'm sorry. You scared me. I'm not used to anybody else being out here this time of the morning." She stretched the other hamstring.

"Yeah, I'm going at it a little earlier today. I had no idea Atlanta would be this hot. I may have to switch my running time."

"Hot? You ain't seen nothing yet. Besides, this can't be as bad as Orlando." She stood up.

"That's true, but I was only in Orlando for a minute. I'm from Chicago, remember?" Quinton smiled. "Who were you talking to?"

Shara froze. "How long have you been here?"

"Long enough to watch you have a serious conversation with nobody else around. It's okay. I talk to myself, too."

"I wasn't talking to myself," she said shyly. "I was talking to God. I always do that at the end of my run."

He stared at her with that intense gaze of his. "What were you talking about?"

"Stuff."

"What stuff?" He looked into her eyes with a slight smile on his lips.

"Private stuff between me and God." She stretched out her quads. "You know, stuff. Just praying for everything we're doing here and for the kids and for Pastor Kendrick and his family."

I guess that's why you didn't want to take me running that morning."

Shara frowned. "Huh?"

"Remember when I was here for my interview

and Mother Hobbs suggested you pick me up to go running in the morning? You gave her the evilest look I've ever seen in my life."

Shara covered her face with her hands. "You saw that?"

Quinton laughed and nodded.

"I didn't think you saw that." She took her hands down and smiled. "It's not that I didn't want to run with you. I cherish my God-time, that's all. My day isn't right without it."

Shara stood on her toes and stretched her calves. "What?"

Quinton was still staring at her. "Nothing. I've never met anyone like you before. That's all."

Shara smoothed back her hair and looked at her watch. "I better hit the showers. I gotta get to class. See you later." She headed for the locker room.

She took a quick shower, put on her clothes, and did her hair and makeup as quickly as she could. She grabbed her bag and headed out the door.

"Oh!" She jumped and almost dropped her bag.

Quinton was standing outside the door.

"Do you purposely sneak up on me and scare me all the time?" Shara put her hand on her chest, waiting for her heart to slow back down to normal.

"Sorry. It's not on purpose. Are you always so jumpy?"

"Only when people sneak up on me."

He laughed nervously. He dug his hands in his pockets and stared down at his feet. "I was wondering if you wanted to get some dinner tonight."

Shara bit her lip. "I . . . uummm. I don't know. I . . ."

"What is up with that?"

"What's up with what?"

"I feel like I'm constantly asking you to go somewhere with me and you're always saying no. Can't you cut a brotha a little slack? Do you have to make this so difficult?"

"Make *what* so difficult?"

Quinton looked at his feet. "You know, I just moved here. I don't really have any friends. I'm trying to get to know some people and hang out."

"You've got Anthony, Malcolm, and all those guys. If I'm making things so difficult, why don't you hang out with them?"

Quinton's voice was soft. "I don't want to be with them. I want to be with you."

Shara stood there not saying anything, looking at him.

Quinton took one step closer to her. She didn't move back, and he took one more step, ever so slight.

He reached out his hand and gently stroked her cheek with his finger.

Shara started breathing faster. Her lips trembled.

He stopped them with his.

Shara could hardly breathe. His lips were so soft and sweet. Her knees went to mush. He kissed her gently and then moved back to look into her eyes again. He seemed to be waiting for a response. The look in his eyes told Shara he was as anxious as she was. She didn't want him to be. But she was frozen and couldn't say or do anything.

He stepped back and put his hand over his chest. "I'm sorry. I shouldn't have—"

Her tongue came unstuck. "Don't be."

"Don't be what?"

"Sorry."

He looked at her hopefully. "No?"

She shook her head. "No."

"Okay." He smiled, biting his bottom lip.

"Okay." She smiled, biting her top one.

They both stood there staring at each other.

Shara looked at her watch. "I . . . I better get to class. I'm already late." She could feel him watching as she walked away. She took a deep breath and turned back around. "Seven o'clock."

"What?"

"I'll meet you at the house at 7:00." She smiled.

"What?"

"Dinner. You asked me to go out to dinner."

"Oh! Yeah. Dinner. Okay. Seven is good. Seven is great. Seven is . . . perfect."

"Okay, see you at seven then."

"Yeah?

She nodded. "Yeah."

Chapter Thirty-one

Every outfit Shara owned was strewn across her bed, hanging on her bathroom door, or in a rejected heap on the floor. She had lost count of the number of times she had changed. At the risk of being teased, she decided to call Keeva for help.

"Hello." A male voice answered the phone.

"Oh! Can I . . . I'm sorry. This is Shara Anderson, a friend of Keeva's. Is she there?"

She thought she heard the man suck his teeth and take a tight breath. She was sure she heard pure venom in his voice when he said, "She's not available right now."

"Oh. Okay, well, could you tell her . . . never mind." Shara hung up the phone. What was his problem?

She flopped back on the bed, lying on her clothes. *Get over it, Shara. You're just going to dinner. Put on some clothes, get in the car, and go.*

She closed her eyes and tried to recapture the feeling of Quinton's lips against hers. She rubbed her cheek softly where his finger had caressed her. She sighed. The phone rang and brought her out of her reverie.

"Shara? Did you just call here?" It was Keeva, sounding irritated.

"Keeeeeeeeeva!" Shara sang her name. "I'm so glad you called me back. I neeeeeed you."

"What's wrong?"

"I looked all over for you at school today, but I couldn't find you."

"Shara, what is going on?"

"He kissed me!"

"What?"

"Quinton kissed me."

"I knew it! I told you! Oh my goodness!"

"Help me," Shara whined.

"What's wrong, Shar?" Keeva's voice was excited and sympathetic at the same time.

"I'm supposed to meet him at Mother Hobbs and he's taking me to dinner but—"

"Oh my God! I knew it! I told you!"

"KEEVA! Please!"

"What's wrong? I thought this is what you wanted. Remember you said—"

"I KNOW!"

"Then what's the problem?"

"I don't know what to wear." Shara described the scene in her bedroom. "Are you laughing? You're laughing. I can't believe you're laughing at me. KEEVA!"

"I'm sorry. Don't worry, girl. This is an easy one. Wear the brown."

"What?"

"The brown outfit you wore when we saw Alvin Ailey. Remember that night?"

"Oooohhhh. Are you sure? You don't think it's too—?"

"Yes, I do, and that's exactly why I think you should wear it."

"Keeva. I don't want to—"

"Shara. Trust me, okay. Have I ever steered you wrong?"

"No."

"Would I steer you wrong on this?"

"I guess not," Shara whined.

"What time are you supposed to be there? Do you want me to come do your makeup?"

"Seven."

"Shara, it's 6:15! What are you doing?"

"Trying to decide what to wear."

"Shara, get up, put on the brown outfit, put on some eyeliner and the spicy brown lipstick, and drive to Mother Hobbs house."

"Okay."

"Can you handle that?"

"Yes."

Keeva laughed. "What's wrong?"

"I'm gonna do something dumb like trip and fall, or have broccoli sticking out of my teeth or I'm gonna say something stupid—"

"Shara, you're not. You're going to be absolutely ravishingly beautiful and you're going to sweep Quinton off his feet more than you already have and it's going to be wonderful. Okay?"

"Okay."

"Now get dressed and go. Call me when you get in, no matter what time it is."

"Yeah, right, so Mark can practically cuss me out again."

"I'm sorry about that. He won't be here. He gets put out at night now."

"Really? What happened?"

"Shara, you're procrastinating. I'm hanging up the phone now so you can get dressed. Have a beautiful time. You deserve it."

"Keeva?"

"Yeah?"

"Thanks."

"Anytime."

Chapter Thirty-two

Shara rang Mother Hobbs' doorbell and stepped back. She was relieved Mother Hobbs answered the door.

"Well, sooky sooky now! Look at you, Miss Thang. You gon' mess that boy's head up looking like that."

Shara put her finger to her lips. "Hush! Don't you *dare* embarrass me."

"Child, please. Quinton can't hear me." Mother Hobbs led her into the house. "He's upstairs back and forth between his room and the bathroom where he's been for the last hour. I've never seen a man take so long to get dressed."

"Really?" Shara was vindicated to know he had experienced the same agony she had.

"I'll be right down," they heard him call from upstairs.

"You look absolutely beautiful." Mother Hobbs started to pat Shara's cheeks, but Shara pulled away.

"Ooowee. I'm sorry, Miss Thang. I didn't mean to mess up your makeup."

"Mother Hobbs, please behave when Quinton comes downstairs. Don't tease me in front of him."

"I would never do that." Mother Hobbs studied Shara. "Look at you. You're all nervous. I don't know which one of y'all is worse."

"Here I come." Quinton could be heard from upstairs again.

Shara patted her curls. Mother Hobbs pulled her hands away from her hair. "You look fine. Relax."

Quinton came down the steps. Shara bit her lip, then made herself stop so she wouldn't mess up her lipstick. He had on a pair of black slacks with an olive green knit shirt that hugged all the muscles in his chest and arms. Thankfully, he slipped a black sports jacket over it on the way down the steps. His mouth dropped open when he saw Shara. Mother Hobbs mysteriously disappeared.

He walked over and kissed her on the cheek. "Wow, you look absolutely beautiful."

"You, too." She shook her head. "I mean, you look very nice, too."

They smiled at each other.

"Ready?" Quinton bit his lip.

Shara nodded.

They called out a good night to Mother Hobbs and walked out the door. Quinton helped her up into the truck. They drove in nervous silence. Shara pulled his CD case out and thumbed through his collection. She put on a Frank Mc-Comb CD.

"Where are we going?" she asked.

"Someplace nice." Quinton smiled.

"Okay." They both seemed to be concentrating on the music.

He finally pulled up at Paschal's Restaurant. He parked and got out to help Shara out of the car.

Shara was glad for a chance to finally get to eat at Paschal's. Everyone always talked about how good the soul food was there. The hostess led them to their table. Shara perused the menu. She saw a lot of things she wanted, but decided to get a salad. She was starving, so she hoped it was a big one. Quinton ordered a slab of ribs, macaroni and cheese, candied yams, and greens. Shara frowned. Those were her favorites.

"What's wrong?"

"Nothing." She should have eaten before she came.

"Are you sure all you want is a salad?"

Shara nodded. She hoped Quinton didn't hear her stomach growl. She sipped on her lemonade. It took the edge off her hunger, but if she didn't eat some real food soon, she was going to get a headache. The waitress brought a basket of bread. Shara slowly picked up a piece and nibbled on it. Quinton picked up a piece and slathered butter on it. It was gone seconds later.

Shara giggled. "Hungry?"

"Starving. Whenever I start running again, my appetite triples."

"Me too."

"Please. A salad? That ain't no appetite."

Shara took another bite of her bread. "So what's up with your place? You've been here almost two months now. You know what? I don't think you really have a place. I think that's what you and Mother Hobbs are telling everybody. I think secretly, you have no intentions of leaving there and she has no intention of letting you go."

"Is that so? I'll have you know that not only do I have a place, but it'll be ready very soon."

"Soon? This must be a castle, as long as it's taking them to finish it. Come clean, Quinton. I bet you're staking out my room at Mother Hobbs' house, too."

"Okay, conspiracy theorist. For real though, the owner decided to renovate the entire building and I didn't want to live there while construction was still going on."

"Umm hmm. Whatever you say."

"Really. Would I lie to you?"

Shara narrowed her eyes at him as if examining him to see if he would. "I guess not. There's one way to tell. Does anyone get to see this place or is its location to remain a secret?"

"You can see it as soon as it's done. In fact, Jenell has seen it because she's started looking at furniture. You can call her and verify that this place does in fact exist."

"I think I'll do that."

"I can't believe you don't believe me."

"I know how great it is living with Mother Hobbs, that's all. I didn't want to move either."

"She is great, isn't she? How'd you meet her anyway?"

Shara told him how they'd met. She talked

about the impact Mother Hobbs had on her
spirituality. She talked a little about her spiritual upbringing and all the mind renewing
she'd had to do to get over it.

"Gee, and I thought the church I came out of
was bad."

"You always talk about how bad it was. I
don't understand what made you go there in
the first place."

Quinton took a sip of his sweet tea. "It was
my mom's church. When my little brother died,
I was really touched by how supportive they
were. You know how everybody is there and
brings food right after a funeral and then after
that, they're nowhere to be found?"

Shara nodded.

"Well, they were always there, even for months
afterward. Some of the women came to clean
the house and bring groceries a couple of times
a week. They showed my mother and me and
my brothers so much love and support."

He picked up another piece of bread. "I was
really angry with God, so the pastor spent a lot
of time with me and really ministered to me.
Their love and concern had a lot to do with me
getting saved. I guess I shouldn't be so hard on
them. When I first got saved, it was great. But
then, the more I started learning about God
and the closer I got to Him, I sorta outgrew
them. Don't get me wrong. I got saved there.
But as far as real growth and taking it to the
next level . . . I couldn't get what I needed
there."

The waitress brought their orders. Quinton
blessed the food so fast, Shara could barely

understand what he was saying. He tore into his food. The smoky barbeque scent of his ribs smelled so good that her stomach churned. She picked at her salad.

He finished his first rib. "I guess God knew what I needed spiritually when he brought me here. I've grown so much hearing Pastor Kendrick in the short time I've been here. Not so much in knowledge—I got that from school. I've grown in spiritual intimacy. I guess you know what I mean. You've been at Kingdom Builders for how long?"

"Huh?"

Quinton put down the rib he was eating. "Why are you doing this to yourself?"

"What?"

"Pretending you're a salad girl like Keeva when you can barely concentrate on what I'm saying because you're so busy staring at my food."

Shara's eyes flew open. She couldn't believe Quinton busted her like that. She knew the look on her face gave her away. They both laughed.

"You want some of mine?" He taunted her, waving a rib under her nose. "Umm umm. These are some of the best ribs I've ever had."

"You are evil, Quinton."

"Why I gotta be evil? You the one frontin'. Tell the truth. You'd rather be eating these ribs than that salad."

"Okay, you got me. Now can you stop waving those ribs under my nose?"

Quinton stopped the waitress. "Excuse me, ma'am. My friend is not enjoying her salad. Can you bring her the same thing I'm having?"

The waitress nodded and took the salad away.

He looked at Shara. "What's that all about?"

Shara shrugged like a little kid caught in the act of some mischief. "What?"

"You've been acting totally disinterested in me for months. But now, you pretend to be a salad girl and you're not really a salad girl."

"And? What's that supposed to mean?"

He grinned. "That you like me more than you let on."

"Whatever, Quinton." She looked at his ribs. "So, are you gonna eat those or what?"

He put his hands over his plate to block her view. "Unh uh, you wanted to order a salad and be cute. You gets none."

"Quinton!"

Shara grabbed another piece of bread and smoothed butter on it, this time eating it almost as fast as he had. Quinton laughed watching her eat it.

After a few minutes, the waitress brought her food. She taunted him. "Aahaa. I got a whole fresh plate. And you can't have none." Shara tore into the ribs. She froze when she felt Quinton staring.

"I knew it. Not only are you not a salad girl, you could probably eat me under the table."

Shara laughed and finished off her first rib. "Yeah, I could take you." She picked up another rib. "I don't know, though. You can put away a lot of food."

"That's what my momma always says." He ate some of his macaroni and cheese.

She liked the look in his eyes when he talked about his mother. "What's your mom like?"

"She is the most incredible woman you could ever meet. You wouldn't think that if you just met her. She's an ordinary, hard-working, single mother. But she loved us so much. She worked herself to the bone making sure our needs were met. She wanted so much for us, but I'm not sure she knew how to push us in the right direction."

"What do you mean?"

"Well, my mother isn't very educated, so I'm not sure she knew how to help us get ahead. She just knew she wanted more for us than she had."

Shara smiled. "You love her a lot, huh?"

"She's my world. I wish I could get her to move down here—her and my brothers."

"She doesn't want to?"

Quinton shook his head. "She loves her church. Plus, my baby brother is . . . you know, 'there.'" He looked down at the table.

Shara didn't know what to say. Quinton was obviously still in a lot of pain over his little brother's death. Shara could see it in his eyes the few times he had mentioned it. She wiped her hands on her napkin and reached across the table. She softly stroked the back of his hand.

He looked up at her and smiled a little. "Sorry."

"Don't be." She continued moving her fingers slowly, tracing the veins on the back of his hands. She rested her hand on his. She propped her chin on her other hand and they sat there looking at each other for a while.

The waitress appeared and started to pick up Shara's plate. "Are you finished with this, ma'am?"

Shara grabbed for her plate. "No!"

Quinton laughed. "Look at the salad girl, now."

She let go of his hand and started eating her ribs again.

He looked hurt. "Gee, nice to know where I stand."

Shara laughed, not putting the rib down.

They bantered back and forth until they both finished their food, and then wiped their hands with the wet-naps the waitress brought. Quinton reached over and wiped some barbeque sauce off Shara's chin. "Messy, messy."

"I think I broke all the girl rules tonight. You're never supposed to eat barbeque with your hands on a first date."

"I don't see you as much of a girl-rules girl."

"I'm not. That's why I ate barbeque with my hands on the first date."

He looked at her with a slight smile on his face. "So does your qualifying this as a first date imply that there might be a second date?"

"Maybe."

"How 'bout a third?"

"Don't push your luck."

He winced. "Ouch." He reached for her hand. "Seriously though, when I told Terrence to leave you alone because you were with me . . ."

"Yeah?"

"Let's just say I was speaking by faith."

Shara blushed. "You so silly."

"Why I gotta be silly? Brotha pouring out his heart and you're stepping on it."

"I'm not stepping on your heart."

"Then how 'bout that third date?

"We haven't even had the second one yet."

"I know. But I don't want to have a second unless I know there's gonna be a third."

"Why not?"

"Because I don't think my heart could take it."

Shara traced circles around his knuckles. He had large, strong hands. He lifted her hand to his lips and kissed it. She didn't pull back.

"Okay." She bit her lip.

"Okay, what?"

"The third date."

"Yeah?"

"Yeah."

The waitress brought back Quinton's credit card he had given her when she brought the check. He came over and pulled Shara's chair back.

"Are you going to be such a gentleman on the third date?" Shara asked as they walked out the door and to his truck.

"Yep, and the fourth, fifth and sixth too."

"Now wait a minute. I didn't say nothing 'bout no fourth, fifth, and sixth dates."

"I know. But after the third date, I won't have anything to worry about."

"Is that so, Quinton Mercer?"

"Yep."

"Okay, we'll see."

He helped her up into the truck. He kissed her hand again before closing her door. When he got in, he smiled as she said, "If you're this much of a gentleman on the third date, I may have to strongly consider that fourth, fifth, and sixth date."

Shara lay back in her seat listening to the music.

"What was that for?" Quinton looked at her with that twinkle in his eye.

"What?"

"That loud, long sigh you just gave."

"Did I?"

"Yep."

"I guess that's how I'm feeling. Good food, great music, comfortable car. Hmmmm." Shara sighed again.

"Is that all?"

"I guess the company's not too bad, either."

"Not too bad, huh?"

"Yeah." She smiled.

"Tired? Ready to call it a night?"

"Honestly, no."

"What you wanna do?"

"I don't know."

"Where do you like to go?"

"Honestly, nowhere. I'm a pretty boring individual."

Quinton rubbed his chin. "So you're telling me that I'm going to have to get pretty creative for this second and third date."

"Yep."

Quinton nodded. "Okay, I'll have to do a little research, then."

They drove in silence for a while, neither one of them wanting to end their evening.

"We could get some coffee," Shara said.

"Sounds good. Where?"

Shara directed him to Joe's Coffee shop in East Atlanta Village. It was one of the places Keeva had taken her on one of their many recent outings. Shara liked it because it lacked the austere bourgie flavor of most of the places Keeva took her. It was eclectic with retro furniture and abstract art on the walls.

Quinton ordered a latte and Shara a mocha. Quinton also ordered a large piece of red velvet cake he said was calling his name. "Share it with me?"

"Sure. It does look good."

Shara followed Quinton over to a comfortable looking couch with a coffee table in front of it and sat down next to him. Her eyes widened as he opened six packets of sugar and dumped them into his latte. "Have a little coffee with your sugar?"

"What can I say?" He gave her his best Kool-Aid smile. "I like sweet things."

"Is that so?"

"Yep."

"You're such a flirt."

"So I've been told."

They chatted and flirted while sipping coffee and nibbling at the red velvet cake. Shara felt like she was high and wondered if it was from the caffeine and sugar or Quinton.

One of the employees started mopping the floor. Shara looked at her watch.

"Oh my, it's almost midnight. We must have

lost track of the time. I guess we better go before they kick us out."

Quinton frowned. "I hate going back to Mother Hobbs house this late at night. I know I'm not a kid, but it seems disrespectful. Did she get upset when you would come in late at night?"

"I never came in late," Shara said.

"So most of your dates ended at a decent hour? I'm flattered."

Shara lowered her eyes. "I didn't go out with anyone while I was living with her. Quite honestly, I haven't gone out with anyone in a real long time."

"Then I'm really flattered. Would I be pushing it to ask why not?"

"Hadn't met anyone worthwhile I guess."

"Now I'm beyond flattered. You better stop before I get the bighead."

Shara smiled. "Since we're asking personal questions, what about you?"

Quinton finished off the cake. "My last relationship ended not too long after my basketball career did. What a coincidence."

"Coincidence?"

"My girlfriend, well fiancée actually—was a trip. We hooked up in my senior year at Arizona when it was real obvious I was going pro. She was always there as long as I was making the money and on top of my game. I guess I should have known something was up when she couldn't make it to my little brother's funeral."

Shara's eyes widened.

"I know. Not cool at all. That's when her true colors started showing. She was all of a sudden busy all the time. She never listened when I needed to talk. When I hurt my knee, she hardly even came to the hospital. She broke up with me not too long after I announced I was quitting. Found out later she was seeing one of my teammates. They're either engaged or married now."

"Wow. That's deep. You haven't been out with anyone since her?"

"I've had a date here and there. Like you said, though, I didn't find anyone worthwhile. I guess I couldn't find anyone I could vibe with on all levels—mental, emotional, and spiritual. You know?"

She nodded. "Yeah, I know."

One of the employees cleared his throat. Quinton stood. "I guess that's our cue. I better get you home."

The ride back to Mother Hobbs' house was too short. The light was on in the living room when they pulled up.

"Uh oh, I think she's waiting up for me," Quinton said.

Shara shook her head. "No, she always stays up late on the weekends watching a movie or reading. She'll be going to bed in about half an hour."

They lingered in the truck for a little while longer, talking and listening to music. When Quinton noticed the light go off in the living room he said, "I better get inside. I don't want to disturb her. You'll have to let me pick you up next time. I don't like you out driving this late."

"I'll be fine. I'm not too far away."

He walked her over to her car where they lingered for a second, facing each other. Quinton held both of her hands and stared at her face.

"Why do you always look at me that way?" Shara asked.

"Because you're beautiful."

Shara could feel the blood rushing to her cheeks. Quinton didn't bother to stop staring at her. He let go of one of her hands and stroked her cheek softly.

"Thanks," he said.

"For what?"

"For finally going out with me and for such a good time."

"Thanks for waiting . . . and for a great time."

He bent and kissed her. His lips seemed even softer and sweeter than they had been that morning and they lingered much longer. He stepped back, biting his bottom lip. He held the door as she got in her car and didn't go inside the house until she was almost all the way down the street.

When Shara got home, there were four messages from Keeva. On the last one, Keeva screeched that she couldn't believe how late it was and Shara still wasn't home. "All right, Shara. I can't hang anymore. Call me tomorrow. Love you, girl."

Shara went straight to bed and fell into the sweetest sleep she'd ever had.

Chapter Thirty-three

"Okay, tell me everything." Keeva showed up at Shara's apartment unannounced late the next afternoon. They sat on Shara's worn couch so she could share the details of her date. Shara felt like a high school girl as she relived the evening for Keeva.

"Shara, you look so happy! I can't believe this. Girl, he is so sweet. You're so lucky."

"We had a good time and all. I don't know about being lucky."

"What do you mean?"

"I mean, I don't know where things go from here. I don't know what happens next and I don't want to be all goo-goo eyed about it."

"Too late for that." Keeva smiled. "Take it slow, go with the flow. In a couple of days, he'll probably call and you guys might even go out again next weekend."

Shara couldn't imagine waiting a couple of days for him to call. She sighed and steered her thoughts to something else. "So what's this about you putting Mark out at night now?"

Keeva sat up. "I told him that I wanted to be celibate until I got married."

"You did? Oh my goodness! And he accepted that?"

"For now. I think he thinks it's a phase I'm going through and will eventually get over."

"I'm proud of you, girl. I know that that was hard to do. Especially since you guys have been together for so long."

"Honestly, it wasn't hard at all. I don't know if it's me, or being depressed, or what. The sex thing doesn't do it for me anymore." Keeva paused for a second. "It's just become a physical act. No romance or love, just, you know."

Shara looked at her blankly. "Actually, I don't know."

"Oh, wow." Keeva's eyes widened. "I never thought of that. I guess you don't . . . Wow." She thought for a second. "That means you're a . . . you've never—"

"No, I've never and I don't plan to until I get married."

"Wow. A real-life virgin at twenty-six."

"What's that supposed to mean?"

"Nothing. I think it's cool. I wish I had waited 'til I got married. Sex is totally overrated. I mean, I guess it's special if you're with someone you're in love with, but—"

"You're not in love with Mark?"

Keeva put her hand over her mouth. "Did I just say that? Oh my God. I can't believe that came out of my mouth. Of course I'm in love with Mark." She paused. "Aren't I?"

Keeva got up and walked over to Shara's dining table. "I was, when we first got together. I think. I mean . . . I don't know, Shara. This is all your fault. You got my head all messed up. I thought I was in love 'til you said all that stuff about what love really was. I kept telling myself you had watched too many movies and had no idea what love was. I had to keep saying that so I wouldn't have to accept the fact that maybe I'm not in love. I have a long-standing habit.

"When I think about you and Quinton and how you guys seem to be so perfect for each other; how you guys have so much in common and believe in and stand for the same things; how he believes in your dreams and you believe in his dreams and your dreams are so intertwined; I see how he looks at you and how you look at him and how sweet and kind and gentle and attentive he is . . . I don't know. Sometimes I wonder if that's how relationships are when you start out and then after you get used to each other, all the magic fades. I mean, do you think it can really be beautiful like that forever?"

Keeva bit her lip. "And then I try to remember whether our relationship started out magical and beautiful like that. I mean, the sex was great back then, but . . . I don't know. I wonder if I could ever have something like what you and Quinton are building."

Keeva pulled her hair. "I guess maybe I need some time to step away from the relationship and really find out what I want, you know?"

Shara nodded hesitantly. She had been

thinking Keeva needed to drop Mark since she met her, but she wasn't about to say that.

Keeva's cell phone rang. She looked at the number. "Speak of the devil." She clicked open the phone. "Yes sweetie? . . . I remember honey. I needed to pick up a book at Shara's. You want me to meet you back at my place? . . . Well, I guess you could pick me up here, but my car . . . Well, it is actually much closer here—around the corner really . . . Okay, honey." She gave him the directions to Shara's apartment.

She frowned. "He is acting so strange. He insisted on taking me out to dinner tonight. He's afraid I won't make it back to the apartment in time for us to make our reservation so he's insisting on picking me up here. Is that okay?"

"Sure, as long as he doesn't come in here cussing at me."

"He won't. He's not like that. I don't know why this is so urgent. Maybe because he's flying out tomorrow for a whole week. I guess he wants to spend some time with me before he leaves."

"Was it my imagination, or was he ridiculously rude to me on the phone last night? Is that just how he is or should I take it personally?"

Keeva sighed. "I think Mark blames you for all the changes in me lately. He attributes my starting to speak my mind and teaching dance classes and wanting to be celibate all to you."

"Oh, isn't that wonderful? So in his mind, I'm the cause of your relationship problems?"

"Yeah, he has no clue things were bad before.

He was happy and it doesn't matter to him that I wasn't."

Shara clenched her teeth.

Keeva asked, "Why do you always do that?"

"What?"

"Whenever I talk about Mark, you get this look on your face like you're going to explode if you don't say something, but then you never say anything."

Shara let out a long breath. "Relationships are sticky. I'm your friend, so on the one hand, I want to say things, but then on the other hand, I feel like it's none of my business. So I keep my mouth shut."

"If you weren't trying so hard to keep your mouth shut, what would you say?"

"Unh uh. I ain't saying nothing. I don't want to be one of those girls that ain't got no man talking 'bout, 'girl, you need to kick him to the curb.'"

They both laughed.

"I think friends should be supportive and listen and not give advice when they're not in the situation," Shara said.

"In other words, you think Mark is horrible for me and I should have let him go a long time ago."

"I didn't say that."

"But that's what you think."

"Keeva, what do you think? That's the real question."

"You're right. I have to figure this out for myself. I guess I've spent so much time going with the flow I never examined whether or not I was happy with him." She frowned at Shara. "Why does being around you cause me to challenge everything going on in my life?"

"Oh, so you're blaming me, too?" Shara asked. "Isn't it better to ask these questions now than to end up being miserable later?"

"I know. It's just hard, that's all."

There was a knock at the door. Shara hopped up to answer it. Mark was as handsome as Keeva was beautiful. He had that same classy style as he sauntered in with beige linen pants and a matching linen shirt on. He was caramel brown with short, black curly hair. The thin frame glasses he wore gave an intelligent look to his handsomeness.

He glanced at Shara. "I'm here for Keeva." He brushed by her into her apartment. Shara looked at his back about to go off, but Keeva looked anxiously at her, so she backed down.

"Come on, Princess, we're going to be late for our reservation." He surveyed Shara's apartment with apparent disdain.

Keeva tried to introduce Shara, but he was back outside as quickly as he had come in. She paused at the door. "Sorry, I'll call you later."

Shara watched Keeva rush out the door to where Mark was standing in the hall waiting impatiently for her.

Not too long after Keeva left, Shara looked around her apartment for something to do. She had cleaned up earlier that morning and had studied a bit before Keeva got there. She thumbed through a notebook, sighing with every turn of the page. She finally shut the notebook. "Oh, forget it."

She picked up the phone and dialed Mother Hobbs' number.

"Hello."

"Hey, Mother Hobbs, can I speak to Quinton?"

"I'm fine, Shara. Thanks for asking. Good to hear from you."

"I'm sorry. I just—"

"You don't have to apologize, baby." Mother Hobbs chuckled. "I understand. Here he is."

Shara froze. Why had she called Quinton?

"Hey," he said.

"Hey." She was more frozen after hearing his voice.

"Shara?"

She made herself say something. "I . . . I just wanted to say hi."

"I'm glad you called." Quinton laughed. "Boy, you're breaking all the girl rules. You called me the very next day after a first date. Doesn't the rulebook say you're not supposed to call me at all? You're supposed to be all nonchalant and wait until I call you."

She relaxed a little. "I told you I never read the girl rulebook. Sounds like you know more about it than me."

"Yeah, I've played and been played in enough relationships to know a little something about the girl rules."

"Is there a boy rulebook too?"

"Yeah, but it's nowhere near as sophisticated as the girl rulebook. It has simple stuff like don't sleep with her best friend and if she comes over while the game is on, say 'yes honey' or 'uh-huh' for at least every fifty words she says."

Shara laughed, relaxing more. "Do either of the rulebooks say anything about how long after the first date you have to wait to have the second date?"

Quinton was silent for a second. "Why do you ask, Shara Anderson?"

She could hear him grinning. "No reason. Just figured if I've committed myself to a second and third date, I should know a little bit about the rules."

"That's the only reason you asked?"

"Yep."

"Oh, that's too bad."

"Why?"

"Because, if you were asking because you were interested in going ahead and getting the second date out of the way so we can get to the all-important third date, then I would have asked you for directions to pick you up so we could catch a movie. But, since you were asking for informational purposes only, I guess I won't be asking you," Quinton teased.

"See, I don't know about that. I'm thinking there must be something in the girl rulebook about waiting at least a week before going out on the second date."

"I tell you what. How about we throw both books out the window and follow our hearts?"

"I don't know about that, either. My heart could get me in a lot of trouble. In fact, I think the reason for the rulebooks is to protect us against what our hearts might lead us into if we have no rules," Shara said.

"And just what might your heart lead you into?"

"Hmmmmm. Why don't you ask me that question on the sixth date?"

"So is that a guaranteed commitment to the sixth date?"

"Sounded like it to me."

"Gee, what'd I do right?"

"Are you coming to pick me up or what?"

"Only if we make a deal," he said.

"What's that?"

"Let's spare ourselves the agony and both wear jeans and T-shirts."

Shara laughed. "That's a deal. I just got all my clothes back in the closet."

"Shara, you're not supposed to tell me that. I might have to get you a copy of the girl rulebook."

She gave him directions to her house. "See you when you get here."

Shara couldn't believe she asked Quinton out on a date. She pulled on her favorite pair of jeans and a T-shirt and waited for him to arrive.

Chapter Thirty-four

Mark drove quietly the entire ride to the restaurant. Keeva wondered what was on his mind. He pulled up at one of their favorite places, Anis. She was impressed. They usually only came here on special occasions like her birthday or their anniversaries.

They sat down at their table. The maitre'd came over and Mark ordered a bottle of expensive champagne.

Keeva raised her eyebrows. "What's the occasion?"

"Do I need a special occasion to treat my Princess well? Things have been strained between us lately and I wanted us to be able to have a good time together for a change."

Even though she had been annoyed with his attitude at Shara's, Keeva vowed to have a good time. If she was going to think of ending the relationship after having invested so much time, she wanted to at least give it a fair chance first.

After the second glass of champagne, she began to relax. She laughed at his corny jokes as if he was straight off of *Def Comedy Jam*.

After dessert, they drove back to her apartment. Mark was quiet again for the entire ride.

"Is something wrong, Mark?"

He looked over at her. "I'm fine, Princess. Just glad to have you back."

She smiled. This did feel like old times.

When they got to the apartment, he walked over to the CD player and put on a Sade CD. He turned down the lights. He was actually setting the mood for the first time in a long time. She realized where this was going. For a moment, she was angry that he was purposely ignoring her desire to be celibate. She relaxed a little though as she remembered his request to wean slowly. He had been behaving since their talk and hadn't even protested about being sent home every evening at 10:00 PM.

She felt a stirring deep inside. It startled her. She hadn't been "in the mood" for a long time.

He held out his hand and invited her to dance. They danced sensuously to the music as he showered her with kisses. She melted in his arms. They began to kiss passionately. He stopped. She gave him a questioning look. For the first time in forever, she didn't want him to stop. She was glad he had and was touched that he was trying to respect her wishes.

He stepped back and led her to the couch. She sat down. He took a deep breath and then fumbled around in his pocket. He pulled out a small, blue box and dropped to his knee. Keeva's eyes widened and her mouth fell open as he opened the box to reveal a beautiful diamond marquis. It was huge. Had to be at least three carats. Her mouth hung locked open as her eyes went from the ring to his earnest face.

He rambled through an explanation of how long they had been together and how much he cared for her. Keeva realized she was barely listening to him when she noticed he had stopped talking and was now anxiously awaiting her reply. He looked so vulnerable, so serious, so intense.

He frowned as a large tear rolled down her cheek. "What's wrong? We talked about this. I thought this was what you wanted." He looked like *he* was about to cry. "I thought we—"

"Of course this is what I want. I . . . I'm just surprised. I'm just so . . . happy. I . . . I didn't expect—"

He ended her stuttering with a kiss. "You just made me the happiest man in the world." He looked into her eyes as he slipped the ring onto her finger. "I am going to make you so happy. We're going to be perfect, you'll see."

He held her tightly and she hugged him back. She hoped that if she held on to him tight enough, the emotions raging inside her would go away. The hug became a kiss and the kiss became more passionate until she found herself being carried to her bedroom. Mark covered her body with kisses as he took off each article of her clothing.

She felt as if she were watching the two of them from the outside and could barely respond. Luckily he didn't seem to notice, probably because of her recent bar on sexual activity.

Her mind kept drifting to her conversation with Shara earlier that afternoon. She tried to shut the thoughts out and tell herself this was the man she was going to spend the rest of her life with—that she should be happy.

She realized Mark was finished when he gave her the usual kiss on the forehead, threw his arm over her waist, and lay facing the wall. In a moment, his breathing became labored and she knew he was asleep.

She stared up at the ceiling as hot tears stung her cheeks. She pried herself out from under his arm and went to the bathroom. She sat on the floor hugging her knees to her chest. There was something so comforting about the coldness of the ceramic tile beneath her bottom. She began to cry, slowly at first, but then began heaving as if the tears were coming from deep in her belly. When there were no tears left, she breathed heavily with her head propped up on her knees.

Her fingers traced circles around her perfectly manicured toenails as she stared forlornly into space. Why couldn't she be happy? She should be in bed, curled up next to Mark, dreaming about the life they would have together. Instead, she was sitting here crying.

Something in her head, or heart, refused to let her believe the lie she had been living for the past three and a half years. Whatever it was, it let her know she couldn't marry Mark. What was she going to do? She had already told him yes—or let him *think* she said yes, and he was so happy. She couldn't bear the thought of breaking his heart. She wouldn't even know what to tell him. It wasn't like she had a real reason.

She slowly pulled herself off the floor and stood to look at herself in the mirror. Her eyes were puffy and red. She had black tear streaks down her cheeks. She took a deep breath, washed her face, and slipped quietly back into the bed. As she fell asleep, she said, "God, help me—please."

At 6:30 the next morning, Mark awoke with a start. He cursed and squinted to see what time it was. He had an obsession with being at the airport two hours before any flight and was scheduled to leave at 8:30. He liked to leave his car at the airport because he hated it whenever Keeva was late picking him up.

After he showered and dressed, he came over to her and kissed her softly on the forehead. "Princess, I'm leaving."

She used the sleep-feigning act she had perfected as a child when she didn't want to get up. "Hmmmmm?" She rolled over and dug deeper under the covers.

"I said I'm leaving. I don't want to be late for my flight. Jade's gonna pick you up later to go get your car. I'll call you this afternoon, okay?"

She turned further away from him and made some mumbly sounds. He laughed and kissed her one more time before he left.

When she was sure he was gone, she got up and went to the window. She saw him emerge from the building and practically skip to his car. He looked so happy.

A tear rolled down her cheek.

How was she going to tell him she couldn't marry him?

Chapter Thirty-five

"Keeva, are you avoiding me? I've barely seen you in the last month." Shara was glad she caught Keeva on the phone early on Saturday before she went to one of her dance classes.

"Of course I'm not avoiding you, silly. Don't act like it's my fault. You're the one who's always busy. Every time I call you, you're gone or on your way out the door. What's up? Wanna hang out today?"

"Well, Quinton and I are about to get together for a run and then he's all jazzed about taking me somewhere special for lunch."

"Quinton, Quinton, Quinton—seems to be all you talk about and all you have time for these days."

"Cut me some slack. I have a lot of dateless years to make up for. I do miss you, though. We can get together this evening. Quinton is taking his 'boys' out for pizza."

"Oh I see. Quinton's busy tonight so you call me."

"Girl, stop tripping."

"You know I'm joking, Shara. I couldn't be happier for you. So when's the wedding?"

"Now you're really tripping. We've only been seeing each other for a month."

"Yeah, but every day for a month is equivalent to about six months of normal dating."

"It hasn't been every day." Shara added sheepishly, "Just every other day."

The last few weeks had been wonderful. Running with Quinton almost daily, dinner at fancy restaurants, a jazz concert at Chastain Park, putt-putt golfing, movies, and *hours* of talking. He had taken her bowling again and given her real lessons. She had even bowled a strike and a few spares. The best part had been studying the Bible and praying together.

"You're pitiful," Keeva said. "You deserve it, though. You held out and waited for the right one without compromising your standards and God sent you exactly what you wanted . . ."

Something in her voice didn't sound right. Shara felt guilty for neglecting her friend. She thought about the fact that Keeva had missed a few Sundays and all the Wednesday night services over the past month. Before that, she had been faithfully attending every Sunday and Wednesday since she had gotten saved. She had even been coming to intercessory prayer some Friday mornings before class. Shara knew better than to believe her when she said school was getting busier, but she had been too caught up in Quinton to press Keeva for the truth.

"Are you okay?" Shara asked. She heard Keeva sigh loudly. "Oh boy—that bad, huh?"

"You know me. Always some drama," Keeva said. "Speaking of drama, how 'bout I cook dinner here tonight? I wouldn't want to burst into tears in a restaurant."

"Tears? Keeva, what's going on?"

"I'll tell you when I see you. 7:00?"

"I'll be there."

"This is my special lunch?"

Quinton pulled up at a building a few blocks from the church. There was scaffolding on the front and some construction workers putting in windows. Compared to the other buildings on the block, it looked great.

"Yep, this is it," he said.

"Oh!" Shara's eyes widened as the identity of their location dawned on her. "This is your place?"

"Yep. Come on up. Jenell had all the stuff delivered this week. She has some serious skills when it comes to decorating."

They climbed four floors to the top floor apartment.

"Sorry. The owner is figuring out how much it would cost to put an elevator in." Quinton opened the door and Shara's mouth flew open as she walked in.

The space was huge and open, much like Keeva's loft. The living area was decorated in earth tones accented with African décor. There was a large television with a lot of electronic equipment attached to it.

"What's all this?"

Quinton pointed at the entertainment center. "DVD, CD player, and stereo with surround sound. Oh and a PlayStation for when my boy, Jamil, comes over." Shara gave him a stern look, but he waved it away. "I know, I know. I spoil him too much."

The dining area had a large table with fresh flowers in a vase on it. Two places were set. "We're dining in? Who's cooking?"

"We are—together. I thought it might be fun."

Shara walked into the kitchen. It was quite spacious with an island and every kitchen appliance available. "Like gadgets, do we?"

"I don't want to hear it. I already told you I was extravagant when it comes to my castle."

Shara looked around as if something was missing. "Where's your bedroom?"

"Why Sister Shara, I'm appalled that you asked me that."

She swatted at him playfully.

He led her through a door out of the apartment. "It would have cost too much and taken too long to join it all together, so I had them do it as a separate suite." He opened a door across the hall. They walked into an office with a large desk, computer, and bookshelves lining the walls filled with books. Quinton opened another door to a huge bedroom with a sitting area and a large walk-in closet. His bathroom had a step down Jacuzzi tub and glass shower. A second door led to a guest bedroom and guest bath. The last door was locked.

"What's in here?"

"Another guest room. I can't find the key."

"Quinton, this ain't no apartment. It's a house."

He led her back to the living area. "Do you like it?"

Shara smiled and stood on her toes to kiss his cheek. "I love it. It's beautiful. Definitely worth the wait."

They walked into the kitchen.

"You can do the salad and the bread. Leave everything else to me." Quinton began pulling vegetables out of the refrigerator.

"What are we having?"

"Seafood Alfredo over angel hair pasta, salad, and garlic bread."

"Sounds good."

"Oh, I almost forgot. I got you something." He walked back into the living room over to the stereo and pulled out a CD. He handed it to her.

She gasped. "Fred Hammond has a new CD out? How could I not know that?"

"What—does he call you before he releases them or something?"

"Yes, actually," she joked. "Seriously though, I always know what Fred is up to. He snuck this one in on me."

"Well, here's the skip button on the CD player. Check it out."

Shara hugged the CD to her chest. "Oh no—listening to a Fred Hammond CD for the first time is a special experience, not to be shared."

Quinton pretended to be hurt. "Is there something going on between you and Fred I should know about?"

She laughed. "It's not like that, silly. I just

love his music. I like to listen to it and read the words and be with God. His music has helped me overcome many a depressed day. It's always guaranteed to take you—"

"Straight to the throne room? I know. It's like he has this key to a room in heaven with nothing but songs in it, and every time he releases a CD, he opens a door and lets a few of those songs out. The lyrics strike a cord deep in your spirit."

Shara stared at him. "It scares me when you—"

"Say what's in your head? Yeah, you scare me too when you think what's in mine." He kissed her. His lips lingered.

"Ummmm." She smiled. "You have the sweetest lips in the world."

"Unh uh, you do." He kissed her again softly.

"Unh uh, you do." She kissed him back.

He pulled away from her and walked back to the kitchen. She put the CD in and followed him, bringing the insert with her.

Quinton grinned when he heard the first song play. "Oh, so I'm Fred Hammond worthy now?"

She giggled and hopped up on the counter to sit, turning through the album insert, scanning the songs.

"What do you think you're doing? You're supposed to be making the salad."

"You invited *me*, remember?"

Quinton scowled, but started chopping a red bell pepper. "Don't think this is how it's gonna be when we . . ."

She lowered the insert and looked at him. "When we what?"

". . . when we uh . . . have our next eat-in date."

She studied his face for a moment, then said, "I expect the food to be ready when I get here next time. I'm starving."

Quinton stood with his mouth open. "You're something, you know that?"

"Yep."

He pulled a peach out of the refrigerator. "Here, I don't want you to spoil your appetite, not that that's possible."

"Whatever, Quinton." Shara pouted.

He bit his lip. "You shouldn't pout like that."

"Why not?" She poked her lips out even further.

"Because . . . it makes me want to kiss you." He walked over and kissed her pouting lips.

"Is that such a bad thing?" She kissed him back. "Hey, I like sitting up here. I'm as tall as you are." She put her arms around his shoulders and kissed him again. He pulled away and walked back over to his chopping board, smiling.

She heard him let out a deep sigh. "What?"

"Nothing. I like you here in my space. Maybe too much," Quinton said.

Shara went back to reading the CD cover as he chopped the vegetables.

Shara was impressed with Quinton's culinary skills. After lunch, she helped him clear the dishes and clean the kitchen. "Oh God, I'm stuffed. I think I just committed a sin. You can't cook like this when we . . ."

"When we what?" Quinton turned around from the sink.

"When we . . . uh have our next eat-in date."

He stared at her for a minute. She stared back. They both smiled.

They finished cleaning and went to the living room. Shara plopped down on the leather couch. Quinton sat in the armchair.

"What are you doing?"

"Nothing." He moved over to the couch, but sat at the other end.

"Hey, I have a CD I want you to hear." He put on the CD and brought the insert to her.

"Nancey Jackson, *Relationships*," she read.

"It's not new, but I don't think you have it in your collection. The theme of the album is having an intimate relationship with God. I pulled it out the other day and it made me think of you."

Shara listened to the lyrics. "Oh, yeah. This is nice. More throne room music." She closed her eyes. They listened until the first song ended. "Where's mine?"

"How do you know I got you one?"

She pouted again.

"Don't start that." He walked over to the entertainment center and pulled out another copy of the CD.

"Thanks, Quint."

"You're getting spoiled, you know that?"

"And whose fault is that?"

He smiled. "Guilty."

Her CD collection had grown exponentially

since they'd started seeing each other. He had introduced her to a lot of artists—gospel and jazz. At first she'd felt funny with him buying her things and paying for everything when they went out. When she saw how insulted he got when she mentioned it, she vowed never to bring it up again. She was actually starting to like it.

When he came back over to the couch, she scooted next to him. He put an arm around her and they listened to the music for a while. She sighed.

"What was that for?" He glanced down at her.

"I don't know. Just feel good I guess. Great atmosphere, great good, good music, comfortable couch . . ."

"That's all?"

"Oh, yeah, the company's not too bad either."

He laughed.

She turned to kiss him. The kiss became a little more passionate than usual and he pulled himself away from her and walked into the kitchen.

"Want something to drink? I'm thirsty all of a sudden."

She followed him into the kitchen with a questioning look on her face. "Why do you do that?"

"What?"

"Run away from me all the time."

He looked at her and chuckled. "Ummm, if you have to ask that question, then my suspicions about you must be true."

"What suspicions?"

"Gee. Now I know I'm blessed." He walked

over to her and put his hands on her shoulders and kissed her on the forehead. "I'm the man in this relationship, so I'm responsible for keeping us out of trouble."

"Trouble?"

He looked at her and allowed time for his meaning to register.

"Ooooohhhhh . . . trouble."

"Yeah . . . trouble."

She squirmed for a second under his gaze.

"I promise to, you know, keep things holy, but you have to promise never to kiss me like that again until . . ."

"Until what?" She traced circles around one of the buttons on his shirt.

He grabbed her hand. "Shara." He let out an exasperated breath. "I don't think you realize the effect you have on me. You can't—"

"Stop worrying, silly." She waved his frustration away. "Nothing's gonna happen. You love God and I love God."

"I know, but . . ."

"But what?"

He bit his lower lip. "But I love you, too."

Her mouth hung open with a slight smile. "Yeah?"

"Yeah."

"Good—'cause I . . . I uh." She bit her upper lip. "I love you, too."

He smiled. "Yeah?"

"Yeah."

He kissed her softly and then held her close. They both sighed together and then laughed.

The phone rang. He looked at the clock and picked up the phone, checking the caller-ID.

"What's up, Jamilly-mil? . . . I ain't forgot. You my dog, man . . . All right, you get the crew together, I'll meet you there . . . Chill man, I'll be there in twenty." He hung up the phone and walked back over to where Shara was standing. He kissed her on the nose.

"I could stay here with you all evening, but it's probably best that I don't. I promised my boys and—"

"I know how they are. I'm going to Keeva's for dinner, anyway. She's cooking for me, too. Although I'm not sure I can eat another bite."

"Yeah, right."

She punched him playfully. "Whatever, Quinton."

Quinton pulled up in the church parking lot and came around to open the door for Shara. He leaned to kiss her but she pulled away. "The kids are over there."

"Oops, my bad." He helped her down and walked her to her car.

"See you tomorrow morning?"

"Yeah."

She turned on her car. "Hey!" she called after him as he walked away.

He turned around.

"Love you." Her smile almost broke her face.

His did too. "Love you, too."

Chapter Thirty-six

When Shara gave Keeva their usual hello hug, Keeva clung to her.

"Hey, are you okay?"

"Yeah, just glad to see you. It's been forever." Keeva stepped back without looking Shara in the eye. "I didn't get a chance to cook yet. Do you want me to order something?"

"No way. I'm still full from lunch at Quinton's."

"Lunch at Quinton's?"

Shara walked over to the couch and plopped down, staring at the ceiling. She blushed as she told Keeva about his apartment and how he had cooked for her.

Keeva was amused at the dreamy look on Shara's face when she talked about him.

Shara's voice even sounded dreamy. "He told me he loved me."

Keeva put her hand over her mouth. "What? Already?"

Shara gasped. "Is there something you want to tell me?"

"What?"

"That large, light reflecting structure that's weighing down your ring finger that wasn't there before. Did you forget to mention something important?"

"Oh, yeah. I just got it back from being sized." Keeva sighed and plopped down on the couch beside her. "Mark asked me to marry him."

Shara studied Keeva's face. "Isn't this the part where you're supposed to blush and tell me excitedly that he proposed, recounting every romantic detail and show me the ring and how beautiful it is and tell me you're so excited about spending the rest of your life with him?"

"That would be the scheduled performance for my *fake* friends. *You* know better."

"So you don't want to marry him?"

"Honestly, no."

"What did he do when you turned him down?"

Keeva looked away. "I didn't."

Shara's eyes bugged out. "No wonder you've been avoiding me. Let me get this straight. You told him you would marry him, but you're sitting here telling me you don't want to."

"Well, I didn't actually *tell* him I would marry him, but that's about the gist of it."

"Keeva, don't you think *he* should be the one you oughta be telling that you don't want to get married?"

"I know."

"And?"

"I don't know what happened. I wasn't expecting it and he was there and he looked so earnest and so serious and I just . . . I didn't want to hurt his feelings, so I sorta said yes. And then we made love—well, had sex—so that didn't seem like an appropriate time to tell him and then he left to go out of town and then he got back and has been so excited . . . I haven't found the right moment to tell him."

"Keeva! You—"

"I know, Shara. I know I'm not being true to myself. I know I'm putting another person's feelings before mine. I know this is your proverbial box you want to let me out of. I know I can't marry him or I'll be miserable for the rest of my life. I know I can't live a lie and that marriage is a very serious thing. I know he's not my soulmate and I know if I marry him, it'll be the worst thing I could have ever done." She paused to take a breath. "Now, what did you want to say?"

"That pretty much covers it." Shara looked her in the eye. "Soooo . . . ?"

"I don't know Shara. Do you always have to be in my face about something?" Keeva snapped.

"Oh, I'm sorry. I guess you'd rather me be like Jade." Shara changed her voice to a high-pitched, valley-girl tone. "Like, ohmigod, Keeva, he proposed? That's *so* exciting. I'm so happy for you. Ooooh, look at your ring. How many carats is it? I can't wait to be a bridesmaid. Ooooh, what color dresses are we going to have? Girl, you are so lucky. Mark is sooooo wonderful. I wish I had a man just like him." Shara put her hands on her hips. "Was that better? Is that what you want? I don't think so, or

Jade would be standing in your living room instead of me."

Keeva clenched her teeth and balled up her fists like she was about to go off on Shara and then burst into tears.

Shara put her arms around her. "I'm sorry, Keeva. I didn't mean all that."

"Yes, you did." Keeva wiped her eyes. "And you're right. That's precisely why I invited you over. I needed someone with some sense to talk some sense into me."

Keeva pulled her hair. "I don't know what to do. I've thought of a million ways to tell him. I wish I could write him a letter and mail him his ring in a box. I don't want to see his face when I tell him."

She stared off into space. "I know I can't marry him, but I am gonna miss him, you know? Even though he's no good for me, he's still . . . *there*. What if I end up like Jade and Heather and all my other hard-up girlfriends who all live in fear that they'll never get married? But then, I know I'd rather be by myself than be in a miserable marriage. As unhappy as I've been with him though, I didn't expect this to hurt so bad."

"What?"

"Breaking up with him. It's not like you say, 'I'm not gonna marry you' and then go back to being girlfriend and boyfriend. When I give him his ring back, that's it. It's over." She sighed. "For the past three years, this was the man I was going to marry. Now all of a sudden, he won't be in my life anymore. Three years is a long time to all of a sudden be over and done with. And I do sort of love him in a weird sort of way. It's not like you can throw those feelings away overnight."

She paused for a minute. "I wonder why he asked me to marry him now. We had always planned to get married after I finished graduate school. I can't help but think it's the sex thing. Since we're engaged, he figures he doesn't have to go home at night anymore. He's also been hinting that since I have to plan the wedding, I won't have time to teach the dance classes anymore. It's more of his control, keeping me in his box."

Shara listened and allowed Keeva to reason with herself.

"I'm gonna miss him, though. I guess I can see why women get a rebound man. You need someone to fill that hole left behind. I don't want to do that, though. I want to be able to fill that hole with me. Really get to know me and spend time with me and love me. Does that make sense?"

Shara nodded.

"And I guess I also want to try to develop, you know . . . a relationship with God. If I can find Him and learn to talk to Him and hear from Him, I know He'll help fill the hole, too."

Shara nodded again, not wanting to interrupt Keeva's introspection.

"So, I guess it's settled. I'm not marrying Mark. I'm gonna marry me instead. And God . . ." She smiled, nodding her head, as if she was satisfied with her decision.

Her smile faded. "Now all I have to do is tell him."

Chapter Thirty-seven

After church on Sunday, Quinton stepped into Pastor Kendrick's office and shut the door behind him. He cleared his throat.

Pastor Kendrick looked up. "Hey Quint-man, what's up?"

Quinton and Pastor Kendrick had gotten close since he'd joined the staff. They ate lunch together almost daily and talked about the church, ministry, and life in general. At least once a week, Quinton had dinner with Pastor Kendrick's family, and the two of them played basketball all the time.

Quinton shifted from side to side, rubbing his hands together.

Pastor Kendrick closed his notebook. "Have a seat, man. Tell me what's on your mind."

Quinton sat on the edge of his chair. Not meeting Pastor Kendrick's eyes, he said, "Uumm, I'm not quite sure how to say this or really what I'm asking, but . . . well, I need some advice of sorts."

"Okay. Shoot."

Quinton took a deep breath. "The last time I dated a woman, I wasn't saved. And now that I am saved, well, I don't know how to uh . . . I don't know what I'm supposed to uh . . ."

Pastor Kendrick held up his hand. "Hey, man, forget talking youth pastor to pastor, and talk to me brother to brother. I may be a pastor, but I'm a man first."

Quinton loosened up a little. "Man, I've never felt this way about anyone. When I was growing up, it was all about getting some." He paused for a minute to gauge Pastor Kendrick's response. When there was none, he decided it was safe to keep talking.

"Then when I was in college, you know, I was this big basketball star. You can't imagine how easy it was, you know to . . . I mean, women throwing it at you. So, being the young stupid kid I was, I got all I could get. Then later I got engaged and still didn't have any restrictions on, well you know . . .

"And then we broke up and I got saved and it was just me and God. So now, I don't know how to date as a Christian. I mean, what's proper, you know? Some people say you should only group date until you get married, others say date only in public places and never be alone together. Others say it's okay to be alone together, but not at night. I want to do this right. I want to be an example for the kids and I would never want to do anything to hurt . . ."

He let out a deep breath and sat back in his seat.

"I thought I knew what love was before, but now *I know* I know. If this isn't love, I don't want to ever be in love, because if real love is any stronger than what I'm feeling right now, I don't know what I'd do. I can barely function. I want to be with her and see her and I think about her all the time . . ."

Quinton felt very vulnerable saying all this, but he had to talk to *someone* about it. Pastor Kendrick had become the big brother he never had.

Pastor Kendrick sat for a few seconds. "I have to be honest. As a pastor, I've never wanted to run my members' lives. I know a lot of pastors who dictate their members' lives down to what they wear and where they're 'allowed' to go. I figure if you have the Word of God and His Spirit in you, He should dictate to you what you do. But since you asked . . ."

He rubbed his goatee. "I think it's safe to start out dating with other people or being out in public. At a certain point, you start to seek God about whether this person is your mate or not. If you believe she is, then things start to change and then it gets difficult. That point between when you decide to get serious, and the time you walk down the aisle and say 'I do' . . . man, I would never want to go through that again. It's pure torture."

Quinton furrowed his eyebrows. This wasn't exactly the advice he was expecting, but he appreciated Pastor Kendrick's honesty. "I thought it was just me."

Pastor Kendrick laughed. "Naw, it ain't just you. It's any man trying to live for God and do things right. The urge is bad enough when you're just trying to 'get some' as you say. When you're actually in *love*, like you appear to be . . . it's ten times worse. It's the natural progression of things. That's the way God made us. You love a person, and everything in you is made to want to take it to that level."

"So what do I do?"

Pastor Kendrick leaned forward as if he was about to tell Quinton the secret to the meaning of life. "You play it safe." He leaned back in his chair, as if he had just preached his best sermon.

"What does that mean?"

"You make sure you don't give the enemy, or your flesh or your natural, God-given desires, any room to make you do something your spirit man doesn't want you to do. Obviously, after you get that serious, group dating only is not realistic. There's no way you can fully get to know someone you want to spend the rest of your life with that way. On the other hand, it's not realistic to think you can sit on the couch late at night hugged up under a blanket watching *Love Jones*. The right answer is somewhere in between."

Quinton nodded.

Pastor Kendrick continued, "You have to decide where that safe place is for you. Some men don't allow a kiss on the cheek or handholding because they know themselves and where that will end up. Others don't even trust themselves to be in a room alone with their future mate. Other men can trust themselves to have private dates at home and they know the evening will end with a hug and kiss at the door. You have to know you and what you would do. And then— stay safe."

Quinton was relieved. It wasn't so bad after all.

Pastor Kendrick had one last bit of advice. "Never overestimate yourself. Never say, 'I wouldn't do this', or 'I'd never do that'. Don't think that you're stronger than you actually are. Never underestimate the power of love and your 'physical nature'. It's more powerful than you think. The minute you think you won't fall is the minute you fall."

Quinton smiled, but then realized how serious Pastor Kendrick was. He made a mental note of this last piece of advice. He stood, feeling as if he had gotten all the help he needed. "Thanks, Pastor. I really want to do right. I wouldn't want to do anything to hurt . . . this woman."

"This woman?" Pastor Kendrick laughed. "Aaawww, man, I thought we was keeping it real. I know good and well who you're talking about. Shoot, the whole church knows."

Quinton's eyes flew open.

That made Pastor Kendrick laugh even harder. "Please, man, I know you guys are trying to be discreet, or *whatever*, but both of you turn complete *fool* when the other one is in the room. Can't talk right, can't walk right, can't do nothing right. Please! You might as well relax and be real, 'cause y'all ain't fooling nobody. Even the kids whisper and make bets about when you're gonna get married."

Quinton didn't realize it was so obvious. He bit his lip.

Pastor Kendrick slapped him on the back. "I couldn't be happier that you guys are together. I think you guys make a great couple and a truly godly couple. I'm excited to see what God will accomplish through the two of you together for the Kingdom."

"Thanks, man. That means a lot to me." He hadn't realized how much Pastor Kendrick's approval would mean to him until that moment. He was happy he had his blessing.

Pastor Kendrick lifted a finger. "One last piece of advice. This may be premature, but two simple words that saved me and Jenell. Short engagement."

"Huh?"

"Christians ain't got no business talking about we're engaged and the wedding is a year from now. You think it's hard now? Wait 'til you know you're definitely getting married. You start imagining your life together, and start that wedding night countdown. It becomes near to impossible. I'm not sure even the godliest of men can stay holy under those circumstances if the engagement is far away."

Pastor Kendrick's phone rang. He smiled as he looked at the caller ID and picked it up. "Hey, you."

Quinton started toward the door.

Pastor Kendrick called behind him, "Hey,

Jenell cooked up a big Sunday dinner. Now that the truth is out, why don't the two of you join us?"

Quinton grinned. "Yeah, man. That sounds great."

Chapter Thirty-eight

A few weeks later, Keeva rolled over, reaching blindly to silence the annoying phone. "Hello?"

"Keev, it's me. Get dressed. I want to take you somewhere."

"Shara, it's 6:30 on a Sunday morning. Are you insane?"

"Come on, Keeva, this is really important. I'll pick you up at 7:15."

Keeva gave Shara the evilest look she could muster when she pulled up at her apartment building. "This better be good."

"It will be. I promise."

Keeva sat in a sleepy daze in the car for a while. She brought her hand to her mouth to cover a yawn.

"Keeva, your finger is empty!"

Keeva finished yawning. "I know. Mark came over last night and I gave the ring back."

"Oh my goodness. Why didn't you tell me? I would have let you rest this morning."

Keeva waved her concern away. "No, it's cool. I'm fine, actually. Anyway, I probably need one of your little surprises right about now."

"Are you okay? How did it go?"

Keeva rolled her eyes. "How do you think?"

She closed her eyes and laid her head back on the headrest, thinking about the previous evening.

She knew giving the ring back would be difficult, but she hadn't expected it would be that bad.

Mark had paced back and forth in her loft. "You get in with these holy rollers and all of a sudden you're throwing away everything we've worked so hard for! What did those people do to you? What about our future together? What about all our plans?"

"Our plans? Those were *your* plans. I don't care about the big house, fancy cars, and country clubs and all that stuff. And I certainly don't want to be a politician's wife like my mom."

"I can't believe you're saying this."

"Mark, I've been unhappy in this relationship for a long time. I've been trying to tell you that. I can't marry you. Why can't you accept that?"

"Because I love you. How can you say you're unhappy? We've had a wonderful four years together."

"You've had four wonderful years. I'm telling you I've been unhappy."

"I can't believe you've let them brainwash you. I've heard about those holy roller cults, but I never imagined you'd get taken in by one. You're too intelligent for that."

"It's not a cult. And this has nothing to do with the church. This is about you and me. Don't bring the church into it."

"How can I not? Our relationship was perfectly fine until you started going there. They've changed you. Why can't you see that? I don't know who you are anymore."

"You never knew who I was before. *I* didn't know who I was before."

Her voice softened. "For the first time in my life, I feel like I'm finding out who I am and know what I want out of life. I've never felt that before. I always did what my parents did, and thought what my parents thought, and accepted the dreams they had for me and let go of my own. Then when we got together, I did what you did, and thought what you thought. Now I want to be my own person. I want to live my own dreams."

"Oh, so this is my fault now? I was controlling you and keeping you from living your dreams? I can't believe I'm hearing this. Why don't you call me when you're making sense."

Keeva jumped, remembering the force with which the door had rattled from his anger.

"Keeva?" Shara looked over at her.

"You know what's funny? When he left, I sat there, waiting to cry, but no tears came. All I felt was . . . relief. I mean—I know it will probably hurt later, but . . ." She let out a long breath. "I don't think it's over in his mind, though. He left screaming for me to call him when I'm making sense. I hope he doesn't try to drag this out."

Shara rubbed her arm.

They pulled up at a large church building.

Keeva read the sign, *New Life Christian Church*. "What's this?"

Shara answered, "This is one of our sister churches. Bishop Thompson really helped Pastor Kendrick out when he was first getting started. I want to show you something."

Keeva was overwhelmed by the size of the church. The sanctuary was huge like a performing arts theater. The choir looked like an army.

They had two dancers on stage during the praise and worship. Keeva was sure that was what Shara wanted her to see. Was that what Shara meant by dancing being about Christ? They were good and it was a nice addition to the praise and worship, but it still wasn't anything like Alvin Ailey.

A large choir sang and then a sign flashed at the bottom of the screens, *Epichoreago Dance Troupe*.

Shara bounced in her seat. "Here we go."

One dancer came out on the stage and the music started. Keeva recognized the song, "Set the Atmosphere," from one of Shara's CD's— Kurt Carr's *Awesome Wonder*. It was one of those songs Shara drove her crazy with, playing it over and over.

The dancer moved passionately to the words

of the song and then was joined by other dancers who came down the aisles. They all met at the front and danced a perfectly choreographed worship scene. Their white satin outfits flowed and billowed with every movement they did.

Tears streamed down Keeva's face. The dancing was beautiful, but it was more than that. Something deep inside of her was stirring, engaging in a dance of its own. She felt as if something were coming alive in her soul, like things were coming together and making sense. She stood while the dancers were still dancing, overwhelmed by the beauty of it. The tears kept flowing and she lifted her hands. She wasn't the only one moved by it. By the time the song reached its climax, others were standing and lifting their hands also.

The CD stopped playing, but the church musicians picked up right where it left off. The dancers kept dancing, improvising. People flowed down to the altar. Keeva didn't know why, but she was drawn also.

She was feeling that God-thing again, coming over her in waves. It was so strong this time she could barely stand up. She started trembling. Bishop Thompson suddenly got up, walked across the stage and stood in front of her. He whispered in her ear and then softly touched her forehead.

Keeva felt a huge wave of the God-thing, and next thing she knew, an usher was helping her up off the floor. She slipped back into her seat beside Shara.

When they got back to the car, Keeva said, "Shara, I'm never going anywhere with you again. I can't believe he pulled a Benny Hinn on me!"

"What?"

"That falling out on the floor thing, like they do on Benny Hinn's show. You know that guy on the Christian television station."

Shara stifled a giggle.

"What happened to me?"

"I don't know. You're the one that fell out on the floor."

"Shara! Explain it to me. I thought that stuff was fake when I saw it on TV."

"You tell *me* what happened."

Keeva put her hand to her cheek. "I was watching the dancers and . . . it spoke to me. When I was watching the lead dancer, it was like something in her was talking to something in me. Then Bishop Thompson came up and whispered something in my ear like he knew me. What was *that*?"

Shara said, "Remember the first time you met Mother Hobbs and you swore I told her something about you, and you asked me if she was psychic? And then when Pastor preached that sermon the day you got saved and you swore I had been talking to him? It's the Holy Spirit talking through a prophetic gift."

"Then he barely touched me and I felt the God-thing like in praise and worship, and—"

"The God-thing?"

"Yeah, that's my name for it. Sometimes in praise and worship, or when Pastor Kendrick is preaching, I feel this thing. It's like waves of . . . I don't know, goodness and warmth and love . . . like electric tingles. Anyway, I felt it when he touched me, but it was much bigger, like a big tidal wave. I felt like I was engulfed in . . . I don't know—the God-thing is all I can say. Then I was getting up. What *is* that?"

Shara smiled. "Actually, the God-thing isn't such a bad name for it. I guess that's really what it is—the presence of God, or the Holy Spirit. What did he whisper in your ear?"

Keeva's eyes sparkled. "That God called me to be His dancer—to dance to display His glory. Not only will I dance, but I will lead a group of dancers. I'll bring life to those I lead, and my dance troupe will bring new life to those that see us dance. Then he said God was releasing His anointing on me to fulfill His purpose for my life."

"Keeva, that's a great word!" Shara slowed down as she approached a stop sign.

"What do you mean?"

"That's what we call it, a word from God. It's like God sending you a message through another person. Sometimes He talks to us through other people to give us direction or to confirm something that we're thinking, but we're not sure it's Him."

"Does that mean that's what my purpose and destiny is?"

"Sounds like that's a part of it. You'll have to seek Him for direction and insight."

"What do you mean, 'seek Him'? I always hear you guys saying 'God said' or 'the Lord told me'. What does that mean? You can actually hear God talking to you?"

Shara wrinkled her nose. "You don't hear an

actual voice. You just get this impression in your spirit."

Keeva frowned.

Shara was quiet for a second as she looked over her shoulder, then sped up to merge onto the freeway. She continued, "It's almost like thoughts inside your head that you hear, but it's not you thinking them, you're hearing them, but they don't sound like a voice, they sound like thoughts. It has this feeling to it though, like the God-thing feeling and you know it's not from you, it has to be from Him."

"Well, how do you know it's Him and not you?"

"I don't know. You just know. There's this scripture that says 'my sheep know my voice.' I guess it's all a part of building a relationship. When I first met you, I couldn't recognize your voice on the phone. You'd have to say, 'this is Keeva.' Now that we're close friends, I could pick out your voice in a noisy room full of people. It's the same way with God. As we familiarize ourselves with hearing His voice by spending time in His presence, it becomes easier and easier to hear Him. Of course, you have to check it with the Word. If it doesn't line up, it's not Him. It takes some time to learn how to hear God and even longer to trust that it's Him speaking. I think the most important thing to realize is that He's always talking and wants to communicate with us about even the smallest details in our lives."

Keeva shook her head. "There's so much to

learn about God, I feel like I'll never understand Him."

"The day you fully understand Him is the day He ceases to be God. I'm sure we'll spend all of eternity still searching out the mysteries of God. He's too awesome for any human mind to understand."

"Yeah, I guess that's part of what makes Him God," Keeva said.

Shara looked at the clock on the dashboard. "You want me to drop you off at home?"

"Nope. It's still early. If you stop driving like I'm Miss Daisy, we can get to our church in time for praise and worship."

Shara smiled. "Our church, huh?"

Keeva nodded. "Yeah. Our church."

Chapter Thirty-nine

Keeva found herself struggling to pay attention to her client. The fall semester was halfway over. She had started her counseling practicum and was working with real people.

She looked at the frumpy woman sitting in front of her. She was a thirty-seven-year-old mother of three and was worried about everything. She worried that her kids weren't getting the best education in their private school and that she wasn't spending enough time with them because they were starting to act out. She was worried that her husband was getting bored with her and that he may have an affair if she couldn't keep him interested. She was concerned that the property values in her exclusive neighborhood weren't rising as fast as in the neighborhood a few blocks over.

Keeva had to work hard not to snap in disdain that the woman's problems weren't real. She pictured herself screaming, *"You want to see problems? Go down to Bankhead Highway and see the kids there whose parents are on crack and would just as soon sell them for their next fix. Check out the sixteen-year-old selling her body so she can get high. All you need to do is get a new hairstyle, put on some makeup, and for God's sake, get some decent clothes. Your kids need a good beatin' or at least to be told 'no' for once in their life. Go home and do all this, and I promise your sad little life will get a lot better."*

Keeva felt guilty for feeling that way. To this woman, her problems were as real as a crack addict's. She imagined her on Oprah, crying into the tissue Oprah handed her. She saw Dr. Phil giving her the advice she needed to make her life better.

"What do you think?" the woman asked.

Keeva looked at her, startled, realizing she hadn't been paying any attention. She recovered quickly. "What I think doesn't really matter now does it, Mrs. Kennedy? What do *you* think? What decisions do you need to make for *you*? What choices will empower you?" She put on her best concerned face.

"You're right. I guess the answers are really deep down. I need to listen to my inner self. I saw that on Oprah the other day. She and Dr. Phil were discussing . . ." she trailed off into another flood of words.

Keeva zoned out again, resisting the temptation to look at her watch. What would Shara do with this patient? She pictured her laying hands on the woman and casting out the spirit of worry and self-pity. She could see Mrs. Kennedy falling out on the floor, slain in the spirit. She must have giggled because Mrs. Kennedy stopped mid-sentence and looked at her in horror.

Keeva froze. She wanted to smack herself. She could hear her mother's voice in her ear chastising her that her daydreaming was going to get her in big trouble one day. *Think girl, think!* "I'm sorry, Mrs. Kennedy, I was imagining something. This is a new therapeutic technique we're using. I want you to close your eyes with me and imagine your husband . . ."

By the time she finished, Mrs. Kennedy was almost on the floor . . . in a fit of laughter.

"We call this technique creative imagery." Keeva coined a new term as it came to her. "I want you to use this every time you're overwhelmed with your problems. Whether it be your husband, your children, the center where you volunteer, whatever it is, use creative imagery to bring the situation to a place where you can handle it." She looked at her watch. "Oh dear, we were having such fun, I lost track of the time. I don't want to be late for my next client."

Sorry for that lie, God. Thankfully, she didn't have anyone else. She couldn't take another person today.

Mrs. Kennedy wiped the tears of laughter away. "Thank you so much, Ms. Banks. I haven't had so much fun and laughed so much in years."

Then you definitely need to get a life.

Keeva felt sorry for her. It was sad that that the most fun she'd had in years was a laugh on the couch with her therapist. Keeva was glad she had been able to help. It felt good to know she had been able to aid in alleviating another person's suffering.

This might not be so bad. Keeva had to shake herself to remember the only reason she had gotten Mrs. Kennedy to laugh was because she had been so bored and annoyed with her that she hadn't paid attention to her meaningless rambling and had had to make up a "therapeutic technique" to save her grade.

Shara had a fit of laughter as Keeva recounted the Mrs. Kennedy story to her later in the church office. Keeva had stopped by before going up to the dance studio.

"Now what did you call it? 'Creative imagery?' What were you thinking about anyway that you weren't paying attention?" Shara asked.

Shara almost fell out of her chair laughing when Keeva recounted the scene of Mrs. Kennedy being slain in the spirit. "Your imagination is out of control, girl. You gotta rein that thing in, or better still, put it to some good use other than tricking your patients."

"Like what?"

"Write stories or plays or choreograph some of those dances you see in your head when your favorite songs are playing. Do something with it, girl, otherwise it's going to keep sneaking up on you at the most inopportune times."

Often, they'd be driving or studying and Keeva would slip into a daydream listening to music. She could actually see images in her head of her and the kids dancing. She smiled as she thought of a piece she and Shanique were working on together. Ever since that day at New Life Christian Center, she had been flooded with creative ideas for choreography.

"See, there you go again. Earth to Keeva. Seriously though Keev, what are you going to do when you've got one Mrs. Housewife right after another one, all day long, every day, five days a week?"

Keeva shuddered. She had been thinking about that a lot since she started her practicum. She couldn't even make it through one patient without taking a trip to her dream world. What would she do when she had to see them all day to pay the bills? She had never actually thought about what it would really be like being a therapist. She did like helping people. It just seemed more meaningful when she was helping her kids.

The door flew open and Danae ran in screaming. "Miss Keeva, Miss Shara! There's a fight on the basketball court. This time it's serious."

Chapter Forty

Keeva and Shara got out to the basketball court in time to see Quinton wrestling T-bone to the ground. Jamil's nose was bleeding and he was yelling obscenities while Anthony held him back from trying to jump on T-bone.

"Quinton?"

"I got it, Shara. You guys go back inside."

She and Keeva stood frozen. Most of the fights never got bad enough for an adult to have to intervene. Usually, at the first sign of an authority figure, the kids would settle down. T-bone, however, had been a problem since he'd gotten involved with the basketball program. He hadn't met the grade requirement, often started fights, and didn't respect any of the adults. Shara had been telling Quinton he needed to be kicked out of the program, but Quinton seemed to think if he kept working with him, he would get better.

Quinton and his boys were becoming a sore

spot between him and Shara. Initially, she admired his dedication and commitment to them, but lately, she had become concerned about it. He spent far too much money on them, and in her opinion, far too much time.

If it wasn't taking Jamil to get sneakers, it was taking Deshawn for a doctor's appointment or Tyreek to the mall, or Tiquan for school clothes. Each of them had his home phone, cell phone, and pager number and used him as their personal taxi and Santa Claus. Shara initially joked about him having a savior complex, but anytime she mentioned it, he got agitated and changed the subject.

Quinton stood T-bone up, still holding on to him.

T-bone was seething, trying to escape Quinton's relentless hold. "You done it now. You think you so great just 'cause you was a basketball star? Your blood will flow red, just like anybody else's," T-bone spat at Quinton. "Jamil, you a dead man. Nobody crosses me and—"

"That's enough!" Quinton's voice bellowed across the court. He looked up at Shara and Keeva.

"Shara, I said go inside."

"Do you want me to call the police?"

"No honey, just do what I told you. Danae, you go with them."

Shara felt chills running up her spine from T-bone's words. She understood Quinton's desire to help him, but this time, he needed to let go. As far as she was concerned, they should have gotten rid of T-bone and his equally belligerent friend, Jermaine, a long time ago.

"You okay?" Keeva asked as they walked back into the office.

"Yeah. I don't like that boy." Shara looked at her watch. "You better go on up. The girls have been waiting and you don't want to have to break up a fight of your own."

"My girls fight? Never."

Keeva hadn't had a fight out of Shanique or Lakita since they'd started taking dance classes. In fact, most of the time, they were inseparable, giggling in some corner about a boy. Shara noticed since they started dancing, a lot of the girls carried themselves with more grace and esteem. They acted prissy and ladylike, as if they were imitating Keeva.

Shara snapped her fingers. "Oh, I almost forgot. Mother Hobbs said Pastor Kendrick wanted to take a few of us out to dinner tonight after we finish up. We're supposed to meet at Justin's at 7:00. You can ride with me and Quinton if you want."

"Wow, nice—what for?"

"I don't know. Mother Hobbs said he had some great news to share with us."

"Cool. I'll meet you in the parking lot after class."

Chapter Forty-one

When Keeva got to the parking lot, Quinton and Shara were already waiting in the truck. As they were pulling off, Anthony came running up. "Hey, can I catch a ride with you guys?"

Anthony and Quinton had become friends and he had started hanging out with the three of them. He hopped in the back seat with Keeva. "Yo, Quint-man, what was up with your boy, T? He's usually bad, but I've never seen him that bad. What's his beef with Jamil?

"I don't know. Kid stuff I guess."

"It seemed like more than that. Talking 'bout your blood flowing red and Jamil's a dead man and stuff. That boy scares me."

"Naw, he's just all mouth."

Keeva watched Shara looking at Quinton. It was obvious he was downplaying things to keep her from being afraid.

"What's the name of this restaurant?" Quinton asked.

"Quinton, you don't think he has a gun or something, do you?" Shara asked.

He looked over at her and rubbed her cheek. "Stop worrying, baby. T-bone is all talk. He's been making threats since he started coming around. He gets mad about any little thing and mouths off. It's nothing." He squeezed Shara's knee.

"Hey! Stop that. You know I'm ticklish." Shara giggled.

Keeva made a face. "Oh boy, here we go. We should have taken your car, Anthony. I don't know how much of 'the Sickenings' I'm going to be able to take."

"Shut up, Keeva." Shara giggled again.

Keeva smiled at how happy her friend was. She wondered when Quinton was going to pop the question. The way they acted, it was just a matter of time.

Her thoughts drifted to Mark. After she first broke off their engagement, he called her relentlessly every day. He stopped by unannounced at odd hours when he knew she'd be home. The first few times she let him in to talk, but after hearing him yell and scream about getting her deprogrammed, she took her key back and stopped answering the door. He even had her mother and father calling. He had obviously convinced them she had lost her mind and joined a cult. The calls eventually trickled off. She hadn't heard from him in about a month.

"Earth to Keeva. Where'd you go this time?" Shara turned around in her seat.

"Just thinking about a dance. You know me." Keeva sighed heavily.

Anthony put a hand on her arm. "Must not have been a happy dance. You okay?"

She nodded at him.

At first it had been difficult and she had missed Mark. Over the past few months though, she had gotten so caught up in dancing and her girls, church, hanging out with the other youth leaders, and school, she hardly thought about him. She smiled to herself as she realized she was happy getting to know herself and getting to know God. She hadn't missed a church service or Bible study since she and Mark broke up. She had even been going to intercessory prayer on Friday mornings. She was really developing a relationship with God, just like Shara had described. She really felt like she was going somewhere with her life now. She wasn't sure where exactly, but since she had started working with the youths, she had that sense of purpose Shara always talked about.

She had asked God to give her some definite direction about what to do next in terms of her career. She asked Him every day to direct her toward what jobs to interview for. She hadn't heard Him answer her and had been meaning to ask Shara more about how to hear His voice. She had to do something soon. Everybody else was interviewing and some had found jobs.

She wasn't nervous though. She had a strange peace that God had it all under control.

"Now you must be thinking about a happy dance. Wish I could unlock that mind of yours. Must be some serious stuff that goes on in there." Anthony watched Keeva grinning to herself.

Shara looked back. "Yeah, Keeva's always dreaming up a masterpiece. I can't wait until the Christmas program."

Keeva wouldn't allow anyone to come near the dance rooms while they were practicing. She kept saying everybody had to wait until the performance at the end of the year. They were planning a combined dance recital, awards ceremony, and dedication for the new track and basketball courts. The kids were very excited about bringing their families and friends.

"Here we go." Quinton parked the truck.

When they walked into the restaurant, Pastor Kendrick, Jenell, and Mother Hobbs were already sitting at a large table. Quinton pulled back Shara's chair and Anthony held Keeva's for her.

"We're still waiting for Nia and Malcolm," Pastor Kendrick said. "Why don't you guys go ahead and order. They should be here any minute."

After Nia and Malcolm arrived and everyone put their orders in, Pastor Kendrick cleared his throat. "First of all, I want to thank everyone for their hard work and dedication this year. God couldn't have sent me a better team. I think God has decided to reward our efforts."

He looked like he was about to burst. "I received official notification today that..." he paused for effect, "... we got the grant."

Everyone cheered at once. The other people in the restaurant looked over to see what all the noise was about.

After everyone calmed down, Pastor Kendrick continued, "I wanted you all to be the first to know, because well, let me slow down some. We're going to be doing some revamping of the allocation of some funds."

He slapped Quinton on the back. "Because Quinton here was so gracious in funding the resurfacing of the track and basketball courts and renovating the dance and martial arts studios, and because he's refused his salary, we have a lot more money than we thought we'd have."

Quinton would have blushed if his skin wasn't so dark. "Man, I told you I didn't want anyone to know about all that. That was supposed to be between me and you."

"Sorry, Quint-man. I'm excited. Cut me some slack."

Pastor Kendrick continued, "Because of the surplus and grant, we have funds for full-time salaries for a few individuals and part-time for others. So here we go. Shara and Keeva will be graduating next year just as the grant starts paying out. Shara, if you're interested and you feel it's God's desire, we'd like you to come on full time as director of our education and tutoring programs. We'll continue the after-school programs and then run a summer enrichment program. After a while, we want to start planning a charter school."

Shara's mouth hung open.

"Keeva, I don't know if we can persuade you to forego your career plans, but we'd like you to head up our dance program. We'll continue the after-school programs and then have a full-time dance academy during the summer. Nia has also told me about the plays you've written for her theatre program. We'd like to have you continue that also. Take your time and really think and pray about it. I know we're asking you to give up a lot, especially since there's no promise of funding beyond the initial five-year period. Let me know what you feel like God is saying."

"Yes!" Keeva bounced in her seat. "Yes! He's saying yes and I'm saying yes."

Everybody laughed. Shara squeezed Keeva's hand. They shared a hug of excitement.

Pastor Kendrick continued, "Anthony, I know that it takes money out of your business when you leave your studios to come teach martial arts for us, so we'd like to compensate you for your time."

Anthony held up his hand. "I can't accept any money, Pastor. My business is going great and my time teaching at the church is actually a tithe. What we can do, though, is use the money to buy uniforms for the kids. I think they'd like that."

Pastor Kendrick nodded. "That sounds great, man. Thanks."

He turned to Nia. "Well, according to the kids, your theatre program is 'da bomb'. We'd like to compensate you for your after-school time, then full-time in the summer."

Nia said, "I wish I could be as noble as Quinton and Anthony and say keep the money, but y'all know teachers don't make nothing. I need all the help I can get."

Everyone laughed.

Shara said, "I hear you, girl."

Pastor Kendrick turned to Malcolm. "Last but not least—our visual arts and creative writing programs. I was going to offer you a part-time position, but I have to look at the numbers now. With Anthony waiving his salary, we can probably bring you on full-time."

"Man, I see God does answer prayer. The starving artist thing is getting *real* old." Malcolm rubbed his hands together like he could feel the money already.

Pastor Kendrick leaned back in his chair and smiled. "I guess that settles it then. I'm so excited I don't know what to do. God couldn't have sent me a better crew. I love y'all, man." Pastor Kendrick sniffled and pretended to start crying and everyone laughed.

Mother Hobbs spoke up. "Pastor, aren't you forgetting someone?"

He looked around. "Oh yeah." He kissed Jenell on the cheek. "My baby here is going to continue the music program and the youth choir at no charge." She kissed him back.

"Don't start that stuff." Mother Hobbs shook her head. "Can't take y'all nowhere."

Everyone laughed.

They all talked excitedly over dinner, making plans and of course, telling stories about their kids. After the waitress cleared their dinner plates, a few people ordered dessert.

Quinton leaned over to Shara. "Wanna share a piece of red velvet cake with me?"

"Just like our first date?" She kissed him and they rubbed noses.

Mother Hobbs humphed. "Now here y'all go. I've told you about all that kissing when people are trying to eat."

They both laughed and blushed.

Nia made a face. "Talk about public displays of affection . . ."

Everyone followed her eyes to a couple at a table not too far away. They were kissing passionately as if no one was in the restaurant but them.

Shara heard Keeva gasp. Obviously, the couple heard her also because they stopped kissing and turned around.

It was Mark . . . with Jade.

Shara could feel Keeva's nails starting to sink into her arm. "Keev?"

"Huh?" She looked down at Shara's arm. "Oh! Sorry, Shara."

Mark sat with his mouth open and eyes wide. Jade ran her fingers through her hair and wiped her mouth. She got up and left the table.

Shara said under her breath, "I can't believe he's going to walk his trifling butt over here and . . ."

Mark stood with his hands in his pockets. "Keeva, it's uh, it's good to uh—"

"Good to see you too, Mark." Keeva's voice was smooth and calm. "Jade didn't leave, did she? I didn't get a chance to say hello."

He cleared his throat. "Yeah, she got paged. She's on call tonight. We'll probably have to uh, leave because she may have to go in to, uh, the hospital." He chuckled and rubbed his hands together. "You know how her, uh, job is . . . you never know when somebody might go into labor." He looked around at the others at the table. All eyes were on him.

"Um hmm, well, too bad your dinner got interrupted. Please tell Jade I said hello." Keeva gave him one of her infamous nice-nasty smiles Shara hadn't seen in a long time. "Do give her a big kiss for me, 'kay?"

"Yeah, uh, I'll do that." He gave a little nod and slunk away from the table. He whispered something to the waitress on the way out the door.

Keeva let out a breath after he was gone.

"You okay, Keeva?" Shara and Anthony asked simultaneously from both sides.

Keeva flagged down the waitress. "I'm so sorry to bug you, but I changed my mind. Could you bring me the biggest hunk of chocolate cake you have?" She smiled as the waitress nodded. "Thank you so much."

Everyone went back to talking again, pretending nothing had happened.

Shara pretended not to hear Anthony whisper, "So is that the guy that ruined things for me?"

She tried not to eavesdrop, but still heard Keeva's answer. "I told you, it's not about him, it's about me."

When she was sure that this exchange was finished, Shara leaned over. "Keev? You all right?"

Keeva took a big bite of her chocolate cake the waitress had just brought. "Ummmm. I am now." She closed her eyes and chewed slowly, humming.

Shara and Anthony both laughed, shaking their heads.

When they got back to the church parking lot, Quinton joked with Anthony as they walked to his car. Shara knew he was allowing her some time to talk to Keeva.

Shara hopped out of the truck and got into the back seat with Keeva. "Well, that was a surprise."

Keeva looked at her. "Come on, Shara, with the brief encounters you had with both of them, was it really?"

"I guess not."

"Actually, they're quite perfect for each other. I'm sure they'll live happily ever after."

Shara smirked. "Please Keeva, you know they'll be battling it out in divorce court ten years from now."

"Ya think? Nah . . . five."

They both laughed.

Shara looked over at Quinton and Anthony. "So what's up with that?"

"Nothing really. He's interested. I'm not. I don't want or need a man right now."

"Isn't that a total switch?"

"What?"

"I'm just thinking back to when we first met. You were with Mark and I was the one that was allergic to men."

"I'm not allergic. I'm enjoying being with me. I think the reason you and Quinton are so disgustingly happy now is because you spent all that time getting to know and love yourself and God first."

"Yeah." Shara sighed, looking dreamy-eyed over at Quinton.

"Oh, I think I'm gonna be sick."

Shara swatted at Keeva. "Whatever! So did you let Anthony down easy? He's such a sweet guy."

"He is nice. I told him the truth. I told him I was coming out of a bad relationship and needed to spend some time healing and becoming the best me that I could be by myself."

"Sounds good. What'd he say?"

Keeva's lips curved into a smile. "That years of practicing martial arts had made him a very patient man and he had seen things in me that let him know I was worth the wait."

Shara sat up in her seat. "Whoa!"

"What can I say, girl?" Keeva batted her eyelashes. "I still got it."

They laughed.

They got out of the truck and Shara gave Keeva a hug. "You sure you're okay?"

Keeva looked her in the eye. "Yeah, honestly, I am."

Shara smiled at her friend. She was amazed at God by how much Keeva had grown emotionally and spiritually since the first time they met.

"What?"

"Nothing. Just proud of you, that's all."

"Whatever, Shara, don't get all corny and mushy on me."

"Love you, girl."

"Yeah, love you too."

Chapter Forty-two

"Hey, Shara. I'm cooking you dinner for our six-month anniversary. Can you be at my place at 6:00?"

"That's the big surprise today? How sweet of you to remember." Shara had grown to love Quinton's early morning phone calls. He seemed to always know the exact minute she finished talking to God but hadn't quite gotten out of the bed to go for a run. She yawned a lazy Saturday morning yawn and then sat up in her bed, realizing what Quinton had said. "You mean I actually get to come to your apartment again?"

"What's that supposed to mean?"

"You haven't invited me over in forever. Not that I mind you taking me out to all these different places. I thought I had been banished from your home."

"You had. I couldn't trust you to behave yourself. I had to keep things safe."

"Whatever, Quinton. Jeans and a T-shirt?"

"No, this is a special occasion. Wear something nice."

"Yeah?"

"Yeah—this is extra special."

Shara hung up the phone and tried to figure out what to wear. She smiled remembering their first date. She decided to wear the brown dress she had worn that night. She'd have to pull on her winter coat over it, though.

Shara could hardly wait until six o'clock to see what Quinton had up his sleeve. After a light sprint up the steps, she knocked on the door of his apartment. She was pleasantly surprised to see candles on the table, already lit. Fred Hammond was playing on the stereo and the air was filled with wonderful smells of food cooking.

Quinton greeted her with a light kiss. "You look beautiful, baby. Dinner is already ready, as you demanded on your last visit here. I'll have everything out in a minute. Make yourself at home." He went back into the kitchen.

Shara looked around. He had new art on the walls and some pictures of what she guessed to be his family. An older woman in a picture *had* to be his mother. He looked just like her. Shara giggled at a young picture of Quinton with a big Afro. She picked up another picture of his mother, him, and three other boys. Two of them were twins. They were caramel brown and didn't bear much resemblance to the others. The youngest one looked exactly like Quinton. Seeing all of them made Shara realize how little

Quinton talked about his family. She didn't even know he had twin brothers.

She put the picture down when he came out with the food.

Quinton had cooked ribs, macaroni and cheese, sweet potatoes, greens, and cornbread.

"Our first date. You remembered."

"How could I forget the first time I got to really see you eat?" He shuddered. "The memory is hard to get rid of."

She punched his arm, but smiled. "You said this was gonna be special, but I didn't expect all this. Where did you learn to cook soul food?"

"The master chef, Delores Mercer." He nodded toward his mother's picture.

They ate, talked, and flirted, as they had on their first date.

"Save some room for dessert," Quinton warned as he watched Shara clean her plate.

"Now you tell me."

Quinton disappeared into the kitchen and returned with a red velvet cake.

"Oh, now I'm really touched."

As they started in on their cake and coffee, they chatted and flirted some more.

After a while, Quinton got a serious look on his face. "Shara, there's something I need to be honest with you about. I've sort of kept something from you for the past few months."

Shara's heart sank into the pit of her stomach. Her mind wandered back to her conversation with her parents a few weeks ago. They had both been on the phone as she told them about how well things were going at the church. Her mother had said her usual, "That's nice, dear." Her father criticized everything and made it clear he didn't approve of their "new-fangled religion."

She had dared to tell them about Quinton and how much she loved him and thought this was the man God sent for her to marry. Her mother sounded happy, but her father, of course, didn't have anything good to say. "You watch out there, baby girl. He sounds too good to be true and things that seem to be too good to be true usually are. Remember—Satan disguises himself as an angel of light."

She was frustrated as always when she hung up the phone with him. Now she wondered if her father was right about another man in her life.

Had Quinton brought her here for this wonderful dinner to soften the blow of some bad news? Had he murdered someone in his gang-banging days in the projects? Did he have AIDS and that's why he always pulled away from kissing her? She looked down at the beautifully decorated cake and thought of all the kitchen appliances.

Was he gay?

Her heart beat so fast she got short of breath.

"Remember when I told you the owner of this building had decided to renovate the entire building? And then when you asked about the other buildings on the block being renovated and I said the same owner was fixing up those buildings too?"

Shara nodded.

Quinton took a deep breath. "Well, I sort of misled you. The mysterious owner is . . . me."

Shara let out a huge breath, and then punched his arm. "You scared me, silly! I thought it was something bad."

Quinton rubbed his arm. "What did you think I was going to say, that I had killed somebody or that I was gay or something?" He laughed.

Shara wondered if Keeva's vivid imagination was rubbing off on her. Then she realized what he had said. "You? *You* own the buildings?"

He nodded sheepishly. "Yeah. When I first started making money, me and a buddy did some real estate deals. We bought abandoned buildings in the projects, got low interest construction loans to fix them up, and then rented them out to Section 8 tenants to pay the mortgages, with a huge profit of course. I own a couple of buildings here and more than a few back in Chicago."

He pointed to the picture of his family. "The twins manage them for me. They've become quite the businessmen and I've helped them buy and renovate a few of their own. I'm going to rent the apartments out to people in the neighborhood here. They'll have to go through some financial management and other classes. Hopefully, they'll be able to eventually buy them as condos. I don't want to just give handouts. I want to empower people to help themselves."

"Why was that such a big secret?"

Quinton hung his head. "I wanted to make sure you loved me for me and not because I have money. When I asked you to marry me, I wanted to know you were saying yes because you love me."

"Quinton, I can't believe you!"

"What?"

"You're not supposed to do it like that!"

"I'm sorry. I know it's insulting to play you for someone that shallow, but after my last relationship—"

"I'm not talking about that, silly! You can't just say 'when I ask you to marry me.' You can't just mention it in conversation like that. You've ruined everything!"

"Woman, what are you talking about?"

Shara pouted. "A woman waits all her life for the perfect man to ask her to marry him. It's supposed to be wonderful and romantic when he proposes to her. You just ruined it! Mentioning it all casual like that. It's supposed to be a big surprise and the happiest moment of her life that she'll never forget."

"You mean like this?" Quinton picked up the remote to the stereo and changed the CD to some soft jazz. He dropped down on one knee and pulled a little blue box out of his pocket.

Shara's mouth flew open and she covered her face with her hands.

"Don't tell me I don't know how to propose."

He looked up at her. "For the past few weeks, I've been in the Bible, trying to write this perfect speech. I had a monologue prepared on the virtuous woman. Then I had this speech on Adam and Eve and how God took her out of him and she was his help-meet. Then I had this other speech about Christ and the church, the perfect example of a man and his bride. I practiced them over and over, but they all ended up sounding corny and stupid, or religious. I finally decided on this.

"When God made you, He put in you everything I needed in a wife. I believe He put in me everything you need in a husband. I feel like everything in our lives up to now was to bring us together in Him, so that we can fulfill the destiny that He ordained for us together. I don't think I can be all that I'm called to be without you by my side. Shara Anderson, I love you with all my heart and can't live another moment unless you promise to be my wife. Will you marry me?"

Shara was dumbstruck. Quinton reached up to wipe the tears falling from her eyes.

"Oh my goodness that was perfect." She sighed. "Yes, Quinton Mercer, I'll marry you."

They stood and embraced, then kissed—passionately. Quinton pulled away. "You kiss me like that again and we're going to have to get married tomorrow."

Shara giggled. Quinton slipped the ring on her finger.

Oh my goodness, it's huge! Quinton, this is too much."

"Don't you dare. I love you and want the best for you."

"No, I mean literally. I don't know if my finger is strong enough to hold this thing."

"I want the whole world to know how much I love you and that you're mine all mine."

They kissed again.

They danced for a while to the music playing, looking into each other's eyes.

"You just made me the happiest man in the world. Wait 'til I tell my momma. She'll be so glad."

Shara looked at the family picture. "That's her?"

Quinton picked up the frame. "Yeah, that's my heart. She has to go to second place now, though. These are the twins, Quintavious and Quintarious, and that's my baby boy, Quintell." He laughed at the look on her face. "Yeah, I know. I'm glad I was born first, before she had to get creative with the names."

"What was her obsession with the Q's?"

"My dad's name was Quinton. She was madly in love with him, so of course named me after him. He left her, though, and broke her heart. The twin's father wasn't around long enough to see them, so I guess she figured he didn't deserve a namesake. They got named after my dad too. Then, my dad came back into the picture for a while. He stayed around long enough to make Quintell, and then broke my mom's heart again. Mine too. My mom got saved not too long after he was born and closed up shop. Probably a good thing because I'm not sure what other 'Q' names she could have come up with."

He chuckled to himself and rubbed Quintell's face on the picture. "Looks exactly like me, doesn't he? I felt like he was a little present from my dad. He didn't stay around, but left a part of himself for me."

Quinton pulled himself away from his thoughts and the picture. "I'm sorry. I'm ruining your perfect proposal going on and on about my dysfunctional family."

"You're not ruining anything, silly. It's important

that I know about your family so I'll know what I'm getting."

"Oh, no. I better stop before you change your mind then."

She kissed him softly. "That's not gonna happen."

He kissed her back, longer this time. Shara felt a tingling in her stomach. She moaned softly. She was the one to pull away this time.

Quinton laughed. "Um hmm. Now you get to feel the torture you're always putting me through."

The phone rang.

Quinton winced. "Sorry. I should have turned it off." He turned the ringer off and came back over to her, but then his pager went off. He looked at it. "Sorry, baby. It's a 911 from Jamil. Let me go ahead and call him back otherwise he'll be showing up at the door."

He dialed the number. "Jamilly-mill, man, you got the worst timing, dog." His smile faded and fear replaced it. "Oh God, Jamil! All right, I'll be there in a minute."

He hung up the phone and picked up his keys. "Shara, listen closely. I want you to call the police and tell them there's been a shooting at the church basketball court."

He saw the panic in her eyes. "Calm down, baby. Nobody's been shot. That's the only way to get them there fast. Listen to me. I want you to stay here. Do *not* leave this apartment until you talk to me directly. I don't care what you hear. Promise me that, okay? Don't go out that door unless you talk to me and I tell you it's safe."

She nodded, hardly able to breathe. "Quinton, be careful . . ."

He kissed her quickly as he walked out the door. "I'll be fine, baby. I'll be back before you know it."

Shara ran to the phone and dialed 911 as he had instructed. After she talked to them, she started praying, pacing back and forth across the living room.

She heard gunshots, too many of them. They came from the direction of the church, right down the street. She screamed, "God, please don't let anything happen to Quinton."

She looked at the ring on her finger.

God wouldn't do that to her, would He?

Chapter Forty-three

Shara's heart beat faster when she heard the ear-piercing cry of an ambulance siren. Her head spun and her stomach churned. She ran to the bathroom and threw up her dinner. Everything was bright red from the red velvet cake. It reminded her of blood. She threw up again.

She grabbed her purse and keys and ran to the door, but remembered her promise to Quinton. She closed the door and called his cell phone, but there was no answer. She paced the floors of the apartment, still praying. She thought of calling Mother Hobbs, but didn't want to worry her when she didn't know what was going on herself. Pastor Kendrick and Jenell were out of town celebrating their wedding anniversary. She dialed Keeva's number.

Keeva promised to get there in fifteen minutes.

When she arrived, Shara opened the door,

her face swollen from crying, her voice ragged from screaming.

Keeva pulled Shara onto the couch and held her. "Shara, everything's gonna be fine." She saw the ring on Shara's hand. "Oh my God!"

That made Shara cry even harder.

Keeva rocked her and started praying. "God, we just commit Quinton into your hands. We thank You for your angels that You have protecting him, lest he even dash his foot against a stone. We thank You that nothing shall by any means harm him and that no weapon formed against him shall prosper . . ."

Hearing Keeva praying scriptures had a calming effect on Shara. She realized if God could so radically save Keeva to the point where Keeva was comforting *her* with the Word and prayer, He could definitely protect Quinton. She stopped crying and wiped her face. She started praying with Keeva.

An hour passed by. Shara didn't realize she had fallen asleep with her head in Keeva's lap until her cell phone phone jolted her awake. She ran to get it.

"Quinton?"

"Miss Shara. It's Jamil. I'm so sorry, Miss Shara. It's all my fault. I'm so sorry." He started crying.

Shara dropped the phone and fell back on the couch. The room grew dim and Keeva's voice sounded far away.

"Shara, what is it?"

Everything was fading to black. Shara put her head between her legs, trying to get some air to her brain before she passed out.

Keeva picked the phone. "Hello? . . . Jamil, it's Miss Keeva . . . slow down, sweetie. What's going on?" She put her hand on her chest. "Shara, he's okay. Quinton's alive."

Shara lay back on the couch trying to catch her breath. She cried tears of relief. She didn't have the strength to get up and motioned for Keeva to bring her the phone.

"Jamil?"

"No, it's me, baby. I'm all right."

She started crying when she heard his voice. "Quinton . . . oh my God. I thought you were dead . . . I heard gun shots . . . then an ambulance . . . oh my God . . ." She sobbed hysterically.

Keeva wrestled the phone from her. "Quinton, where are you?"

Keeva hung up the phone and picked up her purse. She helped Shara to her feet. "Come on, Shar. We're going to the hospital. Quinton is fine. We can bring him home, okay?"

Shara nodded, but continued crying all the way down the steps, into the car, and to the emergency room. When they got there, Keeva talked to a nurse then directed Shara to a room.

She cried harder when she saw Quinton. His face was swollen. One eye was black and blue. He had a large cut over it that had been stitched. The nurse was bandaging it when Shara gasped. "Quinton!"

Quinton motioned for the nurse to move away. Shara stumbled over to him. "Oh, baby, what happened? Look at you."

He tried to smile to make her feel better, but

winced. His top lip was swollen and Shara could see blood on his teeth.

She kissed his bottom lip. "Look at my sweet, sweet lips. Look at my beautiful, chocolate face." She planted little kisses on all the parts of his face and neck that didn't look hurt. "Oh my God, I'm so glad you're alive." She sat gingerly on the edge of the gurney, afraid she would hurt him.

He lifted an arm to hug her, but then winced. He looked down at a large bandage on his arm as if he had forgotten the injury.

"Oh, Quinton, be still, baby. I'm right here."

"I'm sorry I put you through this. I ruined your perfect proposal."

Shara laughed through her tears. He wiped her eyes. She leaned in to hug him, but he winced.

She heard the nurse behind say, "Careful, ma'am. He's got quite a few broken ribs and a bullet wound under that bandage on his arm."

"Bullet?" New tears formed in Shara's eyes.

"Baby, it's okay. It barely grazed me."

Shara looked at the nurse for confirmation as if she didn't believe Quinton. The nurse nodded reassuringly.

She heard a small voice behind her. "Yeah, Miss Shara, Mr. Quinton took a bunch of blows for me, then pushed me out of the way and almost took a bullet for me."

She whipped around to see Jamil. Keeva had her arm around his shoulder. His slender body was trembling.

Shara walked over to him and studied him to see if he was hurt. "Are you okay, Jamil?"

"Yes ma'am, Miss Shara."

"Good." She popped him on the side of his head. "That's for scaring me! The first words out of your mouth on that phone shoulda been Quinton's okay, or Quinton's alive. Not 'I'm so sorry, Miss Shara.'"

He started crying. "Sorry, Miss Shara."

She pulled him to her and hugged him. "It's okay, Jamil. I'm sorry. I was just scared. Miss Shara's sorry for hitting you." She kissed the spot where she had popped him.

She pulled Jamil away from her and started fussing. "How long have I been telling you to stay away from T-bone and them? I know that's who did this. If you had just listened to me—"

"Shara, that's enough!" Quinton yelled at her. Keeva led a sniffling Jamil out of the room.

She walked back over to the bed, her eyes blazing. "You have no right to yell at me, Quinton Mercer." She punched his good arm.

"Ow!"

The nurse moved over to protect him. Her face looked like she had seen enough ghetto drama in the ER to know this could turn ugly.

Quinton motioned to her that everything was okay. "Shara, have you lost your mind? I've had enough of a beating for one night."

"Quinton, I thought you were dead. You scared the *hell* out of me!"

"Obviously, not all of it." He chuckled, rubbing his arm.

She punched him again. "It's not funny. You propose to me and then almost get yourself killed? What's wrong with you? You and your savior complex."

Quinton laughed, wincing at the pain.

"Quinton, stop laughing! What's funny?"

"Minister Shara Anderson-soon-to-be-Mercer, standing here, cursing me out, that's what's funny. Come here, woman. Calm down before the nurse calls security on you."

She sat on the edge of the stretcher and started crying again.

He pulled her close. "I'm sorry, baby. I didn't mean to scare you. Where's your faith? You know God wouldn't let anything happen to me. We got a destiny to live out together."

"Faith? Even Jesus said He wouldn't put God to the test by throwing himself down off a mountain. What does faith have to do with your stupidity?"

"I know, Shara. Please stop fussing. You're making my head hurt." He tried to kiss her but couldn't purse his upper lip. She giggled through her tears and kissed his lower one.

He made a sour face. "Did you throw up or something?"

She covered her mouth. "When I heard the gun shots and the ambulance, I got so scared, I threw up my whole dinner."

"Woman, I can't believe you wasted all that good food I cooked for you."

She caught herself before punching him in the arm again.

Her face got serious. "I don't know what I would have done if you were dead. I can't imagine spending the rest of my life without you."

He bit his lip. "Does that mean you'll still marry me?"

"Of course, silly. I love you." A mischievous

look came across her face. "Besides, I'd have to be crazy to let a rich man like you go."

Quinton tried to make a shocked face, but couldn't. "Ooowee this hurts."

"Ma'am, he's going to need plenty of pain medicine," The nurse said. "We gave him a big dose here, but he'll need another by morning. You may not even be able to sleep in the same bed for a while because you could hurt him."

"Oh, we're not married yet." She tried to embarrass the nurse for her assumption.

The nurse shrugged and left.

"Quinton, I *am* going to have to stay with you tonight to make sure you're okay." She frowned at the face he made. "What? I'll be in the guest room. Are you afraid I'm gonna jump your bones or something?"

"No—I'm not sure I can handle knowing you're sleeping in the room next to me." He laughed. "I might jump *your* bones." He winced at the pain his laughter caused him.

"Yeah, right. Not in your condition. If it makes you feel any better, I'll sleep in the room on the end."

"No!"

She jumped.

He softened. "I mean . . . it's not ready yet. I'll be all right with you in the next room."

"Okay, baby. Whatever you want." Shara eyed him strangely.

Chapter Forty-four

It took Shara, Keeva, and Jamil forever to get Quinton up the stairs leading up to his apartment. He groaned with every step. "I knew I should have put an elevator in here. That's what I get for being cheap."

Keeva looked at Shara questioningly. Shara gave her an 'I'll tell you later' look.

When they finally got into the apartment, Quinton asked, "Keeva, are you going to be all right getting home?"

"I'll be fine, Quint. Jamil's gonna walk me back down to the car."

"Jamilly-mil, you come straight back upstairs, you hear me? You know how to pull out the folding bed in the couch. And no PlayStation either. You go right to sleep. We'll call your mom when she gets off work in the morning."

"Yes, sir."

"When you come back up, go in the guest bedroom and pull off those sheets you had last time you were here. Make up the bed for Miss Shara."

"Yes, sir."

"Jamil, stop playing. You don't have to talk to me like that in front of Miss Shara. She's family now." He held up Shara's hand to show Jamil. "I did it, man. Just like I told you."

"What?" Shara pretended to be mad, but was enjoying seeing the paternal side of Quinton with Jamil.

"Don't be mad, Shara. I had to get a little advice from my boy, Jamil. You know he's the original player."

"Yeah, Miss Shara. I had to help him out. He was gonna come at you with some old corny sermon about Adam and Eve and Jesus and the church. It was lame."

They all laughed.

Keeva hugged Jamil. "Where were you when my ex-fiancé needed some romance pointers? Come on, walk me down, so you can go to bed." She rubbed his head. "You've had enough excitement and need some rest."

Shara gave Keeva a big hug before she left. "Thanks, girl, I couldn't have made it without you here. Look at you trying to be an intercessor."

Keeva laughed and held her tight. "I learned from the best." She whispered in her ear, "Girl, the ring is too much. Call me tomorrow."

Jamil was a little longer than Shara thought he should have been and a terrifying thought crossed her mind. "Quinton, it was T-bone and Jermaine that did this, right?"

Quinton nodded and looked at the floor. He

looked like he was preparing himself to hear Shara say, "I told you so."

Shara remembered T-bone's menancing threats to both Quinton and Jamil. "What if they try to come after Jamil or . . . after you?"

"They won't, Shara."

"How do you know?"

"They're going to jail, where they'll be for a long time. Not only did the cops witness them shooting at us, they found a big stash of drugs in T-bone's car. We won't have to worry about them anymore."

She was horrified picturing Quinton being shot at and started crying again.

"Baby? What's wrong? I'm fine." He pulled her close to him. "You love me, huh?"

"Yeah, I love you, silly. Don't ever do anything like this again."

"I won't, baby, I promise."

"Yeah, right. Until Jamil, or Jacquell, or Deshawn, or another one of your boys gets in trouble again."

He pulled away from her to look her in the eye. "What do you suggest, Shara? That I just let something bad happen to them?"

"I didn't mean it like that, Quinton. I just . . . I don't want anything to happen to you."

"It won't, baby. God's got me."

Shara thought for a minute. "Drugs? Does that mean Jamil—?"

"He used to. He stopped . . . not too long after he started your track program." He held her close. "Good ol' Miss Shara. Saving the lives of today's youth."

Jamil walked back in. "Ooops! 'Scuse me. I

guess y'all *should* be celebrating your engagement right about now."

"Jamil, you know it ain't like that, man. We
gotta wait till we get married. If I wasn't hurt,
Miss Shara would be going home right now.
She'll be in the guestroom, I'll be in my room.
Go on and change the bed for her."

Shara helped Quinton into his bedroom and
tried to help him take his shirt off.

"You're gonna have to cut it off. Hurts too
much to lift my arms."

She found a pair of scissors on his desk and
started cutting the bloody shirt. She gasped as
she saw the large bruises on his chest and back.
Her eyes filled with tears.

"Do I need to get Jamil to help me out?"
Quinton asked gently.

"No baby, I'm okay." She went into the bathroom and wet a towel to clean off the dried
blood. She started to feel that tingling in her
stomach again as she washed his arms and
chest. She softly kissed a bruise on his shoulder.

He pulled away. "Really, do I need to get
Jamil to help me out?"

She giggled. "I promise I'll behave. I wouldn't
want to take advantage of a crippled man."

He laughed, wincing.

"Baby, I'm sorry. Let me get you into bed."

"Oooh, I like the way that sounds. How long
do you think it's gonna take to plan this wedding?"

"Hush, Quinton. You just worry about getting better." She led him to the bed and helped

him sit down. "I'm gonna get Jamil to help you get your pants off."

"Yeah, you do that."

After Jamil helped Quinton into a T-shirt and some basketball shorts, Shara came back in the room and sent Jamil to bed. She brought Quinton two pain pills and some water. "Take these before you go to sleep."

"Baby, that's too much. They just gave me some at the hospital."

"I know. I want you to be able to sleep 'til morning."

He swallowed the pills. "Leave the door open."

"Scared of the dark?"

"No silly, just leave it open, okay?"

She kissed him on the forehead and went next door. She changed into a T-shirt and some sweats he had given her that were way too long. She left her door open, too. She felt closer to him that way. She snuggled under the covers. How long *would* it take her to plan a wedding? She drifted off to sleep.

She awoke to loud yelling. Her heart froze. It was Quinton's voice.

"Quintell!"

She ran in the room and tried to wake him. His eyes were open, but he looked at her without recognition.

"Where's Quintell?"

"Quinton, baby, wake up. You're having a bad dream."

"Momma, where's Quintell?"

She tried to shake him, but he wouldn't come

Sherri L. Lewis

out of his trance. Had she given him too much pain medicine?

"Quinton, please, you're scaring me."

"Quintell! Momma, where is Quintell? Did I get here in time? Am I too late?"

He thrashed in the bed. The bandage on his arm was soaked through, red.

"Quinton, wake up!"

"Just tell me where Quintell is. Please! Where's Quintell?"

Shara burst into tears. "He's gone, Quinton. Quintell is gone."

Jamil ran into the room. "Miss Shara, what's wrong?"

"Quintell, you're all right! Oh God, I knew I could save you. Come here, man. I knew you'd be back. I knew I could save you." Quinton held out his arms for Jamil.

Jamil looked at Shara as if he didn't know what to do and didn't understand what was going on. He walked over to the bed and sat down. Quinton held him and rocked him back and forth crying Quintell's name over and over. He stopped rocking and pulled Jamil away from him and looked at him.

"Quintell?"

Jamil shook his head slowly with tears flowing down his face. "No, man. I'm Jamil."

Shara brushed Jamil's tears away. "Go back to bed, sweetie. Quinton's going to be okay."

"But, Miss Shara—"

"Jamil, do as I say. You can play with the Play-Station, okay?"

He obediently turned to walk away, but stopped with a worried look when he heard Quinton yell,

"NO! Quintell, come back! Please don't leave me again. Quintell!"

Shara pushed Jamil out the door and closed it behind him. She walked back over to the bed and turned on the light.

"Quinton, wake up! You're having a reaction to the pain medicine. Wake up, baby, you're hurting yourself!"

"Momma, I'm sorry. I didn't mean to lose Quintell. I'm sorry, Momma."

He cried in Shara's arms as she rocked him. He kept crying Quintell's name and telling his mother he was sorry.

After he fell asleep, Shara was afraid to move, not wanting to wake him. She lay there praying, wondering what Quinton had been talking about. Was it *just* the pain medicine?

Chapter Forty-five

Shara awoke to a feathery soft kiss on her cheek.

"I knew I couldn't trust you. Woman, what are you doing in my bed? Did I miss the wedding or something?"

She stared at him.

"What?"

"Quinton, you don't remember waking up last night?"

"What are you talking about?"

Shara sat up and swung her legs over the side of the bed. She recounted the events of the night before.

"Jamil heard me?"

"He came in here. You hugged him and called him Quintell."

Quinton held his face in his hands. "Oh God, I didn't." He looked up. "Where is he now?"

"He went back to bed. I heard him playing

PlayStation until about two in the morning."
They both looked over at the clock. It was 5:30.

"Oh God. I'm so sorry, Shara. I didn't mean
to scare you. Oh God. I can't believe I . . ." He
held his face in his hands again.

Shara noticed that his body started heaving.
She heard a muffled cry.

"Quinton?"

"Give me a minute, Shara. Could you—"

"Step out? No, Quinton, talk to me."

"Shara, just let me—"

"No, Quinton!" She pulled his hands away
from his face and held his chin so he had to
meet her eyes. "We're going to be married. No
secrets. Talk to me, baby. What's going on?"

Shame filled his eyes. He covered his face
again and started crying. It was the most pain-
ful sound Shara had ever heard. She felt like
her heart was being ripped open. She held him
and rocked him until he stopped crying. His
voice was hoarse.

"Is that why you went to save Jamil last
night?"

"I couldn't lose another one. I couldn't bury
another baby brother."

"Oh, honey. I'm sorry." Shara kissed his face
softly, stopping the tears. "Quint, is there something you need to talk about? I'm going to be
your wife. Trust me, baby. Whatever it is—don't
hold it in anymore."

He got up slowly and walked over to his
dresser. He opened the top drawer and pulled
out a key. He walked out the bedroom door, indicating for her to follow.

He opened the door to the last bedroom and held it for Shara to walk inside.

She gasped at what she saw.

There were bunk beds in the room with Superhero bedspreads. There was a little chair and desk with Curious George books on it.

He explained without looking her in the eye. "Quintell and I shared a bedroom until I left for college. The twins were inseparable, so when he came along, mom just stuck him in the room with me."

He smiled a faraway smile. "When he was little, he would climb in the bed with me and sleep curled up in a little ball up under me. When he got older, he would keep me awake all night asking questions. He got on my nerves, but when I left for college, I missed him so much." Quinton rubbed the bunk bed.

There were pictures everywhere. Anywhere Shara turned, Quintell's little chocolate face was staring back at her at all different ages. There were a lot of pictures of him and Quinton together. There was a large blow-up of Quinton in his Magic jersey with Quintell grinning beside him. They looked so much alike it was scary.

Quinton's voice was filled with pain. "That was the last time I saw him alive. He came to visit me in Orlando. He had been getting in a lot of trouble with the guys in the neighborhood, so mom sent him to visit me until things cooled off. The only problem was, I couldn't watch him. I had to go to practice and go to games, and then I had my girl. I didn't make time for him."

Quinton rubbed his chin. "He wanted to come live with me, but . . . I didn't want him 'cramping my style.' I was too busy being a rich superstar athlete to be there for my baby brother. The night before he was killed, he called, begging me to come visit. He said he was afraid something was going to happen to him. He wouldn't let me off the phone until I promised to make a plane reservation for that weekend. He wanted me to come the next day, but I had a game."

Quinton fingered a worn piece of paper on the wall. It was a program for a basketball game. "Orlando Magic vs. Houston Rockets—March 27, 1998." He fingered another worn piece of paper next to it. It was an obituary with Quintell's face smiling on the front. It read, "Quintell Mercer, January 14, 1983—March 27, 1998."

Tears streamed down Quinton's face. "I was too late. If I had just gotten there when he begged me to, I could have saved him. My mom had already picked out the house she wanted, and I was supposed to close on it that weekend. If I had gotten the house before then, he wouldn't have even been in that neighborhood that night."

He hung his head. "But I was too busy playing basketball."

He sat in the little chair and fingered one of the Curious George books. "He always made me read this to him. When he was little, I used to call him curious Quintell. He was the cutest thing in the world. He worshipped the ground I walked on."

Quinton's voice cracked. "And I let him

down." He pounded the table. "For a stupid basketball game!"

He started weeping that gut-wrenching cry again. Shara went over to him and held him in her arms. She didn't know what to say.

"That's why I couldn't play anymore. I put that stupid game before my baby brother and it cost him his life. For what? Some stupid money? Fame and fortune? Was any of that worth his life? He was only fifteen years old. After I quit, I swore I'd never pick up a basketball again."

Shara's voice was soft. "Quinton, you didn't know."

"It doesn't matter. I should have been there for him."

Shara held him for a while, thinking. That explained all the money he had given to help the church youth programs, and his undying devotion to his boys.

"I know, Shara. I know I can't bring him back, no matter how much time and money I devote to these boys. I guess I feel like it's blood money. Quintell's blood money. I feel like I owe it to them. If I can't save him, at least I can save them. That's why every time Jamil or any of them calls, I'm there. I don't want to ever feel like I should have been there *ever* again. Do you understand, baby?"

She nodded and kissed him. "I understand, baby. I just don't think—"

"I know, Shara. Please . . . give me some time to heal. I never told anyone this before. My mother doesn't know anything about the phone call. She doesn't know Quintell wanted to come live with me. I don't think she'd ever forgive me."

"I doubt that, Quint."

He laughed.

"What?" She hoped he wasn't about to become delirious again.

"That's what my mom used to call us. All of us. She could never get the name right for who she was yelling at. She'd yell, 'Come here, Quintavious, no Quintarious, no Quintell, no . . . Quint! Get in here.' We'd all come running, hoping not to be the one she was calling for."

Quinton chuckled with a faraway look in his eyes. "It was always one of the twins. I was too busy trying to be grown and responsible and Quintell was a perfect angel . . ."

He looked upward. "He's my little angel. I like to think of him up there with the cloud of witnesses, cheering me on. At first I was real worried about his . . . eternal soul, you know? But when I sat down and talked to the pastor at my mom's church, he told me Quintell came to visit him the week before he died. He had told the pastor he didn't know why, but he wanted to get saved. The pastor sat him down and talked to him about it and led him to Christ. When Pastor Williams told me about that, I cried and cried. That's what made me give *my* life to Christ, right there in his office. The thought that Quintell was in heaven, and that God made sure he would get there right before he died . . ."

Quinton let out a deep sigh. "I'm tired, baby. Take me back to bed?"

Shara led him by the hand, careful to close

the door tightly behind her. "Want me to lock it?"

"No, baby. No more locked doors in our lives."

She tucked him into his bed.

"Stay with me 'til I fall asleep?" She got in bed, but stayed on top of the sheets while he lay under them.

He laid his head on her chest. "Ummm. I could get used to this. How 'bout we skip the wedding and elope?"

She laughed softly, stroking his hair gently with her fingers.

"Quinton?"

"Hmmm?"

"What made you pick up a basketball again?"

She felt him sigh.

"When I came back home for good after quitting, Pastor Williams called me into his office. My mother told him she was concerned because I was depressed and never wanted to leave my room. I had created a little Quintell shrine like the one here.

"He told me he was sorry Quintell had died, and he didn't know why God had allowed him to die. He said I had two choices. I could either let his death destroy me, or I could allow God to use my pain. He quoted what has become my favorite scripture about Joseph . . . what Satan meant for evil, God meant for good. Just like Pastor preached in his sermon that Sunday. Joseph went through a lot of pain, but it ended him up somewhere where he could deliver a whole nation of people. I guess Jamil and my boys are my little nation. For every soul

God saves through me, I get to get some re-
venge on the kingdom of darkness for taking
Quintell."

"Quinton?"

"Hmmm?"

"I love you."

"Me too, baby."

She heard his breathing become labored and
knew he had fallen asleep. She didn't want to
wake him, so she stayed there and fell asleep,
too.

Epilogue

Pastor Kendrick announced proudly, "You may kiss the bride." Everyone applauded as Quinton leaned over to kiss Shara. The applause got louder as the kiss lasted for a while.

Quinton whispered in Shara's ear, "That's the last kiss I'll have to run away from."

She giggled and blushed, whispering back, "Can't we skip the reception?"

They both laughed. It had been a long six months, but they had survived by "keeping it safe."

It had actually passed by pretty quickly. Shara had worked hard in school and had graduated a few weeks ago, the programs at the church were in full swing, and they had trained for a marathon together to relieve some of their pent up "frustrations."

As they sat at the head table at the reception, Shara looked around at everyone she loved who came to share their special day. Keeva was at her right hand as her maid of honor. Nia and Danielle were her bridesmaids. Quinton was flanked by his best man, Anthony, and his groomsmen, Quintavious and Quintarious.

Mother Hobbs also joined them at the head table. She had been given a special seat of honor at the wedding as the mother of the bride *and* groom. She cried tears of joy throughout almost the entire wedding.

Shara's parents and Quinton's mother were sitting together at the table closest to theirs. Shara was overjoyed at how well her mom and Quinton's mother got along. Her father was initially grumpy about not being asked to perform the ceremony. Shara didn't know if it was Quinton's mom's feistiness rubbing off or what, but Shara's mom fussed at her father until he was ashamed. He hadn't said another word about Shara's "new-fangled Pastor" for the rest of their visit to "the city."

When the time came, he graciously danced her around on the dance floor for their father-daughter dance, looking as proud as a father could.

Shara smiled at Quinton dancing with his mother. She had been down to visit quite a few times in the last six months. Quinton had started seeing a pastoral counselor to deal with his guilt and grief over Quintell's death. The therapist had suggested his mother be present for some of the sessions. He had done quite well and on her last visit back in March, she had returned to Chicago with a box filled with the remnants of Quinton's "Quintell shrine." The room had been redecorated as a guest room where the twins had been staying for the past few days.

Quinton's "boys" had attributed his sudden decrease in time and money spent on them to his engagement and impending marriage to Shara. There was no need to tell them Quinton no longer saw the need to rescue Quintell in each of them. He still took them for the occasional pizza party and bought sneakers for the one with the highest grades, but they were now only allowed to call his cell or pager for the most extreme of emergencies. Luckily, there had been none.

Shara's brother had been grinning at her the entire day. David wouldn't believe she was marrying the infamous Quinton Mercer until he actually met him in person. Shara knew he would spend the next few weeks telling everyone he saw about how he got a chance to play basketball with an ex-Pro player a few days before the wedding.

Shara looked over at Keeva who was smiling and blushing as Anthony whispered something in her ear. They had become close friends over the past few months. Anthony had proven to be as patient as promised and hadn't pressured Keeva for anything further than friendship. Shara could tell she was falling for him though. Keeva insisted she was enjoying her singleness and didn't want to commit to a relationship just yet, but Shara was figuring on a year before she was asked to be Keeva's matron of honor.

Shara smiled thinking back on the Christmas dance recital. That night solidified Keeva's decision to take the position as the dance instructor. The entire audience was awestruck after each beautifully choreographed piece until the final piece brought the house down. Keeva and company brought to life Kirk Franklin's "Lamb of God." The altar was crammed with people crying and worshipping, and some of the kids' parents and siblings got saved. Keeva said she was overwhelmed that displaying God through dance could have that kind of effect on people.

Dancing had an effect on her girls, too. Danae and Shanique were tied for the highest grades of all of the kids in the entire youth program. They were both praying that by the time they finished high school, they'd get full scholarships to Spelman, so they could be "just like Miss Keeva." Shanique wanted to go to be a teacher, and Danae changed career choices almost daily. Her latest announcement was she wanted to be a pediatrician. Most of the other girls were maintaining their B averages as expected.

Shara looked around at the many tables filled with "their kids". She was proud of each one of them and how much they'd grown in the last year. Lakita just finished a semester at Georgia Perimeter College. She had applied to transfer to Georgia State University so she could get a Bachelor's Degree in early childhood education. She had informed Pastor Kendrick that the church needed a daycare and pre-school and that when she finished school, she was going to run it.

Jamil, under the rigorous tutelage of Quinton, was the star basketball player on his high school team. Even though he often bragged about Jamil's skills on the court, Quinton constantly reminded him that his education was more important than basketball. Jamil had been the recipient of the last few pairs of sneakers for having the highest grades. He could always be heard talking about going to Morehouse to become a "bidness man," like Quinton.

The mentoring program was a big hit and a lot of the older teens were spending the summer shadowing people in the perspective careers. Tyreek talked about becoming a lawyer while Deshawn wanted to be a stockbroker. Sometimes Shara wished they had started working with them sooner so they wouldn't have to work so hard now to play catch-up. She was excited for her middle school and junior high kids that would get the chance to maintain A and B averages throughout high school and be more prepared for college.

A representative from the school district had even come to visit the program to see what was responsible for the increased testing scores in the kids from their particular neighborhood. Shara had been overjoyed when other churches in nearby neighborhoods came over for meetings to find out how they could duplicate the program in other communities.

As she looked at each of the kids, she was sad for a second as she thought of Tangee. She had no idea what had become of her. She had tried to call her mother several times, but she always hung up on her. Shara was disappointed Tangee hadn't tried to contact her. She thought she would have at least tried to write.

Shara smiled as she saw Pastor Kendrick and Jenell making eyes at each other at their table. Jenell was glowing and her nose was already spreading. She still joked it was Shara's fault she was now four months pregnant. Shara had insisted on babysitting the kids on Valentine's Day weekend so they could get away. Jenell was just starting to show. She kept teasing that Shara would be the next one in the church to get pregnant. Shara and Quinton both decided they wanted to wait at least two years before even thinking about thinking about starting a family. They already had a lot of children.

Shara smiled as Quinton tapped her father on the shoulder to indicate it was his turn to dance with Shara.

"Hey." Quinton grinned, biting his lower lip.

"Hey." Shara grinned, biting her upper one.

He stroked her cheek softly and kissed her gently.

"Ummmm. You have the sweetest lips in the world."

"Unh uh, you do." She kissed him back.

"Unh uh, you do." He kissed her again and held her close.

They danced in blissful silence for a few minutes.

"How long do we have to stay here?" Shara asked impatiently.

"Shara, this is your wedding reception." Quinton laughed. "You can't leave early. All these people came all this way just to be with us." He kissed her on the nose. "Soon enough baby, soon enough."

She snuggled into his chest. She couldn't have ever dreamed she could ever be this happy in life. They had a late morning flight planned for tomorrow morning to Aruba where they would spend seven blissful days. Shara had fussed that she didn't see the point of going that far and spending that much money when she had no intention of leaving their suite, but Quinton had insisted nothing was too good for her. He said, "Woman, I plan to spoil you for as long as I live, so you might as well get used to it."

"What was that for?" Quinton kissed her neck.

"What?"

"That long sigh you just gave." He grinned.

"I don't know. Beautiful day, good food, good music, family and friends . . ."

"That's it?" He pretended to be hurt.

"Oh yeah, the company's not too bad either."

He laughed and kissed her. "I love you, Shara Mercer."

She smiled. "Ummmm, I love the sound of that." She kissed him back. "I love you, too, Quinton Mercer."

He pulled her close again and they danced for the rest of the song, as if no one else was in the room with them, dreaming of their future and destiny together.

Reader's Group Guide

1. Keeva has made decisions about her career and future based on her parents' and society's expectations. How does that affect her ability to perform in school and her pursuit of that career? Shara challenges her to decide on her future based on God's purpose for her life. How can people discover God's purpose for their lives? How are people affected by living without a sense of purpose and destiny?

2. Shara has a great sense of purpose and an intimate relationship with God, but she has no social life. Mother Hobbs stresses to her the importance of balance in her life. What do you think is responsible for Shara's lack of balance? How can Christians maintain balance in their Christian walk?

3. Shara often uses the terms relationship with God and intimacy with God. What do these terms mean and how does one

develop a relationship and intimacy with God?

4. Shara often speaks of how her super-religious upbringing affected her ability to have a true relationship with God. She describes "churchianity" as opposed to Christianity and how it makes the power of God of no effect. How do religious rules and church rituals affect our relationship with God? What are some examples of "churchianity" that affect one's relationship with God?

5. Shara keeps a "vision notebook" of the dreams God has given her. When she meets with Pastor Kendrick about the ideas God has given her, he pulls out a notebook with his written vision for the church. Why is it important to "write the vision down"?

6. Keeva is attracted to Shara's Christianity because she doesn't act religious and doesn't try to push God down her throat. Shara was concerned that she wasn't doing enough to bring Keeva to Christ. What do you think is the proper way to minister to the unsaved?

7. How does Shara's father's attitude toward boys in her early years and her experience with her first boyfriend affect her building a relationship with Quinton? Why do you think she was able to overcome her past to develop a relationship with him?

8. Shara talks about the divorce rate in this country as 50% and attributes it to the fact that many people form relationships based on surface attributes only such as physical appearance and sexual attraction. What are the most important foundations for relationship building? What is the importance of factoring in purpose and destiny when picking a mate? Keeva says she thinks Shara and Quinton are so happy because Shara had a strong relationship with God before meeting him. How can our relationship with God affect our relationship with a potential mate?

9. Quinton describes his former Pastor's criticism of his "methods" in dealing with youths. In reaching out to minister to young people, do you think Christians compromise when adapting so called "worldly" styles of music and entertainment to reach out to them?

10. Quinton talks with Pastor Kendrick about proper guidelines for Christian dating. What do you think is appropriate for Christian singles where dating is concerned? Should Christians date? What are guidelines for showing affection? How should Christian singles "keep things safe" as Quinton asked?

11. Keeva has experiences with Mother Hobbs, Pastor Kendrick, and the pastor of the church she visited with Shara saying things to her or about her that they knew without

knowing her. How can the active operation of the gifts of the Spirit lead people to salvation and toward knowing and fulfilling the purpose and destiny?

12. How does Quinton's brother's death affect his work ethic and his relationship with his "boys"? How does unresolved grief affect people's relationships with others?

Urban Christian His Glory Book Club!

Established January 2007, *UC His Glory Book Club* is another way by which to introduce **Urban Christian** and its authors. We are an online book club supporting Urban Christian authors by purchasing, reading, and providing written reviews of the authors' books. *UC His Glory Book Club* welcomes both men and women of the literary world who have a passion for reading Christian based fiction.

UC His Glory Book Club is the brainchild of Joylynn Jossel, author and Executive Editor of Urban Christian and Kendra Norman-Bellamy, copy editor for Urban Christian. The book club will provide support, positive feedback, encouragement, and a forum whereby members can openly discuss and review the literary works of Urban Christian authors. In the future, we anticipate broadening our spectrum of services to include online author chats, author spotlights, interviews with your favorite Urban Christian author(s), special online groups for *UC His Glory Book Club* members, ability to post reviews on the website and amazon.com, membership ID cards, *UC His Glory* Yahoo! Group, and much more.

Even though there will be no membership fees attached to becoming a member of *UC His Glory Book Club*, we do expect our members to be active, committed, and to follow the guidelines of the Book Club.

UC His Glory Book Club members pledge to:

- Follow the guidelines of *UC His Glory Book Club*.
- Provide input, opinions, and reviews that build up, rather than tear down.
- Commit to purchasing, reading and discussing featured book(s) of the month.
- Respect the Christian beliefs of *UC His Glory Book Club*.
- Believe that Jesus is the Christ, Son of the Living God

We look forward to the online fellowship.

Many Blessings to You!

Shelia E. Lipsey
President
UC His Glory Book Club

**Visit the official Urban Christian Book Club website at www.uchisglorybookclub.net

Coming Soon

Selling My Soul

By Sherri L. Lewis

One

The door to flight 1748 from Johannesburg, South Africa to Washington DC's Reagan National airport opened, and for the first time in over two years, I stepped onto American soil. I couldn't believe I was back.

What I really couldn't believe was that I didn't want to be back. After such a long time away, I was excited about seeing my mom, my best friend, Monica, and maybe my baby sister. Other than that, I wanted to go back to Africa.

I had actually thought about it. Come back, head up to Baltimore to spend a week or so with Moms, fly down to Atlanta to visit Monnie, and then book another flight back to what felt more like home to me than anywhere I had ever lived. And back to the man I had tried so hard not to fall in love with.

The two years I spent in Mozambique had changed my life forever. What started out as a mission trip became an incredible life journey,

Sherri L. Lewis

and I wasn't sure I could go back to life as usual in the States.

Attention in the terminal, flight 1423 is now boarding for . . .

The first thing I noticed when I walked off the plane was how fast everyone moved. The tangible sense of frenzied, chaotic, hurriedness unnerved me. While I walked at what felt like a normal pace, it seemed like everyone raced by me, bumping into me, giving me dirty looks for getting in their way. It was weird to hear everyone speaking English. I had gotten used to hearing Portuguese and tribal dialects.

As I strolled toward customs, I couldn't help but glance at the placard advertisements on the wall. Every ad seemed to have sexual overtones. What did a woman with long, sexy legs in a short, red dress with pouty lips have to do with life insurance? People whizzed by me dressed in designer suits that cost enough to feed an entire village for a month. They were talking on cell phones and not even taking the time to acknowledge the people they walked past. Rushing toward nothing.

After a long trek from the gate, I sat on the floor in customs, exhausted from more than thirty hours of travel. It was taking forever, but I was excited that in a few minutes, I would finally get to lay eyes on my mom. She waited just a few hundred yards away, on the other side of the stupid customs gate. Monica, unfortunately, was much farther away. She had moved to Atlanta while I was gone, so I wouldn't get to see her until one of us could plan a trip.

Two weeks before I left for Africa, Monica's

life fell apart. I remember the day she called me, hysterical after catching her husband in bed with his best friend. His best *male* friend. She got depressed, as anyone would, and had to get away from her life, so she moved to Atlanta. I couldn't imagine my life here without her. We had been best friends for the past seven years, and before I left for Africa, talked to each other daily and hung out every weekend.

When I finally cleared customs and came through the little gate, I scanned the crowd looking for my mom. For the last month, I dreamed about getting one of her hugs. My mother gave the kind of hugs that could melt all your problems away. The more nervous I got about the re-entry process—that culture shock of coming back to the States after having lived in another country and culture for two years—the more I knew my mom's hugs would make everything all right.

My eyes finally landed on my baby sister, Tiffany. I looked all around her, but didn't see my mother.

"Trina!" She smiled and waved at me. Over here."

I was glad to feel happy to see her. We didn't always get along and rarely saw things eye to eye, but seeing her face comforted me.

"Tiffy!" I ran over and grabbed her. We hugged, and I held on to her for a few seconds.

We pulled apart, and I pinched her cheeks. "How's my baby girl?"

She rolled her eyes at my calling her that. I couldn't help it. All during her pregnancy with Tiffany, my mother told me she was bringing me home a baby girl to take care of. I guess she was trying to avoid sibling rivalry or something. It worked. I was the devoted big sister that had always taken care of my baby sister. Me and mom probably spoiled her too much, because now, she was a grown adult, thirty years old, and still thought she should be taken care of.

"Look at you, girl." Tiffany studied me from head to toe. I was wearing a classic Mozambiquan *capelana* skirt tied around my waist, a T-shirt, and sandals. She studied my hair. Of course I couldn't be bothered with perming my hair while I was in Africa. After being there six months, I cut off the damaged, straight ends, and let it go natural. Tiffany stuck her fingers in my afro. "I guess they ain't got no perm or pressing combs in Africa, huh?" She looked down at my unshaven legs. "I guess they ain't got no razors either."

I had to laugh and hugged her again.

Tiffany was her usual fashionable self. She'd had an obsession with clothes, makeup, and hair since she was a teenager. She had chopped off all her hair and wore a short, spiky cut that looked frozen into sharp, geometrical points with some kind of shiny varnish. She sported flared jeans with high heels and a red, cleavage-bearing top. At five feet-nine, she stood only two inches shorter than me and looked model perfect in whatever clothes she put on. It amazed me that she was always broke, but always looked like a million bucks.

"Where's Moms? She in the car?"

"She couldn't make it." Tiffany glanced downward and to the right, a gesture which surfaced when she lied or felt guilty about something. Which unfortunately happened quite often. "She's a little sick and stayed home. I'm gonna drive you up there later."

"A little sick? What do you mean?" I couldn't imagine any kind of sickness keeping Moms from greeting me at the airport after not seeing me for so long. Every time I had talked to her over the past month, that's all she talked about. How she couldn't wait to see me the second I stepped off the plane.

"Just a little sick." Tiffany's eyes did the down and to the right routine, and I got worried. If Moms was sick enough not to meet me and Tiffany was lying, something had to be wrong.

"Tiffy, don't play with me. What's going on?"

"Just come on, girl. We'll see her in a little while." Tiffany grabbed one of my huge suitcases and walked ahead of me toward the exit. I wasn't gonna press her because whenever she was evasive about something and I kept questioning her, we ended up in an argument. It was usually about her owing me money, or something stupid she did with some guy, or some bad life decision she had made. What could she possibly be keeping from me about Moms?

She turned around to look at me. "Why is this bag so light?" She lifted it in the air with ease.

"I gave everything away before I left. I only brought back a few things I bought over there for you and Moms and a couple of souvenirs for me."

She looked at me like I was crazy. "You gave

all your clothes away? Why?" She looked me up and down. "You'll gain your weight back in a few weeks. Then you gon' be mad that you left all them clothes over there." She continued on ahead of me, mumbling under her breath, "Went over to Africa and lost her mind . . . giving all them clothes away. If you wanted to give clothes away, you could have brought them back and given them to me."

I shook my head, not even caring to explain that unlike her—with her endless wardrobe of high fashion—I had left my clothes with people who barely had anything.

"Tiffy, slow down." The difficulty of maneuvering through the thronging crowd made me a little dizzy. The air here even felt different.

"Sorry, girl." When we got closer to the entrance, she stood my bag next to me and said, "Why don't you wait here; I'll go get the car."

I nodded and watched her model walk, sashaying her hips toward the door. She turned back and looked at me, biting her lip. "I forgot to tell you. I've been driving your car for a while."

I let out a deep breath. "What happened, and how long is a while?"

Her eyes flickered down and to the right.

"Never mind. Just go get it."

I couldn't believe how quickly tension crept back into my shoulders. I had been warned that after about a week or so of being back, I would start to feel the stress of life in America, but I had only been back fifteen minutes, and my peace was draining by the second.

Undoubtedly, Tiffany's car had been repossessed, and she was driving mine. Hopefully, it hadn't been too long because Tiffany didn't believe in car maintenance—oil changes, tire rotation, spark plugs, all that necessary stuff. Tiffany must have thought cars ran on magic. Every car that she had ever owned had either been repossessed or had died on the side of the road from lack of maintenance. I could only pray that she hadn't been driving my car so long that her neglect had damaged it.

While I waited for her, I glanced at a newsstand filled with fashion magazines, celebrity gossip rags, and sports magazines. Everything seemed so trivial and superficial. Where was the real news about the millions of AIDS-orphaned children all over Africa, the genocide in Darfur, and kids getting their arms chopped off for blood diamonds in Senegal? Who in the world was Rihanna, and why did she seem to be so important?

My eyes fell on The *Washington Times*. My heart dropped as I read the large front-page headline: CHURCH SEX SCANDAL. Americans only cared about gossip and drama. I hated it. Especially when it involved the church.

I glanced down at the picture of two men in handcuffs, being led away by policemen. One guy had turned his head to shield hs face, but the other had been captured dead on.

I gasped. It was the head deacon at Love and Faith Christian Center, the church where I had gotten saved, and the church that Monica had been a member of before she moved to Atlanta.

Her husband, Kevin, had been the minister of music there for years, but after everything that happened with them, he had moved to Atlanta about a year after she went.

I'd had limited phone and Internet access while in my remote little village in Mozambique, but from the little Monica had told me, Kevin had gotten involved in a ministry in Atlanta that helped people get delivered from homosexuality, and their marriage had been restored. Before going to Africa, that might have sounded strange and honestly, unbelievable to me. But after seeing miracles there like blind people seeing, deaf people hearing, and dead people coming back to life, I knew anything was possible with God.

I pulled out some money to purchase the newspaper so I could get a better idea of what was going on. I scanned the article. The head deacon at Love and Faith and the pastor of their daughter church in Alexandria, Virginia, had been arrested the day before. The men were accused of molesting little boys in the church for as long as twenty years. I remembered Monica telling me that Kevin had been molested at the church when he was ten years old. I was sure that it had been by one of those men. The article said the arrest came after the ministry council governing the churches received a letter from a man who had been molested there as a child. He had finally spoken out after God had begun taking him through a healing process.

Monica had told me that as part of his therapy, Kevin had mailed a letter to the Bishop's council overseeing Love and Faith Christian Center. In spite of his fears that his celebrity status as a gospel artist would be affected by the admission, he couldn't stand the thought of any more boys being molested. He felt guilty that he had kept the secret for so long. I was glad they kept the source of the letter confidential in the article. Monica would die if the truth about Kevin's past life got out.

I read the article further. Since the ministry council had begun their investigation, they discovered that several boys at Love and Faith DC and Alexandria had been molested. They expected that as the investigation continued, more would come forward.

My stomach churned. Twenty years? How had they gotten away with it that long? How come no one came forward before Kevin had? How many other men's lives had been affected like Kevin's? How could their pastor, Bishop Walker, not have known what was going on?

Did Monica know that the men had been arrested? How was she going to handle it when she found out? Was it possible to keep Kevin's past out of the press or would he be exposed and affected by this as well? If he were exposed, how would Monica handle it?

I tucked the newspaper into the front pocket of my suitcase, grabbed both bags, and ambled slowly toward the front door to look for my sister and my car.

I was ready to go home. I had hoped to be able to relax for a few days when I got back, but already I had issues to take care of. First order of business was getting up to Baltimore to see how my mother was doing. Second, I had to call Monica to find out what was really going on.